TALES OF
THE WOLD NEWTON
UNIVERSE

PHILIP JOSÉ FARMER

TALES OF THE WOLD NEWTON UNIVERSE

EDITED BY WIN SCOTT ECKERT
AND CHRISTOPHER PAUL CAREY

TITAN BOOKS

TALES OF THE WOLD NEWTON UNIVERSE
Print edition ISBN: 9781781163047
E-book edition ISBN: 9781781163054

Published by Titan Books
A division of Titan Publishing Group Ltd
144 Southwark Street, London SE1 0UP

First edition: October 2013
1 3 5 7 9 10 8 6 4 2

TALES OF
THE WOLD NEWTON
UNIVERSE

TABLE OF CONTENTS

THE WOLD NEWTON TALES
OF PHILIP JOSÉ FARMER
INTRODUCTION BY WIN SCOTT ECKERT AND CHRISTOPHER PAUL CAREY

What precisely makes a tale a Wold Newton tale?

In short, a Wold Newton tale must involve a character whom Philip José Farmer identified as a member of the Wold Newton Family, and/or it must add to our knowledge of the secret history that Farmer uncovered, which has come to be known as the "Wold Newton Universe." It can also be a crossover story, but that is not required.

In recent years, generic crossover stories have come to be mistakenly referred to as "Wold Newton" tales. A mere crossover is not enough.

A few examples are likely in order.

Farmer's *The Peerless Peer* (reissued by Titan Books in 2011) is an unabashed Wold Newton Universe novel. The two leads, Sherlock Holmes and Lord Greystoke, are Wold Newton Family members. It is also, obviously, a crossover.

Farmer's short story "Skinburn," included in the present volume, features the son of a man Farmer identified as a Wold

Newton Family member. Since the son is also a Wold Newton Family member, "Skinburn" is a Wold Newton tale, although it does not feature any crossovers.

"The Freshman," another short tale in this volume, has a crossover between a descendant of a character seen in Edgar Rice Burroughs' Lord Greystoke stories, and H. P. Lovecraft's Cthulhu mythos. Since the continuity of the Greystoke tales is a subset of the larger Wold Newton Universe, and since Farmer also discovered that the Cthulhu mythos tales take place in the wider Wold Newton secret history (he noted this in "The Fabulous Family Tree of Doc Savage: Another Excursion into Creative Mythography" in his biography *Doc Savage: His Apocalyptic Life* [1973]), "The Freshman" is a Wold Newton Universe story.

In contrast, a comic-book crossover between Marvel Comics' Spider-Man and Red Sonja (*Marvel Team-Up* #79, March 1979) is not a Wold Newton tale. Via a chain of crossovers links, the story can be shown to take place in a "Crossover Universe" that encompasses the Wold Newton Universe (Farmer included Robert E. Howard's Solomon Kane as an ancestor of the Wold Newton Family, and the Red Sonja character is a variant of a Howard heroine), but it is not, in and of itself, a Wold Newton story.[1]

To make matters even more complicated, Cay Van Ash's authorized Fu Manchu novel, *Ten Years Beyond Baker Street: Sherlock Holmes Matches Wits With the Diabolical Dr. Fu Manchu*, features a crossover match-up between two prominent Wold

---

[1] For more on this, see Win Scott Eckert's *Crossovers: A Secret Chronology of the World*, Volumes 1 and 2, Black Coat Press, 2010.

Newton Family members, the Great Detective and the Devil Doctor. One might argue that this qualifies as a Wold Newton novel, but it's also instructive to remember that although Van Ash was privy to Dr. Petrie's notes, which formed the basis of this novel, he was not aware of the wider "secret history" events that form the basis of the Wold Newton Universe continuity.

With all this in mind, a primer on Farmer's discoveries regarding the Wold Newton Family is in order.

The Wold Newton Family takes its name from the cosmic event that spawned it. On December 13, 1795, at 3:00 P.M., a meteor came plunging to the Earth, landing near the English village of Wold Newton. The impact site became part of the local folklore in the countryside of the Yorkshire Wolds in the East Riding of Yorkshire. Pieces of the Wold Cottage meteorite[2] are held in the Natural History Museum in London, and in 1799, Edward Topham built a brick monument to commemorate the event:

HERE

ON THIS SPOT, DEC[R] 13TH, 1795

FELL FROM THE ATMOSPHERE

AN EXTRAORDINARY STONE

IN BREADTH 28 INCHES

IN LENGTH 30 INCHES

---

[2] The meteorite is named after the Wold Cottage, the house owned by Edward Topham, who was a poet, playwright, landowner, and local magistrate. Apparently Magistrate Topham was instrumental in the Wold Cottage meteorite's role in promoting worldwide acceptance of the fact that some stones are not of this Earth. The Wold Cottage is still privately owned, and is currently the site of an excellent bed and breakfast; nearby is the Wold Top Brewery, where one can procure the local brew, Falling Stone Bitter.

AND

WHOSE WEIGHT WAS 56 POUNDS

THIS COLUMN

IN MEMORY OF IT

WAS ERECTED BY

EDWARD TOPHAM

1799

History also records that several people observed the object in the sky. "Topham's shepherd was within 150 yards of the impact and a farmhand named John Shipley was so near that he was forcibly struck by mud and earth as the falling meteorite burrowed into the ground."[3] A contemporaneous account observes that:

In the afternoon of the 13th of December, 1795, near the Wold Cottage, noises were heard in the air, by various persons, like the report of a pistol; or of guns at a distance at sea; though there was neither any thunder or lightning at the time:—two distinct concussions of the earth were said to be perceived:—and an hissing noise, was also affirmed to be heard by other persons, as of something passing through the air;—and a labouring man plainly saw (as we are told) that something was so passing; and beheld a stone, as it seemed, at last, (about ten yards, or thirty feet, distant from the ground) descending, and striking into the ground, which flew up all about him:

---

[3] See the *Wold Cottage* website, <fernlea.tripod.com/woldcottage.html>.

and in falling, sparks of fire, seemed to fly from it.

Afterwards he went to the place, in company with others; who had witnessed part of the phænomena, and dug the stone up from the place, where it was buried about twenty-one inches deep.

It smelt, (as it is said,) very strongly of sulphur, when it was dug up: and was even warm, and smoked:— it was found to be thirty inches in length, and twenty-eight and a half inches in breadth. And it weighed fifty-six pounds.

—Edward King, ESQ. F.R.S. and F.A.S, *Remarks Concerning Stones Said To Have Fallen from the Clouds, Both in These Days, and in Ancient Times* (1796)

What many historians fail to adequately record is the presence of eighteen other persons in the immediate vicinity at the time of the Wold Newton meteor strike. We know about these eighteen people through the extraordinary and singular work of one historian. This historian, in fact, engaged in a rather in-depth treatment of the subject in two scholarly biographical tomes. However, despite the fact that this historian's biographies are often appropriately shelved in the Biography section of libraries, his revelations are generally regarded as fictional.

The historian to whom we refer, of course, is Philip José Farmer, and the biographies of which we speak are *Tarzan Alive: A Definitive Biography of Lord Greystoke* (1972) and *Doc Savage: His Apocalyptic Life* (1973). In the course of his researches into the life of Lord Greystoke, Farmer extensively traced the jungle lord's ancestry, and came to discover the ape-man was closely related to several other august historical personages. The nexus of this relationship was the Wold Cottage meteor strike in 1795.

As Farmer uncovered, seven couples and their coachmen "were riding in two coaches past Wold Newton, Yorkshire... A meteorite struck only twenty yards from the two coaches... The bright light and heat and thunderous roar of the meteorite blinded and terrorized the passengers, coachmen, and horses... They never guessed, being ignorant of ionization, that the fallen star had affected them and their unborn." (*Tarzan Alive*, Addendum 2, pp. 247–248.)

The eighteen present were:[4]

COACH PASSENGERS (14)

JOHN CLAYTON, 3rd Duke of Greystoke, and his wife, ALICIA RUTHERFORD – *ancestors of the jungle lord*

SIR PERCY BLAKENEY, and his (second) wife, ALICE CLARKE RAFFLES – *Blakeney is from Baroness Emmuska Orczy's* The Scarlet Pimpernel *and sequels*

FITZWILLIAM DARCY, and his wife, ELIZABETH BENNET – *from Jane Austen's* Pride and Prejudice

GEORGE EDWARD RUTHERFORD (THE 11TH BARON TENNINGTON),

---

[4] It has since been revealed, by researchers inspired by Farmer's original discoveries, that there were several more persons present that fateful day, not named by Farmer. These are named in the present volume's "The Wild Huntsman."

and his wife, ELIZABETH CAVENDISH – *ancestors of Professor George Edward Challenger, from* The Lost World *by Edward Malone, edited for publication by Sir Arthur Conan Doyle*

HONORÉ DELAGARDIE, and his wife, PHILIPPA DRUMMOND – *ancestors of Hugh "Bulldog" Drummond from H. C. "Sapper" McNeile's (and later Gerard Fairlie's) novels*

DR. SIGER HOLMES, and his wife, VIOLET CLARKE – *ancestors of Sherlock Holmes, from the stories and novels by John H. Watson, M.D., edited for publication by Sir Arthur Conan Doyle*

SIR HUGH DRUMMOND, and his wife, LADY GEORGIA DEWHURST – *ancestors of Hugh "Bulldog" Drummond from H. C. "Sapper" McNeile's (and later Gerard Fairlie's) novels*

COACHMEN (4)

LOUIS LUPIN – *ancestor of Arsène Lupin, from novels and stories by Maurice Leblanc*

ALBERT LECOQ – *ancestor of Monsieur Lecoq, from the novels by Émile Gaboriau*

ALBERT BLAKE – *ancestor of Sexton Blake, from the stories by Harry Blythe and countless others*

1 UNNAMED by Farmer

The meteor's ionized radiation caused a genetic mutation in those present, endowing many of their descendants with extremely high intelligence and strength. As Farmer stated, the meteor strike was "the single cause of this nova of genetic splendor, this outburst of great detectives, scientists, and explorers of exotic worlds, this last efflorescence of true heroes in an otherwise degenerate age."[5] (*Tarzan Alive*, Addendum 2, pp.230–231.)

In addition to the jungle lord and the man of bronze, Farmer concluded that influential people whose lives were chronicled in popular literature were part of the Wold Newton Family, including Solomon Kane (a pre-meteor strike ancestor); Captain Blood (a pre-meteor strike ancestor); The Scarlet Pimpernel (present at meteor strike); Fitzwilliam Darcy and his wife, Elizabeth Bennet (present at meteor strike); Sherlock Holmes and his nemesis Professor Moriarty (aka Captain Nemo); Phileas Fogg; Monsieur Lecoq; The Time Traveller; Allan Quatermain; A. J. Raffles; Professor Challenger; Arsène Lupin; Bulldog Drummond and his archenemy, Carl Peterson; the evil Fu Manchu and his adversary, Sir Denis Nayland Smith; Sir Richard Hannay; G-8; Lord Peter Wimsey; The Shadow; Sam Spade; Doc Savage's friend and associate Monk Mayfair, his cousin Pat Savage, and his daughter Patricia Wildman; The Spider; Nero Wolfe; Mr. Moto; The Avenger; Philip Marlowe; James Bond; Lew Archer; Travis McGee; and many more.

Farmer's researches, uncovering the cosmic explanation

---

[5] Of course, not all the Wold Newton Family members were heroes. Some turned the genetic advantages with which they had been blessed toward decidedly nefarious pursuits.

for the almost superhuman nature and abilities of these amazing men and women, heroes and villains, are meticulous, well-sourced, and representative of all his historical endeavors. He not only studied the jungle lord's life, but he actually met and interviewed the ape-man himself,[6] after spending uncounted hours poring over Burke's *Peerage* to uncover his real name, titles, arms, and forebears. He applied a similar depth of focus when researching the life of Doc Savage, discovering Doc's real name, ancestors, and current relatives, as well as the family arms.

After writing the two biographies, Farmer continued to chronicle previously unrevealed exploits of Wold Newton Family members in novels and short stories; often these tales have been mistaken for fiction, but they are entirely consistent with the information he had already uncovered, and many are similarly sourced from newly discovered, and unpublished, manuscripts and diaries.

Among the first of these was *The Adventure of the Peerless Peer*, edited by Farmer in 1974 from Dr. John H. Watson's unpublished manuscript. Another, *The Other Log of Phileas Fogg*, was first published in 1973 (reissued by Titan Books in 2012), and derived from Phileas Fogg's secret notes.

Although Farmer's *Time's Last Gift* (1972; revised 1977)

---

[6] On September 1, 1970, Philip José Farmer conducted "An Exclusive Interview with Lord Greystoke." (Originally published as "Tarzan Lives" in *Esquire*, April 1972; reprinted in Farmer's *Tarzan Alive: A Definitive Biography of Lord Greystoke*, University of Nebraska Press/Bison Books, 2006.) The interview ostensibly took place in Libreville, Gabon, West Africa, but Farmer later revealed that the interview actually occurred in Chicago. ("I Still Live!" in *Farmerphile: The Magazine of Philip José Farmer* no. 3, Christopher Paul Carey and Paul Spiteri, eds., January 2006; reprinted in the Farmer collection *Up From the Bottomless Pit and Other Stories*, Subterranean Press, 2007.)

and the related Khokarsa trilogy—*Hadon of Ancient Opar*[7] (1974), *Flight to Opar* (1976), and *The Song of Kwasin* (2012; coauthored with Christopher Paul Carey)—are set in prehistoric times, they also recount the real-life histories of Wold Newton Family members. This might at first seem to be a contradiction, since the Wold Cottage meteor strike that gave rise to the Wold Newton Family occurred in 1795 A.D. whereas the events of *Time's Last Gift* and the Khokarsa trilogy take place circa 12,000 B.C. and 10,000 B.C. respectively.

The answer to this seeming paradox, however, may be found in *Time's Last Gift*. In that novel, a man named John Gribardsun travels back in time as a member of an anthropological expedition from the year 2070 A.D. to 12,000 B.C. He appears in *Hadon of Ancient Opar* under the identity of Sahhindar, the Gray-Eyed Archer God, also known as the god of plants, bronze, and Time. As a member of the Wold Newton Family, Gribardsun introduced the mutated genes of his lineage to the prehistoric peoples of Khokarsa and other lands, and since both Hadon of Opar and Kwasin of Dythbeth—the heroes of the Khokarsa trilogy—can count him as an ancestor, this means they themselves are both members of the Wold Newton Family, despite having been born 12,000 years before the meteor fell to Earth near Wold Newton, Yorkshire in December 1795.

And thus the Wold Newton Family enters prehistory.

But who exactly is John Gribardsun? Farmer leaves plenty

---

[7] *Time's Last Gift* and *Hadon of Ancient Opar* are both now available in Titan Books' Wold Newton series.

of clues to his true identity in *Time's Last Gift*, although such hints are neither overbearing nor do they distract from the novel's compelling narrative, and the reader should not feel embarrassed at having missed them. In fact, the author buried them deep for a reason. He could not risk the world knowing the truth, and, although he had come into an arrangement with "Gribardsun" to publish his memoirs in the guise of fiction, Farmer was honor-bound by the agreement to remain within certain very well-defined parameters. Gribardsun had to ensure that the author would not reveal clues that might endanger him or his loved ones. For this reason, Farmer withheld publication of the novel's epilogue until the revised edition of *Time's Last Gift* appeared in 1977, by which time Gribardsun must have felt he had slipped far enough off the radar that no one could conceivably follow the clues to him or his family. This newly appended epilogue (also included in the Titan Books edition) revealed that the jungle lord whom Farmer called Gribardsun was married to a beautiful blonde named Jane. The reader should also consider the account in that novel of the Duke of Pemberley, the British peer who was born in 1872 and "raised in indeterminate circumstances" in the jungles of West Africa, and who one member of the time travel expedition to 12,000 B.C. believes is one and the same as John Gribardsun. Incidentally, the 1872 birthdate serves as both a red herring and a clue to Gribardsun's identity, as readers of Farmer's *Tarzan Alive: A Definitive Biography of Lord Greystoke* are well aware.

Farmer continued his exploration of the Wold Newton Family in *Ironcastle* (1976), his translation and retelling of J. H.

Rosny Aîné's *L'Étonnant Voyage de Hareton Ironcastle* (1922), which includes several prominent Wold Newton references. Farmer's *The Lavalite World* (1977), the fifth entry in the World of Tiers series,[8] also solidly connects to the Wold Newton series. Here Farmer's protagonist, Kickaha, aka Paul Janus Finnegan, is revealed to be closely related to both the aforementioned Phileas Fogg and to Hardin Blaze Fog, a relative of "the famous Confederate war hero and Western gunfighter Dustine 'Dusty' Edward Marsden Fog," whose exploits were chronicled in fictionalized form by author J. T. Edson.

Farmer also wrote several Wold Newton short stories and pieces in the 1970s: "Skinburn," "The Problem of the Sore Bridge—Among Others," "The Freshman," "After King Kong Fell," "A Scarletin Study," "The Doge Whose Barque Was Worse Than His Bight," "The Obscure Life and Hard Times of Kilgore Trout," "Extracts from the Memoirs of 'Lord Greystoke,'" and others more peripherally connected to the series.

He also continued to write short biographical pieces, including "A Reply to 'The Red Herring,'" "The Two Lord Ruftons," "The Great Korak-Time Discrepancy," "The Lord Mountford Mystery," "From ERB to Ygg," "A Language for Opar," and "Jonathan Swift Somers III, Cosmic Traveller in a Wheelchair: A Short Biography by Philip José Farmer (Honorary Chief Kennel Keeper)."[9]

---

[8] *The Maker of Universes* (1965), *The Gates of Creation* (1966), *A Private Cosmos* (1968), *Behind the Walls of Terra* (1970), *The Lavalite World* (1977), *Red Orc's Rage* (1991), and *More Than Fire* (1993).

[9] These have been collected in *Myths for the Modern Age: Philip José Farmer's Wold Newton Universe*, Win Scott Eckert, ed., MonkeyBrain Books, 2005.

Farmer returned to the Wold Newton series in a big way in the 1990s, starting the decade with the authorized novel *Escape from Loki: Doc Savage's First Adventure* (1991), and rounding it out with the authorized *The Dark Heart of Time: A Tarzan Novel* (1999). 2009 saw the publication of the Wold Newton series novel *The Evil in Pemberley House*, coauthored with Win Scott Eckert, and in 2012 the concluding novel of the Khokarsa trilogy, *The Song of Kwasin*, coauthored with Christopher Paul Carey, at last saw print.

Farmer passed away on February 25, 2009, after the completion of *The Evil in Pemberley House* and *The Song of Kwasin* but before publication.

In 2010, Wold Newton fiction was authorized by Farmer's estate, and new stories based on his research appeared.

Those works included in the present volume are marked with an asterisk.

The Worlds of Philip José Farmer 1: Protean Dimensions, Michael Croteau, ed., Meteor House, 2010.

"A Kick in the Side" by Christopher Paul Carey

"Is He in Hell?" by Win Scott Eckert

The Worlds of Philip José Farmer 2: Of Dust and Soul, Michael Croteau, ed., Meteor House, 2011.

"Kwasin and the Bear God" by Philip José Farmer and Christopher Paul Carey*

"For the Articles" by Bradley H. Sinor

"Into Time's Abyss" by John Allen Small*

The Worlds of Philip José Farmer 3: Portraits of a Trickster, Michael Croteau, ed., Meteor House, 2012.

"The Last of the Guaranys" by Octavio Aragão & Carlos Orsi*

"The Wild Huntsman" by Win Scott Eckert*

Exiles of Kho: A Tale of Lost Khokarsa by Christopher Paul Carey, Meteor House, 2012.

The Scarlet Jaguar, a Pat Wildman adventure by Win Scott Eckert, Meteor House, 2013.

Philip José Farmer's novels of the Nine, *A Feast Unknown* (1969), *Lord of the Trees* (1970), and *The Mad Goblin* (1970) (all part of Titan Books' Wold Newton series under the subheading "Secrets of the Nine—Parallel Universe"), present an interesting conundrum for followers of Farmer's Wold Newton mythos, and may have also added to the impression among some readers that the Wold Newton biographies, novels, and stories are works of fiction. The books recount the ongoing battle of the ape-man Lord Grandrith and the man of bronze Doc Caliban against the Nine, a secret cabal of immortals bent on amassing power and manipulating the course of world events.

These novels are sourced from the memoirs of Lord Grandrith and Doc Caliban, and cover the exploits of Grandrith and Caliban. Grandrith is also a jungle lord, while Caliban is also a man of bronze. However, unlike cousins Lord Greystoke and Doc Wildman (the real name of the man whose exploits were published in pulp novels under the fictional name "Doc Savage"), Grandrith and Caliban are half-brothers. They share a common history that is not based on the Wold Newton meteor strike. One

widely accepted explanation for the discrepancy is that Lord
Grandrith and Doc Caliban exist in a universe that is parallel,
but very similar, to the Wold Newton Universe. As described in
Win Scott Eckert's afterword to Titan Books' new edition of *The
Mad Goblin* ("A Feast Revealed: A Chronology of Major Events
Pertinent to Philip José Farmer's Secrets of the Nine Series"), the
alternate universe shares a common past with the Wold Newton
Universe, but diverged from it circa 26,000 B.C.

The parallel universe theory is supported by Farmer's
fragment of a fourth Nine novel, *The Monster on Hold*. The
fragment was introduced by Farmer at the 1983 World Fantasy
Convention, and was published in the convention program.[10]
During a series of adventures in which Doc Caliban continues
to battle the forces of the Nine, he "begins to suffer from a
recurring nightmare and has dreams alternating with these in
which he sees himself or somebody like himself. However, this
man, whom he calls The Other, also at times in Caliban's dreams
seems to be dreaming of Caliban."

Later, when Caliban has descended below the surface
into a labyrinthine series of miles-deep caverns in search of the
extra-dimensional entity known as Shrassk, a being that had
been invoked and then imprisoned by the Nine in the eighteenth
century, Caliban has another vision of The Other: "The Other was
standing at the entrance to a cave. He was smiling and holding up

---

[10] Reprinted in *Myths for the Modern Age: Philip José Farmer's Wold Newton Universe*,
Win Scott Eckert, ed., MonkeyBrain Books, 2005; and in *Pearls from Peoria*, Paul
Spiteri, ed., Subterranean Press, 2006. An additional fragment of the novel, entitled
"Down to Earth's Centre," has since been located in Mr. Farmer's "Magic Filing
Cabinet," and was published in *Farmerphile: The Magazine of Philip José Farmer* no.
12, Win Scott Eckert and Paul Spiteri eds., April 2008.

one huge bronze-skinned hand, two fingers forming a V."

"One huge bronze-skinned hand."

The Other is Doc Wildman, communicating to Caliban across the dimensional void.

The presence of Doc Wildman in the caverns deep beneath New England, at the gate held open by the Shrassk entity, as observed by Doc Caliban across the dimensional nexus, strongly indicates that there also exists a secret organization of the Nine in Farmer's universe (i.e., Wildman and Greystoke's dimension, known as the Wold Newton Universe). Since the two universes diverged circa 26,000 B.C., the Nine in each universe have some immortal members in common, members who were alive when the universes divided.

The present volume's "The Wild Huntsman" brings the two universes back together.

Win Scott Eckert is the coauthor with Philip José Farmer of the Wold Newton novel The Evil in Pemberley House, *about Patricia Wildman, the daughter of a certain bronze-skinned pulp hero. Pat Wildman's adventures continue in Eckert's sequel,* The Scarlet Jaguar. *He is the editor of and contributor to* Myths for the Modern Age: Philip José Farmer's Wold Newton Universe, *a 2007 Locus Awards finalist. He has coedited three Green Hornet anthologies, and his tales of Zorro, The Green Hornet, The Avenger, The Phantom, The Scarlet Pimpernel, Captain Midnight, The Domino Lady, and Sherlock Holmes, can be found in the pages of various character-themed anthologies, as well as in the annual series* The

Worlds of Philip José Farmer *and* Tales of the Shadowmen. *His critically acclaimed, encyclopedic two-volume* Crossovers: A Secret Chronology of the World 1 & 2 *was recently released, and* A Girl and Her Cat *(coauthored with Matthew Baugh), the first new Honey West novel in over forty years, is due in 2013. Find him online at www.winscotteckert.com.*

Christopher Paul Carey is the coauthor with Philip José Farmer of The Song of Kwasin, *and the author of* Exiles of Kho, *a prelude to the Khokarsa series. His short fiction may be found in such anthologies as* The Worlds of Philip José Farmer 1: Protean Dimensions, The Worlds of Philip José Farmer 2: Of Dust and Soul, Tales of the Shadowmen: The Vampires of Paris, Tales of the Shadowmen: Grand Guignol, *and* The Avenger: The Justice, Inc. Files. *He is an editor with Paizo Publishing on the award-winning* Pathfinder Roleplaying Game, *and the editor of three collections of Farmer's fiction. Visit him online at www.cpcarey.com.*

THE
GREAT DETECTIVE
AND OTHERS

THE PROBLEM OF THE SORE
BRIDGE—AMONG OTHERS
BY HARRY MANDERS
EDITED BY PHILIP JOSÉ FARMER

This tale is unique in the extent to which its tentacles reach down into the shrouded deeps of the Wold Newton Universe. Enthusiasts of literary crossovers will be sure to revel in an adventure in which gentleman burglar A. J. Raffles takes on three unsolved cases of the Great Detective. Other readers may find their interest piqued by the reference in the story to "a worm unknown to science." A quite similar phrase appears in Sir Arthur Conan Doyle's "The Problem of Thor Bridge" in reference to one of the aforementioned unsolved cases. It is surely no coincidence that the identical phrase crops up again in Farmer's *Escape from Loki: Doc Savage's First Adventure.*

In that novel, the sixteen-year-old future Man of Bronze is shot down over war-torn France in World War I and seeks refuge in the abandoned chateau of one Baron de Musard (whose name also happens to make an appearance in the final tale in this anthology, Win Scott Eckert's "The Wild Huntsman"). There, in a secret chamber dedicated to the dark rites of its former residents,

Savage observes "a long whitish worm moving slowly over the spine bones" of an infant that has been sacrificed upon an unholy altar. Savage thinks that "it was, as far as he was aware, a worm unknown to science." Exactly what one of the strange worms that Raffles encounters in the story at hand was doing in 1918 occupied France has caused much speculation among Farmer's readers. Those interested in exploring this mystery further are encouraged to seek out Christopher Paul Carey's article on the subject, "The Green Eyes Have It—Or Are They Blue?" (*Myths for the Modern Age: Philip José Farmer's Wold Newton Universe*, MonkeyBrain Books, 2005).

Note that according to Farmer's *Tarzan Alive: A Definitive Biography of Lord Greystoke*, Raffles is not only a resident of the Wold Newton Universe; he is also "Tarzan's gray-eyed cousin," making him a full-blooded Wold Newton Family member—as are Sherlock Holmes and Doc Savage, of course.

Harry "Bunny" Manders was an English writer whose other profession was that of gentleman burglar, circa 1890–1900. Manders' adored senior partner and mentor, Arthur J. Raffles, was a cricket player rated on a par with Lord Peter Wimsey or W. G. Grace. Privately, he was a second-story man, a cracksman, a quick-change artist and confidence man whose only peer was Arsène Lupin. Manders' narratives have appeared in four volumes titled (in America) The Amateur Cracksman, Raffles, A Thief in the Night, *and* Mr. Justice Raffles. *"Raffles" has become incorporated into the English language (and a number of others) as a term for a gentleman burglar or dashing upper-crust Jimmy Valentine. Mystery story aficionados, of course, are thoroughly acquainted with the incomparable, though tragically flawed, Raffles and his sidekick, Manders.*

After Raffles' death in the Boer War, Harry Manders gave up crime and became a respectable journalist and author. He married, had children, and died in 1924. His earliest works were agented by E. W. Hornung, Arthur Conan Doyle's brother-in-law. A number of Manders' posthumous works have been agented by Barry Perowne. One of his tales, however, was forbidden by his will to be printed until fifty years after his death. The stipulated time has passed, and now the public may learn how the world was saved without knowing that it was in the gravest peril. It will also discover that the paths of the great Raffles and the great Holmes did cross at least once.

The Boer bullet that pierced my thigh in 1900 lamed me for the rest of my life, but I was quite able to cope with its effects. However, at the age of sixty-one, I suddenly find that a killer that has felled far more men than bullets has lodged within me. The doctor, my kinsman, gives me six months at the most, six months which he frankly says will be very painful. He knows of my crimes, of course, and it may be that he thinks that my suffering will be poetic justice. I'm not sure. But I'll swear that this is the meaning of the slight smile which accompanied his declaration of my doom.

Be that as it may, I have little time left. But I have determined to write down that adventure of which Raffles and I once swore we would never breathe a word. It happened; it really happened. But the world would not have believed it then. It would have been convinced that I was a liar or insane.

I am writing this, nevertheless, because fifty years from now the world may have progressed to the stage where such things as I tell of are credible. Man may even have landed on the moon by then, if he has perfected a propeller which works in the ether as well as in the air. Or if he discovers the same sort of drive that brought… well, I anticipate.

I must hope that the world of 1974 will believe this adventure. Then the world will know that, whatever crimes Raffles and I committed, we paid for them a thousandfold by what we did that week in the May of 1895. And, in fact, the world is and always will be immeasurably in our debt. Yes, my dear doctor, my scornful kinsman, who hopes that I will suffer pain as punishment, I long ago paid off my debt. I only wish that you could be alive to read these words. And, who knows, you may live to be a hundred and may read this account of what you owe me. I hope so.

2

I was nodding in my chair in my room at Mount Street when the clanging of the lift gates in the yard startled me. A moment later, a familiar tattoo sounded on my door. I opened it to find, as I expected, A. J. Raffles himself. He slipped in, his bright blue eyes merry, and he removed his Sullivan from his lips to point it at my whisky and soda.

"Bored, Bunny?"

"Rather," I replied. "It's been almost a year since we stirred our stumps. The voyage around the world after the Levy affair was stimulating. But that ended four months ago. And since then…"

"Ennui and bile!" Raffles cried. "Well, Bunny, that's all over! Tonight we make the blood run hot and cold and burn up all green biliousness!"

"And the swag?" I said.

"Jewels, Bunny! To be exact, star sapphires, or blue corundum, cut *en cabochon*. That is, round with a flat underside. And large, Bunny, vulgarly large, almost the size of a hen's egg, if my informant was not exaggerating. There's a mystery about them, Bunny, a mystery my fence has been whispering with his Cockney speech into my ear for some time. They're dispensed by a Mr. James Phillimore of Kensal Rise. But where he gets them, from whom he lifts them, no one knows. My fence has hinted that they may not come from manorial strongboxes or milady's throat but are smuggled from Southeast Asia or South Africa or Brazil, directly from the mine. In any event, we are going to do some reconnoitering tonight, and if the opportunity should arise…"

"Come now, A. J.," I said bitterly. "You *have* done all the needed reconnoitering. Be honest! Tonight we suddenly find that the moment is propitious, and we strike? Right?"

I had always been somewhat piqued that Raffles chose to do all the preliminary work, the casing, as the underworld says, himself. For some reason, he did not trust me to scout the layout.

Raffles blew a huge and perfect smoke ring from his Sullivan, and he clapped me on the shoulder. "You see through me, Bunny! Yes, I've examined the grounds and checked out Mr. Phillimore's schedule."

I was unable to say anything to the most masterful man I have ever met. I meekly donned dark clothes, downed the rest of the whisky, and left with Raffles. We strolled for some distance, making sure that no policemen were shadowing us, though we had no reason to believe they would be. We then took the last train to Willesden at 11:21. On the way I said, "Does Phillimore live near old Baird's house?"

I was referring to the money lender killed by Jack Rutter,

the details of which case are written in *Wilful Murder*.

"As a matter of fact," Raffles said, watching me with his keen steel-gray eyes, "it's the *same* house. Phillimore took it when Baird's estate was finally settled and it became available to renters. It's a curious coincidence, Bunny, but then all coincidences are curious. To man, that is. Nature is indifferent."

(Yes, I know I stated before that his eyes were blue. And so they were. I've been criticized for saying in one story that his eyes were blue and in another that they were gray. But he has, as any idiot should have guessed, gray-blue eyes which are one color in one light and another in another.)

"That was in January, 1895," Raffles said. "We are in deep waters, Bunny. My investigations have unearthed no evidence that Mr. Phillimore existed before November, 1894. Until he took the lodgings in the East End, no one seems to have heard of or even seen him. He came out of nowhere, rented his third-story lodgings—a terrible place, Bunny—until January. Then he rented the house where bad old Baird gave up the ghost. Since then he's been living a quiet-enough life, excepting the visits he makes once a month to several East End fences. He has a cook and a housekeeper, but these do not live in with him."

At this late hour, the train went no farther than Willesden Junction. We walked from there toward Kensal Rise. Once more, I was dependent on Raffles to lead me through unfamiliar country. However, this time the moon was up, and the country was not quite as open as it had been the last time I was here. A number of cottages and small villas, some only partially built, occupied the empty fields I had passed through that fateful night. We walked down a footpath between a woods and a field, and we came out on the tarred woodblock road that had been laid only four years before. It now had the curb that had been lacking then, but there was still only one pale lamppost across the road from the house.

Before us rose the corner of a high wall with the moonlight shining on the broken glass on top of the wall. It also outlined the sharp spikes on top of the tall green gate. We slipped on our masks. As before, Raffles reached up and placed champagne corks on the spikes. He then put his covert-coat over the corks. We slipped over quietly, Raffles removed the corks, and we stood by the wall in a bed of laurels. I admit I felt apprehensive, even more so than the last time. Old Baird's ghost seemed to hover about the place. The shadows were thicker than they should have been.

I started toward the gravel path leading to the house, which was unlit. Raffles seized my coattails. "Quiet!" he said. "I see somebody—something, anyway—in the bushes at the far end of the garden. Down there, at the angle of the wall."

I could see nothing, but I trusted Raffles, whose eyesight was as keen as a Red Indian's. We moved slowly alongside the wall, stopping frequently to peer into the darkness of the bushes at the angle of the wall. About twenty yards from it, I saw something shapeless move in the shrubbery. I was all for clearing out then, but Raffles fiercely whispered that we could not permit a competitor to scare us away. After a quick conference, we moved in very slowly but surely, slightly more solid shadows in the shadow of the wall. And in a few very long and perspiration-drenched minutes, the stranger fell with one blow from Raffles' fist upon his jaw.

Raffles dragged the snoring man out from the bushes so we could get a look at him by moonlight. "What have we here, Bunny?" he said. "Those long curly locks, that high arching nose, the overly thick eyebrows, and the odor of expensive Parisian perfume? Don't you recognize him?"

I had to confess that I did not.

"What, that is the famous journalist and infamous duelist, Isadora Persano!" he said. "Now tell me you have never heard of him, or her, as the case may be?"

"Of course!" I said. "The reporter for the *Daily Telegraph*!"

"No more," Raffles said, "He's a freelancer now. But what the devil is he doing here?"

"Do you suppose," I said slowly, "that he, too, is one thing by day and quite another at night?"

"Perhaps," Raffles said. "But he may be here in his capacity of journalist. He's also heard things about Mr. James Phillimore. The devil take it! If the press is here, you may be sure that the Yard is not far behind!"

Mr. Persano's features curiously combined a rugged masculinity with an offensive effeminacy. Yet the latter characteristic was not really his fault. His father, an Italian diplomat, had died before he was born. His English mother had longed for a girl, been bitterly disappointed when her only-born was a boy, and, unhindered by a husband or conscience, had named him Isadora and raised him as a girl. Until he entered a public school, he wore dresses. In school, his long hair and certain feminine actions made him the object of an especially vicious persecution by the boys. It was there that he developed his abilities to defend himself with his fists. When he became an adult, he lived on the continent for several years. During this time, he earned a reputation as a dangerous man to insult. It was said that he had wounded half a dozen men with sword or pistol.

From the little bag in which he carried the tools of the trade, Raffles brought a length of rope and a gag. After tying and gagging Persano, Raffles went through his pockets. The only object that aroused his curiosity was a very large matchbox in an inner pocket of his cloak. Opening this, he brought out something that shone in the moonlight.

"By all that's holy!" he said. "It's one of the sapphires!"

"Is Persano a rich man?" I said.

"He doesn't have to work for a living, Bunny. And since he hasn't been in the house yet, I assume he got this from a fence. I also assume that he put the sapphire in the matchbox because a pickpocket isn't likely to steal a box of matches. As it was, *I* was about to ignore it!"

"Let's get out of here," I said. But he crouched staring down at the journalist with an occasional glance at the jewel. This, by the way, was only about a quarter of the size of a hen's egg. Presently, Persano stirred, and he moaned under the gag. Raffles whispered into his ear, and he nodded. Raffles, saying to me, "Cosh him if he looks like he's going to tell," undid the gag.

Persano, as requested, kept his voice low. He confessed that he had heard rumors from his underworld contacts about the precious stones. Having tracked down our fence, he had contrived easily enough to buy one of Mr. Phillimore's jewels. In fact, he said, it was the first one that Mr. Phillimore had brought in to fence. Curious, wondering where the stones came from, since there were no reported thefts of these, he had come here to spy on Phillimore.

"There's a great story here," he said. "But just what, I haven't the foggiest. However, I must warn you that…"

His warning was not heeded. Both Raffles and I heard the low voices outside the gate and the scraping of shoes against gravel.

"Don't leave me tied up here, boys," Persano said. "I might have a little trouble explaining satisfactorily just what I'm doing here. And then there's the jewel…"

Raffles slipped the stone back into the matchbox and put it into Persano's pocket. If we were to be caught, we would not have the gem on us. He untied the journalist's wrists and ankles and said, "Good luck!"

A moment later, after throwing our coats over the broken glass, Raffles and I went over the rear rail. We ran crouching into a dense woods about twenty yards back of the house. At the other side at some distance was a newly built house and a newly laid road. A moment later, we saw Persano come over the wall. He ran by, not seeing us, and disappeared down the road, trailing a heavy cloud of perfume.

"We must visit him at his quarters," said Raffles. He put his hand on my shoulder to warn me, but there was no need. I too had seen the three men come around the corner of the wall. One took a position at the angle of the wall; the other two started toward our woods. We retreated as quietly as possible.

Since there was no train available at this late hour, we walked to Maida Vale and took a hansom from there to home. Raffles went to his rooms at the Albany and I to mine on Mount Street.

When we saw the evening papers, we knew that the affair had taken on even more bizarre aspects. But we still had no inkling of the horrifying metamorphosis yet to come.

I doubt if there is a literate person in the West—or in the Orient, for that matter—who has not read about the strange case of Mr. James Phillimore. At eight in the morning, a hansom cab from Maida Vale pulled up before the gates of his estate. The housekeeper and the cook and Mr. Phillimore were the only occupants of the house. The area outside the walls was being surveilled by eight men from the Metropolitan Police Department. The cab driver rang the electrically operated bell at the gate. Mr. Phillimore walked out of the house and down the gravel path to the gate. Here he was observed by the cab driver, a policeman near the gate, and another in a tree. The latter could see clearly the entire front yard and house, and another man in a tree could clearly see the entire back yard and the back of the house.

Mr. Phillimore opened the gate but did not step through it. Commenting to the cabbie that it looked like rain, he added that he would return to the house to get his umbrella. The cabbie, the policemen, and the housekeeper saw him reenter the house. The housekeeper was at that moment in the room which occupied the front part of the ground floor of the house. She went into the kitchen as Mr. Phillimore entered the house. She did, however, hear his footsteps on the stairs from the hallway which led up to the first floor.

She was the last one to see Mr. Phillimore. He did not come back out of the house. After half an hour Mr. Mackenzie, the Scotland Yard inspector in charge, decided that Mr. Phillimore had somehow become aware that he was under surveillance. Mackenzie gave the signal, and he with three men entered the gate, another four retaining their positions outside. At no time was any part of the area outside the walls unobserved. Nor was the area inside the walls unscrutinized at any time.

The warrant duly shown to the housekeeper, the policemen entered the house and made a thorough search. To their astonishment, they could find no trace of Mr. Phillimore. The six-foot-six, twenty-stone[1] gentleman had utterly disappeared.

For the next two days, the house—and the yard around it—was the subject of the most intense investigation. This established that the house contained no secret tunnels or hideaways. Every cubic inch was accounted for. It was impossible for him not to have left the house; yet he clearly had not done so.

"Another minute's delay, and we would have been

---

[1] Two hundred and eighty pounds.

cornered," Raffles said, taking another Sullivan from his silver cigarette case. "But, Lord, what's going on there, what mysterious forces are working there? Notice that no jewels were found in the house. At least, the police reported none. Now, did Phillimore actually go back to get his umbrella? Of course not. The umbrella was in the stand by the entrance; yet he went right by it and on upstairs. So, he observed the foxes outside the gate and bolted into his briar bush like the good little rabbit he was."

"And where is the briar bush?" I said.

"Ah! That's the question," Raffles breathed. "What kind of a rabbit is it which pulls the briar bush in after it? That is the sort of mystery which has attracted even the Great Detective himself. He has condescended to look into it."

"Then let us stay away from the whole affair!" I cried. "We have been singularly fortunate that none of our victims have called in your relative!"

Raffles was a third or fourth cousin to Holmes, though neither had, to my knowledge, even seen the other. I doubt that the sleuth had even gone to Lord's, or anywhere else, to see a cricket match.

"I wouldn't mind matching wits with him," Raffles said. "Perhaps he might then change his mind about who's the most dangerous man in London."

"We have more than enough money," I said. "Let's drop the whole business."

"It was only yesterday that you were complaining of boredom, Bunny," he said. "No, I think we should pay a visit to our journalist. He may know something that we, and possibly the police, don't know. However, if you prefer," he added contemptuously, "you may stay home."

That stung me, of course, and I insisted that I accompany him. A few minutes later, we got into a hansom, and Raffles told the driver to take us to Praed Street.

4

Persano's apartment was at the end of two flights of Carrara marble steps and a carved mahogany banister. The porter conducted us to 10-C but left when Raffles tipped him handsomely. Raffles knocked on the door. After receiving no answer within a minute, he picked the lock. A moment later, we were inside a suite of extravagantly furnished rooms. A heavy odor of incense hung in the air.

I entered the bedroom and halted aghast. Persano, clad only in underwear, lay on the floor. The underwear, I regret to say, was the sheer black lace of the *demimondaine*. I suppose that if brassieres had existed at that time he would have been wearing one. I did not pay his dress much attention, however, because of his horrible expression. His face was cast into a mask of unutterable terror.

Near the tips of his outstretched fingers lay the large matchbox. It was open, and in it writhed *something*.

I drew back, but Raffles, after one soughing of intaken

breath, felt the man's forehead and pulse and looked into the rigid eyes.

"Stark staring mad," he said. "Frozen with the horror that comes from the deepest of abysses."

Emboldened by his example, I drew near the box. Its contents looked somewhat like a worm, a thick tubular worm, with a dozen slim tentacles projecting from one end. This could be presumed to be its head, since the area just above the roots of the tentacles was ringed with small pale-blue eyes. These had pupils like a cat's. There was no nose or nasal openings or mouth.

"God!" I said shuddering. "What is it?"

"Only God knows," Raffles said. He lifted Persano's right hand and looked at the tips of the fingers. "Note the fleck of blood on each," he said. "They look as if pins have been stuck into them."

He bent over closer to the thing in the box and said, "The tips of the tentacles bear needlelike points, Bunny. Perhaps Persano is not so much paralyzed from horror as from venom."

"Don't get any closer, for heaven's sake!" I said.

"Look, Bunny!" he said. "Doesn't that thing have a tiny shining object in one of its tentacles?"

Despite my nausea, I got down by him and looked straight at the monster. "It seems to be a very thin and slightly curving piece of glass," I said. "What of it?"

Even as I spoke, the end of the tentacle which held the object opened, and the object disappeared within it.

"That *glass*," Raffles said, "is what's left of the *sapphire*. It's eaten it. That piece seems to have been the last of it."

"Eaten a sapphire?" I said, stunned. "Hard metal, blue corundum?"

"I think, Bunny," he said slowly, "the sapphire may only have looked like a sapphire. Perhaps it was not aluminum oxide but something hard enough to fool an expert. The interior may have been filled with something softer than the shell. Perhaps the shell held an embryo."

"What?" I said.

"I mean, Bunny, is it inconceivable, but nevertheless true, that that thing might have *hatched* from the jewel?"

5

We left hurriedly a moment later. Raffles had decided against taking the monster—for which I was very grateful—because he wanted the police to have all the clues available.

"There's something very wrong here, Bunny," he said. "Very sinister." He lit a Sullivan and added in a drawl, "Very *alien*!"

"You mean un-British?" I said.

"I mean… un-Earthly."

A little later, we got out of the cab at St. James' Park and walked across it to the Albany. In Raffles' room, smoking cigars and drinking Scotch whisky and soda, we discussed the significance of all we had seen but could come to no explanation, reasonable or otherwise. The next morning, reading the *Times*, the *Pall Mall Gazette*, and the *Daily Telegraph*, we learned how narrowly we had escaped. According to the papers, Inspectors Hopkins and Mackenzie and the private detective Holmes had entered Persano's rooms two minutes after we had left. Persano had died while on the way to the hospital.

"Not a word about the worm in the box," Raffles said. "The police are keeping it a secret. No doubt, they fear to alarm the public."

There would be, in fact, no official reference to the creature. Nor was it until 1922 that Dr. Watson made a passing reference to it in a published adventure of his colleague. I do not know what happened to the thing, but I suppose that it must have been placed in a jar of alcohol. There it must have quickly perished. No doubt the jar is collecting dust on some shelf in the backroom of some police museum. Whatever happened to it, it must have been disposed of. Otherwise, the world would not be what it is today.

"Strike me, there's only one thing to do, Bunny!" Raffles said, after he'd put the last paper down. "We must get into Phillimore's house and look for ourselves!"

I did not protest. I was more afraid of his scorn than of the police. However, we did not launch our little expedition that evening. Raffles went out to do some reconnoitering on his own, both among the East End fences and around the house in Kensal Rise. The evening of the second day, he appeared at my rooms. I had not been idle, however. I had gathered a supply of more corks for the gatetop spikes by drinking a number of bottles of champagne.

"The police guard has been withdrawn from the estate itself," he said. "I didn't see any men in the woods nearby. So, we break into the late Mr. Phillimore's house tonight. If he is late, that is," he added enigmatically.

As the midnight chimes struck, we went over the gate once

more. A minute later, Raffles was taking out the pane from the glass door. This he did with his diamond, a pot of treacle, and a sheet of brown paper, as he had done the night we broke in and found our would-be blackmailer dead with his head crushed by a poker.

He inserted his hand through the opening, turned the key in the lock, and drew the bolt at the bottom of the door open. This had been shot by a policeman who had then left by the kitchen door, or so we presumed. We went through the door, closed it behind us, and made sure that all the drapes of the front room were pulled tight. Then Raffles, as he did that evil night long ago, lit a match and with it a gas light. The flaring illumination showed us a room little changed. Apparently, Mr. Phillimore had not been interested in redecorating. We went out into the hallway and upstairs, where three doors opened onto the first-floor hallway.

The first door led to the bedroom. It contained a huge canopied bed, a mid-century monster Baird had bought secondhand in some East End shop, a cheap maple tallboy, a rocking chair, a thunder mug, and two large overstuffed leather armchairs.

"There was only one armchair the last time we were here," Raffles said.

The second room was unchanged, being as empty as the first time we'd seen it. The room at the rear was the bathroom, also unchanged.

We went downstairs and through the hallway to the kitchen, and then we descended into the coal cellar. This also contained a small wine pantry. As I expected, we had found nothing. After all, the men from the Yard were thorough, and what they might have missed, Holmes would have found. I was about to suggest to Raffles that we should admit failure and leave before somebody saw the lights in the house. But a sound from upstairs stopped me.

Raffles had heard it, too. Those ears missed little. He held up a hand for silence, though none was needed. He said, a moment later, "Softly, Bunny! It may be a policeman. But I think it is probably our quarry!"

We stole up the wooden steps, which insisted on creaking under our weight. Thence we crept into the kitchen and from there into the hallway and then into the front room. Seeing nobody, we went up the steps to the first floor once more and gingerly opened the door of each room and looked within. While we were poking our heads into the bathroom, we heard a noise again. It came from somewhere in the front of the house, though whether it was upstairs or down we could not tell.

Raffles beckoned to me, and I followed, also on tiptoe, down the hall. He stopped at the door of the middle room, looked within, then led me to the door of the bedroom. On looking in (remember, we had not turned out the gaslights yet), he started. And he said, "Lord! One of the armchairs! It's gone!"

"But—but... who'd want to take a chair?" I said.

"Who, indeed!" he said, and ran down the steps with no attempt to keep quiet. I gathered my wits enough to order my feet to get moving. Just as I reached the door, I heard Raffles outside shouting, "There he goes!" I ran out onto the little tiled veranda. Raffles was halfway down the gravel path, and a dim figure was plunging through the open gate. Whoever he was, he had had a key to the gate.

I remember thinking, irrelevantly, how cool the air had become in the short time we'd been in the house. Actually, it was not such an irrelevant thought since the advent of the cold air had caused a heavy mist. It hung over the road and coiled through the woods. And, of course, it helped the man we were chasing.

Raffles was as keen as a bill-collector chasing a debtor, and he kept his eyes on the vague figure until it plunged into a grove. When I came out its other side, breathing hard, I found Raffles standing on the edge of a narrow but rather deeply sunk brook. Nearby, half shrouded by the mist, was a short and narrow footbridge. Down the path that started from its other end was another of the half-built houses.

"He didn't cross that bridge," Raffles said. "I'd have heard him. If he went through the brook, he'd have done some splashing, and I'd have heard it. But he didn't have time to double back. Let's cross the bridge and see if he's left any footprints in the mud."

We walked Indian file across the very narrow bridge. It bent a little under our weight, giving us an uneasy feeling. Raffles said, "The contractor must be using as cheap materials as he can get away with. I hope he's putting better stuff into the houses. Otherwise, the first strong wind will blow them away."

"It does seem rather fragile," I said. "The builder must be a fly-by-night. But nobody builds anything as they used to do."

Raffles crouched down at the other end of the bridge, lit a match, and examined the ground on both sides of the path.

"There are any number of prints," he said disgustedly. "They undoubtedly are those of the workmen, though the prints of the man we want could be among them. But I doubt it. They're all made by heavy workingmen's boots."

He sent me down the steep muddy bank to look for prints on the south side of the bridge. He went along the bank north of the bridge. Our matches flared and died while we called out the results of our inspections to each other. The only tracks we saw were ours. We scrambled back up the bank and walked a little way onto the bridge. Side by side, we leaned over the excessively thin railing to stare down into the brook. Raffles lit a Sullivan, and the pleasant odor drove me to light one up too.

"There's something uncanny here, Bunny. Don't you feel it?"

I was about to reply when he put his hand on my shoulder. Softly, he said, "Did you hear a groan?"

"No," I replied, the hairs on the back of my neck rising like the dead from the grave.

Suddenly, he stamped the heel of his boot hard upon the plank. And then I heard a very low moan.

Before I could say anything to him, he was over the railing. He landed with a squish of mud on the bank. A match flared under the bridge, and for the first time I comprehended how thin the wood of the bridge was. I could see the flame through the planks.

Raffles yelled with horror. The match went out. I shouted, "What is it?" Suddenly, I was falling. I grabbed at the railing, felt it dwindle out of my grip, struck the cold water of the brook, felt the planks beneath me, felt them sliding away, and shouted once more. Raffles, who had been knocked down and buried for a minute by the collapsed bridge, rose unsteadily. Another match flared, and he cursed. I said, somewhat stupidly, "Where's the bridge?"

"Taken flight," he groaned. "Like the chair!"

He leaped past me and scrambled up the bank. At its top he stood for a minute, staring into the moonlight and the darkness beyond. I crawled shivering out of the brook, rose even more unsteadily, and clawed up the greasy cold mud of the steep bank. A minute later, breathing harshly, and feeling dizzy with unreality, I was standing by Raffles. He was breathing almost as hard as I.

"What *is* it?" I said.

"*What* is it, Bunny?" he said slowly. "It's something that can change its shape to resemble almost anything. As of now, however, it is not what it is but *where* it is that we must determine. We must find it and kill it, even if it should take the shape of a beautiful woman or a child."

"What are you talking about?" I cried.

"Bunny, as God is my witness, when I lit that match under the bridge, I saw one brown eye staring at me. It was embedded in a part of the planking that was thicker than the rest. And it was not far from what looked like a pair of lips and one malformed ear. Apparently, it had not had time to complete its transformation. Or, more likely, it retained organs of sight and hearing so that it would know what was happening in its neighborhood. If it scaled off all its organs of detection, it would not have the slightest idea when it would be safe to change shape again."

"Are you insane?" I said.

"Not unless you share my insanity, since you saw the same things I did. Bunny, that thing can somehow alter its flesh and bones. It has such control over its cells, its organs, its bones—which somehow can switch from rigidity to extreme flexibility—that it can look like other human beings. It can also metamorphose to look like objects. Such as the armchair in the bedroom, which looked exactly like the original. No wonder that Hopkins and Mackenzie and even the redoubtable Holmes failed to find Mr. James Phillimore. Perhaps they may even have sat on him while resting from the search. It's too bad that they did not rip into the chair with a knife in their quest for the jewels. I think that they would have been more than surprised.

"I wonder who the original Phillimore was? There is no record of anybody who could have been the model. But perhaps it based itself on somebody with a different name but took the name of James Phillimore from a tombstone or a newspaper account of an American. Whatever it did on that account, it was also the bridge that you and I crossed. A rather sensitive bridge, a sore bridge, which could not keep from groaning a little when our hard boots pained it."

I could not believe him. Yet I could *not* not believe him.

6

Raffles predicted that the thing would be running or walking to Maida Vale. "And there it will take a cab to the nearest station and be on its way into the labyrinth of London. The devil of it is that we won't know what, or whom, to look for. It could be in the shape of a woman, or a small horse, for all I know. Or maybe a tree, though that's not a very mobile refuge.

"You know," he continued after some thought, "there must be definite limitations on what it can do. It has demonstrated that it can stretch its mass out to almost paper-thin length. But it is, after all, subject to the same physical laws we are subject to as far as its mass goes. It has only so much substance, and so it can get only so big. And I imagine that it can compress itself only so much. So, when I said that it might be the shape of a child, I could have been wrong. It can probably extend itself considerably but cannot contract much."

As it turned out, Raffles was right. But he was also wrong. The thing had means for becoming smaller, though at a price.

"Where could it have come from, A. J.?"

"That's a mystery that might better be laid in the lap of Holmes," he said. "Or perhaps in the hands of the astronomers. I would guess that the thing is not autochthonous. I would say that it arrived here recently, perhaps from Mars, perhaps from a more distant planet, during the month of October, 1894. Do you remember, Bunny, when all the papers were ablaze with accounts of the large falling star that fell into the Straits of Dover, not five miles from Dover itself? Could it have been some sort of ship which could carry a passenger through the ether? From some heavenly body where life exists, intelligent life, though not life as we terrestrials know it? Could it perhaps have crashed, its propulsive power having failed it? Hence, the friction of its too-swift descent burned away part of the hull? Or were the flames merely the outward expression of its propulsion, which might be huge rockets?"

Even now, as I write this in 1924, I marvel at Raffles' superb imagination and deductive powers. That was 1895, three years before Mr. Wells' *War of the Worlds* was published. It was true that Mr. Verne had been writing his wonderful tales of scientific inventions and extraordinary voyages for many years. But in none of them had he proposed life on other planets or the possibility of infiltration or invasion by alien sapients from far-off planets. The concept was, to me, absolutely staggering. Yet Raffles plucked it from what to others would be a complex of complete irrelevancies. And I was supposed to be the writer of fiction in this partnership!

"I connect the events of the falling star and Mr. Phillimore because it was not too long after the star fell that Mr. Phillimore suddenly appeared from nowhere. In January of this year Mr. Phillimore sold his first jewel to a fence. Since then, once a month, Mr. Phillimore has sold a jewel, four in all. These look like star sapphires. But we may suppose that they are not such because of our experience with the monsterlet in Persano's matchbox. Those pseudo jewels, Bunny, are eggs!"

"Surely you do not mean that?" I said.

"My cousin has a maxim which has been rather widely quoted. He says that, after you've eliminated the impossible, whatever remains, however improbable, is the truth. Yes, Bunny, the race to which Mr. Phillimore belongs lays eggs. These are, in their initial form, anyway, something resembling star sapphires. The star shape inside them may be the first outlines of the embryo. I would guess that shortly before hatching, the embryo becomes opaque. The material inside, the yolk, is absorbed or eaten by the embryo. Then the shell is broken and the fragments are eaten by the little beast.

"And then, sometime after hatching, a short time, I'd say, the beastie must become mobile, it wriggles away, it takes refuge in a hole, a mouse hole, perhaps. And there it feeds upon cockroaches, mice, and, when it gets larger, rats. And then, Bunny? Dogs? Babies? And then?"

"Stop," I cried. "It's too horrible to contemplate!"

"Nothing is too horrible to contemplate, Bunny, if one can do something about the thing contemplated. In any event, if I am right, and I pray that I am, only one egg has so far hatched. This was the first one laid, the one that Persano somehow obtained. Within thirty days, another egg will hatch. And this time the thing might get away. We must track down all the eggs and destroy them. But first we must catch the thing that is laying the eggs.

"That won't be easy. It has an amazing intelligence and adaptability. Or, at least, it has amazing mimetic abilities. In one month it learned to speak English perfectly and to become well acquainted with British customs. That is no easy feat, Bunny. There are thousands of Frenchmen and Americans who have been here for some time who have not yet comprehended the British language, temperament, or customs. And these are human beings, though there are, of course, some Englishmen who are uncertain about this."

"Really, A. J.!" I said. "We're not all that snobbish!"

"Aren't we? It takes one to know one, my dear colleague, and I am unashamedly snobbish. After all, if one is an Englishman, it's no crime to be a snob, is it? Somebody has to be superior, and we know who that someone is, don't we?"

"You were speaking of the thing," I said testily.

"Yes. It must be in a panic. It knows it's been found out, and it must think that by now the entire human race will be howling for its blood. At least, I hope so. If it truly knows us, it will realize that we would be extremely reluctant to report it to the authorities. We would not want to be certified. Nor does it know that we cannot stand an investigation into our own lives.

"But it will, I hope, be ignorant of this and so will be trying to escape the country. To do so, it will take the closest and fastest means of transportation, and to do that it must buy a ticket to a definite destination. That destination, I guess, will be Dover. But perhaps not."

At the Maida Vale cab station, Raffles made inquiries of various drivers. We were lucky. One driver had observed another pick up a woman who might be the person—or thing—we were chasing. Encouraged by Raffles' pound note, the cabbie described her. She was a giantess, he said, she seemed to be about fifty years old, and, for some reason, she looked familiar. To his knowledge, he had never seen her before.

Raffles had him describe her face feature by feature. He said, "Thank you," and turned away with a wink at me. When we were alone, I asked him to explain the wink.

"She—it—had familiar features because they were Phillimore's own, though somewhat feminized," Raffles said. "We are on the right track."

On the way into London in our own cab, I said, "I don't understand how the thing gets rid of its clothes when it changes shape. And where did it get its woman's clothes and the purse? And its money to buy the ticket?"

"Its clothes must be part of its body. It must have superb control; it's a sentient chameleon, a superchameleon."

"But its money?" I said. "I understand that it has been selling its eggs in order to support itself. Also, I assume, to disseminate its young. But from where did the thing, when it became a woman, get the money with which to buy a ticket? And was the purse a part of its body before the metamorphosis? If it was, then it must be able to detach parts of its body."

"I rather imagine it has caches of money here and there," Raffles said.

We got out of the cab near St. James' Park, walked to

Raffles' rooms at the Albany, quickly ate a breakfast brought in by the porter, donned false beards and plain-glass spectacles and fresh clothes, and then packed a Gladstone bag and rolled up a traveling rug. Raffles also put on a finger a very large ring. This concealed in its hollow interior a spring-operated knife, tiny but very sharp. Raffles had purchased it after his escape from the Camorra deathtrap (described in *The Last Laugh*). He said that if he had had such a device then, he might have been able to cut himself loose instead of depending upon someone else to rescue him from Count Corbucci's devilish automatic executioner. And now a hunch told him to wear the ring during this particular exploit.

We boarded a hansom a few minutes later and soon were on the Charing Cross platform waiting for the train to Dover. And then we were off, comfortably ensconced in a private compartment, smoking cigars and sipping brandy from a flask carried by Raffles.

"I am leaving deduction and induction behind in favor of intuition, Bunny," Raffles said. "Though I could be wrong, intuition tells me that the thing is on the train ahead of us, headed for Dover."

"There are others who think as you do," I said, looking through the glass of the door. "But it must be inference, not intuition, that brings them here." Raffles glanced up in time to see the handsome aquiline features of his cousin and the beefy but genial features of his cousin's medical colleague go by. A moment later, Mackenzie's craggy features followed.

"Somehow," Raffles said, "that human bloodhound, my

cousin, has sniffed out the thing's trail. Has he guessed any of the truth? If he has, he'll keep it to himself. The hardheads of the Yard would believe that he'd gone insane, if he imparted even a fraction of the reality behind the case."

7

Just before the train arrived at the Dover station, Raffles straightened up and snapped his fingers, a vulgar gesture I'd never known him to make before.

"Today's the day!" he cried. "Or it should be! Bunny, it's a matter of unofficial record that Phillimore came into the East End every thirty-first day to sell a jewel. Does this suggest that it lays an egg every thirty days? If so, then it lays another *today*! Does it do it as easily as the barnyard hen? Or does it experience some pain, some weakness, some tribulation and trouble analogous to that of human women? Is the passage of the egg a minor event, yet one which renders the layer prostrate for an hour or two? Can one lay a large and hard star sapphire with only a trivial difficulty, with only a pleased cackle?"

On getting off the train, he immediately began questioning porters and other train and station personnel. He was fortunate enough to discover a man who'd been on the train on which we suspected the thing had been. Yes, he had noticed something disturbing. A woman had occupied a compartment by herself, a very large woman, a Mrs. Brownstone. But when the train had pulled into the station, a huge man had left her compartment. She was nowhere to be seen. He had, however, been too busy to do anything about it even if there had been anything to do.

Raffles spoke to me afterward. "Could it have taken a hotel room so it could have the privacy needed to lay its egg?"

We ran out of the station and hired a cab to take us to the nearest hotel. As we pulled away, I saw Holmes and Watson talking to the very man we'd just been talking to.

The first hotel we visited was the Lord Warden, which was near the railway station and had a fine view of the harbor. We had no luck there, nor at the Burlington, which was on Liverpool Street, nor the Dover Castle, on Clarence Place. But at the King's Head, also on Clarence Place, we found that he—it—had recently been there. The desk clerk informed us that a man answering our description had checked in. He had left exactly five minutes ago. He had looked pale and shaky, as though he'd had too much to drink the night before.

As we left the hotel, Holmes, Watson, and Mackenzie entered. Holmes gave us a glance that poked chills through me. I was sure that he must have noted us in the train, at the station, and now at this hotel. Possibly, the clerks in the other hotels had told him that he had been preceded by two men asking questions about the same man.

Raffles hailed another cab and ordered the driver to take us along the waterfront, starting near Promenade Pier. As we rattled along, he said, "I may be wrong, Bunny, but I feel that Mr. Phillimore is going home."

"To Mars?" I said, startled. "Or wherever his home planet may be?"

"I rather think that his destination is no farther than the vessel that brought him here. It may still be under the waves, lying on the bottom of the straits, which is nowhere deeper than twenty-five fathoms. Since it must be airtight, it could be like Mr. Campbell's and Ash's all-electric submarine. Mr. Phillimore could be heading toward it, intending to hide out for some time. To lie low, literally, while affairs cool off in England."

"And how would he endure the pressure and the cold of twenty-five fathoms of sea water while on his way down to the vessel?" I said.

"Perhaps he turns into a fish," Raffles said irritatedly.

I pointed out the window. "Could that be he?"

"It might well be *it*," he replied. He shouted for the cabbie to slow down. The very tall, broad-shouldered, and huge-paunched man with the great rough face and the nose like a red pickle looked like the man described by the agent and the clerk. Moreover, he carried the purplish Gladstone bag which they had also described.

Our hansom swerved toward him; he looked at us; he turned pale; he began running. How had he recognized us? I do not know. We were still wearing the beards and spectacles, and he had seen us only briefly by moonlight and matchlight when we were wearing black masks. Perhaps he had a keen sense of odor, though how he could have picked up our scent from among the tar, spices, sweating men and horses, and the rotting garbage floating on the water, I do not know.

Whatever his means of detection, he recognized us. And the chase was on.

It did not last long on land. He ran down a pier for private craft, untied a rowboat, leaped into it, and began rowing as if he were training for the Henley Royal Regatta. I stood for a moment on the edge of the pier; I was stunned and horrified. His left foot was in contact with the Gladstone bag, and it was melting, flowing *into* his foot. In sixty seconds, it had disappeared except for a velvet bag it contained. This, I surmised, held the egg that the thing had laid in the hotel room.

A minute later, we were rowing after him in another boat while its owner shouted and shook an impotent fist at us. Presently, other shouts joined us. Looking back, I saw Mackenzie, Watson, and Holmes standing by the owner. But they did not talk long to him. They ran back to their cab and raced away.

Raffles said, "They'll be boarding a police boat, a steam-driven paddlewheeler or screwship. But I doubt that it can catch up with *that*, if there's a good wind and a fair head start."

That was Phillimore's destination, a small single-masted sailing ship riding at anchor about fifty yards out. Raffles said that she was a cutter. It was about thirty-five feet long, was fore-and-aft rigged, and carried a jib, forestaysail, and mainsail—according to Raffles. I thanked him for the information, since I knew nothing and cared as much about anything that moves on water. Give me a good solid horse on good solid ground any time.

Phillimore was a good rower, as he should have been with

that great body. But we gained slowly on him. By the time he was boarding the cutter *Alicia*, we were only a few yards behind him. He was just going over the railing when the bow of our boat crashed into the stern of his. Raffles and I went head over heels, oars flying. But we were up and swarming up the rope ladder within a few seconds. Raffles was first, and I fully expected him to be knocked in the head with a belaying pin or whatever it is that sailors use to knock people in the head. Later, he confessed that he expected to have his skull crushed in, too. But Phillimore was too busy recruiting a crew to bother with us at that moment.

When I say he was recruiting, I mean that he was splitting himself into three sailors. At that moment, he lay on the foredeck and was melting, clothes and all.

We should have charged him then and seized him while he was helpless. But we were too horrified. I, in fact, became nauseated, and I vomited over the railing. While I was engaged in this, Raffles got control of himself. He advanced swiftly toward the three-lobed monstrosity on the deck. He had gotten only a few feet, however, when a voice rang out.

"Put up yore dooks, you swells! Reach for the blue!"

Raffles froze. I raised my head and saw through teary eyes an old grizzled salt. He must have come from the cabin on the poopdeck, or whatever they call it, because he had not been visible when we came aboard. He was aiming a huge Colt revolver at us.

Meanwhile, the schizophrenic transformation was completed. Three little sailors, none higher than my waist, stood before us. They were identically featured, and they looked exactly like the old salt except for their size. They had beards and wore white-and-blue-striped stocking caps, large earrings in the left ear, red-and-black-striped jerseys, blue calf-length baggy pants, and they were barefooted. They began scurrying around, up came the anchor, the sails were set, and we were moving at a slant past the great Promenade Pier.

The old sailor had taken over the wheel after giving one of the midgets his pistol. Meanwhile, behind us, a small steamer, its smokestack belching black, tried vainly to catch up with us.

After about ten minutes, one of the tiny sailors took over the wheel. The old salt and one of his duplicates herded us into the cabin. The little fellow held the gun on us while the old sailor tied our wrists behind us and our legs to the upright pole of a bunk with a rope.

"You filthy traitor!" I snarled at the old sailor. "You are betraying the entire human race! Where is your common humanity?"

The old tar cackled and rubbed his gray wirelike whiskers.

"Me humanity? It's where the lords in Parliament and the fat bankers and the church-going factory owners of Manchester keep theirs, me fine young gentleman! In me pocket! Money talks louder than common humanity any day, as any of your landed lords or great cotton spinners will admit when they're drunk in the privacies of their mansion! What did common humanity ever do for me but give me parents the galloping consumption and make me sisters into drunken whores?"

I said nothing more. There was no reasoning with such a beastly wretch. He looked us over to make sure we were secure, and he and the tiny sailor left. Raffles said, "As long as Phillimore remains—like Gaul—in three parts, we have a chance. Surely, each of the trio's brains must have only a third of the intelligence of the original Phillimore I hope. And this little knife concealed in my ring will be the key to our liberty. I hope."

Fifteen minutes later, he had released himself and me. We went into the tiny galley, which was next to the cabin and part of the same structure. There we each took a large butcher's knife and a large iron cooking pan. And when, after a long wait, one of the midgets came down into the cabin, Raffles hit him alongside the head with a pan before he could yell out. To my horror, Raffles then squeezed the thin throat between his two hands, and he did not let loose until the thing was dead.

"No time for niceties, Bunny," he said, grinning ghastily as he extracted the jewel-egg from the corpse's pocket. "Phillimore's a type of Boojum. If he succeeds in spawning many young, mankind will disappear softly and quietly, one by one. If it becomes necessary to blow up this ship and us with it, I'll not hesitate a moment. Still, we've reduced its forces by one-third. Now let's see if we can't make it one hundred percent."

He put the egg in his own pocket. A moment later, cautiously, we stuck our heads from the structure and looked out. We were in the forepart, facing the foredeck, and thus the old salt at the wheel couldn't see us. The other two midgets were working in the rigging at the orders of the steersman. I suppose that the thing actually knew little of sailsmanship and had to be instructed.

"Look at that, dead ahead," Raffles said. "This is a bright clear day, Bunny. Yet there's a patch of mist there that has no business being there. And we're sailing directly into it."

One of the midgets was holding a device which looked much like Raffles' silver cigarette case except that it had two rotatable knobs on it and a long thick wire sticking up from its top. Later, Raffles said that he thought that it was a machine which somehow sent vibrations through the ether to the spaceship on the bottom of the straits. These vibrations, coded, of course, signaled the automatic machinery on the ship to extend a tube to the surface. And an artificial fog was expelled from the tube.

His explanation was unbelievable, but it was the only one extant. Of course, at that time neither of us had heard of wireless, although some scientists knew of Hertz's experiments with oscillations. And Marconi was to patent the wireless telegraph the following year. But Phillimore's wireless must have been far advanced over anything we have in 1924.

"As soon as we're in the mist, we attack," Raffles said.

A few minutes later, wreaths of gray fell about us, and our faces felt cold and wet. We could barely see the two midgets working furiously to let down the sails. We crept out onto the deck and looked around the cabin's corner at the wheel. The old tar was no longer in sight. Nor was there any reason for him to be at the wheel. The ship was almost stopped. It obviously must be over the space vessel resting on the mud twenty fathoms below.

Raffles went back into the cabin after telling me to keep an eye on the two midgets. A few minutes later, just as I was beginning to feel panicky about his long absence, he popped out of the cabin.

"The old man was opening the petcocks," he said. "This ship will sink soon with all that water pouring in."

"Where is he?" I said.

"I hit him over the head with the pan," Raffles said. "I suppose he's drowning now."

At that moment, the two little sailors called out for the old sailor and the third member of the trio to come running. They were lowering the cutter's boat and apparently thought there wasn't much time before the ship went down. We ran out at them through the fog just as the boat struck the water. They squawked like chickens suddenly seeing a fox, and they leaped down into the boat. They didn't have far to go since the cutter's deck was now only about two feet above the waves. We jumped down into the boat and sprawled on our faces. Just as we scrambled up, the cutter rolled over, fortunately away from us, and bottom up. The lines attached to the davit had been loosed, and so our boat was not dragged down some minutes later when the ship sank.

A huge round form, like the back of a Brobdingnagian turtle, broke water beside us. Our boat rocked, and water shipped in, soaking us. Even as we advanced on the two tiny men, who jabbed at us with their knives, a port opened in the side of the great metal craft. Its lower part was below the surface of the sea, and suddenly water rushed into it, carrying our boat along with it. The ship was swallowing our boat and us along with it.

Then the port had closed behind us, but we were in a metallic and well-lit chamber. While the fight raged, with Raffles and me swinging our pans and thrusting our knives at the very agile and speedy midgets, the water was pumped out. As we were to find out, the vessel was sinking back to the mud of the bottom.

The two midgets finally leaped from the boat onto a metal

platform. One pressed a stud in the wall, and another port opened. We jumped after them, because we knew that if they got away and got their hands on their weapons, and these might be fearsome indeed, we'd be lost. Raffles knocked one off the platform with a swipe of the pan, and I slashed at the other with my knife.

The thing below the platform cried out in a strange language, and the other one jumped down beside him. He sprawled on top of his fellow, and within a few seconds they were melting together.

It was an act of sheer desperation. If they had had more than one-third of their normal intelligence, they probably would have taken a better course of action. Fusion took time, and this time we did not stand there paralyzed with horror. We leaped down and caught the thing halfway between its shape as two men and its normal, or natural, shape. Even so, tentacles with the poisoned claws on their ends sprouted, and the blue eyes began to form. It looked like a giant version of the thing in Persano's matchbox. But it was only two-thirds as large as it would have been if we'd not slain the detached part of it on the cutter. Its tentacles also were not as long as they would have been, but even so we could not get past them to its body. We danced around just outside their reach, cutting the tips with knives or batting them with the pans. The thing was bleeding, and two of its claws had been knocked off, but it was keeping us off while completing its metamorphosis. Once the thing was able to get to its feet, or, I should say, its pseudopods, we'd be at an awful disadvantage.

Raffles yelled at me and ran toward the boat. I looked at him stupidly, and he said, "Help me, Bunny!"

I ran to him, and he said, "Slide the boat onto the thing, Bunny!"

"It's too heavy," I yelled, but I grabbed the side while he pushed on its stern; and somehow, though I felt my intestines would spurt out, we slid it over the watery floor. We did not go very fast, and the thing, seeing its peril, started to stand up. Raffles stopped pushing and threw his frying pan at it. It struck the thing at its head end, and down it went. It lay there a moment as if stunned, which I suppose it was.

Raffles came around to the side opposite mine, and when we were almost upon the thing, but still out of reach of its vigorously waving tentacles, we lifted the bow of the boat. We didn't raise it very far, since it was very heavy. But when we let it fall, it crushed six of the tentacles beneath it. We had planned to drop it squarely on the middle of the thing's loathsome body, but the tentacles kept us from getting any closer.

Nevertheless, it was partially immobilized. We jumped into the boat and, using its sides as a bulwark, slashed at the tips of the tentacles that were still free. As the ends came over the side, we cut them off or smashed them with the pans. Then we climbed out, while it was screaming through the openings at the ends of the tentacles, and we stabbed it again and again. Greenish blood flowed from its wounds until the tentacles suddenly ceased writhing. The eyes became lightless; the greenish ichor turned black-red and congealed. A sickening odor, that of its death, rose from the wounds.

8

It took several days to study the controls on the panel in the vessel's bridge. Each was marked with a strange writing which we would never be able to decipher. But Raffles, the ever redoubtable Raffles, discovered the control that would move the vessel from the bottom to the surface, and he found out how to open the port to the outside. That was all we needed to know.

Meantime, we ate and drank from the ship's stores which had been laid in to feed the old tar. The other food looked nauseating, and even if it had been attractive, we'd not have dared to try it. Three days later, after rowing the boat out onto the sea—the mist was gone—we watched the vessel, its port still open, sink back under the waters. And it is still there on the bottom, for all I know.

We decided against telling the authorities about the thing and its ship. We had no desire to spend time in prison, no matter how patriotic we were. We might have been pardoned because of our great services. But then again we might, according to Raffles, be shut up for life because the authorities would want to keep the whole affair a secret.

Raffles also said that the vessel probably contained devices which, in Great Britain's hands, would ensure her supremacy. But she was already the most powerful nation on Earth, and who knew what Pandora's box we'd be opening? We did not know, of course, that in twenty-three years the Great War would slaughter the majority of our best young men and would start our nation toward second-classdom.

Once ashore, we took passage back to London. There we launched the month's campaign that resulted in stealing and destroying every one of the sapphire-eggs. One had hatched, and the thing had taken refuge inside the walls, but Raffles burned the house down, though not until after rousing its human occupants. It broke our hearts to steal jewels worth in the neighborhood of a million pounds and then destroy them. But we did it, and so the world was saved.

Did Holmes guess some of the truth? Little escaped those gray hawk's eyes and the keen gray brain behind them. I suspect that he knew far more than he told even Watson. That is why Watson, in writing *The Problem of Thor Bridge*, stated that there were three cases in which Holmes had completely failed.

There was the case of James Phillimore, who returned into his house to get an umbrella and was never seen again. There was the case of Isadora Persano, who was found stark mad, staring at a worm in a matchbox, a worm unknown to science. And there was the case of the cutter *Alicia*, which sailed on a bright spring morning into a small patch of mist and never emerged, neither she nor her crew ever being seen again.

A SCARLETIN STUDY

BY JONATHAN SWIFT SOMERS III
EDITED BY PHILIP JOSÉ FARMER

BEING A REPRINT FROM THE REMINISCENCES OF
JOHANN H. WEISSTEIN, DR. MED., LATE OF THE
AUTOBAHN PATROL MEDICAL DEPARTMENT.

It is little wonder that Philip José Farmer ended up editing the following story, keen as he was for both mysteries and puns. In his Wold Newton biography *Doc Savage: His Apocalyptic Life*, Farmer makes it clear that Ralph von Wau Wau—the famous canine detective whose intelligence and skills rival those of Sherlock Holmes himself—is indeed a resident of the Wold Newton Universe.

Some readers new to the following tale might wonder why the name Ralph von Wau Wau seems so strangely familiar. They need look no further than Spider Robinson's brilliantly funny and appropriately pun-filled Callahan stories, in which, by permission of the editor, Ralph has frequently appeared as a character. Similarly, Jonathan Swift Somers III might be familiar to some as the favorite author of Simon Wagstaff, the protagonist of Farmer's novel *Venus on the Half-Shell* (Titan Books, 2013).

In "Jonathan Swift Somers III: Cosmic Traveller in a Wheelchair," a biographical sketch on the present story's author, Farmer writes the following:

"There is no doubt that Somers modeled his fictional dog, Ralph von Wau Wau, on his own pet. Or is there doubt? The Bellener Street Irregulars[2] insist that there is a real von Wau Wau. In fact, Somers is not the real author of the series of tales about this Hamburg police dog who became a private eye. The Irregulars maintain that Somers is only the literary agent for Johann H. Weisstein, Dr. Med., and for Cordwainer Bird, the two main narrators in the Wau Wau series. Weisstein and Bird are the real authors.

"When asked about this, Somers only replied, 'I am not at liberty to discuss the matter.'"

---

[2] A society dedicated to the study of the canine detective Ralph von Wau Wau.

FOREWORD

Ralph von Wau Wau's first case as a private investigator is not his most complicated or curious. It does, however, illustrate remarkably well my colleague's peculiar talents. And it is, after all, his first case, and one should proceed chronologically in these chronicles. It is also the only case I know of in which not the painting but the painter was stolen. And it is, to me, most memorable because through it I met the woman who will always be for me The Woman.

Consider this scene. Von Wau Wau, his enemy, Detective-Lieutenant Strasse, myself, and the lovely Lisa Scarletin, all standing before a large painting in a room in a Hamburg police station. Von Wau Wau studies the painting while we wonder if he's right in his contention that it is not only a work of art but a map. Its canvas bears, among other things, the images of Sherlock Holmes in lederhosen, Sir Francis Bacon, a green horse, a mirror, Christ coming from the tomb, Tarzan, a waistcoat, the Wizard of Oz in a balloon, an ancient king of

Babylon with a dietary problem, and a banana tree.

But let me begin at the beginning.

HERR RALPH VON WAU WAU

In the year 1978 I took my degree of Doctor of Medicine at the University of Cologne and proceeded to Hamburg to go through the course prescribed for surgeons in the Autobahn Patrol. Having completed my studies there, I was duly attached to the Fifth North-Rhine Westphalia Anti-Oiljackers as assistant surgeon. The campaign against the notorious Rottenfranzer Gang brought honors and promotions to many, but for me it was nothing but misfortune and disaster. At the fatal battle of the Emmerich Off-Ramp, I was struck, on the shoulder, by a missile which shattered the bone. I should have fallen into the hands of the murderous Rottenfranzer himself but for the devotion and courage shown by Morgen, my paramedic aide, who threw me across a Volkswagen and succeeded in driving safely across the Patrol lines.

At the base hospital at Hamburg (and it really is base), I seemed on the road to recovery when I was struck down with an extremely rare malady. At least, I have read of only one case similar to mine. This was, peculiarly, the affliction of another doctor, though he was an Englishman and he suffered his wounds a hundred years before on another continent. My case was written up in medical journals and then in general periodicals all over the world. The affliction itself became known popularly as "the peregrinating pain," though the scientific name, which I prefer for understandable reasons, was "Weisstein's Syndrome." The popular name arose from the fact that the occasional suffering it caused me did not remain at the site of the original wound. At times, the pain traveled downward and lodged in my leg. This was a cause célèbre, scientifically speaking, nor was the mystery solved until some years later. (In *The Wonder of the Wandering Wound*, not yet published.)

However, I rallied and had improved enough to be able to walk or limp about the wards, and even to bask a little on the veranda when smog or fog permitted, when I was struck down by *Weltschmerz*, that curse of Central Europe. For months my mind was despaired of, and when at last I came to myself, six months had passed. With my health perhaps not irretrievably ruined, but all ability to wield the knife as a surgeon vanished, I was discharged by a paternal government with permission to spend the rest of my life improving it. (The health, not the life, I mean.) I had neither kith nor kin nor kinder and was therefore as free as the air, which, given my small social security and disability pension, seemed to be what I was expected to eat. Within a few months the state of my finances had become so alarming that I was forced to completely alter my lifestyle. I decided to look around for some considerably less pretentious and expensive domicile than the Hamburg Hilton.

On the very day I'd come to this conclusion, I was standing at the Kennzeichen Bar when someone tapped me on the shoulder. Wincing (it was the wounded shoulder), I turned around. I recognized young blonde Stampfert, who had been an anesthetist under me at the Neustadt Hospital. (I've had a broad experience of women in many nations and on three continents, so much so in fact that I'd considered entering gynecology.) Stampfert had a beautiful body but a drab personality. I was lonely, however, and I hailed her enthusiastically. She, in turn, seemed glad to see me, I suppose because she wanted to flaunt her newly acquired engagement ring. The first thing I knew, I had invited her to lunch. We took the bus to the Neu Bornholt, and on the way I outlined my adventures of the past year.

"Poor devil!" she said. "So what's happening now?"

"Looking for a cheap apartment," I said. "But I doubt that it's possible to get a decent place at a reasonable rate. The housing shortage and its partner, inflation, will be with us for a long time."

"That's a funny thing," Stampfert said. "You're the second… person… today who has said almost those exact words."

"And who was the first?"

"Someone who's just started a new professional career," Stampfert said. "He's having a hard go of it just now. He's looking for a roommate to share not only expenses but a partnership. Someone who's experienced in police work. You seem to fit the bill. The only thing is…"

She hesitated, and I said, "If he's easy to get along with, I'd be delighted to share the expenses with him. And work is something I need badly."

"Well, there's more to it than that, though he is easy to get along with. Lovable, in fact."

She hesitated, then said, "Are you allergic to animals?"

I stared at her and said, "Not at all. Why, does this man have pets?"

"Not exactly," Stampfert said, looking rather strange.

"Well, then, what is it?"

"There is a dog," she said. "A highly intelligent… police dog."

"Don't tell me this fellow is blind?" I said. "Not that it will matter, of course."

"Just color-blind," she said. "His name is Ralph."

"Yes, go on," I said. "What about Herr Ralph?"

"That's his first name," Stampfert said. "His full name is Ralph von Wau Wau."

"What?" I said, and then I guffawed. "A man whose last name is a dog's bark?" (In Germany "wau wau"—pronounced vau vau—corresponds to the English "bow wow.")

Suddenly, I said, "Ach!" I had just remembered where I had heard, or rather read, of von Wau Wau.

"What you're saying," I said slowly, "is that the dog is also the fellow who wants to share the apartment and is looking for a partner?"

Stampfert nodded.

2

THE SCIENCE OF ODOROLOGY

And so, fifteen minutes later, we entered the apartment building at 12 Bellener Street and took the elevator to the second story. Stampfert rang the bell at 2K, and a moment later the door swung in. This operation had been effected by an electrical motor controlled by an on-off button on a control panel set on the floor in a corner. This, it was obvious, had been pressed by the paw of the dog now trotting toward us. He was the largest police dog I've ever seen, weighing approximately one hundred and sixty pounds. He had keen eyes which were the deep lucid brown of a bottle of maple syrup at times and at other times the opaque rich brown of a frankfurter. His face was black, and his back bore a black saddlemark.

"Herr Doktor Weisstein, Herr Ralph von Wau Wau," said Stampfert.

He grinned, or at least opened his jaws, to reveal some very long and sharp teeth.

"Come in, please, and make yourself at home," he said.

Though I'd been warned, I was startled. His mouth did not move while the words came from his throat. The words were excellent standard High German. But the voice was that of a long-dead American movie actor. Humphrey Bogart's, to be exact.

I would have picked Basil Rathbone's, but *de gustibus non disputandum*. Especially someone with teeth like Ralph's. There was no mystery or magic about the voice, though the effect, even to the prepared, was weird. The voice, like his high intelligence, was a triumph of German science. A dog (or any animal) lacks the mouth structure and vocal chords to reproduce human sounds intelligibly. This deficiency had been overcome by implanting a small nuclear-powered voder in Ralph's throat. This was connected by an artificial-protein neural complex to the speech center of the dog's brain. Before he could activate the voder, Ralph had to think of three code words. This was necessary, since otherwise he would be speaking whenever he thought in verbal terms. Inflection of the spoken words was automatic, responding to the emotional tone of Ralph's thoughts.

"What about pouring us a drink, sweetheart?" he said to Stampfert. "Park it there, buddy," he said to me, indicating with a paw a large and comfortable easy chair. I did so, unsure whether or not I should resent his familiarity. I decided not to do so. After all, what could, or should, one expect from a dog who has by his own admission seen *The Maltese Falcon* forty-nine times? Of course, I found this out later, just as I discovered later that his manner of address varied bewilderingly, often in the middle of a sentence.

Stampfert prepared the drinks at a well-stocked bar in the

corner of the rather large living room. She made herself a tequila with lemon and salt, gave me the requested double Duggan's Dew o' Kirkintilloch on the rocks, and poured out three shots of King's Ransom Scotch in a rock-crystal saucer on the floor. The dog began lapping it; then seeing me raise my eyebrows, he said, "I'm a private eye, Doc. It's in the best tradition that P.I.'s drink. I always try to follow human traditions—when it pleases me. And if my drinking from a saucer offends you, I can hold a glass between my paws. But why the hell should I?"

"No reason at all," I said hastily.

He ceased drinking and jumped up onto a sofa, where he sat down facing us. "You two have been drinking at the Kennzeichen," he said. "You are old customers there. And then, later, you had lunch at the Neu Bornholt. Doctor Stampfert said you were coming in the taxi, but you changed your mind and took the bus."

There was a silence which lasted until I understood that I was supposed to comment on this. I could only say, "Well?"

"The babe didn't tell me any of this," Ralph said somewhat testily. "I was just demonstrating something that a mere human being could not have known."

"Mere?" I said just as testily.

Ralph shrugged, which was quite an accomplishment when one considers that dogs don't really have shoulders.

"Sorry, Doc. Don't get your bowels in an uproar. No offense."

"Very well," I said. "How did you know all this?"

And now that I came to think about it, I did wonder how he knew.

"The Kennzeichen is the only restaurant in town which gives a stein of Lowenbrau to each habitué as he enters the bar," von Wau Wau said. "You two obviously prefer other drinks, but you could not turn down the free drink. If you had not been at the Kennzeichen, I would not have smelled Lowenbrau on your breath. You then went to the Neu Bornholt for lunch. It serves a salad with its house dressing, the peculiar ingredients of which I detected with my sense of smell. This, as you know, is a million times keener than a human's. If you had come in a taxi, as the dame said you meant to do, you would be stinking much more strongly of kerosene. Your clothes and hair have absorbed a certain amount of that from being on the streets, of course, along with the high-sulfur coal now burned in many automobiles. But I deduce—olfactorily—that you took instead one of the electrically operated, fuel-celled, relatively odorless buses. Am I correct?"

"I would have said that it was amazing, but of course your nose makes it easy for you," I said.

"An extremely distinguished colleague of mine," Ralph said, "undoubtedly the most distinguished, once said that it is the first quality of a criminal investigator to see through a disguise. I would modify that to the *second* quality. The first is that he should smell through a disguise."

Though he seemed somewhat nettled, he became more genial after a few more laps from the saucer. So did I after a few more sips from my glass. He even gave me permission to smoke, provided that I did it under a special vent placed over my easy chair.

"Cuban make," he said, sniffing after I had lit up. "*La Roja Paloma de la Revolucion.*"

"Now that is astounding!" I said. I was also astounded to find Stampfert on my lap.

"It's nothing," he said. "I started to write a trifling little monograph on the subtle distinctions among cigar odors, but I realized that it would make a massive textbook before I was finished. And who could use it?"

"What are you doing here?" I said to Stampfert. "This is business. I don't want to give Herr von Wau Wau the wrong impression."

"You didn't used to mind," she said, giggling. "But I'm here because I want to smoke, too, and this is the only vent he has, and he told me not to smoke unless I sat under it."

Under the circumstances, it was not easy to carry on a coherent conversation with the dog, but we managed. I told him that I had read something of his life. I knew that his parents had been the property of the Hamburg Police Department. He was one of a litter of eight, all mutated to some degree since they and their parents had been subjected to scientific experiments. These had been conducted by the biologists of *das Institut und die Tankstelle fur Gehirntaschenspielerei.* But his high intelligence was the result of biosurgery. Although his brain was no larger than it should have been for a dog his size, its complexity was comparable to that of a human's. The scientists had used artificial protein to make billions of new nerve circuits in his cerebrum. This had been done, however, at the expense of his cerebellum or hindbrain. As a result, he had very little subconscious and hence could not dream.

As everybody now knows, failure to dream results in a progressive psychosis and eventual mental breakdown. To rectify this, Ralph created dreams during the day, recorded them audiovisually, and fed them into his brain at night. I don't have space to go into this in detail in this narrative, but a full description will be found in *The Case of the Stolen Dreams*. (Not yet published.)

When Ralph was still a young pup, an explosion had wrecked the Institute and killed his siblings and the scientists responsible for his sapiency. Ralph was taken over again by the Police Department and sent to school. He attended obedience school and the other courses requisite for a trained *Schutzhund* canine. But he was the only pup who also attended classes in reading, writing, and arithmetic.

Ralph was now twenty-eight years old but looked five. Some attributed this anomaly to the mutation experiments. Others claimed that the scientists had perfected an age-delaying elixir which had been administered to Ralph and his siblings. If the explosion had not destroyed the records, the world might now have the elixir at its disposal. (More of this in *A Short Case of Longevity*, n.y.p.)

Ralph's existence had been hidden for many years from all except a few policemen and officials sworn to silence. It was believed that publicity would reduce his effectiveness in his detective work. But recently the case had come to the attention of the public because of Ralph's own doing. Fed up with being a mere police dog, proud and ambitious, he had resigned to become a private investigator. His application for a license had, of course, resulted in an uproar. Mass media persons had descended on Hamburg in droves, herds, coveys, and gaggles. There was in fact litigation against him in the courts, but pending the result of this, Ralph von Wau Wau was proceeding as if he were a free agent. (For the conclusion of this famous case, see *The Caper of Kupper, the Copper's Keeper*, n.y.p.)

But whether or not he was the property of the Police Department, he was still very dependent upon human beings. Hence, his search for a roommate and a partner. I told him something about myself. He listened quietly and then said, "I like your odor, buddy. It's an honest one and uncondescending. I'd like you to come in with me."

"I'd be delighted," I said. "But there is only one bedroom…"

"All yours," he said. "My tastes are Spartan. Or perhaps I should say canine. The other bedroom has been converted to a laboratory, as you have observed. But I sleep in it on a pile of blankets under a table. You may have all the privacy you need, bring all the women you want, as long as you're not noisy about it. I think we should get one thing straight though. I'm the senior partner here. If that offends your human chauvinism, then we'll call it quits before we start, amigo."

"I foresee no cause for friction," I replied, and I stood up to walk over to Ralph to shake hands. Unfortunately, I had forgotten that Stampfert was still on my lap. She thumped into the floor on her buttocks and yelled with pain and indignation. It was, I admit, stupid—well, at least an unwise, action. Stampfert, cursing, headed toward the door. Ralph looked at my outstretched hand and said, "Get this straight, mac. I never shake hands or sit up and beg."

I dropped my hand and said, "Of course."

The door opened. I turned to see Stampfert, still rubbing her fanny, going out the door.

"*Auf Wiedersehen*," I said.

"Not if I can help it, you jerk," she said.

"She always did take offense too easily," I said to Ralph.

I left a few minutes later to pick up my belongings from the hotel. When I re-entered his door with my suitcases in hand, I suddenly stopped. Ralph was sitting on the sofa, his eyes bright, his huge red tongue hanging out, and his breath coming in deep happy pants. Across from him sat one of the loveliest women I have ever seen. Evidently she had done something to change his mood because his manner of address was now quite different.

"Come in, my dear Weisstein," he said. "Your first case as my colleague is about to begin."

3

THE STATEMENT OF THE CASE

An optimist is one who ignores, or forgets, experience. I am an optimist. Which is another way of saying that I fell in love with Lisa Scarletin at once. As I stared at this striking yet petite woman with the curly chestnut hair and great lustrous brown eyes, I completely forgot that I was still holding the two heavy suitcases. Not until after we had been introduced, and she looked down amusedly, did I realize what a foolish figure I made. Red-faced, I eased them down and took her dainty hand in mine. As I kissed it, I smelled the subtle fragrance of a particularly delightful— and, I must confess, aphrodisiacal—perfume.

"No doubt you have read, or seen on TV, reports of Mrs. Scarletin's missing husband?" my partner said. "Even if you do not know of his disappearance, you surely have heard of such a famous artist?"

"My knowledge of art is not nil," I said coldly. The tone of my voice reflected my inward coldness, the dying glow of delight on first seeing her. So, she was married! I should have known on seeing her ring. But I had been too overcome for it to make an immediate impression.

Alfred Scarletin, as my reader must surely know, was a wealthy painter who had become very famous in the past decade. Personally, I consider the works of the so-called Fauve Mauve school to be outrageous nonsense, a thumbing of the nose at commonsense. I would sooner have the originals of the *Katzenjammer Kids* comic strip hung up in the museum than any of the maniac creations of Scarletin and his kind. But, whatever his failure of artistic taste, he certainly possessed a true eye for women. He had married the beautiful Lisa Maria Mohrstein only three years ago. And now there was speculation that she might be a widow.

At which thought, the warm glow returned.

A. Scarletin, as I remembered, had gone for a walk on a May evening two months ago and had failed to return home. At first, it was feared that he had been kidnapped. But, when no ransom was demanded, that theory was discarded.

When I had told Ralph what I knew of the case, he nodded.

"As of last night there has been a new development in the case," he said. "And Mrs. Scarletin has come to me because she is extremely dissatisfied with the progress—lack of it, rather—that the police have made. Mrs. Scarletin, please tell Doctor Weisstein what you have told me."

She fixed her bright but deep brown eyes upon me and in a voice as lovely as her eyes—not to mention her figure—sketched in the events of yesterday. Ralph, I noticed, sat with his head cocked and his ears pricked up. I did not know it then, but he had asked her to repeat the story because he wanted to listen to her inflections again. He could detect subtle tones that would escape the less sensitive ears of humans. As he was often to say, "I cannot only *smell* hidden emotions, my dear Weisstein, I can also *hear* them."

"At about seven last evening, as I was getting ready to go out…" she said.

With whom? I thought, feeling jealousy burn through my chest but knowing that I had no right to feel such.

"…Lieutenant Strasse of the Hamburg Metropolitan Police phoned me. He said that he had something important to show me and asked if I would come down to headquarters. I agreed, of course, and took a taxi down. There the sergeant took me into a room and showed me a painting. I was astounded. I had never seen it before, but I knew at once that it was my husband's work. I did not need his signature—in its usual place in the upper right-hand corner—to know that. I told the sergeant that and then I said, 'This must mean that Alfred is still alive! But where in the world did you get it?'

"He replied that it had come to the attention of the police only that morning. A wealthy merchant, Herr Lausitz, had died a week before. The lawyer supervising the inventory of his estate found this painting in a locked room in Lausitz's mansion. It was only one of many valuable objects d'art which had been stolen. Lausitz was not suspected of being a thief except in the sense that he had undoubtedly purchased stolen goods or commissioned the thefts. The collection was valued at many millions of marks. The lawyer had notified the police, who identified the painting as my husband's because of the signature."

"You may be sure that Strasse would never have been able to identify a Scarletin by its style alone," Ralph said sarcastically.

Her delicate eyebrows arched.

"Ach! So that's the way it is! The lieutenant did not take it kindly when I told him that I was thinking of consulting you. But that was later.

"Anyway, I told Strasse that this was evidence that Alfred was still alive. Or at least had been until very recently. I know that it would take my husband at least a month and a half to have painted it—if he were under pressure. Strasse said that it could be: one, a forgery; or, two, Alfred might have painted it before he disappeared. I told him that it was no forgery; I could tell at a glance. And what did he mean, it was painted some time ago? I knew exactly—from day to day—what my husband worked on."

She stopped, looked at me, and reddened slightly.

"That isn't true. My husband visited his mistress at least three times a week. I did not know about her until after he disappeared, when the police reported to me that he had been seeing her... Hilda Speck... for about two years. However, according to the police, Alfred had not been doing any painting in her apartment. Of course, she could have removed all evidence, though Strasse tells me that she would have been unable to get rid of all traces of pigments and hairs from brushes."

What a beast that Scarletin was! I thought, how could anybody married to this glorious woman pay any attention to another woman?

"I have made some inquiries about Hilda Speck," Ralph

said. "First, she has an excellent alibi, what the English call ironclad. She was visiting friends in Bremen two days before Scarletin disappeared. She did not return to Hamburg until two days afterward. As for her background, she worked as a typist-clerk for an export firm until two years ago when Scarletin began supporting her. She has no criminal record, but her brother has been arrested several times for extortion and assault. He escaped conviction each time. He is a huge obese man, as ugly as his sister is beautiful. He is nicknamed, appropriately enough, *Flusspferd*. (Hippopotamus. Literally, riverhorse.) His whereabouts have been unknown for about four months."

He sat silent for a moment, then he went to the telephone. This lay on the floor; beside it was a curious instrument. I saw its function the moment Ralph put one paw on its long, thin but blunt end and slipped the other paw snugly into a funnel-shaped cup at the opposite end. With the thin end he punched the buttons on the telephone.

A police officer answered over the loudspeaker. Ralph asked for Lt. Strasse. The officer said that he was not in the station. Ralph left a message, but when he turned off the phone, he said, "Strasse won't answer for a while, but eventually his curiosity will get the better of him."

It is difficult to tell when a dog is smiling, but I will swear that Ralph was doing more than just exposing his teeth. And his eyes seemed to twinkle.

Suddenly, he raised a paw and said, quietly, "No sound, please."

We stared at him. None of us heard anything, but it was

evident he did. He jumped to the control panel on the floor and pushed the on button. Then he dashed toward the door, which swung inward. A man wearing a stethoscope stood looking stupidly at us. Seeing Ralph bounding at him, he yelled and turned to run. Ralph struck him on the back and sent him crashing against the opposite wall of the hallway. I ran to aid him, but to my surprise Ralph trotted back into the room. It was then that I saw the little device attached to the door. The man rose unsteadily to his feet, glaring. He was just above minimum height for a policeman and looked as if he were thirty-five years old. He had a narrow face with a long nose and small close-set black eyes.

"Doctor Weisstein," Ralph said. "Lieutenant Strasse."

Strasse did not acknowledge me. Instead, he tore off the device and put it with the stethoscope in his jacket pocket. Some of his paleness disappeared.

"That eavesdropper device is illegal in America and should be here," Ralph said.

"So should talking dogs," Strasse said. He bowed to Mrs. Scarletin and clicked his heels.

Ralph gave several short barks, which I found out later was his equivalent of laughter. He said, "No need to ask you why you were spying on us. You're stuck in this case, and you hoped to overhear me say something that would give you a clue. Really, my dear Lieutenant!"

Strasse turned red, but he spoke up bravely enough.

"Mrs. Scarletin, you can hire this… this… hairy four-footed Holmes…"

"I take that as a compliment," Ralph murmured.

"...if you wish, but you cannot discharge the police. Moreover, there is grave doubt about the legality of his private investigator's license, and you might get into trouble if you persist in hiring him."

"Mrs. Scarletin is well aware of the legal ramifications, my dear Strasse," Ralph said coolly. "She is also confident that I will win my case. Meantime, the authorities have permitted me to practice. If you dispute this, you may phone the mayor himself."

"You... you!" Strasse sputtered. "Just because you once saved His Honor's child!"

"Let's drop all this time-wasting nonsense," Ralph said. "I would like to examine the painting myself. I believe that it may contain the key to Scarletin's whereabouts."

"That is police property," Strasse said. "As long as I have anything to say about it, you won't put your long nose into a police building. Not unless you do so as a prisoner."

I was astonished at the hatred that leaped and crackled between these two like discharges in a Van de Graaff generator. I did not learn until later that Strasse was the man to whom Ralph had been assigned when he started police work. At first they got along well, but as it became evident that Ralph was much the more intelligent, Strasse became jealous. He did not, however, ask for another dog. He was taking most of the credit for the cases cracked by Ralph, and he was rising rapidly in rank because of Ralph. By the time the dog resigned from the force, Strasse had become a lieutenant. Since then he had bungled two cases, and the person responsible for Strasse's rapid rise was now obvious to all.

"Pardon me," Ralph said. "The police may be holding the painting as evidence, but it is clearly Mrs. Scarletin's property. However, I think I'll cut through the red tape. I'll just make a complaint to His Honor."

"Very well," Strasse said, turning pale again. "But I'll go with you to make sure that you don't tamper with the evidence."

"And to learn all you can," Ralph said, barking laughter. "Weisstein, would you bring along that little kit there? It contains the tools of my trade."

4

LIGHT IN THE DARKNESS,
COURTESY OF VON WAU WAU

On the way to the station in the taxi (Strasse having refused us use of a police vehicle), Ralph told me a little more of Alfred Scarletin.

"He is the son of an American teacher who became a German citizen and of a Hamburg woman. Naturally, he speaks English like a native of California. He became interested in painting at a very early age and since his early adolescence has tramped through Germany painting both urban and rural scenes. He is extremely handsome, hence, attracts women, has a photographic memory, and is an excellent draftsman. His paintings were quite conventional until the past ten years when he founded the Fauve Mauve school. He is learned in both German and English literature and has a fondness for the works of Frank Baum and Lewis Carroll. He often uses characters from them in his paintings. Both writers, by the way, were fond of puns."

"I am well aware of that," I said stiffly. After all, one does not like to be considered ignorant by a dog. "And all this means?"

"It may mean all or nothing."

About ten minutes later, we were in a large room in which many articles, the jetsam and flotsam of crime, were displayed. Mrs. Scarletin led us to the painting (though we needed no leading), and we stood before it. Strasse, off to one side, regarded us suspiciously. I could make no sense out of the painting and said so even though I did not want to offend Mrs. Scarletin. She, however, laughed and said my reaction was that of many people.

Ralph studied it for a long time and then said, "It may be that my suspicions are correct. We shall see."

"About what?" Strasse said, coming closer and leaning forward to peer at the many figures on the canvas.

"We can presume that Mrs. Scarletin knows all her husband's works—until the time he disappeared. This appeared afterward and so we can presume that he painted it within the last two months. It's evident that he was kidnaped not for ransom but for the money to be made from the sale of new paintings by Scarletin. They must have threatened him with death if he did not paint new works for them. He has done at least one for them and probably has done, or is doing, more for them.

"They can't sell Scarletins on the open market. But there are enough fanatical and unscrupulous collectors to pay very large sums for their private collections. Lausitz was one such. Scarletin is held prisoner and, we suppose, would like to escape. He can't do so, but he is an intelligent man, and he thinks of a way to get a message out. He knows his paintings are being sold, even if he isn't told so. Ergo, why not put a message in his painting?"

"How wonderful!" Mrs. Scarletin said and she patted Ralph's head. Ralph wagged his tail, and I felt a thrust of jealousy.

"Nonsense!" Strasse growled. "He must have known that the painting would go to a private collector who could not reveal that Scarletin was a prisoner. One, he'd be put in jail himself for having taken part in an illegal transaction. Two, why would he suspect that the painting contained a message? Three, I don't believe there is any message there!"

"Scarletin would be desperate and so willing to take a long chance," Ralph said. "At least, it'd be better than doing nothing. He could hope that the collector might get an attack of conscience and tell the police. This is not very likely, I'll admit. He could hope that the collector would be unable to keep from showing the work off to a few close friends. Perhaps one of these might tell the police, and so the painting would come into the hands of the police. Among them might be an intelligent and well-educated person who would perceive the meaning of the painting. I'll admit, however, that neither of these theories is likely."

Strasse snorted.

"And then there was the very slight chance—which nevertheless occurred—that the collector would die. And so the legal inventory of his estate would turn up a Scarletin. And some person just might be able to read the meaning in this—if there is any."

"Just what I was going to say," Strasse said. "Even if what you say happened did happen," he continued, "his kidnapers wouldn't pass on the painting without examining it. The first thing they'd suspect would be a hidden message. It's so obvious."

"You didn't think so a moment ago," Ralph said. "But you are right… in agreeing with me. Now, let us hypothesize. Scarletin, a work of art, but he wishes to embody in it a message. Probably a map of sorts which will lead the police—or someone else looking for him—directly to the place where he is kept prisoner.

"How is he to do this without detection by the kidpnapers? He has to be subtle enough to escape their inspection. *How* subtle depends, I would imagine, on their education and perceptivity. But too subtle a message will go over everybody's head. And he is limited in his choice of symbols by the situation, by the names or professions of his kidnapers—if he knows them—and by the particular location of his prison—if he knows that."

"If, if, if?" Strasse said, throwing his hands up in the air.

"If me no ifs," Ralph said. "But first let us consider that Scarletin is equally at home in German or English. He loves the pun-loving Carroll and Baum. So, perhaps, due to the contingencies of the situation, he is forced to pun in both languages."

"It would be like him," Mrs. Scarletin said. "But is it likely that he would use this method when he would know that very few people would be capable of understanding him?"

"As I said, it was a long shot, Madame. But better than nothing."

"Now, Weisstein, whatever else I am, I am a dog. Hence, I am color-blind." (But not throughout his career. See *The Adventure of the Tired Color Man*, to be published.) "Please describe the colors of each object on this canvas."

Strasse sniggered, but we ignored him. When I had finished, Ralph said, "Thank you, my dear Weisstein. Now, let us separate the significant from the insignificant. Though, as a matter of fact, in this case even the insignificant is significant. Notice the two painted walls which divide the painting into three parts—like Gaul. One starts from the middle of the left-hand side and curves up to the middle of the upper edge. The other starts in the middle of the right-hand side and curves down to the middle of the lower side. All three parts are filled with strange and seemingly unrelated—and often seemingly unintelligible—objects. The Fauve Mauve apologists, however, maintain that their creations come from the collective unconscious, not the individual or personal and so are intelligible to everybody."

"Damned nonsense!" I said, forgetting Lisa in my indignation.

"Not in this case, I suspect," Ralph said. "Now, notice that the two walls, which look much like the Great Wall of China, bear many zeros on their tops. And that within the area these walls enclose, other zeros are scattered. Does this mean nothing to you?"

"Zero equals nothing," I said.

"A rudimentary observation, Doctor, but valid," Ralph said. "I would say that Scarletin is telling us that the objects within the walls mean nothing. It is the central portion that bears the message. There are no zeros there."

"Prove it," Strasse said.

"The first step first—if one can find it. Observe in the upper right-hand corner the strange figure of a man. The upper half is, obviously, Sherlock Holmes, with his deerstalker hat, cloak, pipe—though whether his meditative briar root or disputatious clay can't be determined—and his magnifying glass in hand. The lower half, with the lederhosen and so on, obviously indicates a

Bavarian in particular and a German in general. The demi-figure of Holmes means two things to the earnest seeker after the truth. One, that we are to use detective methods on this painting. Two, that half of the puzzle is in English. The lower half means that half of the puzzle is in German. Which I anticipated."

"Preposterous!" Strasse said. "And just what does that next figure, the one in sixteenth-century costume, mean?"

"Ah, yes, the torso of a bald and bearded gentleman with an Elizabethan ruff around his neck. He is writing with a pen on a sheet of paper. There is a title on the upper part of the paper. Doctor, please look at it through the magnifying glass which you'll find in my kit."

5

MORE DAWNING LIGHT

I did so, and I said, "I can barely make it out. Scarletin must have used a glass to do it. It says *New Atlantis*."

"Does that suggest anything to anybody?" Ralph said.

Obviously it did to him, but he was enjoying the sensation of being more intelligent than the humans around him. I resented his attitude somewhat, and yet I could understand it. He had been patronized by too many humans for too long a time.

"The great scholar and statesman Francis Bacon wrote the *New Atlantis*," I said suddenly. Ralph winked at me, and I cried, "Bacon! Scarletin's mistress is Hilda Speck!"

(*Speck* in German means *bacon*.)

"You have put one foot forward, my dear Weisstein," Ralph said. "Now let us see you bring up the other."

"The Bacon, with the next two figures, comprise a group separate from the others," I said. "Obviously, they are to be considered as closely related. But I confess that I cannot make much sense out of Bacon, a green horse, and a house with an attic window from which a woman with an owl on her shoulder leans. Nor do I know the significance of the tendril which connects all of them."

"Stuck in the mud, eh, kid?" Ralph said, startling me. But I was to get used to his swift transitions from the persona of Holmes to Spade and others and back again.

"Tell me, Doc, is the green of the oats-burner of any particular shade?"

"Hmm," I said.

"It's Nile green," Lisa said.

"You're certainly a model client, sweetheart," Ralph said. "Very well, my dear sawbones, does this mean nothing to you? Yes? What about you, Strasse?"

Strasse muttered something.

Lisa said, "*Nilpferd!*"

"Yes," Ralph said. "*Nilpferd.* (Nile-horse.) Another word for hippopotamus. And Hilda Speck's brother is nicknamed *Hippopotamus.* Now for the next figure, the house with the woman looking out the attic and bearing an owl on her shoulder. Tell me, Strasse, does the Hippo have any special pals? One who is, perhaps, Greek? From the city of Athens?"

Strasse sputtered and said, "Somebody in the department has been feeding you information. I'll…"

"Not at all," Ralph said. "Obviously, the attic and the woman with the owl are the significant parts of the image. *Dachstube* (attic) conveys no meaning in German, but if we use the English translation, we are on the way to light. The word has two meanings in English. If capitalized, Attic, it refers to the ancient Athenian language or culture and, in a broader sense, to Greece as a whole. Note that the German adjective *attisch* is similar to the English *Attic*. To clinch this, Scarletin painted a woman with an owl on her shoulder. Who else could this be but the goddess of wisdom, patron deity of Athens? Scarletin was taking a chance on using her, since his kidnapers, even if they did not get beyond high school, might have encountered Athena. But they might not remember her, and, anyway, Scarletin had to use some redundancy to make sure his message got across. I would not be surprised if we do not run across considerable redundancy here."

"And the tendrils?" I said.

"A pun in German, my dear Doctor. *Ranke* (tendril) is similar to *Ranke* (intrigues). The three figures are bound together by the tendril of intrigue."

Strasse coughed and said, "And the mirror beneath the house with the attic?"

"Observe that the yellow brick road starts from the mirror and curves to the left or westward. I suggest that Scarletin means here that the road actually goes to the right or eastward. Mirror images are in reverse, of course."

"What road?" Strasse said.

Ralph rolled his eyes and shook his head.

"Surely the kidnapers made my husband explain the symbolism?" Lisa said. "They would be very suspicious that he might do exactly what he did do."

"There would be nothing to keep him from a false explanation," Ralph said. "So far, it is obvious that Scarletin has named the criminals. How he was able to identify them or to locate his place of imprisonment, I don't know. Time and deduction—with a little luck—will reveal all. Could we have a road map of Germany, please?"

"I'm no dog to fetch and carry," Strasse grumbled, but he obtained a map nevertheless. This was the large Mair's, scale of 1:750,000, used primarily to indicate the autobahn system. Strasse unfolded it and pinned it to the wall with the upper part of Germany showing.

"If Scarletin had put, say, an American hamburger at the beginning of the brick road, its meaning would have been obvious even to the *dummkopf* kidnapers," Ralph said. "He credited his searchers—if any—with intelligence. They would realize the road has to start where the crime started—in Hamburg."

He was silent while comparing the map and the painting. After a while the fidgeting Strasse said, "Come, man! I mean, dog! You…"

"You mean Herr von Wau Wau, yes?" Ralph said.

Strasse became red-faced again, but after a struggle he said, "Of course. Herr von Wau Wau. How do you interpret this, this mess of a mystery?"

"You'll note that there are many figures along the yellow brick road until one gets to the large moon rising behind the castle. All these figures have halos over their heads. This puzzled me until I understood that the halos are also zeros. We are to pay no attention to the figures beneath them.

"But the moon behind the castle? Look at the map. Two of

the roads running southeast out of Hamburg meet just above the city of Luneburg. A *burg* is a castle, but the *Lune* doesn't mean anything in German in this context. It is, however, similar to the English *lunar*, hence the moon. And the yellow brick road goes south from there.

"I must confess that I am now at a loss. So, we get in a car and travel to Luneburg and south of it while I study the map and the painting."

"We can't take the painting with us; it's too big!" Strasse said.

"I have it all in here," Ralph said, tapping his head with his paw. "But I suggest we take a color Polaroid shot of the painting for you who have weak memories," and he grinned at Strasse.

6

FOLLOW THE YELLOW BRICK ROAD

Strasse did not like it, but he could not proceed without Ralph, and Ralph insisted that Mrs. Scarletin and I be brought along. First, he sent two men to watch Hilda Speck and to make sure she did not try to leave town—as the Americans say. He had no evidence to arrest her as yet, nor did he really think—I believe— that he was going to have any.

The dog, Lisa, and I got into the rear of a large police limousine, steam-driven, of course. Strasse sat in the front with the driver. Another car, which kept in radio contact with us, was to follow us at a distance of a kilometer.

An hour later, we were just north of Luneburg. A half-hour later, still going south, we were just north of the town of Uelzen. It was still daylight, and so I could easily see the photo of the painting which I held. The yellow road on it ran south of the moon rising behind the castle (Luneburg) and extended a little south of a group of three strange figures. These were a hornless sheep (probably a female), a section of an overhead railway, and an archer with a medieval Japanese coiffure and medieval clothes.

Below this group the road split. One road wound toward the walls in the upper and lower parts of the picture and eventually went through them. The other curved almost due south to the left and then went through or by some more puzzling figures.

The first was a representation of a man (he looked like the risen Jesus) coming from a tomb set in the middle of some trees. To its right and a little lower was a waistcoat. Next was what looked like William Penn, the Quaker. Following it was a man in a leopard loincloth with two large apes at his heels.

Next was a man dressed in clothes such as the ancient Mesopotamian people wore. He was down on all fours, his head bent close to the grass. Beside him was a banana tree.

Across the road was a large hot-air balloon with a bald-headed man in the wicker basket. On the side of the bag in large letters were: O.Z.

Across the road from it were what looked like two large Vikings wading through a sea. Behind them was the outline of a fleet of dragon-prowed longships and the silhouette of a horde of horn-helmeted bearded men. The two leaders were approaching a body of naked warriors, colored blue, standing in horse-drawn chariots.

South of these was a woman dressed in mid-Victorian clothes, hoopskirts and all, and behind her a mansion typical of the pre-Civil War American south. By it was a tavern, if the drunks lying outside it and the board hanging over the doorway meant anything. The sign was too small to contain even letters written under a magnifying glass.

A little to the left, the road terminated in a pair of hands tearing a package from another pair of hands.

Just before we got to Uelzen, Strasse said, "How do you know that we're on the right road?"

"Consider the sheep, the raised section of railway, and the Japanese archer," Ralph said. "In English, *U* is pronounced exactly like the word for the female sheep—*ewe*. An elevated railway is colloquially an *el*. The Japanese archer could be a Samurai, but I do not think so. He is a *Zen* archer. Thus, *U*, *el*, and *zen* or the German city of Uelzen."

"All of this seems so easy, so apparent, now that you've pointed it out," I said.

"Hindsight has twenty/twenty vision," he said somewhat bitterly.

"And the rest?" I said.

"The town of Esterholz is not so difficult. Would you care to try?"

"Another English-German hybrid pun," I said, with more confidence than I felt. "*Ester* sounds much like *Easter*, hence the risen Christ. And the wood is the *holz*, of course. *Holt*, archaic English for a small wood or copse, by the way, comes from the same Germanic root as *holz*."

"And the *Weste* (waistcoat)?" Ralph said.

"I would guess that that means to take the road west of Esterholz," I said somewhat more confidently.

"Excellent, Doctor," he said. "And the Quaker?"

"I really don't know," I said, chagrined because Lisa had been looking admiringly at me.

He gave his short barking laughter and said, "And neither do I, my dear fellow! I am sure that some of these symbols, perhaps most, have a meaning which will not be apparent until we have studied the neighborhood."

Seven kilometers southeast of Uelzen, we turned into the village of Esterholz and then west onto the road to Wrestede. Looking at the hands tearing loose the package from the other pair, I suddenly cried out, "Of course! Wrestede! Suggesting the English, *wrested*! The hands are *wresting* the package away! Then that means that Scarletin is a prisoner somewhere between Esterholz and Wrestede!"

"Give that man the big stuffed teddy bear," Ralph said. "OK, toots, so where is Scarletin?"

I fell silent. The others said nothing, but the increasing tension was making us sweat. We all looked waxy and pale in the light of the sinking sun. In half an hour, night would be on us.

"Slow down so I can read the names on the gateways of the farms," Ralph said. The driver obeyed, and presently Ralph said, "Ach!"

I could see nothing which reminded me of a Quaker.

"The owner of that farm is named Fuchs (fox)," I said.

"Yes, and the founder of the Society of Friends, or The Quakers, was George Fox," he said.

He added a moment later, "As I remember it, it was in this area that some particularly bestial—or should I say human?—murders occurred in 1845. A man named Wilhelm Graustock was finally caught and convicted."

I had never heard of this case, but, as I was to find out,

Ralph had an immense knowledge of sensational literature. He seemed to know the details of every horror committed in the last two centuries.

"What is the connection between Herr Graustock and this figure which is obviously Tarzan?" I said.

"Graustock is remarkably similar in sound to Greystoke," he said. "As you may or may not know, the lord of the jungle was also Lord Greystoke of the British peerage. As a fact, Graustock and Greystoke both mean exactly the same thing, a gray stick or pole. They have common Germanic roots. Ach, there it is! The descendants of the infamous butcher still hold his property, but are, I believe, singularly peaceful farmers."

"And the man on all fours by a banana tree?" Strasse growled. It hurt him to ask, but he could not push back his curiosity.

Ralph burst out laughing again. "Another example of redundancy, I believe. And the most difficult to figure out. A tough one, sweetheart. Want to put in your two pfennigs' worth?"

"Aw, go find a fireplug," Strasse said, at which Ralph laughed even more loudly.

"Unless I'm mistaken," Ralph said, "the next two images stand for a word, not a thing. They symbolize *nebanan* (next door). The question is, next door to what? The Graustock farm or the places indicated by the balloon and the battle tableau and the antebellum scene? I see nothing as yet which indicates that we are on or about to hit the bullseye. Continue at the same speed driver."

There was silence for a minute. I refused to speak because of my pride. Finally, Lisa said, "For heaven's sake, Herr von Wau

Wau, I'm dying of curiosity! How did you ever get *nebanan*?"

"The man on all fours with his head close to the ground looks to me like ancient Nebuchadnezzar, the Babylonian king who went mad and ate grass. By him is the banana (*Banane*) tree. Collapse those two words into one, à la Lewis Carroll and his portmanteau words, and you have *nebanan* (next to)."

"This Scarletin is crazy," Strasse said.

"If he is, he has a utilitarian madness," Ralph said.

"You're out of your mind, too!" Strasse said triumphantly. "Look!" And he pointed at a name painted on the wall. Neb Bannons.

Ralph was silent for a few seconds while Strasse laughed, and then he said, quietly, "Well, I was wrong in the particular but right in the principle. Ach! Here we are! Maintain the same speed driver! The rest of you, look straight ahead, don't gawk! Someone may be watching from the house, but they won't think it suspicious if they see a dog looking out of the window!"

I did as he said, but I strained out of the corners of my eyes to see both sides of the road. On my right were some fields of barley. On my left I caught a glimpse of a gateway with a name over it in large white-painted letters: Schindeler. We went past that and by a field on my left in which two stallions stood by the fence looking at us. On my right was a sign against a stone wall which said: Bergmann.

Ralph said delightedly, "That's it!"

I felt even more stupid.

"Don't stop until we get around the curve ahead and out of sight of the Schindeler house," Ralph said.

A moment later, we were parked beyond the curve and pointed west. The car which had been trailing us by several kilometers reported by radio that it had stopped near the Graustock farm.

"All right!" Strasse said fiercely. "Things seem to have worked out! But before I move in, I want to make sure I'm not arresting the wrong people. Just how did you figure this one out?"

"Button your lip and flap your ears, sweetheart," Ralph said. "Take the balloon with O.Z. on it. That continues the yellow brick road motif. You noticed the name Bergmann (miner)? A Bergmann is a man who digs, right? Well, for those of you who may have forgotten, the natal or Nebraskan name of the Wizard of Oz was Diggs."

Strasse looked as if he were going to have an apoplectic fit. "And what about those ancient Teutonic warriors and those naked blue men in chariots across the road from the balloon?" he shouted.

"Those Teutonic warriors were Anglo-Saxons, and they were invading ancient Britain. The Britons were tattooed blue and often went into battle naked. As all educated persons know," he added, grinning. "As for the two leaders of the Anglo-Saxons, traditionally they were named Hengist and Horsa. Both names meant *horse*. In fact, as you know, *Hengst* is a German word for stallion, and *Ross* also means horse. Ross is cognate with the Old English *hrossa*, meaning horse."

"God preserve me from any case like this one in the future!" Strasse said. "Very well, we won't pause in this madness! What does this pre-Civil War house with the Southern belle before it and the tavern by it mean? How do you know that it means that Scarletin is prisoner there?"

"The tableau suggests, among other things, the book and the movie *Gone With the Wind*," Ralph said. "You probably haven't read the book, Strasse, but you surely must have seen the movie. The heroine's name is Scarlett O'Hara, right, pal? And a *tavern* in English is also an *inn*. Scarlett-inn, get it?"

A few minutes later Ralph said, "If you don't control yourself, my dear Strasse, your men will have to put you in a straitjacket."

The policeman ceased his bellowing but not his trembling, took a few deep breaths, followed by a deep draught from a bottle in the glove compartment, breathed schnapps all over us, and said, "So! Life is not easy! And duty calls! Let us proceed to make the raid upon the farmhouse as agreed upon!"

7

NO EMERALD CITY FOR ME

An hour after dusk, policemen burst into the front and rear doors of the Schindeler house. By then it had been ascertained that the house had been rented by a man giving the name of Albert Habicht. This was Hilda Speck's brother, Albert Speck, the Hippopotamus. His companion was a Wilhelm Erlesohn, a tall skinny man nicknamed *die Giraffe*. A fine zoological pair, both now behind bars.

Hilda Speck was also convicted but managed to escape a year later. But we were to cross her path again. (*The Case of the Seeing Eye Man.*)

Alfred Scarletin was painting another canvas with the same message but different symbols when we collared his kidnapers. He threw down his brush and took his lovely wife into his arms, and my heart went into a decaying orbit around my hopes. Apparently, despite his infidelity, she still loved him.

Most of this case was explained, but there was still an important question to be answered. How had Scarletin known where he was?

"The kidnaping took place in daylight in the midst of a large crowd," Scarletin said. "Erlesohn jammed a gun which he had in his coat pocket against my back. I did as he said and got into the back of a delivery van double-parked nearby. Erlesohn then rendered me unconscious with a drug injected by a hypodermic syringe. When I woke up, I was in this house. I have been confined to this room ever since, which, as you see, is large and has a southern exposure and a heavily barred skylight and large heavily barred windows. I was told that I would be held until I had painted twelve paintings. These would be sufficient for the two men to become quite wealthy through sales to rich but unscrupulous collectors. Then I would be released.

"I did not believe them of course. After the twelve paintings were done, they would kill me and bury me somewhere in the woods. I listened often at the door late at night and overheard the two men, who drank much, talking loudly. That is how I found out their names. I also discovered that Hilda was in on the plot, though I'd suspected that all along. You see, I had quit her only a few days before I was kidnaped, and she was desperate because she no longer had an income.

"As for how I knew where I was, that is not so remarkable. I have a photographic memory, and I have tramped up and down Germany painting in my youth and early middle age. I have been along this road a number of times on foot when I was a teenager. In fact, I once painted the Graustock farmhouse. It is true that I had forgotten this, but after a while the memory came back. After all, I looked out the window every day and saw the Graustock farm.

"And now, tell me, who is the man responsible for reading my message? He must be an extraordinary man."

"No man," I said, feeling like Ulysses in Polyphemus' cave.

"Ach, then, it was you, Lisa?" he cried.

"It's yours truly, sweetheart," the voice of Humphrey Bogart said.

Scarletin is a very composed man, but he has fainted at least once in his life.

THE CONCLUSION

It was deep in winter with the fuel shortage most critical. We were sitting in our apartment trying to keep warm by the radiations from the TV set. The Scotch helped, and I was trying to forget our discomfort by glancing over my notes and listening to the records of our cases since the Scarletin case. Had Ralph and I, in that relatively short span of time, really experienced the affair of the aluminum crèche, the adventures of the human camel and the Old-School Thai, and the distressing business with the terrible Venetian, Granelli? The latter, by the way, is being written up under the title: *The Doge Whose Barque Was Worse Than His Bight*.

At last, I put the notes and records to one side and picked up a book. Too many memories were making me uncomfortable. A long silence followed, broken when Ralph said, "You may not have lost her after all, my dear Weisstein."

I started, and I said, "How did you know I was thinking of *her*?"

Ralph grinned (at least, I think he was grinning). He said, "Even the lead-brained Strasse would know that you cannot forget her big brown eyes, her smiles, her deep rich tones, her figure, and her et cetera. What else these many months would evoke those sighs, those moping stares, those frequent attacks of insomnia and absentmindedness? It is evident at this moment that you are not at all as deep in one of C. S. Forester's fine sea stories as you pretend.

"But cheer up! The fair Lisa may yet have good cause to divorce her artistic but philandering spouse. Or she may become a widow."

"What makes you say that?" I cried.

"I've been thinking that it might not be just a coincidence that old Lausitz died after he purchased Scarletin's painting. I've been sniffing around the painting—literally and figuratively—and I think there's one Hamburger that's gone rotten."

"You suspect Scarletin of murder!" I said. "But how could he have killed Lausitz?"

"I don't know yet, pal," he said. "But I will. You can bet your booties I will. Old murders are like old bones—I dig them up."

And he was right, but that adventure was not to happen for another six months.

THE DOGE WHOSE BARQUE WAS
WORSE THAN HIS BIGHT

BY JONATHAN SWIFT SOMERS III
EDITED BY PHILIP JOSÉ FARMER

In his Wold Newton biography *Doc Savage: His Apocalyptic Life*, Philip José Farmer himself sets up this next installment from the case files of Ralph von Wau Wau:

"Cordwainer Bird [is] a mainstream novelist and a militant foe of evil. Though he is nowhere as tall as his ancestors and relatives, the Scarlet Pimpernel, Rudolf Rassendyll, the Shadow, and Doc Savage, et al., he has their heroic spirit and their dedication to fighting wickedness. But unlike these heroes of an earlier age, who fought to preserve The Establishment, he fights to destroy The Establishment. One of The Establishments, anyway.

"Harlan Ellison, in 'The New York Review of Bird' (see *Weird Heroes #2: A New American Pulp*, Byron Preiss, editor, Pyramid, 1975), writes of Bird's first campaign in this war...

"Bird, after his conquest of the secret rulers of New York, fell in with Ralph von Wau Wau... And while in Venice... Ralph and Bird became good friends..."

"A Scarletin Study," the first of the Ralph von Wau Wau series, appeared in the March 1975 issue of The Magazine of Fantasy and Science Fiction. *Those interested in biographical details about the author may refer to Kilgore Trout's* Venus on the Half-Shell *(December 1974, and January 1975 issues of* The Magazine of Fantasy and Science Fiction; *Dell Publications, February 1975).[3] Since then, your inquisitive editor has unearthed some information unprovided by Trout. Somers was born in Petersburg, Illinois, on January 26, 1910. His grandfather was a judge; his father, an aspiring but unpublished poet. Their epitaphs and a fragment of Somers III's blank verse epic can be found in Edgar Lee Masters'* The Spoon River Anthology. *Somers III was partially paralyzed by polio at the age of ten. Though he has never been out of his native town, he often soars from his wheelchair to freewheel via the exploits of his fictional heroes. The two most*

---

[3]*Venus on the Half-Shell* is available from Titan Books in the Grandmaster Series, published under Philip José Farmer's byline.

popular are John Clayter, spaceman extraordinaire, *and Ralph von Wau Wau, unique private eye. Ralph, it's true, hasn't exactly stepped into Sherlock Holmes' or Sam Spade's shoes. He isn't built for it. But he is unmatchable at sniffing out evil. And how many male detectives, totally unclothed, can enter a ladies' restroom without causing an uproar?*

It was on a bitterly cold night and frosty morning toward the end of the winter of '79 that I was awakened by a long wet tongue licking my face. It was Ralph von Wau Wau. The streetlight under which our Volkswagen was parked shone upon his eager face and told me that something was amiss. Rather, I'd missed a miss.

"Come, Weisstein, come!" he cried. "The dame is afoot!"

He spoke in English, for some reason preferring its use when we were alone.

"Good heavens!" I said. "Surely, you can't mean Fraulein Saugpumpe?"

He chuckled and then switched from Basil Rathbone's voice to the one he preferred when he was especially sarcastic. You would swear that you were hearing Humphrey Bogart in *The Maltese Falcon*.

"Who else have we been watching for five straight days and nights, sweetheart?" he said. "Pippi Longstocking? She just went around the corner. Get on the stick, Doc, and step on the gas. Or would you prefer to keep on dreaming of Frau Scarletin?"

He pressed the specially installed button on the dashboard. The door swung shut. He can open and close the door by bending his paw at right angles to his leg and pulling the handle out. But he usually uses the mechanism actuated by the dashboard and a toggle switch under the fender. Those familiar with our adventures will remember that we fitted the Volkswagen with this device during the rather horrendous events of *The Hind of the Baskerbergs*.

I started the motor and put the gear into first. As we drove away from the curb, headlights suddenly struck us and a loud deep horn blared. I slammed on the brakes, and Ralph bounced into the dashboard and fell on the floor. The huge diesel truck roared by, missing our left fender by an inch.

"Are you hurt?" I said as Ralph climbed back to the seat.

"No, but you're going to be, pal. Unless you take your mind off that skirt and get with it."

"I really prefer that you not refer to Frau Scarletin in that manner," I said stiffly.

"My apologies, my dear fellow," he said, reverting to his favorite alternate voice. "I had no intention of insulting one who, for you, will always be The Woman. But please do concentrate on the business at hand. Our quarry is a slippery one, a real fox, no pun intended."

I had by then driven the car around the corner. No sooner done than I pulled over to the curb and stopped.

"She's getting into a taxi," I said.

"I'm not blind," Ralph said. "Undoubtedly, she's heading for the airport."

"However could you know that?" I cried.

"To anyone else, she would merely be going to the opera. She's dressed for it, she has no luggage, only a small purse, and in forty minutes *Fidelio* begins. But it is not the magnificent Beethoven she is interested in.

"I was in the alley a half a block away when she came out of the door of her apartment building. Fortunately, the wind was in my favor. I was able to obtain an excellent olfactory profile of her. She'd been drinking heavily. Now, we know from the *Polizei* psychological profile of her that when she is relaxed she drinks California brandy. Though she'd also been smoking heavily, I was able to detect through the odor of American cigarettes—Camels, I believe—the telltale molecules of four-year-old California brandy stored in re-used white oak barrels.

"Without fear of contradiction I can state that the emitted fumes were of a brandy of 84 proof: pH, 4.48; total acid, 14.3; aldehydes, 5.9; esters, 1.6; fusel oil, 45.5; furfural, 0.18…"

I pulled the car from the curb to follow the taxi, crying at the same time, "Spare me the details, Ralph! I know your nose is an ambulatory chemical-analysis laboratory!"

He chuckled. "If you had memorized the profile as I have, my dear Weisstein, you would recall that she is terrified of flying. Only in extreme emergencies will she travel otherwise than by car or train. She can only overcome her neurosis by imbibing considerable amounts of alcohol. When she entered the building six hours ago, she looked contented and she had been drinking moderate quantities of Armagnac. It's apparent that she's received a phone call necessitating an airplane flight. You do follow my line of reasoning, my good fellow?"

He paused, grinning, his tongue hanging out, a triumphant light in his big brown eyes.

"And I suppose you know where that is?" I said somewhat testily. I was, I admit, in a bad mood.

I had been interrupted almost at the climax, if I may use the word, of a most pleasant dream. It would be indiscreet to go into its details.

"*Its citizens are a race apart, comparable only to themselves,*" he said.

"Venice!" I cried, recognizing Goethe's phrase. "But how...?"

I shot the VW into a parking space near Dammtorstrasse 28. Saugpumpe's taxi had stopped before the *Staatsoper* and she was getting out.

"Ha!" I said. "For once, you have erred, Ralph! She *is* attending the opera!"

"Really?" he said. "Have you also forgotten that the police report stated that she is tone deaf?"

"Whenever did that keep people from going to the opera?" I replied. "Perhaps she is meeting a gentleman inside, enduring what is to her a meaningless gibberish for the sake of male companionship."

He switched to Bogart. (From now on, I will refrain from identifying his differing voices except when necessary. I trust the reader can distinguish from the style of speech whether he is speaking in the persona of the Great Detective or the hard-boiled dick of San Francisco.)

"Bushwa, pal. She's shaking her tail, I mean, ducking her shadow. She still thinks she's the meat in a Hamburger police bun. She doesn't know the shami—that's the plural of shamus, sweetheart—were pulled off five days ago."

I groaned. Perhaps Ralph preferred English because only in that language can one make appropriate—or inappropriate—puns preserving the peculiar flavor of those two immortal mythics. Personally, I prefer Dr. Thorndyke.

A few minutes later, we were standing by the entrance to the opera house. We were in Guise No. 3, I with dark glasses and a cane, holding a leash attached to Ralph's harness. We stood there twelve minutes, the only interruption being a doorman who asked if he could do anything for us. I told him that we were waiting for my wife.

Presently a man in evening clothes came out, passing us with only a glance. The doorman whistled a taxi for him, and he was carried off.

"He looked mad," I said. "Perhaps his date stood him up."

"That was Saugpumpe, you simp! Get the lead out! Hump it! We'll lose her!" And he dragged me along willy-nilly behind him. Ralph weighs one hundred and sixty pounds, about seventy pounds more than the average German shepherd dog. Besides, his father was half Canadian timber wolf.

As we got into the VW, he said, "I smelled her. OK, I apologize. I keep forgetting you don't have my keen nose. That disguise would've fooled me, too, if I'd just eyeballed her. Maybe.

Didn't you dig that hipswaying? She was trying to walk like a man and almost succeeded."

"I thought he might just be a little, you know, on the ambiguous side," I said.

"Always the gent, ain't you, Doc?"

As we drove away, I said, "How do you know she's going to Venice?"

"That's where the long green, the loot, the mazuma is just now. And where the carrion is, the hyenas gather. In this case, Giftlippen and his sidekick, Smigma. Things must be about ready to pop open. Otherwise, Giftlippen wouldn't have called in his old lady."

"But," I said, "Giftlippen and Smigma are dead! They were blown to bits last year at Marienbad when the Czech police ambushed them. You know that. You set up the trap for them."

"How many wooden pfennigs have you got in the bank, Doc?"

2

As Ralph had predicted, her taxi went straight to the Northern Aircross, the airport at Fuhlsbüttel. I hope my foreign readers will forgive me if I mention, with some pride, that it is the oldest airport in Europe. It also has some of the longest lines at the ticket counter in the world. Ralph stayed in the car while I waited by the counter and ascertained that Saugpumpe was indeed going to Venice. Fortunately, she was so intoxicated that her normal perceptiveness was missing. She didn't notice me. Also, I suppose she must have been sure she had eluded her shadows, if any.

She was still in her male clothes, passing as a Herr Kleinermann Wasnun. I returned to the parking lot, where I got out of the trunk our forged IDs and other papers. Among these was a health certificate from a licensed veterinarian, required for a seeing-eye dog traveling to a foreign country. I wrote in the date since it is invalid if issued over fifteen days before leaving. I then muzzled Ralph, another requirement; and with a suitcase which is always packed for such emergencies, we proceeded to buy a ticket. (A blind man's dog travels free.) Of course, we couldn't board Saugpumpe's airliner. Even she would have thought it suspicious that we would have been at the opera and on her plane, too. She took a Lufthansa directly to the Lido Airport, and we left on an Albanian airliner to Rome. Not, however, before I had phoned Lisa Scarletin. When I hung up, I found that Ralph had been eavesdropping.

"You look like one of Dracula's victims," he said. "She really chewed you out, didn't she?"

"Yes. She said this was the last time. She gave me seven days more. If the case isn't wrapped up by then, I can either abandon it and return to Hamburg. Or..."

"Or forget the wedding bells, heh? Well, Doc, you can't blame her. She hardly ever gets to see you, and you lead a very dangerous life. Besides, women regard their competitors as bitches, but a male dog... unforgivable! I won't crowd you. You're a big boy now. You can make your own decision."

"Either way, I lose!" I cried.

"That's life for you." But his involuntary whine betrayed him. He was as upset as I.

The flight was pleasant enough, though marred by three minor incidents. One was when a scowling Albanian commented, in his native Gheg, about us. I leaned down to Ralph, who was lying in the aisle by my seat, as regulations required. "What did he say?"

"How the hell can I talk with this muzzle on?" he said.

Reassured that I could hear him—after all, the voder in his throat doesn't depend upon his lip movements—he said, "Something about a capitalist dog."

"What?" I said. "I shall certainly complain to the stewardess. After all, the Albanian Airline is trying to drum up business, and they certainly won't get any goodwill if they allow their passengers to be insulted."

"For cripes' sake, pipe down!" he said. "He was referring to *me*. And quit talking. They're staring at us."

Sometime later he rose while I was eating. Through a lifted lip, he said, "How's the rabbit stew?"

"Delicious. But I can't give you some. You know I can't unmuzzle you to eat."

"It ain't rabbit, Doc. It's *cat*!"

I suddenly lost my appetite. And I was furious, but I could not complain. I didn't want to draw any more attention to myself. Besides, how could I explain that I knew the difference between cat and rabbit without admitting that I was well acquainted with the taste of both?

About an hour before we landed at Rome, Ralph again put his head on my lap. "I can't stand it anymore," he said. "I gotta go!"

"Number 1 or Number 2?" I said.

"Do you want a demonstration in the aisle? Let me into the toilet before I bust."

It was most embarrassing, but Ralph insisted on the intensity of the urgency in terms which would affront the more delicate of my readers. In fact, they affronted me. Even more furious, I rose and tap-tapped my way down the aisle with the leash in my other hand. The passengers started, but they assumed of course that I was the one in need. Once at the door of the toilet, which fortunately was in the rear, I observed that no one was looking. I quickly opened the door and Ralph bounded in and sat down on the seat. I shut the door, but a few seconds later it occurred to me that if anyone did look back he might be surprised. I went into the toilet quickly and locked the door.

"I was wondering what you were doing out there," Ralph said. "I don't know what the Albanians consider a low sanitation level, but they might object to a mere canine using their facilities."

"Hurry up," I said. "The other toilet's occupied, and somebody might want to use this one at any moment. If he should see us emerge together from this place, well…"

"Can it, Doc! No pun intended. I've been able to adapt to living as a human in most respects. But I am a dog, and in some things I'll always be a dog. For Homo sap, Number 1 relief is a continuous process, quickly done. For me, it's intermittent, and it's long, though highly pleasurable. So keep your shirt on."

I sweated, and then at last Ralph was finished, and I opened the door. And what I'd dreaded, happened. A fat, frowzy, and elderly woman was waiting outside. Her expression of impatience, and perhaps of some slight pain, became astonishment. Then revulsion. She poured out a flood of furious protest mixed with some invectives, I'm sure, though I didn't understand a word of it. Ralph growled, and even though muzzled he scared her. She backed up, screaming for the stewardess. There was quite a commotion for a while. I got back to my seat and sat down, and then the stewardess, speaking German, asked me for an explanation.

"It's simple," I said. "The dog was suffering, and so I took him where he would no longer have to suffer."

"But that is for the passengers," she said, though she was having difficulty repressing a smile.

"The dog is a passenger," I said. "And I didn't see any sign forbidding use by animals. Besides, he's much cleaner than her," and I pointed to the fat woman glaring at us from across the aisle.

"Oh, you mustn't say that!" she said. "She's a commissar!"

But she returned to the woman; they talked for a while, and that was the last I heard of that. However, after disembarking, Ralph pulled me up alongside the woman, who was trudging across the field carrying a large attaché case. He lifted his lip, said something, and then dropped back. She looked back, this time with a frightened look, and then broke into a waddling run.

"All right," I said. "What did you say?"

"Do you know the Albanian for *up yours*?"

"Ralph," I said, "that was stupid. We've had a lot of publicity. She might put two and two together and..."

"And come up with *vier*," he said. (I should explain that the German word for *four* sounds much like the British English *fear*.)

"Anyway," he continued, "she'll convince herself she was mistaken. It's been my experience that nobody really believes in a talking dog until he's been around me for a while."

"Nevertheless, that was stupid. It could jeopardize our mission."

"I'm human, all too human. Likely to give way to self-destructive impulses. I apologize again. You're entitled to that remark. God knows how many times I've called you stupid. I've regretted it later, of course. After all, it's not your fault you don't have my high IQ."

For the reader who knows nothing about Ralph—though it seems incredible in this day of global TV—I'll recapitulate his career. Ralph was the result of experiments by psychobiologists at an institute in Hamburg. They were able to raise the intelligence of various animals through the implantation of an artificial protein. These developed into billions of cerebral nerve synapses, making the brain not much larger but immensely more complex.

German shepherd dogs were not the only experimental animals at the institute. The scientists had succeeded in raising the intelligence of all their subjects and also increased the size of many. The sentient beasts had included donkeys, bears, otters, rodents of various kinds, and a gorilla.

The person believed to be chiefly responsible for the IQ-raising techniques was Professor Pierre Sansgout. He was a biologist who had been fired from the University of Paris because he preferred German beer to French wine.

Blackballed everywhere in his native country, he had gone to work for the Hamburg institute. Apparently, the explosion that killed everyone but Ralph at the institute was Sansgout's fault. From the few notes escaping destruction, it was learned that his pet project was the mutation of bees which would directly produce mead. According to a note, he had done this, and the alcoholic content of this mead was eighty percent. However, he, and the institute as a whole, had become victims of oversuccess. The source of the explosion was traced to a giant hive on his laboratory table.

Ralph was now twenty-nine but was as vigorous as a man of the same age. No one knew how his lifespan had been extended. The explosion had also destroyed the records. There was speculation that the scientists had discovered an age-delaying "elixir" which had been injected into the beasts. But no one really knew.

Ralph was a pup when the explosion occurred. Legally, he was a *Schutzhund*, the property of the Hamburg Police Department. He came close to being destroyed—"murdered," Ralph said—by the HPD because of his slow growth, which matched the pace of a human infant. But when he uttered a few words while on the way to the gas chamber, he was saved. The HPD realized what they had and gave him an education.

Investigation revealed that a voder had been implanted in his throat. This was connected to cerebral circuits which enabled him to switch it off and on and converted his linguistic thoughts into spoken words. As he grew older, larger voders were implanted. At the present, the voder contained circuits enabling him to speak with a perfect accent all twelve of the world's great languages and a number of the minor.

However, Ralph wasn't fluent in all of these. He had not as yet mastered all. Nor could he speak all of these with perfect grammar or a large vocabulary. But he was learning. The voder also contained different voice circuits. Hence, he had two male, one female, and one child's voice. He could also whistle, meow like a cat, utter ten different bird calls, and the decibel level ranged from that of a bullhorn to a whisper.

Every four years, the voder had to be removed and its tiny atomic battery replaced.

On becoming a juvenile, Ralph went to work for the HPD. He soon became famous because of his success in solving crimes. Eventually, he tired of this and applied for freedom and a license as a private detective. Those familiar with my chronicles will know that he had to endure a trial to establish his legal right to become a German citizen. Ralph won, but he also had to pay back the HPD for the expenses of his education. Thus, though he often earned fabulous fees, he was still sending large monthly amounts to the HPD.

A bitter aggravation of his financial distress had been brought about by the very villain we were tracking, Giftlippen, Baron Rottenfranzer. Before taking up a criminal career, Giftlippen had been an eminent literary critic and an affluent literary agent. Though a native and resident of the tiny principality of Liechtenstein, his influence was enormous all over the world. When Ralph's novel, *Some Humans Don't Stink*, came out, Giftlippen had turned thumbs down on it. His venomously unfair and viciously scornful articles had resulted in small sales for the book. (He even had the audacity to claim that it was authored by a ghost writer.)

Recently, we'd heard that the English translation was selling well. But the American royalties had not yet arrived. I once asked Ralph how it was possible for a distinguished and highly educated man like Giftlippen to become a crook.

"From literary critic to criminal is only a short, almost inevitable, step," Ralph had replied bitterly.

Smigma had been a noted Polish author of didactic fairy tales. He was also Giftlippen's good friend and client. His fiction, however, was only a sideline. He was a high official in the communist propaganda bureau. Then a strange thing happened after he'd suffered brain damage in a car crash. He found himself unable to utter a falsehood. This, of course, rendered him unfit for writing propaganda or fiction. (This characteristic would trip him up in *The Case of the Jesting Pilot*.) It also made him dangerous to the state. He fled Poland and joined Giftlippen.

In the case titled *A Scarletin Study*, I recount my own career as a physician for the Autobahn Patrol Medical Department. During an encounter with the murderous Rottenfranzer Gang—oil-hijacking specialists—I suffered a wound which hospitalized me. I retired and took up private practice without much success. During this time I met Ralph, who was looking for a human to share the expenses of his apartment. I abandoned my practice and became Ralph's full-time partner.

It was an exciting life, but now I had to make a choice

between Lisa and Ralph. She would accept no more excuses that I was sorely needed by Ralph.

While we were waiting for our plane, Ralph explained why we were going to Venice.

"Here's the setup, Doc. Venice has slowly been sinking at the rate of 2.08 centimeters annually since 1920. It doesn't sound like much, but Venice is flush with the surface of the sea. In addition, the tides and seiches that sweep through the lagoon from the Adriatic cause a lot of trouble. And the atmospheric pollution from the factories of Mestre, the nearest mainland city, is destroying the art treasures, the building exteriors, the paintings, the statues, et cetera.

"The islands of Venice are sinking because of withdrawal of water through wells. The water-bearing strata are subsiding. And it won't do any good to pump water back in, according to the scientists. Venice seemed doomed.

"Meanwhile, a short time ago, a savior, or a man who claims to be a savior, appears. He's a strange man with a strange story. His name *was* Giuseppe Granelli. He was born and raised in the back woods of the Italian Alps. His village was destroyed in a landslide. He was the sole survivor, though crippled for life. But during his convalescence he had a selcouth experience."

"Selcouth? What does that mean?" I said.

"It's an archaic English word meaning *unusual* or *strange*, my unlearned colleague. Granelli had a series of visions which revealed to him that he is the reincarnation of the most famous Doge of Venice, Enrico Dandolo, died 1205. He adopted the name and came to Venice in his wheelchair. There he proclaimed his real identity and his mission and organized the Venice Uplift Foundation. Despite the sound of its title, it is not an organization to raise money to buy a bra for the goddess of the sea."

"Spare me," I murmured.

"Dandolo's ideas for salvation sound feasible, though they'll cost a hell of a lot of money. He aroused vast enthusiasm. Mazuma pours in from art lovers, rich and poor, from all over the world. We kicked in twenty marks ourselves, remember, Doc? Had to skip a few meals but we considered it worth it."

"*You* did," I said. "Lisa was upset when I took her out to a Colonel Sanders' instead of the Epicurean's Club."

"Economics always wins over esthetics. Anyway, the Fund's funds are kept in a Venetian bank. So far, eighty million dollars American, and more coming in. And in two days the various festivals will start, including the traditional Marriage of the Sea of the Doge."

"And you think this vast sum will tempt Giftlippen? And he'll attempt a robbery during the confusion of the festivals?"

"Bingo! Give the man a kewpie doll! Look, I could be wrong. But it'll be the first time. Why should Giftlippen's mistress suddenly take off for Venice? It's because Giftlippen isn't dead, and he needs her for more than just sexual satisfaction."

"And Saugpumpe will lead us to Giftlippen?"

"We'll nail him. And we'll be financially independent. The reward offered for him, dead or alive, by the West German government has not been withdrawn. He's supposed to have perished, but the bureaucrats haven't gotten around to canceling the offer. It's still in effect, legally, and if we get him, we can legally collect. Five million marks. Think of that. You'll take your half and marry Mrs. Scarletin with your head held high. You won't be a down-at-the-heels quack marrying a rich widow."

"I don't care for your choice of words," I said. But it was an automatic response. I had gotten used to Ralph's taking his resentments out on me. Even though he had proved a hundred times that he was smarter and more educated and competent than most humans, he was still patronized by many. To them, he was just a freak. There were many who didn't believe that he was just a freak. There were many who didn't believe that he was truly sentient. I've even read articles where it was hinted that he couldn't speak at all, that I was a ventriloquist. The worst, in his eyes, were those who talked down to him, who insisted on petting him. He couldn't stand this. Not even I was allowed to pat his head. Lisa was the only exception so far.

He had once explained to me why she was granted this privilege.

"Dogs are inherently pack animals. I don't mean beasts of burden. I mean members of a pack. In a pack there's always one leader to whom the others defer and make submissive gestures. This is in the wild state, you comprehend, my dear fellow. But domesticated dogs have the same instincts, which is why they adapted to human society so well and why dogs have become the favorite pets of most people. But they're all psychologically mixed up by domestication. Some are one-man dogs, and will allow only their master or mistress to pet them. Other dogs will allow any familiar human or stranger to pet them. Every human is, to them, a pack leader.

"I have the same instincts, but I am also, in a sense, human. I regard myself as the leader, whether the pack is Canis or Homo. But there's something about Mrs. Scarletin, call it charisma or whatever, that makes me want her to pet me. It's humiliating, in a way, because I'm more intelligent, more perceptive, and stronger. But that's the way it is."

"That's the way it is with me, too," I said.

Coming in at 12,000 feet, I could see the whole of the Laguna Veneta and much of the mainland in the late April sun. Two islands form part of the barriers which almost seal off the lagoon from the Adriatic: the Lido and Pellestrina. The former looks like an extended human shinbone; the latter is little more than a semi-deserted thin flat reef, now frequently awash. Between the two is a strait through which the high tide poured to send water swirling around the islanders' ankles.

Within the lagoon were the 116 closely spaced islands. A motor and train causeway connected Venice to the mainland. Smoke poured from the stacks of hundreds of factories in Mestre.

We sank down, then came in low over the Lido. Looking down, I could see the famous golf course at the western end. A minute later, we had landed on the airport at the other end. The Lido is, I believe, the only island on which vehicles are permitted. We took a Fiat taxi to our hotel. Since we did not have much money, and wanted to be inconspicuous, we had reserved a room at the Rivamare, a third-rate hotel facing the Adriatic. The Lido was crowded and festive, as were all the major islands. We were lucky to get rooms at this time, when Labor Day, Ascension, Corpus Christi, and the Marriage of the Sea coincided on May 1. Moreover, the Doge Dandolo had been attracting large crowds even out of season.

The taxi driver cheated me, which infuriated me. But since I was supposed to be blind, I couldn't protest. I ordered a bottle of Falerno, two bowls of *burrida*, and a dish of *capotano* for me and of *fegatino* for Ralph. We finished them off with *cassata siciliana*, a rich cake with ice cream.

I then spent some time on the phone, calling hotels on the main island. Finally, the clerk at the Danieli informed me that a Herr Wasnun was registered there. We at once took a *vaporetto*, a steamboat, to the Riva degli Schiavone, a promenade facing the lagoon by the Canale di San Marco. A cluster of hotels was along here. The most famous, and expensive, was the Danieli.

"George Sand and Alfred de Musset stayed there in Room 13," Ralph said. "The Doge Dandolo resides there. More to the point, Fraulein Saugpumpe is there. She didn't have any trouble getting a room there; it had been reserved for her for a long time. So I suspect that our quarry, Giftlippen, is also residing there. The *arschloch* always did travel in style.

"Also, you'll notice that the Banco di Manin is nearby. That's where the Fund's money is deposited. But I suspect that Giftlippen has more in store for Venice than just cleaning out a bank. I have to give him credit; he does think big."

We were on the point of strolling to the Danieli when our

attention was attracted by a commotion on the waterfront. At first we thought it was a brawl, a fight between the supporters of Dandolo and his opposition. A number of Italians decried him because of the stand of the Church. As I said, Dandolo claimed to be a reincarnation of the greatest of the Doges. Reincarnation is contrary to Catholic theology, of course, and the Pope had denounced Dandolo as a heretic and a fraud. Despite this, the majority of Catholics supported the Doge. They wanted Venice saved. Moreover, they regarded this affair as one more event in the love-hate relationship between the Pope and the Italian people.

"If they can give the man in the Vatican the finger, without endangering their immortal souls, they'll gladly do it," Ralph had commented.

The news media had crackled with reports of brawls between the pro- and anti-Dandolists. But the melee, the screaming and shouting and cursing and fistfighting, were not caused by theological disagreement. After we got close, we saw that it was a mob scene being filmed for a movie. Suddenly, two men and a woman were pushed into the water, a man yelled, "Cut!" and silence clamped like a giant hand over the mouths of the actors.

But only for a moment. The director began yelling— screaming, rather—and I suddenly realized that the screaming had been done mostly by him. He had an extremely shrill voice, one which carried like a factory whistle for a long distance. He was an extraordinary person, one who'd attract attention anywhere. He was only four feet high but looked as if he were thirty-five years old. As I found out later, he was actually forty-five. He had long straight hair as black as the bottom of an oil well. His eyes were a beautiful robin's-egg blue. His face was hawklike but handsome. The stocky body was perfectly proportioned. So, though he was often referred to as a "giant dwarf," he was actually a midget, though too tall even to deserve that appellation.

It would be indiscreet to record the scorn, the invective, the denunciations of incompetency he hurled at the actors. Suffice it to say that he gave them the worst tongue-lashing I've ever heard. Also, the most entertaining. The man was an artist, a poet, extemporaneously pouring out Demosthenics which must have cut the actors to the heart yet made me want to fall on the marble walk with laughter. Of course, I wasn't the recipient of the words and so could enjoy them.

The assistant director argued with him that the scene had been extremely vigorous and loud. There was nothing phony-looking about it.

"Yeah!" the little man screamed. "Everybody knows you Italians are very dramatic! You can ask somebody to please pass the antipasto, and you look and sound as if you're threatening murder and mayhem! But everybody knows you're mostly bluff and bluster and you just like to hear the sound of your own voices! You're all soap opera characters in real life and about as convincing!

"What I want is sincerity, understand, sincerity! I want you to be really mad at each other! Hate each other's guts. Don't just shake your fists! Slam each other in the breadbasket! Twist a few balls; that'll get some sincerity out of you.

"OK! Take your places and this time do it for real. Think

of your opponent as someone who's spit on the Pope *and* balled your mother. He has knocked up your sister and won't marry her. He's also the editor of a newspaper, and he's just put in big headlines that your aunt is running a whorehouse. As if that isn't enough, he's revealed that your daughter has run off with a married man, a *German* tourist!"

At this point the actors began yelling at him. His voice rose again, blanketing out the others like a lid put on a pot of steaming soup. By this time, the three who'd fallen into the water had climbed out. They stood near him, dripping with the stinking sewage-clotted liquid. One of them was a tall woman with a beautiful face and a superb figure. Her scanty wet clothes clung tightly to her body. All of a sudden, I was no longer in a hurry.

One of the actors was talking to the director. It seemed that he was the agent for the actors' union and he was protesting that they were not being paid to hurt each other.

"I'll pay you! I'll pay you!" the little man screamed. "Godalmighty! Every time I want you to do something extra, put a little sincerity into your shams, you want more *lire*! Are you sure you're not members of the Mafia? It's extortion, pure essence of extortion, blackmail, financial rape, a currency copulation, *lira* lewdness, a Giovanni jazzing! You're bankrupting me!

"OK! Let's shoot it again and do it right this time. You think film grows like spaghetti! Do you think at all? Look, I'll tell you what'll make you mad enough to shuck off your insincerity like a stripteaser drops her panties! Think of your opponent as me! And I've just told you you're the illegitimate son of a Sicilian!"

That did it. No Italian will admit that Sicilians are real

Italians, or so I've often been told by them. The North Italians look down upon the South Italians, and both look down on the Sicilian. I don't know who the Siciliano looks down on. The Maltese, perhaps.

The mob held a brief but spirited discussion. The agent said a few words to the director, something like "*Ah fahng goo*," and all, including the cameraman, walked off. For a moment, the big midget was speechless, then he shouted, "You're fired! Discharged for incompetency! Come back, do you hear? Come back or I'll put barnacles on your gondolas! Oh, my God, why did I ever come to this garlic swamp?"

Yelling, he hurled the camera into the canal and stamped around as if he would leave his footprints in the marble.

"Childish tantrums," I said to Ralph.

Ralph said, "I know who he is! He's the famous, or infamous, Cordwainer Bird!"

Immediately I recognized him. Bird was an American, an inhabitant of Los Angeles who had, in recent years, been much in the world's eyes. Originally, he had been a science-fiction writer, author of works well known in his peculiar genre. These included such strange titles as *I Have No Can and I Must Go*, *Pane Deity* or *Up Your Window*, *The Breast That Spouted Cholesterol into the Arteries of the World*, *The Whining of Whopped Whippets*, and *Dearthbird Stories*.

At the same time, he had managed to rise to the top as a TV and movie writer. But his inability to tolerate tampering with his scripts by the producers, their mothers-in-law and mistresses, directors, actors, and studio floorsweepers had gotten him into trouble. After several incidents in which he almost strangled some powerful producers, he was blackballed in Hollywood.

Simultaneously, he was frustrated in his efforts to impress the literary critics of New York. He wrote several mainstream novels which the "East Coast Literary Mafia"—as he called it—reviled. He became destitute, which was the normal state of most science-fiction writers. But he was a fighter, and he vowed to smash the Manhattan cartel, which existed to encourage native Gothamites whose shoddy works counterfeited emotions and destroyed the imagination of readers. He sold his stately mansion in Sherman Oaks at a loss and hitchhiked to New York. There he engaged in a guerrilla war with the critics and their allies, the publishers, distributors, and truck drivers' union.

And here he was, Cordwainer Bird, apparently making his own movie.

At that moment he saw us. He stopped, stared, then bounded grinning toward us.

"Wow! What a magnificent dog!" he said to me. "Is it all right to pet him?"

I wasn't surprised at this request. Many people desire to do this. And Bird's reputation as an ardent canophile was well known.

"There's only one person he's permitted to do so," I said. "But you can try. He won't bite, though."

Bird reached out a hand. I was surprised and, I must admit, somewhat jealous, when Ralph submitted to his stroking.

"Holy Moly!" Bird said. "I think I'm in love! Listen, I don't want to offend you, but I'd like to buy him! Name your price."

This was too much for Ralph. He growled and lifted his

lip, baring teeth that would have given a hungry leopard second thoughts. The idea of being sold, as if he were just an animal, offended him.

"Hey!" Bird said. "He acts like he knows what I'm saying!" Coaxingly, he said, "Come on, pal. I wouldn't hurt your feelings for anything. Say, what's his name?"

He thrust out his hand again and stroked Ralph's ear.

"He's not for sale," I said. I tugged at the leash and Ralph trotted on ahead of me. But he kept looking back as if he regretted having to leave.

Suddenly, Bird was in front of me. Before I could resist, he had removed my large dark glasses and ripped off my false mustache.

"Ah, ha!" he said. "I thought so! *Herr Weisstein und der wunderhund*, Ralph von Wau Wau! I might've thought another German shepherd could be as big as Ralph. But it was evident he understood every word I spoke. Wow! Weisstein and von Wau Wau!"

"You sure blew it, sweetheart," Ralph said to me.

I sputtered with indignation. "Really," I said. "What could I have done? What did I do to give us away? It was your reaction that aroused his suspicions."

"Never mind that." He spoke to Bird. "For Pete's sakes, be a pal and give him his glasses and mustache. We're on a case!"

Bird smote his forehead with his hand. "Holy Jumping Moses! You're right! I am a dummy."

Unfortunately, the hand with which he struck his forehead was holding the mustache. It stuck to it when his hand came away. He handed me the glasses and then started to look around. "Where'd it go?"

I ripped it off his skin and replaced it with trembling hands. "By now all of Venice must be on to us," I said.

He looked quickly around. "No, nobody's looking this way. You're okay. So far. Listen, I don't want to horn in if I'm not welcome. But I've been looking for some real excitement. Life has been an emotional downhill slide since I cleaned out the New York establishment. I'd like to be dealt in this. I have certain talents which you could use. And it'd be a great honor to work with the great von Wau Wau. I'd do it for nothing, too. But don't tell my agent I said so."

"The best thing you could do for us would be to swear to keep silent about us," I said frostily.

I spoke to Ralph. "Isn't that so?"

"My dear fellow," Ralph said. "It *isn't* so. We're up against a great criminal, the deadliest biped in Europe. I've studied Mr. Bird's exploits in New York, and I believe we could use him with great advantage to our mission."

I was struck dumb with astonishment. Ralph had always said he wouldn't dream of taking in another partner. He had enough to do to put up with me. Of course, he was jesting when he spoke so disparagingly of me. But though he liked me, perhaps— dare I say—even loved me, he resented having to depend upon a human. As he once said, "Weisstein, you are my hands." Of course, he had to spoil it by adding, "And all thumbs, alas!"

But there was some sense in what he said. We could use a man of Cordwainer Bird's caliber. By which I mean that, though he looked like he was a BB gun, he shot a .44 Magnum. Besides, if he got mad at us, he could expose us. And that might be fatal.

At an outdoor restaurant we outlined to him our mission over a bottle of *soave* and a plate of *baccala*. Bird, however, refused the wine. He neither smoked nor drank, he said. He didn't seem to like it that Ralph lapped up the wine from the platter by my feet, but he said nothing.

"Bend an ear, buddy," Ralph said. "You're in the midst of shooting a flicker. You'll have to forget about that now. Can you stand the expense, all that money tied up?"

"No sweat," Bird said. "I'm backing and producing this myself. I'll show those Hollywood phonies a thing or two. I wrote the script myself, too. It was originally titled *Deaf in Venice*. But I decided on a more eye-catching title. I'm great on that, you know. How about *Ever Since I Met Her in Venice, I've Had Trouble with My He-ness*?"

"You'll need a wide screen," I said.

At that moment, we heard a blare of trumpets and a banging of drums. Everybody got up from their tables and ran to the crowd pouring out of the hotels and streets. I called to a man hurrying by, and he said, *"Il Doge Dandolo!"*

We stood up and looked out across the Canale di San Marco. A boat had appeared from around the island of San Giorgio Maggiore. I recognized it at once, having seen it many times on TV. It was magnificent, coated with gold, propelled by sixty oarsmen, an exact replica of a late medieval barque. On a platform in the stern stood some people dressed, like the oarsmen, in twelfth-century Venetian costumes. After a while, we could see the Doge himself. He sat in a wheelchair, an extraordinarily large one, also coated with gold. It was said to be self-propelled with a steam engine fueled by a small atomic reactor. As the barque stopped by the *riva*, a gang of flunkies from the Danieli Hotel ran out and placed an ornately carved gangplank onto the boat.

Ralph said, "Watch for Saugpumpe, amigo. I'll nose around and try to pick up the scents of Giftlippen and Smigma."

I released the leash and he trotted over to the crowd cheering on the quay. Bird left on his task, a rather distasteful one. He had to dive down into the stinking waters and recover his camera. Ralph had said that he could pose as a TV-news cameraman. He could take pictures which we could study later, hoping to identify our quarry in the crowds. Also, posing as a newsman, he could be seen everywhere without arousing suspicion.

I remained on my chair to observe both the crowd and the hotel entrance. I had difficulty not keeping my attention strictly on Dandolo. He was a huge man with a disproportionately large head. His features were exactly those of the late Doge whose reincarnation he claimed to be. They were immobile, waxy, their deadness the result of the landslide which had buried him for three days. He could, however, move his lips and jaws. He always wore fur gloves, reportedly to conceal hideous scars. A tigerskin robe covered his legs.

The wheelchair and its occupant rolled off the platform and down the gangplank. He was surrounded by his retainers and the hurrahing crowd, but I got up on my chair to get a good view. Before I remembered that I was supposed to be blind and hastily got down, I saw him clearly. By his side was his chief assistant and valet, Bruto Brutini, a small bespectacled man, prim-faced, bald and bearded.

He carried an ornately chased golden bowl full of shelled walnuts and pecans. Dandolo dropped his hands into this and threw a dozen at a time into his mouth. His addiction to nuts was well known.

Presently, the *riva* was almost deserted, the crowd having collected around the hotel entrance. Ralph came back and allowed me to leash him again. "Order another bottle of *soave*," he said, his tongue hanging out. "That was dry work."

"Any luck?"

"No, damn it. For one thing, both Dandolo and Smigma were too heavily perfumed. It overrode every other odor in the crowd. I wonder why they used perfume instead of taking a bath. Perhaps it's because that's what the old doges did. Dandolo is said to be a stickler for authenticity."

Cordwainer Bird rose out of the water, shoved the camera onto the stone, and walked dripping to us. He looked excited; his robin's-egg blue eyes shone.

"You aren't going to believe this. But I was under the barque when it came in."

"You bumped your head?" I said.

He stared. "Yeah. How'd you know?"

"A wish fulfillment," Ralph said, staring at me. I blushed. There was no fooling him. He knew that I was jealous, though I had tried not to show any sign of such an unworthy feeling. He claimed that he could smell emotions in humans, that they caused a subtle change of body odor. He would have made a great psychiatrist, not only because of his olfactory and emotional sensitivity and high intellect. People have no hesitancy in revealing all to a dog.

"Oh?" Bird said. "Listen, you guys, I did bump my head, but not on the bottom of the barque. I rammed it into metal six feet below the barque! Curved metal!"

"What was it?" I said.

"Hell, man, it was a submarine!"

I gasped, and Ralph whined.

"Yeah, there's a tiny submarine attached to the bottom of the barque!"

5

"Donnerwetter!" Ralph said, reverting in his surprise to his native tongue. Then, "Of course, what a blockhead I am! All the clues were in front of my nose, and I failed to smell them! How humiliating!"

"What are you talking about?" I said.

"The Doge Dandolo is Giftlippen!"

"However did you deduce that?"

"You mean *infer*, not deduce, don't you?" he said. "How often must I point out the difference? Actually, to be exact, I *gathered*. Check your Webster's."

"For crying out loud!" Bird said. "This is no time for lexical lessons! What's going on?"

"I had thought that Giftlippen would be here because of the Venice Uplift Fund millions," Ralph said. "But I erred again in underestimating that archvillain. He created the fund in order to steal it. But I'm sure that's part of a much bigger rip-off. Exactly what, I don't as yet know."

"But… the clues?" I said.

"It's too early to tell you. Besides, I think I also know the true identity of Giftlippen. It's only a theory, you understand. I prefer not to say anything about it until theory has become fact. But we may proceed on my premise that Dandolo is indeed Giftlippen, who is… never mind that now."

"If this is true," I said, "we must inform the Venetian police."

Simultaneously, Ralph said, "Don't be a sap, pal," and Bird said, "You're out of your gourd."

"One, the police would claim the reward," Ralph said. "And we need the money badly. Two, Giftlippen has a habit of bribing a strategically situated policeman or official to tip him off. Sometimes, he even plants one of his own men in a high place long before he pulls a job. The Venetian fuzz may be safe, but we can't take a chance."

"We'll give the big cheese our own *shazam*!" Bird cried.

Bird, I found out later, often reverted in moments of intense excitement to the speech he'd picked up from the comic books he'd read when a youth. Hence, his sometimes old-fashioned and often obscure phrases.

(For the benefit of my German readers, I'll explain that *shazam* was a word endemic in, I believe, the Captain Marvel comic books. Uttered by the captain and his juvenile partner, Billy Batson, it gave them superman powers. The American audience will have no trouble recognizing it. Neither will the French, who take comics seriously and even grant Ph.D. degrees for theses on this subject.)

"This turn of events pulls the rug from under us,

sweethearts," Ralph said. "If Giftlippen or Smigma eyeball us, we'll be candidates for the morgue. This blind-man-and-his-seeing-eye-dog act isn't going to fool them. Not after our Kuwait adventure, heh, Weisstein?"

He was referring to that series of extraordinary events which I have chronicled as *The Shakedown of the Shook Sheik*.

Ralph suddenly growled. Bird said, "Oh, oh!"

I turned. We were surrounded by seven Arabs. All wore dark glasses and were dressed in flowing robes. The faces of two were shrouded by their hoods, or whatever Arabs call them. But they were not concealed enough to prevent me from distinguishing the massive waxen features of the Doge under a fake beard and the prunish lineaments of his assistant. They were all barefoot, and the wind was blowing from us to them. That accounted for their being able to take Ralph by surprise. Their wide loose sleeves had been pulled over their hands, but we could see the silencers attached to automatics.

"You three gentlemen will walk onto the barque with us," Smigma said in a thin high voice with a Polish accent. "Believe me, at the first sign of making a break, we will shoot you down."

I looked around. A number of oarsmen were coming toward us. They would block off the view of the passersby. If we were shot, they'd doubtless just pick us up and carry us off as if we were drunks—a not uncommon sight during the festivals.

That Smigma had addressed us as "three gentlemen" told me that they knew Ralph's identity.

We said nothing as we were conducted up the gangplank to the center of the boat. A hatch was raised and we were prodded down a ladder into a narrow cabin. Ralph could manage a ladder by himself. Another hatch gave entrance to the submarine attached to the bottom of the barque. We went past the small control room to a cell near the bow and were locked inside. This was so confined that we had no room to sit down. After a few minutes, we felt the craft begin moving and could detect faint vibrations as the propellers pushed us toward an unknown destination.

Ralph quit cursing himself for a dunderhead in six languages, including the Scandinavian. "I suspect, my esteemed but also dumb colleagues," he said, "that Saugpumpe led us into this trap. Giftlippen would want to get me, his most dangerous antagonist, out of the way before he proceeded with his dastardly plot. So, he allowed his mistress to remain under our observation until the last moment."

The only sound then was Bird banging his forehead on the steel bulkhead and muttering, "You cretin, you! Taken like a babe in diapers! Oh, the ignominy of it all!"

After a while, Ralph said, "You'll suffer even more brain damage if you keep that up." That was his way of subtly calling Bird a blockhead. There was one thing about Ralph. Though he had little hesitation in self-reproach, he hesitated even less in reproaching others.

We could do nothing. We couldn't even see the control room, since our door was windowless. After an hour, we felt the sub slow down. Then it stopped, the door was opened, and we were ushered up the ladder. We emerged into a vast cavern illuminated by floodlights. The cave had no visible entrance, which meant that it was beneath the surface of the sea. Our craft lay next to a stone platform; almost level with the water. Near it was docked a much larger submarine. Like our vessel, it had no conning tower. Beyond it was a blue sausage-shaped bag of rubber or plastic about sixty feet long and ten feet wide.

Ralph said, "Aha! That sub is a World War I U-boat! I recognize it. It was stolen from the Kiel Marine Museum a year ago! Giftlippen plans far ahead of time, the cunning fellow. He's removed the conning towers because of the extreme shallowness of the lagoon. Otherwise, the towers would project above the surface."

"And the bag?" I said.

"To be towed behind the U-boat. It must contain a metal skeleton to keep it from collapsing. Also, compartments to be flooded for submersion. Plus others for transporting the loot and much of his gang back from Venice. Doubtless, he has a large crew planted there, ready to carry out his foul plot."

Prodded by a rifle, we crossed the platform into a tunnel hewn out of rock. This led us for thirty paces to stairs also cut out of the rock. We ascended these into another tunnel made of stone blocks. A man pulled a lever; a section of the wall ground open. We entered a dungeon filled with rusty instruments of torture, a disheartening sight, passed through it and up a narrow, winding stone staircase, and came out through another wall-door into a kitchen. It looked exactly like the kitchen of a medieval castle, which, indeed, it was.

After traversing a wide stone corridor, we came into a vast unfurnished room. We climbed up dusty staircases and presently were locked inside a twelfth-story stone cell. I looked through the steel bars of a small square opening in the southeast wall. The castle was set on a hill about fifty feet high. Since the rest of the country hereabouts was so flat, I deduced that the hill was artificial. The builder of the castle had piled earth here centuries ago.

The seaward side had been cut to make a perpendicular front and then a stone-block wall had been erected against it to prevent erosion (I couldn't see this from my window, of course, but I found out these details later).

The castle was about half a mile from the shore. An arm of the lagoon a hundred yards wide extended from the shore to the base of the hill. It was the avenue for the sub which had brought us here. Once it, too, had been lined with great stone blocks, but many of these had fallen. A number jutted above the water just below the walls.

Ralph stood up on his hind legs by me. "You can see the islands from here," he said.

Normally, he wouldn't have been able to see that far. Dogs are shortsighted. But he was wearing contact lenses.

"Well, I know where we are," he said. "In the ruined and long-abandoned castle of Il Seno. He was a thirteenth-century Venetian, confined by the Council of Ten to his castle. The Council didn't mind his piracy as long as it was restricted to non-Venetian vessels. But Il Seno wasn't very discriminating.

"His name, by the way, means 'The Bight' in Italian. And this little recess in the land was also called Il Seno. It's still referred to by the locals as Il Seno del Seno. The Bight of the Bight. And here we are, the bitten among the bighters. A bitter pun, if you will excuse me."

"The desperate among the desperadoes," Bird said. "Okay, now what'll we do?"

At that moment the Judas window in the steel door opened. Giftlippen's enormous head appeared beyond it. "Have you any complaints about the accommodations?" he said in a deep baritone voice. He spoke in German with a Liechtensteiner accent.

"Cut the comedy, crook," Ralph said. "What I want to know is what do you intend for us? I would have thought you'd have kaputted us at once."

"What? And deprive me of the esthetic pleasure of forcing you to watch the rape of Venice?" Giftlippen said. "You, who screwed up my greatest coup? No, my shaggy friend, ever since you thwarted me in Kuwait, I've been planning this very scenario. I want you to view, as helpless spectators, my second-greatest coup. Actually, my greatest, since the Kuwait caper was a failure.

"You'll see the whole thing. Here"—he handed a long telescope to me—"and you won't be able to do a damned thing about it."

He broke into a weird blood-chilling cackling. Bird said, "Sounds just like my uncle, Kent Allard, alias Lamont Cranston. I've heard Giftlippen has a fabulous collection of old radio-show records."

"It *is* a recording," Ralph said enigmatically.

"Tomorrow is the ceremony of the Marriage of the Sea," Giftlippen said. "Ah, wait until you see the priceless wedding gifts the Venetians will be giving me. Of course, they don't know about their generosity yet, and I regret to say that it will be one hundred percent involuntary. But it's the gift that counts, not the intention."

"And after the wedding?" Ralph said.

"Do you know the history of this chamber?" Giftlippen said. "It's rather grim. This is the place where the daughter of a noble starved to death. Il Seno abducted her, locked her in it, and told her she could eat when she agreed to share his bed. She refused. I think it only esthetically appropriate that my greatest enemy suffer a like fate."

He paused to chomp on some nuts.

"Legend has it that she ate her own flesh before she expired. A classic case of diminishing returns. Now! There are three of you, and I have a wager with my esteemed colleague, Smigma, that one of you will put off the inevitable for a while by dining upon the other two. My money is on you, von Wau Wau. You're a dog, and dogs are always hungry. Your canine heritage will triumph over the human. You'll eat your friends, though you may weep walrus tears while doing so."

"By the heavens!" I cried. "You're a fiend! You're not human, you foul beast!"

"I'll go along with that, pal," Ralph said.

Bird snatched the telescope from me and drove its end through the window into the huge face. Giftlippen cried out and fell away. Smigma's face, a safe distance away, succeeded his. He cursed us in Polish, and then the window was slammed shut.

"At least, he'll never forget Cordwainer Bird," the little man said. "His nose crumpled up like a paper cup!"

"I doubt he was hurt," Ralph said. But he refused to elaborate on that statement.

"Hell, they haven't built the cell that can keep me in!" Bird said. He began inspecting the room, testing the steel bars, tapping the walls. Presently he went back to the bars, of which there were three. They were about a half-inch in diameter, a foot long, and set into holes drilled in the stone. Bird grabbed one with both hands and braced his feet against the wall. He pulled mightily, the muscles coiling like pythons beneath his skintight shirt. The shirt split along the biceps and across the back under the pressure. The bar bent as he pulled. Sweat ran out, soaked his clothes, and fell onto the floor to form a little pool. And the bar popped out.

Bird fell backward but twisted and somehow landed on his feet. "Like a cat!" he cried, and then, "Begging your pardon, Ralph!"

"My dear fellow, I don't share the common canine prejudice against felines," Ralph said. "Oh, occasionally my instincts catch me off guard when a cat runs by, and I go after him. But reason quickly reasserts itself."

"That's quite a feat of strength," I said. "But even if you get the other bars out, so what? It's a fall of a hundred feet to the base of the castle. And fifty more if you should miss the slight projection of the cliff. Not to mention the boulders sticking out of the sea at the bottom."

"There are birds that can fly but can't dive. And birds that can dive but can't fly. This Bird can do both."

"I admire your confidence but deplore your lack of good sense," I said.

"Don't be such a Gloomy Gus, sweetheart," Ralph said. "Anyway, it's better to go out like a smashed bulb than flicker away while your battery dies by agonizing degrees."

"It's no wonder Giftlippen denigrated your novel," I said.

"The most unkindest cut of all," Ralph said, wincing.

Bird laughed and bent, literally, to the Herculean task of ripping out the other bars. After much groaning and panting and screech of steel riven from stone, plus a miniature Mediterranean of perspiration on the floor, the way was open.

"Disbarred like a shyster!" Bird cried triumphantly. The window was too small for any person of normal size to wriggle through. Bird, however, wasn't handicapped in this respect. In fact, what some would regard as a handicap was in this case an advantage. If he'd been larger, he could not have gotten through the window.

"But how in the world can you launch yourself from the ledge?" I said. "The window is flush with the outer wall. By no means can you attain an upright position on it. Surely, you don't plan on dropping headfirst from it?"

Bird eyed the opening, said, "Get out of the way," and backed to the door, which was directly opposite the window.

"I'll get you guys out of this mess," he said. "Never fear."

As I shouted a protest, he ran at blinding speed across the room and dived through the window. I'll swear he had no more than half an inch clearance on all sides. I expected to see him bash his head against the stone, much like those cartoon characters who attempt a similar feat. But he sailed through and disappeared. For a moment we stood stupefied, like drunken stand-ins; then we rushed to the window. I got there first and stuck my head through the window. Behind me, Ralph cried, "For heaven's sake, Weisstein! Tell me, tell me, is he all right?"

"So far, so good," I said. "He's still falling."

Even as I cried out to Ralph, Bird cleared the edge of the cliff by a hair's breadth. Then he was hurtling down alongside the cliff. I expected to see him strike one of the two boulders at the sea's edge. But he shot between the two, disappeared, and the water spouted up after him.

I said, "He went in cleanly. But who knows what the impact of the water after that fall will be? And if the bottom is shallow…?"

I waited for a sign of him while Ralph, reverting in his excitement, barked. I looked at my watch. Twenty seconds since he had plunged through the blue-green surface. Sixty seconds. At one hundred and thirty seconds, I withdrew my head and looked sadly at Ralph. "He didn't come up."

"Look again."

I turned just in time to see a black head break loose. And, a moment later, a brown arm wave at me. "He made it!" I shouted. "He made it!" I grabbed Ralph's two front paws, pulled him upright, and we danced around and around together.

Finally, Ralph said, "You're not following properly. Let me down."

I did so. Ralph recovered his breath, then said, *"Voilà un homme!"*

For the benefit of my readers who don't understand French, this means, "What a man!" I recognized it as the phrase uttered by Napoleon after meeting the great Goethe. And, unworthy emotion, jealousy struck again.

Ralph, of course, smelled it. "My dear fellow," he said, "there's no blame attached to you. I'm sure that if you weren't too big to get through the window, you would have tried it. If you'd also been crazy. Bird was small enough, and insane enough, to attempt it. Let us hope that…"

At that moment a strangled cry came from the door. We turned to see Smigma staring stricken through the Judas window.

Everything happened very quickly after that. Giftlippen, still in his Arabian robes and cloud of perfume, stormed in. He was followed by armed men. I was astounded to see that Ralph was right. His nose was untouched. The archvillain looked through the window, whirled, and shouted, "We can still get him!" He gave orders for some men to go after him in the mini-submarine and others to go in a helicopter. We were then conducted downstairs to another tower room. My hands were tied behind my back. The door was slammed shut and bolted.

A half-hour passed. Suddenly, the door was unbolted and opened. Giftlippen and Smigma came in with six men. The former's face as impassive and pale as ever, but the latter's was twisted and red. Giftlippen roared, "The Yankee runt got away! But the chopper's still looking for him! He won't dare to come out from the coastal bush until nightfall! By then it'll be too late! I'm moving the schedule up! Too bad! It would have been esthetically appropriate to pull off this job during the Marriage!

But you and your friends have no sense of the beautiful, von Wau Wau! So, instead of marrying the bride, we abduct her! Ha! Ha!"

We were hustled back to the cave. The large submarine and the giant plastic bag were gone. Presently we were outbound on the mini-sub. When the boat stopped, an hour had passed according to my luminous watch. Ralph said little during the transit, and I uttered nothing except a few groans. My thoughts, I must admit, were not, like his, directed to means of getting us out of this mess. I could only curse myself for my stubborn and stupid resistance to Lisa. Why had I not said yes, I will marry you at once, abandon this dangerous life? I could now be sharing connubial bliss, not to mention the delights, with Lisa, surely the daintiest thing in slacks that ever walked this planet.

On the other hand, Ralph would have been alone, would have died without a single friend to give him moral support at the fatal moment. How sad to die companionless. And how I would have grieved, have been stricken with remorse, have cursed myself for a coward, if I had not been at his side. On the other hand, there was Lisa… such were my thoughts during that gloomy trip in our dark narrow cell.

The craft stopped with a bump. The cell door was opened to let us into the control room. A man snapped the leash on Ralph's harness while another held a gun to his head. A man wearing a gas mask climbed the short ladder, opened the hatch, and looked out. He removed the mask and shouted down, "All clear!" I followed Ralph to emerge on the deck of the barque by the Riva degli Schiavoni.

Ralph sniffed and said, "There's a strange odor in the air."

I could smell nothing except the sewage-laden canal waters. What struck me was the silence. Except for the distant drone of a helicopter and the faraway chug of a *vaporetto*, there was not a sound. The loud babble of the festive crowds was gone. No wonder. Everywhere I looked, bodies sprawled unmoving upon the *riva* and the plaza of St. Mark.

"Great Scott!" I cried. "Are they all dead?"

"Fortunately, no," Ralph said. "That strange odor is the residue of an anesthetic gas. That helicopter must have laid down a cloud of it, rendering all the citizens unconscious. Undoubtedly, all the islands nearby, including the Lido, were also subjected to the gas."

Ralph and I were taken to the poopdeck. The end of his leash was looped through an oarhole and tied. I was made to stand by him; a guard with a Browning automatic rifle was stationed about six feet from us.

Giftlippen strode up to us, his robes flapping in the stiff breeze which had sprung up. He gestured toward the city with his gloved hands.

"You are indeed privileged," he said. "You'll be the only non-participant witnesses to the crime of, not the century, but of the ages. Unfortunately, you won't be able to report it. But I am allowing you enough time to savor its full flavor. And to contemplate what idiots you were to think you could outwit me. Within one hour, we will have the greatest treasures, those that can be moved, anyway, stowed away."

He waved a hand at the big submarine, which was just to the north of us. Men were lowering paintings, statuettes, chests, and boxes into the giant sausage behind it.

Motorboats roared up, docked, and discharged other treasures: bags of jewels, figurines, statuettes, reliquaries, and paintings. All beautiful, priceless, unique. Among the paintings I recognized N. B. Schiavone's *The Adoration*, Titian's *The Annunciation*, Bellini's *Madonna of the Trees*, Vecchio's *Saint Barbara*.

Due to their limited time, the bandits could not take the care needed in moving these fragile works. Fortunately, all had been sprayed with Giftlippen's plastic as part of his professed pollution-prevention program. This saved them from being scratched or chipped. But it broke my heart to see them so roughly handed down into the hatches of the giant bag.

Giftlippen said, "The VUF funds have been removed from the bank. In fact, all the banks nearby have been looted. I'll hold the works of art for several years, then ransom them. But the world is going to pay me for those I've had to leave behind. You see, they've all been sprayed. What the authorities don't know, as yet, is that the plastic is actually acidic. It will in time eat up the paintings and the surfaces of the statues, whether stone or bronze. I shall inform them of this and then demand a large—exorbitant, in fact—sum for the formula of the solvent to neutralize the acid effect. Only I know this."

"What is to prevent the Venetians from removing the acidic plastic?" Ralph said.

"They can't dissolve the plastic by any known means," Giftlippen said triumphantly. "Scraping it off will cause a friction which will accelerate the acidic effect." He paused. "Magnificent, isn't it? I expect to reap a profit, tax free, of about three billion American dollars."

Again, he broke into that hideous freezing cachinnation.

"And all the time, while a worldwide search is being made for me, I'll be watching them, almost within arm's reach of them."

A moment later, men brought aboard two large tables and set them down on the middeck. Others put piles of plates and tableware on the tables. Still others staggered up laden with baskets full of bottles of wine. Four men deposited two huge kettles on a table. Another set by them an enormous bowl of antipasto. Saugpumpe removed the kettle lids, and I smelled spaghetti and spaghetti sauce.

Good heavens, I thought. Surely they are not so confident that they are going to have a leisurely meal on the return trip?

Ralph said, "You have about a hundred and fifty men in your band? Do they share in the profits? Or do you intend to rid yourself of most of them? I would think a bomb planted on the barque, set to go off after you've escaped in the mini-sub, would eliminate forty or so. And you must be thinking of flooding the compartments in the bag which will carry most of the others."

I expected Giftlippen to react violently to this. Even if Ralph's speculations were unfounded, the crew might become very suspicious. Enough to decide to make sure there was no double-cross by killing him.

But he only laughed again. He said, "You'd make a great criminal, von Wau Wau. But then crooks and cops are only two sides of a coin, aren't they? And you can't always be sure which is obverse; which, reverse."

He spoke to the guard. "Shoot them if they try to communicate to anybody but me or Smigma."

He walked away, leaving us, me, at least, with gloomy thoughts. Ah, Lisa, I will never see you again!

The gangsters were using small motorcycles towing long, low wagons. Both were collapsible and apparently had been transported here in the plastic bag. They were busy, roaring off into the city and returning with wagons laden with treasures.

Presently, the *vaporetto* I'd heard chug-chugged up and docked. Its deck was filled with men and piles of objects.

"How long can they go undetected?" I said. "Surely, the causeway into Venice will be full of cars and the train loaded with tourists? If the traffic is stalled because of the gas, won't the authorities at Mestre investigate?"

"Giftlippen has undoubtedly cut all lines of communication," he said. "And bribed some officials in Mestre to create confusion and delay."

"And Bird, if he survived, won't be able to venture out from the bush until dark," I said. "By then it'll all be over. Still, Giftlippen knows that Bird can reveal his secret. He surely isn't going to return to the castle."

"Not unless Bird is caught. You must realize, my dear fellow, that the chopper has undoubtedly laid down a cloud of the anesthetic gas over the area in which Bird is hiding. When the gas is blown away, a search will be made on the ground for the unconscious Bird. If he isn't found, Giftlippen will take an alternate route to safety. He must be impatiently waiting for a radio message that Bird has been snared."

At that moment Smigma gave a shout and hurried up to Giftlippen. He was holding a walkie-talkie. They conferred for a moment. Smigma was smiling broadly. After a minute, Giftlippen walked to us. He said, "Your athletic, but stupid, colleague has been captured! He'll be taken back to a tower cell. From there he can witness your end. It'll make a fine display, and his agony will be increased by knowing that you will be in the explosion!"

"Ah," Ralph said quietly. "You *are* going to blow up the barque! And we'll be in the casualty list?"

"If there's enough of you left to identify," Giftlippen said. "You see, by the time the barque is halfway across the lagoon, airplanes and helicopters from Mestre will be over the area. My agents there can stall an investigation only so long. A time bomb in the barque will go off. Investigators will find only pieces of bodies and the art treasures left from the 'accidental' explosion. The barque will contain only works of lesser value."

Cackling, he walked away. He began shouting at the men who were coming aboard laden with paintings and boxes. I almost felt sorry for them. They would also be victims of the man's diabolical cunning.

"Ralph," I said, "this is it…"

Ralph whined, his nose pointed toward the open hatch, his nostrils expanding.

"What is it?" I said.

"What I'd hoped for. *I am Sir Oracle, and when I ope my lips, let no dog bark!*"

I recognized the quotation as from Shakespeare's *The Merchant of Venice*, Act I, scene i. But what he meant by it, I didn't know. He was always doing this to me, making obscure references through quotations. Very aggravating.

"*If I can catch him once upon the hip, I will feed the ancient grudge I bear him.*" This was also from *The Merchant of Venice.*

"What in heaven's name are you getting at?" I said.

"Look at Giftlippen and Smigma. They're jumping with joy. *Some there be that shadows kiss; Such have but a shadow's bliss.*"

"Will you stop that?" I said. "And enlighten me?"

"*I would not have given him for a wilderness of monkeys.*"

"It's *it*, not *him*," I said. "Same play, Act III, scene i, line 130, I believe."

"*But, since I am a dog, beware of my fangs.*"

"Act III, scene iii, line 6," I said. "Ralph, this is no time to show off."

The guard was looking at us curiously. Ralph winked and said, "A bird in the hatch is worth two in the bush."

"Oh!" I said. "You mean…?"

I jumped, and Ralph started. Simultaneously, at least a dozen explosions in the city gouted flame and fragments. As their reverberations died, Smigma shouted at the men to get aboard. They hurried up, bearing their loads, onto the barque, the U-boat, and the floating bag.

"He's started fires to make a diversion," I said, staring at the thick black plumes of smoke. "Listen, Ralph! Now's your chance to make a break for it! Snap your leash and run like mad! I'll knock down our guard, keep him from shooting!"

"What, and leave you, my dear friend?" Ralph said. "No! I am touched at your offer of sacrifice. But we'll play this game out together, lose or win, side by side."

I am not ashamed to record that these words of loyalty and love almost made me cry.

A helicopter swept over, and the men cheered. Then, laughing joyously, they disappeared into the U-boat and the bag. Those who came aboard the barque did not, as I had expected, grab the oars and start rowing. The barque started moving as if by magic. But it was the tiny submarine attached to it that was the motive power. It wasn't progressing very fast. It would at this rate only get a few miles from the island before the police showed up. The crew must have known that, but they didn't seem worried. I surmised that Giftlippen must have given them some sort of explanation to put them at ease.

Saugpumpe beat on a gong and yelled at them to come eat and drink, to celebrate their ill-gotten wealth. Poor fools, they crowded around the tables and dished themselves up heaps of spaghetti and antipasto. They grabbed the numerous bottles of wine and toasted each other and their leader. Giftlippen had retreated to the poopdeck to sit on the wheelchair and eat nuts while Smigma and Saugpumpe helped fill the plates and uncapped the bottles.

Within fifteen minutes, the men had become very drunk. Far too drunk for the alcohol alone to account for it, even at the rate they drank. They were whooping and yelling, staggering around, speaking slurredly, and singing off-key.

"Giftlippen is helping us, though he doesn't know it," Ralph muttered. "He's cutting down the odds against us. When the time comes for action, move swiftly, Weisstein. We'll still be unarmed. And I don't know when the bomb will go off. Or where it is, either."

We had gone about two miles when one of the men yelled louder than the others. Everybody followed the direction of his finger. There were small objects above Venice, moving so slowly they had to be helicopters.

Giftlippen arose. Smigma and the woman looked at him. He nodded. Some of the men abruptly collapsed and lay snoring heavily on the deck. Others were glaze-eyed and looking around stupidly.

Our guard had not drunk or eaten anything. Obviously he was in on the plot. At the moment, he was watching the aircraft.

"Back up to me and spread your bonds as far as they'll go!" Ralph whispered.

I did so, and his teeth snapped down on them, the lips brushing wetly against my wrists. He had the powerful jaws of a German shepherd and even more strength than the average because of his size and the genes of his wolf grandfather. Two snaps, and the thin ropes were severed.

"Stand still! Wait!" Ralph said. "The timing must be of the exquisite!"

I couldn't see him, but I could imagine him moving back to get some slack in his leash. It had a concealed breakaway in it, designed for just such emergencies as this.

Giftlippen was nearing the hatch. Smigma and the woman were by the table. I supposed they were anticipating objections from the crew. Both now held submachine guns they had picked up from under the table. A dozen more men had crashed upon the deck. Those still on their feet were swaying or reeling crazily around.

Of the U-boat and the bag it was towing, there was no sign. It must have dived as soon as possible.

Giftlippen stopped and looked at his wristwatch. "We have ten minutes before the bomb goes off!" he shouted. "Everybody below!"

The guard turned for one last check to us. I did not move. Still carrying his rifle, he hurried toward the hatch. Smigma and Saugpumpe threw down their weapons and trotted toward it also. Giftlippen turned and yelled at us, *"Bon voyage!"* and he broke into that maniacal laughter.

"Ready, set, GO!" Ralph said. He lunged; the leash snapped; he sped past me, a black and brownish-gray blur, silent death.

Smigma and Saugpumpe yelled and stopped. Giftlippen whirled so fast he fell down, his feet caught in the floor-length robe. The guard spun, firing the rifle before he had completed his circle. Ralph gave a bound, and his jaws closed on the man's throat.

I was already charging across the deck, intending to pick up the automatic rifle. But as I did, I saw Cordwainer Bird pop up from the hatch.

The guard was on his back, his throat torn open. Ralph wasted no time on him. He sped growling toward Giftlippen, who was back on his feet by now. Smigma and the woman turned and ran back toward their weapons. Giftlippen yanked a huge automatic pistol from beneath his robe and pointed it at Ralph. I yelled a warning to him, but Ralph didn't have a chance unless Giftlippen missed him. At that short range, it was not likely.

Bird had seen this, however, and he made a split-second choice. Instead of going after the others, he hurled himself at Giftlippen. In what is called in American football a blocker's tackle, I believe, or perhaps it was an illegal clip, his shoulder took Giftlippen's feet from under him. Giftlippen flew backward screaming, and crashed upon the deck. His automatic skittered, spinning out of his reach.

Bird was up on his feet as if he were made of rubber. Ralph ran by him, his target Smigma and Saugpumpe. Bird, passing by the fallen man to assist Ralph, kicked out sideways. The side of his foot struck Giftlippen in the face, and he collapsed again.

I picked up the rifle and fired several rounds into the air to get the attention of the villains. Everybody ignored me. Ralph leaped high and knocked Smigma sprawling. Saugpumpe bent down to get her submachine gun, but Bird was flying through the air. As if he were broad jumping, his feet preceded him. She rose and turned to fire at us, just in time to receive Bird's feet in her face. She performed a splendid, if involuntary, backward somersault. Thereafter, she took no interest in the proceedings.

"I always wanted to do that to a woman!" Bird yelled exultantly from the deck where he had fallen. "Anyway, she looked like my sixth wife, the bitch!"

Smigma had gotten to his feet. Ralph crouched for another leap. Smigma grabbed the nearest thing he could find for a weapon, the enormous bowl of antipasto. He lifted it above his head, and the contents spilled down, blinding him. Smigma, shrieking, cast the bowl hard but missed Ralph. Ralph leaped, but this time not for the throat. He grabbed the man's arm and bit down. Then the two were thrashing around on the deck.

Giftlippen rose, crouching. I stared in horror at his face. It had been broken by Bird's kick, literally crumbled. As I stood frozen, he reached up and tore away the rest of the covering. I could not believe my eyes. Then he quickly doffed his robe and kicked off his slippers. I was even more incredulous. This state of shock, I am ashamed to admit, was my undoing. Before I could lift my rifle and start firing, his hand moved and the sinking sun glittered on something streaking toward me.

The fellow, if I may call him that, had depended upon the shock of recognition to paralyze me. It succeeded just long enough for him to pluck a knife from the scabbard at his belt and hurl it. I felt a shock in my right arm; the rifle clattered on the deck; I was suddenly weak. I looked down. The knife had penetrated the muscle of my right shoulder. It wasn't a fatal wound, but it certainly was unnerving.

Giftlippen, chattering, was on me then, had knocked me down, had gone on. I sat up while Bird and Ralph ran toward the poopdeck. I groped for the weapon, could not find it, and thus was unable to prevent Giftlippen's escape.

He was quick, oh, so quick! Even the speedy Bird and the swift Ralph could not catch him in time. He had leaped into the wheelchair, punched some buttons on the control panel, and then was gone. Hidden, rather, I should say. Panels had slid up from the sides of the enormous wheelchair and closed over him. Behind a glass port, his mouth worked devilishly. The two giant front teeth, incisors like daggers, or perhaps I should say, a rodent's, gleamed.

His hands moved again, and the muzzles of two automatic rifles sprang out of the sides. I rolled off the slight elevation of the poopdeck, falling to the deck. Bullets chopped off pieces of the teakwood and then were spraying the deck. Bird dived down the hatch, head first, the deck exploding around him. Ralph raced forward and then rolled in toward me, safe from the fire.

He looked at the protruding dagger. "Are you hurt, buddy?"

"Not severely," I said. "But what next?"

"He could hold us here, but he'll abandon ship at once. The bomb's too close to going off. Ah, there he goes!"

The rifles had suddenly ceased their terrifying racket. A few seconds later, there was a splash. Ralph stood on his hind legs. He said, "All clear now."

I stood up. There was no sign of the wheelchair or the thing that had been in it. But it was obvious where they had gone. The railing had been destroyed by the rifle fire to make a passage to the sea.

"There's no use trying to get him now," he said. "That wheelchair is obviously submersible, and it's also jet-propelled. He'll go underwater to the shore. But, unless he has another disguise cached away somewhere, he will be easily spotted."

"Yes," I said. "There's nothing that will attract more attention than a six-foot-six-inch-high squirrel."

There was no opportunity for explanations. Somewhere in the barque, a time bomb was ticking away. We could have escaped in the mini-sub, but that would have meant leaving sixty or so people to perish. They did deserve to die, but we would not abandon them. It was impossible to carry them into the submarine in the little time left. Besides, there wasn't room for that many.

Bird stuck his head out of the hatch. Ralph shouted at him to look for the bomb. There was only five minutes left. We would help him after we secured Smigma and Saugpumpe.

Bird said, "Right on!" and he disappeared.

Both the culprits were still unconscious. I tied up the woman while Ralph stood guard in case the man aroused. Then I used his belt to bind him. He was a sorry-looking mess, covered with lettuce, mushrooms, anchovies, sliced peppers, and a garlicky oil.

Ralph chuckled and said, "I smote the saladed Polack."

"A slightly altered line from a speech by Horatio, *Hamlet*,

Act I, scene i," I said. "Good heavens, Ralph, this is no time for your atrocious puns."

We hastened below deck where we found Bird frantically opening boxes. Though handicapped by my wound, I pitched in. Ralph, cursing his lack of hands, paced back and forth.

"Jumping jellybeans!" Bird said. "Only two minutes to go!"

"It's too late to get into the sub," I said. I was sweating profusely, but I like to think that that was caused by my wound, not panic.

"Sixty more seconds, and we'll have to jump into the sea," Ralph said. "Wait! I have it! Quiet, you two! Absolutely quiet!"

We stood still. The only sound was the lapping of the waves against the hull. Ralph stood, ears cocked, turning this way and that. He had a much keener sense of hearing than we two humans. Even so, if the timing mechanism was not clockwork or if it was covered with some insulating material...

Suddenly, he barked. Then he said, "Damn! My instincts again! That box on the pile by you, Doc! Third one under!"

I toppled off the top two with one hand while Bird and Ralph danced around. "Forty-five seconds!" Bird shrilled.

The third box was of cardboard, its top glued down. Bird jumped in and tore it open savagely. Ralph stood up on his hind legs to look within. All three of us stared at a curious contrivance. It was of plastic, cube-shaped, and had two small cubes on its top. On the inner side of the left-hand one was a metal disk. Moving slowly from the inner wall of the other one was a thin cylinder of steel. Its tip was only about two-sixteenths of an inch from the disk.

As we stared, the slender cylinder moved a sixteenth of an inch.

"Quick, Weisstein, the needle!"

I snatched my handkerchief from my pocket, but I wasn't quick enough to satisfy Bird. He grabbed it from me and interposed a corner between the disk and cylinder. One more second, and the electrical contact would have been made. I shudder even now as I write of this and a certain sphincter muscle tightens up.

Bird threw the bomb overboard. "Whew! Okay, I'll get the sub going, and we'll mosey back to Venice. But first, *what* the hell was Giftlippen? I know what I saw, but I still don't believe it."

"I had suspected for some time that it was Nucifer," Ralph said. "There were clues, though only I had the background to interpret them. You see, one of the institute animals supposedly wiped out by the explosion was a giant squirrel. Nucifer, Professor Sansgout called him. Nut-bearing. From the Latin.

"Obviously, he wasn't killed. He took to a life of crime, murdered the real Giftlippen, and took over his gang. Smigma joined the gang after Giftlippen was well launched on his career, you know. He may have been surprised to find that his friend and agent was now a giant rodent. On the other hand, Giftlippen was always a little squirrelly. I should feel bad about the Liechtensteiner's murder... but, after the way he murdered my book... well, no matter.

"Anyway, when Giftlippen—Nucifer, I mean—decided on the Venetian caper, he set up a whole new identity. He triggered off that landslide... cold-blooded massacre of the villagers...

and emerged as Granelli, the reincarnation of Doge Dandolo.

"But now he was in the public eye. So, he put on a wax-and-putty head to conceal his bestial features and gloves to disguise his paws. He stayed in a wheelchair when on display, covering his unhuman legs with the tigerskin. He stuck his bushy tail down a hole in the chair's seat. When he was in that Arabian costume, he strapped his tail to a leg, as you saw.

"He also made sure that his distinctive squirrel's odor was covered by a heavy perfume. He knew that I was on his trail and that I could expose him after one whiff."

"But why did Smigma also use perfume?"

"Same reason. After Smigma's accident, he suffered a metabolic imbalance, you know. He emitted a cheesy odor which even humans could detect.

"The immobile features, the covering of the legs, the gloves, the perfume all suggested to me his true identity. His addiction to nuts cinched the matter."

"Elementary," I said.

"No, alimentary."

Bird started away. I said, "Wait a minute. However did you manage to appear so conveniently—for us—inside the barque?"

"Easy," Bird said, grinning. Then: "Well, I won't lie to you; it wasn't a breeze. I swam toward the sea to give the impression I was escaping that way. But I returned, working my way through the fallen blocks of stone. Then I swam through the tunnel to the cave. I almost didn't make it. I got to the mini-sub before the bandits came down. I hid in its engine room, behind the batteries. When everybody left the sub, I came out. I used the sub's radio to send a fake message that I'd been captured. I was taking a chance. If the chopper overheard me, they'd warn Smigma. But Smigma turned the walkie-talkie off right after he got my message.

"First, though, I listened in on him and the chopper. That way, I learned the code words they were using for identification. Giftlippen's—Nucifer's—was California. Isn't that strange? No other names of states were used."

"The squirrel's a double-dyed villain," Ralph said. "But he has a sense of humor. California has the world's biggest collection of nuts."

Nucifer eluded detection. Smigma later escaped from prison and rejoined Nucifer. How Ralph and I caught up with them is described in *The Four Musicians of Bremen*.

Bird used the walkie-talkie to summon the police. They arrested the few crooks in the cave. I say few because, as Ralph had suspected, the gang in the plastic bag had been drowned by their compatriots in the U-boat.

All the art treasures were recovered. And it turned out that Nucifer had lied about the acidic effect of the plastic spray. The authorities would have had no way of knowing this, of course, and undoubtedly would have paid millions for a useless formula.

We stayed two weeks for the festivities in our honor. We were made honorary citizens of Venice, and a local artist was commissioned to cast in bronze a commemorative monument of us. It can be seen today in St. Mark's Square. It's well done, though it always causes children, unacquainted with our story, to ask why the dog is grabbing the big squirrel by its tail. Artists, like TV/

movie directors, feel no obligation to be historically accurate.

While we were waiting at the Lido Airport, I made another long-distance call to Lisa. Ralph paced back and forth nervously, whining now and then despite his vow to repress this canine characteristic. Cordwainer Bird sat on a bench nearby, writing in longhand his latest novel, *Adrift Just Off the Eyelets of My Buster Browns*. Both, seeing my approach, stopped what they were doing. Bird rose from the bench, though not very far.

"She gave the final ultimatum, Ralph," I said. "It's either she or you. I had to make the final decision right there."

"No need to tell me what it is," he said. "If your long face wasn't enough, the odor of resignation mixed somewhat with that of repressed joy, would inform me."

"Then it's goodbye," I said, choking.

"*Das Ewig-Weibliche/Zieht uns hinan*," he said.

"*The Eternal-Feminine/Draws us on*," I said. "The last line of Goethe's *The Gothic Chamber*. He was a wise man."

"A very horny one, too. I'll miss you, Doc. It'll be a new and exciting life in Los Angeles—provided I can get my citizenship papers in the States. But…"

The loudspeaker blared, informing us in Italian, French, German, and English that passengers for Hamburg must enter customs. At least, I thought that was what was said. Like airport announcers everywhere, he managed to make almost everything unintelligible, no matter what the language.

Bird said, "I'll go change our reservations for the plane to LA." He held out his hand. "Sorry about this, Doctor. I don't like to rip off Ralph from you. But it's your decision."

"Don't blame yourself," I said. "Sooner or later, it would have come. But be sure to get in touch with me."

"I'm not much for letter writing. Ralph'll have to do that. *Auf Wiedersehen*, Doc."

He walked away. I looked at Ralph. Then my German reserve shattered, and I knelt down and put my arms around that furry neck and wept. Ralph whined, and he said, "Come on, buck up, sweetheart. You know it's all for the best. You'll lead a dog's life, it's true. But that ain't necessarily bad. Take it from one who knows."

I stroked his ears, shed a few more tears, then rose. "*Auf Wiedersehen*. Though I have this feeling that I'll never see you again."

"Hit the road, Doc, before my guts lose their anchors. *Gott!* If only I had tear ducts! You humans don't know how lucky you are. But we'll see each other now and then. Maybe sooner than you think."

I picked up my bags and walked away, never once looking back. I thought he was just talking to make me feel better. I didn't know how prophetic his words were. Or how distressed I would be to see him. But that is all chronicled in the bewildering adventure of adulation and adulteration, private sin and public confession, branding irons and preachers: *The Scarletin Letter*.

PULP
INSPIRATIONS

SKINBURN

BY PHILIP JOSÉ FARMER

Philip José Farmer's preface to "Skinburn" states that pulp
devotees "might deduce Kent Lane's identity from his fire opal
ring and his name." The implication is that Lane got the fire opal
ring from his father, whom Farmer identified, in *Doc Savage:
His Apocalyptic Life*, as Wold Newton Family member Allard
Kent Rassendyll—the real name of the man whose exploits were
immortalized in the pages of the long-running pulp magazine
The Shadow (1931–1949). While many who are casually familiar
with The Shadow might identify his alter-ego as man-about-
town Lamont Cranston, pulp aficionados know that he was, in
truth, aviator and adventurer Kent Allard. Kent Lane's mother
is The Shadow's friend and companion, Margo Lane, who made
her way into the pulp series in 1941 after being introduced as a
radio character in 1937.

PREFACE

It makes no difference in the story itself, but devotees of old pulp-magazine fiction might deduce Kent Lane's identity from his fire opal ring and his name. The surname implies, of course, that his parents were never married. I have plans for Lane, who will carry on his distinguished father's career, though in a less violent manner.

This story is about Love, which means that it is also about Hate. One of the themes that run through much of my work is that for every advantage you gain there is a disadvantage, that the gods, or whoever, require payment, that the universe in all its aspects, which include the human psyche, is governed by a check and balance system.

"Your skin tingles every time you step outdoors?" Dr. Mills said. "And when you stand under the skylight in your apartment? But only now and then when you're standing in front of the window, even if the sunlight falls on you?"

"Yes," Kent Lane said. "It doesn't matter whether or not it's night or day, the skies are cloudy or clear, or the skylight is open or closed. The tingling is strongest on the exposed parts of my body, my face and hands or whatever. But the tingling spreads from the exposed skin to all over my body, though it's much weaker under my clothes. And the tingling eventually arouses vaguely erotic feelings."

The dermatologist walked around him. When he had completed his circuit, he said, "Don't you ever tan?"

"No, I just peel and blister. I usually avoid burning by staying out of the sun as much as possible. But that isn't doing me any good now, as you can see. I look as if I'd been on the beach all day. That makes me rather conspicuous, you know. In my work, you can't afford to be conspicuous."

The doctor said, "I know."

He meant that he was aware that Lane was a private detective. What he did not know was that Lane was working on a case for a federal government agency. CACO—Coordinating Authority for Cathedric Organizations—was short of competent help. It had hired, after suitable security checks, a number of civilian agents. CACO would have hired only the best, of course, and Lane was among these.

Lane hesitated and then said, "I keep getting these phone calls."

The doctor said nothing. Lane said, "There's nobody at the other end. He, or she, hangs up just as soon as I pick the phone up."

"You think the skinburn and the phone calls are related?"

"I don't know. But I'm putting all unusual phenomena into one box. The calls started a week after I'd had a final talk with a lady who'd been chasing me and wouldn't quit. She has a Ph.D. in bioelectronics and is a big shot in the astronautics industry. She's brilliant, charming, and witty, when she wants to be, but very plain in face and plane in body and very nasty when frustrated. And so…"

He was, he realized, talking too much about someone who worked in a top-secret field. Moreover, why would Mills want to hear the sad story of Dr. Sue Brackwell's unrequited love for Kent Lane, private eye? She had been hung up on him for some obscure psychological reason and, in her more rational moments, had admitted that they could never make it as man and wife, or even as man and lover, for more than a month, if that. But she was not, outside of the laboratory, always rational, and she would not take no from her own good sense or from him. Not until he had gotten downright vicious over the phone two years ago.

Three weeks ago, she had called him again. But she had said nothing to disturb him. After about five minutes of light chitchat about this and that, including reports on their health, she had said goodbye, making it sound like an *ave atque vale*, and had hung up. Perhaps she had wanted to find out for herself if the sound of his voice still thrilled her. Who knew?

Lane became aware that the doctor was waiting for him to finish the sentence. He said, "The thing is, these phone calls occurred at first when I was under the skylight and making love. So I moved the bed to a corner where nobody could possibly see it from the upper stories of the Parmenter Building next door.

"After that, the phone started ringing whenever I took a woman into my apartment, even if it was just for a cup of coffee. It'd be ringing before I'd get the door open, and it'd ring at approximately three-minute intervals thereafter. I changed my phone number twice, but it didn't do any good. And if I went to the woman's apartment instead, her phone started ringing."

"You think this lady scientist is making these calls?"

"Never! It's not her style. It must be a coincidence that the calls started so soon after our final conversation."

"Did your women also hear the phone?"

Lane smiled and said, "Audiohallucinations? No. They heard the phone ringing, too. One of them solved the problem by tearing her phone out. But I solved mine by putting in a phone jack and disconnecting the phone when I had in mind another sort of connection."

"That's all very interesting, but I fail to see what it has to do with your skin problem."

"Phone calls aside," Lane said, "could the tingling, the peeling and blistering, and the mild erotic reaction be psychosomatic?"

"I'm not qualified to say," Mills said. "I can, however, give you the name of a doctor whose specialty is recommending various specialists."

Lane looked at his wristwatch. Rhoda should be about done with her hairdresser. He said, "So far, I'm convinced I need a dermatologist, not a shrink. I was told you're the best skin doctor in Washington and perhaps the best on the East Coast."

"The world, actually," Dr. Mills said. "I'm sorry. I can do nothing for you at this time. But I do hope you'll inform me of new developments. I've never had such a puzzling, and, therefore, interesting, case."

Lane used the phone in the ground-floor lobby to call his fiancée's hairdresser. He was told that Rhoda had just left but that she would pick him up across the street from the doctor's building.

He got out of the building just in time to see Rhoda drive his MG around the corner, through a stoplight, and into the path of a pickup truck. Rhoda, thrown out by the impact (she was careless about using her safety belt), landed in front of a Cadillac. Despite its locked brakes, it slid on over her stomach.

Lane had seen much as an adviser in Vietnam and as a member of the San Francisco and Brooklyn Police Departments.

He thought he was tough, but the violent and bloody deaths of Leona and Rhoda within four months was too much. He stood motionless, noting only that the tingling was getting warmer and spreading over his body. There was no erotic reaction, or, if there were, he was too numb to feel it. He stood there until a policeman got the nearest doctor, who happened to be Mills, to come out and look at him. Mills gave Lane a mild sedative, and the cop sent him home in a taxi. But Lane was at the morgue an hour later, identified Rhoda, and then went to the precinct station to answer some questions.

He went home prepared to drink himself to sleep, but he found two CACO agents, Daniels and Lyons, waiting for him. They seemed to have known about Rhoda's death almost as quickly as he, and so he knew that they had been shadowing him or Rhoda. He answered some of their questions and then told them that the idea that Leona and Rhoda might be spies was not worth a second's consideration. Besides, if they were working for SKIZO, or some other outfit, why would SKIZO, or whoever, kill their own agents?

"Or did CACO kill them?" Lane said.

The two looked at him as if he were unspeakably stupid.

"All right," Lane said. "But there's absolutely no evidence to indicate that their deaths were caused by anything but pure accident. I know it's quite a coincidence..."

Daniels said, "CACO had both under surveillance, of course. But CACO saw nothing significant in the two women's behavior. However, that in itself is suspicious, you know. Negative evidence demands a positive inquiry."

"That maxim demands the investigation of the entire world," Lane said.

"Nevertheless," Lyons said, "SKIZO must've spotted you by now. They'd have to be blind not to. Why in hell don't you stay out from under sunlamps?"

"It's a skin problem," Lane said. "As you must know, since you've undoubtedly bugged Dr. Mills' office."

"Yeah, we know," Daniels said. "Frankly, Lane, we got two tough alternatives to consider. Either you're going psycho, or else SKIZO is on to you. Either way…"

"You're thinking in two-valued terms only," Lane said. "Have you considered that a third party, one with no connection at all with SKIZO, has entered the picture?"

Daniels cracked his huge knuckles and said, "Like who?"

"Like whom, you mean. How would I know? But you'll have to admit that it's not only possible but highly probable."

Daniels stood up. Lyons jumped up. Daniels said, "We don't have to admit anything. Come along with us, Lane."

If CACO thought he was lying, CACO would see to it that he was never seen again. CACO was mistaken about him, of course, but CACO, like doctors, buried mistakes.

On leaving the apartment building, Lane immediately felt the warm tingling on his face and hands and, a few seconds later, the spreading of the warmth to his crotch. He forgot about that a moment later when Daniels shoved him as he started to get into the back seat of the CACO automobile. He turned and said, "Keep your dirty hands off me, Daniels! Push me, and I may just walk off. You might have to shoot me to stop me, and you wouldn't want to do that in broad daylight, would you?"

"Try it and find out," Daniels said. "Now shut up and get in or get knocked in. You know we're being observed. Maybe that's why you're making a scene."

Lane got into the back seat with Lyons, and Daniels drove them away. It was a hot June afternoon, and evidently the CACO budget did not provide for cars with air-conditioning. They rode with the windows down while Lyons and Daniels asked him questions. Lane answered all truthfully, if not fully, but he was not concentrating on his replies. He noticed that when he hung his hand out of the window, it felt warm and tingling.

Fifteen minutes later, the big steel doors of an underground garage clanged shut behind him. He was interrogated in a small room below the garage. Electrodes were attached to his head and body, and various machines with large staring lenses were fixed on him while he was asked a series of questions. He never found out what the interpreters of the machines' graphs and meters thought about his reactions to the questions. Just as the electrodes were being detached, Smith, the man who had hired Lane for CACO, entered. Smith had a peculiar expression. He called the interrogators to one side and spoke to them in a low voice. Lane caught something about "a telephone call." A minute later, he was told he could go home. But he was to keep in touch, or, rather, keep himself available for CACO. For the time being, he was suspended from service.

Lane wanted to tell Smith that he was quitting CACO, but he had no desire to be "detained" again. Nobody quit CACO; it let its employees go only when it felt like it.

Lane went home in a taxi and had just started to pour himself a drink when the doorman called up.

"Feds, Mr. Lane. They got proper IDs."

Lane sighed, downed his Scotch and, a few minutes later, opened the door. Lyons and two others, all holding .45 automatic pistols, were in the hall.

Lyons had a bandage around his head and some Band Aids on one cheek and his chin. Both eyes were bloodshot.

"You're under arrest, Lane," Lyons said.

In the chair in the interrogation room, attached once again to various machines, Lane answered everything a dozen times over. Smith personally conducted the questioning, perhaps because he wanted to make sure that Lyons did not attack Lane.

It took Lane ten hours to piece together what had happened from occasional comments by Smith and Lyons. Daniels and Lyons had followed Lane when he had been released from CACO HQ. Trailing Lane by a block, Daniels had driven through a stoplight and into the path of a hot rod doing fifty miles an hour. Daniels had been killed. Lyons had escaped with minor injuries to the body but a large one to the psyche. For no logical reason, he blamed Lane for the accident.

After the interrogation, Lane was taken to a small padded room, given a TV dinner, and locked in. Naked, he lay down on the padded floor and slept. Three hours later, two men woke him up and handed him his clothes and then conducted him to Smith's office.

"I don't know what to do with you," Smith said. "Apparently, you're not lying. Or else you've been conditioned somehow to give the proper—or perhaps I should say, improper—responses and reactions. It's possible, you know, to fool the machines, what with all the conscious control of brain waves, blood pressure, and so on being taught at universities and by private individuals."

"Yes, but you know that I haven't had any such training," Lane said. "Your security checks show that."

Smith grunted and looked sour.

"I can only conclude," he said, "from the data that I have, that you are involved in counter-espionage activity."

Lane opened his mouth to protest, but Smith continued, "Innocently, however. For some reason, you have become the object of interest, perhaps even concern, to some foreign outfit, probably Commie, most probably SKIZO, CACO's worst enemy. Or else you are the focus of some wildly improbable coincidences."

Lane couldn't think of anything to say to that. Smith said, "You were released the first time because I got a phone call from a high authority, a very high authority, telling me to let you go. By telling, I mean ordering. No reasons given. That authority doesn't have to give reasons.

"But I made the routine checkback, and I found out that the authority was fake. Somebody had pretended to be him. And the code words and the voice were exactly right. So, somehow, somebody, probably SKIZO, has cracked our code and can duplicate voices so exactly that even a voiceprint check can't tell the difference between the fake and the genuine. That's scary, Lane."

Lane nodded to indicate that he agreed it was scary. He

said, "Whoever is doing this must have a damn good reason to reveal that he knows all this stuff. Why would a foreign agent show such a good hand just to get me out of your clutches—uh, custody? I can't do anyone, foreign agent or not, any good. And by revealing that they know the code words and can duplicate voices, they lose a lot. Now the code words will be changed, and the voices will be double-checked."

Smith drummed his fingers on the desktop and then said, "Yes, we know. But this extraordinary dermal sensitivity... these automobile accidents..."

"What did Lyons report about his accident?"

"He was unaware of anything wrong until Daniels failed to slow down on approaching the stoplight. He hesitated to say anything, because Daniels did not like backseat drivers, although Lyons was, as a matter of fact, in the front seat. Finally, he was unable to keep silent, but it was too late. Daniels looked up at the signal and said, 'What in hell you talking about?' and then the other car hit them."

Lane said, "Apparently Daniels thought the signal was green."

"Possibly. But I believe that there is some connection between the phone calls you got while with your women and the one I got from the supposed high authority."

"How could there be?" Lane said. "Why would this, this person, call me up just to ruin my lovemaking?"

Smith's face was as smooth as the face on a painting, but his fingers drummed a tattoo of desperation. No wonder. A case which could not even give birth to a hypothesis, let alone a theory, was the ultimate in frustration.

"I'm letting you go again, only this time you'll be covered with my agents like the North Pole is with snow in January," Smith said.

Lane did not thank him. He took a taxi back to his apartment, again feeling the tingling and warmth and mildly erotic sensations on the way to the taxi and on the way out of it.

In his rooms, he contemplated his future. He was no longer drawing pay from CACO, and CACO would not permit him to go to work for anybody else until this case was cleared up. In fact, Smith did not want him to leave his apartment unless it was absolutely necessary. Lane was to stay in it and force the unknown agency to come to him. So how was he to support himself? He had enough money to pay the rent for another month and buy food for two weeks. Then he would be eligible for welfare. He could defy Smith and get a job at nondetective work, say, a carryout boy at a grocery store or a car salesman. He had experience in both fields. But times were bad, and jobs of any kind were scarce.

Lane became angry. If CACO was keeping him from working, then it should be paying him. He phoned Smith, and, after a twelve-minute delay, during which Smith was undoubtedly checking back that it was really Lane phoning, Smith answered.

"I should pay you for doing nothing? How could I justify that on the budget I got?"

"That's your problem."

Lane looked up, because he had carried the phone under the skylight and his neck started tingling. Whoever was observing him at this moment had to be doing it from the Parmenter Building. He called Smith back and, after a ten-minute delay, got him.

"Whoever's laying a tap-in beam on me is doing it from any of the floors above the tenth. I don't think he could angle in from a lower floor."

"I know," Smith said. "I've had men in the Parmenter Building since yesterday. I don't overlook anything, Lane."

Lane had intended to ask him why he had overlooked the fact that they were undoubtedly being overheard at this moment. He did not do so because it struck him that Smith wanted their conversations to be bugged. He was keen to appear overconfident so that SKIZO, or whoever it was, would move again. Lane was the cheese in the trap. However, anybody who threatened Lane seemed to get hurt or killed, and Smith, from Lane's viewpoint, was threatening him.

During the next four days, Lane read Volume IV of the Durants' *The Story of Civilization*, drank more than he should have, exercised, and spent a half-hour each day, nude, under the skylight. The result of this exposure was that the skin burned and peeled all over his body. But the sexual titillation accompanying the dermal heat made the pain worth it. If the sensations got stronger each day, he'd be embarrassing himself, and possibly his observers, within a week.

He wondered if the men at the other end of the beam (or beams) had any idea of the gratuitous sexuality their subject felt. They probably thought that he was just a horny man with horny thoughts. But he knew that his reaction was unique, a result of something peculiar in his metabolism or his pigment or his whatever. Others, including Smith, had been under the skylight, and none had felt anything unusual.

The men investigating the Parmenter Building had detected nothing suspicious beyond the fact that there was nothing suspicious.

On the seventh day, Lane phoned Smith. "I can't take this submarine existence any longer. And I have to get a job or starve. So, I'm leaving. If your stormtroopers try to stop me, I'll resist. And you can't afford to have a big stink raised."

In the struggle that followed, Lane and the two CACO agents staggered into the area beneath the skylight. Lane went down, as he knew he would, but he felt that he had to make some resistance or lose his right to call himself a man. He stared up into the skylight while his hands were cuffed. He was not surprised when the phone rang, though he could not have given a reasonable explanation of why he expected it.

A third agent, just entering, answered. He talked for a moment, then turned and said, "Smith says to let him go. And we're to come on home. Something sure made him change his mind."

Lane started for the door after his handcuffs were unlocked. The phone rang again. The same man as before answered it. Then he shouted at Lane to stop, but Lane kept on going, only to be halted by two men stationed at the elevator.

Lane's phone was being monitored by CACO agents in the basement of the apartment building. They had called up to report that Smith had not given that order. In fact, no one had actually called in from outside the building. The call had come from somewhere within the building.

Smith showed up fifteen minutes later to conduct the search throughout the building. Two hours later, the agents were told to quit looking. Whoever had made that call imitating Smith's voice and giving the new code words had managed, somehow, to get out of the building unobserved.

"SKIZO, or whoever it is, must be using a machine to simulate my voice," Smith said. "No human throat could do it well enough to match voiceprints."

Voices!

Lane straightened up so swiftly that the men on each side of him grabbed his arms.

Dr. Sue Brackwell!

Had he really talked to her that last time, or was someone imitating her voice, too? He could not guess why; the mysterious Whoever could be using her voice to advance whatever plans he had. Sue had said that she just wanted to talk for old times' sake. Whoever was imitating her might have been trying to get something out of him, something that would be a clue to... to what? He just did not know.

And it was possible that this Whoever had talked to Sue Brackwell, imitating his, Lane's, voice.

Lane did not want to get her into trouble, but he could not afford to leave any possible avenue of investigation closed. He spoke to Smith about it as they went down the elevator. Smith listened intently, but he only said, "We'll see."

Glumly, Lane sat on the back seat between two men, also glum, as the car traveled through the streets of Washington. He looked out the window and through the smog saw a billboard advertising a rerun of *The Egg and I*. A block later, he saw another billboard, advertising a well-known brand of beer. SKY-BLUE

WATERS, the sign said, and he wished he were in the land of sky-blue waters, fishing and drinking beer.

Again, he straightened up so swiftly that the two men grabbed him.

"Take it easy," he said. He slumped back down, and they removed their hands. The two advertisements had been a sort of free association test, provided only because the car had driven down this route and not some other it might easily have taken. The result of the conjunction of the two billboards might or might not be validly linked up with the other circuits that had been forming in the unconscious part of his mind. But he now had a hypothesis. It could be developed into a theory which could be tested against the facts. That is, it could be if he were given a chance to try it.

Smith heard him out, but he had only one comment. "You're thinking of the wildest things you can so you'll throw us off the track."

"What track?" Lane said. He did not argue. He knew that Smith would go down the trail he had opened up. Smith could not afford to ignore anything, even the most far-fetched of ideas.

Lane spent a week in the padded cell. Once, Smith entered to talk to him. The conversation was brief.

"I can't find any evidence to support your theory," Smith said.

"Is that because even CACO can't get access to certain classified documents and projects at Lackalas Astronautics?" Lane said.

"Yeah. I was asked what my need to know was, and I couldn't tell them what I really was trying to find out. The next thing I'd know, I'd be in a padded cell with regular sessions with a shrink."

"And so, because you're afraid of asking questions that might arouse suspicions of your sanity, you'll let the matter drop?"

"There's no way of finding out if your crazy theory has any basis."

"Love will find a way," Lane said.

Smith snorted, spun around, and walked out.

That was at 11 A.M. At 12:03, Lane looked at his wristwatch (since he was no longer compelled to go naked) and noted that lunch was late. A few minutes afterward, an Air Force jet fighter on a routine flight over Washington suddenly dived down and hit CACO HQ at close to one thousand miles an hour. It struck the massive stone building at the end opposite Lane's cell. Even so, it tore through the fortress-like outer walls and five rooms before stopping.

Lane, in the second subfloor, would not have been hit if the wreck had traveled entirely through the building. However, flames began to sweep through, and guards unlocked his door and got him outside just in time. On orders transmitted via radio, his escorts put him into a car to take him across the city to another CACO base. Lane was stiff with shock, but he reacted quickly enough when the car started to go through a red light. He was down on the floor and braced when the car and the huge diesel met. The others were not killed. They were not, however, in any condition to stop him. Ten minutes later, he was in his apartment.

Dr. Sue Brackwell was waiting for him under the skylight.

She had no clothes on; even her glasses were off. She looked very beautiful; it was not until much later that he remembered that she had never been beautiful or even passably pretty. He could not blame his shock for behaving the way he did, because the tingling and the warmth dissolved that. He became very alive, so much so that he loaned sufficient life to the thing that he pulled down to the floor. Somewhere in him existed the knowledge that "she" had prepared this for him and that no man might ever experience this certain event again. But the knowledge was so far off that it influenced him not at all.

Besides, as he had told Smith, love would find a way. He was not the one who had fallen in love. Not at first. Now, he felt as if he were in love, but many men, and women, feel that way during this time.

Smith and four others broke into the apartment just in time to rescue Lane. He was lying on the floor and was as naked and red as a newborn baby. Smith yelled at him, but he seemed to be deaf. It was evident that he was galloping with all possible speed in a race between a third-degree burn and an orgasm. He obviously had a partner, but Smith could neither see nor hear her.

The orgasm might have won if Smith had not thrown a big pan of cold water on Lane.

Two days afterward, Lane's doctor permitted Smith to enter the hospital room to see his much-bandaged and somewhat-sedated patient. Smith handed him a newspaper turned to page two. Lane read the article, which was short and all about EVE. EVE—Ever Vigilant Eye—had been a stationary-orbit surveillance satellite which had been sent up over the East Coast two years ago. EVE had exploded for unknown reasons, and the accident was being investigated.

"That's all the public was told," Smith said. "I finally got through to Brackwell and the other bigwigs connected with EVE. But either they were under orders to tell me as little as possible or else they don't have all the facts themselves. In any event, it's more than just a coincidence that she—EVE, I mean—blew up just as we were taking you to the hospital."

Lane said, "I'll answer some of your questions before you ask them. One, you couldn't see the holograph because she must've turned it off just before you got in. I don't know whether it was because she heard you coming or because she knew, somehow, that any more contact would kill me. Or maybe her alarms told her that she had better stop for her own good. But it would seem that she didn't stop or else did try to stop but was too late.

"I had a visitor who told me just enough about EVE so I wouldn't let my curiosity carry me into dangerous areas after I got out of here. And it won't. But I can tell you a few things and know it won't get any further.

"I'd figured out that Brackwell was the master designer of the bioelectronics circuit of a spy satellite. I didn't know that the satellite was called EVE or that she had the capability to beam in on ninety thousand individuals simultaneously. Or that the beams enabled her to follow each visually and tap in on their speech vibrations. Or that she could activate phone circuits with a highly variable electromagnetic field projected via the beam.

"My visitor said that I was not, for an instant, to suppose

that EVE had somehow attained self-consciousness. That would be impossible. But I wonder.

"I also wonder if a female designer-engineer-scientist could, unconsciously, of course, design female circuits? Is there some psychic influence that goes along with the physical construction of computers and associated circuits? Can the whole be greater than the parts? Is there such a thing as a female gestalt in a machine?"

"I don't go for that metaphysical crap," Smith said.

"What does Brackwell say?"

"She says that EVE was simply malfunctioning."

"Perhaps man is a malfunctioning ape," Lane said. "But could Sue have built her passion for me into EVE? Or given EVE circuits which could evolve emotion? EVE had self-repairing capabilities, you know, and was part protein. I know it sounds crazy. But who, looking at the first apeman, would have extrapolated Helen of Troy?

"And why did she get hung up on me, one out of the ninety thousand she was watching? I had a dermal supersensitivity to the spy beam. Did this reaction somehow convey to EVE a feeling, or a sense, that we were in rapport? And did she then become jealous? It's obvious that she modulated the beams she'd locked on Leona and Rhoda so that they saw green where the light was really red and did not see oncoming cars at all.

"And she worked her modulated tricks on Daniels and that poor jet pilot, too."

"What about that holograph of Dr. Brackwell?"

"EVE must've been spying on Sue, also, on her own creator,

you might say. Or—and I don't want you to look into this, because it won't do any good now—Sue may have set all this up in the machinery, unknown to her colleagues. I don't mean that she put in extra circuits. She couldn't get away with that; they'd be detected immediately, and she'd have to explain them. But she could have put in circuits which had two purposes, the second of which was unknown to her colleagues. I don't know.

"But I do know that it was actually Sue Brackwell who called me that last time and not EVE. And I think that it was this call that put into EVE's mind, if a machine can have a mind in the human sense, to project the much-glamorized holograph of Sue. Unless, of course, my other theory is correct, and Sue herself was responsible for that."

Smith groaned and then said, "They'll never believe me if I put all this in a report. For one thing, will they believe that it was only free association that enabled you to get *eye in the sky* from 'The egg and I' and 'Sky-blue waters'? I doubt it. They'll think you had knowledge you shouldn't have had and you're concealing it with that incredible story. I wouldn't want to be in your shoes. But then, I don't want to be in my shoes.

"But why did EVE blow up? Lackalas says that she could be exploded if a destruct button at control center was pressed. The button, however, was not pressed."

"You dragged me away just in time to save my life. But EVE must have melted some circuits. She died of frustration—in a way, that is."

"What?"

"She was putting out an enormous amount of energy for

such a tight beam. She must have overloaded."

Smith guffawed and said, "She was getting a charge out of it, too? Come on!"

Lane said, "Do you have any other explanation?"

THE FRESHMAN
BY PHILIP JOSÉ FARMER

Philip José Farmer, in his preface to "The Freshman," refers to the possibility of more in the "degrees" series coming to him in dreams. It's unknown whether additional tales manifested to Farmer in this manner, but at least we have this amusing story, in which he cannot resist connecting the Miskatonic University freshman in question to Lord Greystoke's Africa—Greystoke being, of course, a prominent member of the Wold Newton Family, as demonstrated in Farmer's biography *Tarzan Alive*. The Miskatonic student is Bukawai, who comes from a long line of witch doctors. The ancestor of the Bukawai seen here was a witch doctor of the same name, and was featured in Edgar Rice Burroughs' *Jungle Tales of Tarzan*.

PREFACE

I began reading H. P. Lovecraft's stories about the Cthulhu mythos when I was a young boy. His grim peeps into the Necronomicon *and into the shuddery horrors of the extremely ancient elder ones fascinated me. When I got older I still liked to read them, though I wasn't gung-ho about them. But I'd never had any desire to write a story which would be part of the Cthulhu cycle.*

Then, one night, some years ago, I had a dream in which I, a sixty-year-old man, was a freshman at a strange college and was attending a rush party given by a more-than-strange fraternity. There was something sinister about the whole affair, a sense of mounting danger. Just as the face of one of the frat brothers began to melt and he broke into a cackling laughter and I knew that something horrible was going to happen to me, I awoke.

I remember most of my dreams, and that was one I'd never forget. But it led to this story, "The Freshman," and may lead to others, "The Sophomore," "The Junior," "The Senior," "The M.A. Candidate," "The Ph.D." and who knows what else in the course of degrees.

The long-haired youth in front of Desmond wore sandals, ragged blue jeans, and a grimy T-shirt. A paperback, *The Collected Works of Robert Blake*, was half stuck into his rear pocket. When he turned around, he displayed in large letters on the T-shirt, M.U. His scrawny Fu Manchu mustache held some bread crumbs.

His yellow eyes—surely he suffered from jaundice—widened when he saw Desmond. He said, "This ain't the place to apply for the nursing home, pops." He grinned, showing unusually long canines; and then turned to face the admissions desk.

Desmond felt his face turning red. Ever since he'd gotten into the line before a table marked *Toaahd Freshmen A-D*, he'd been aware of the sidelong glances, the snickers, the low-voiced comments. He stood out among these youths like a billboard in a flower garden, a corpse on a banquet table.

The line moved ahead by one person. The would-be students were talking, but their voices were subdued. For such young people, they were very restrained, excepting the smart aleck just ahead of him.

Perhaps it was the surroundings that repressed them. This gymnasium, built in the late nineteenth century, had not been repainted for years. The once-green paint was peeling. There were broken windows high on the walls; a shattered skylight had been covered with boards. The wooden floor bent and creaked, and the basketball goal rings (?) were rusty. Yet M.U. had been league champions in all fields of sports for many years. Though its enrollment was much less than that of its competitors, its teams somehow managed to win, often by large scores.

Desmond buttoned his jacket. Though it was a warm fall day, the air in the building was cold. If he hadn't known better, he would have thought that the wall of an iceberg was just behind him. Above him the great lights struggled to overcome the darkness that lowered like the underside of a dead whale sinking into sea depths.

He turned around. The girl just back of him smiled. She wore a flowing dashiki covered with astrological symbols. Her black hair was cut short; her features were petite and well-arranged but too pointed to be pretty.

Among all these youths there should have been a number of pretty girls and handsome men. He'd walked enough campuses to get an idea of the index of beauty of college students. But here... There was a girl, in the line to the right, whose face should have made her eligible to be a fashion model. Yet, there was something missing.

No, there was something added. A quality undefinable

but... Repugnant? No, now it was gone. No, it was back again. It flitted on and off, like a bat swooping from darkness into a grayness and then up and out.

The kid in front of him had turned again. He was grinning like a fox who'd just seen a chicken.

"Some dish, heh, pops? She likes older men. Maybe you two could get your shit together and make beautiful music."

The odor of unwashed body and clothes swirled around him like flies around a dead rat.

"I'm not interested in girls with Oedipus complexes," Desmond said coldly.

"At your age you can't be particular," the youth said, and turned away.

Desmond flushed, and he briefly fantasized knocking the kid down. It didn't help much.

The line moved ahead again. He looked at his wristwatch. In half an hour he was scheduled to phone his mother. He should have come here sooner. However, he had overslept while the alarm clock had run down, resuming its ticking as if it didn't care. Which it didn't, of course, though he felt that his possessions should, somehow, take an interest in him. This was irrational, but if he was a believer in the superiority of the rational, would he be here? Would any of these students?

The line moved jerkily ahead like a centipede halting now and then to make sure no one had stolen any of its legs. When he was ten minutes late for the phone call, he was at the head of the line. Behind the admissions table was a man far older than he. His face was a mass of wrinkles, gray dough that had been incised with fingernails and then pressed into somewhat human shape. The nose was a cuttlefish's beak stuck into the dough. But the eyes beneath the white chaotic eyebrows were as alive as blood flowing from holes in the flesh.

The hand which took Desmond's papers and punched cards was not that of an old man's. It was big and swollen, white, smooth-skinned. The fingernails were dirty.

"The Roderick Desmond, I assume."

The voice was rasping, not at all an old man's cracked quavering.

"Ah, you know me?"

"Of you, yes. I've read some of your novels of the occult. And ten years ago I rejected your request for xeroxes of certain parts of *the* book."

The name tag on the worn tweed jacket said: R. Layamon, COTOAAHD. So this was the chairman of the Committee of the Occult Arts and History Department.

"Your paper on the non-Arabic origin of al-Hazred's name was a brilliant piece of linguistic research. I knew that the name wasn't Arabic or even Semitic in origin, but I confess that I didn't know the century in which the word was dropped from the Arabian language. Your exposition of how it was retained only in connection with the Yemenite, al-Hazred, and that its original meaning was not *mad* but *one-who-sees-what-shouldn't-be-seen* was quite correct."

He paused, then said smiling, "Did your mother complain when she was forced to accompany you to Yemen?"

Desmond said, "No-n-n-o-body forced her."

He took a deep breath and said, "But how did you know she…?"

"I've read some biographical accounts of you."

Layamon chuckled. It sounded like nails being shifted in a barrel. "Your paper on al-Hazred and the knowledge you display in your novels are the main reasons why you're being admitted to this department despite your sixty years."

He signed the forms and handed the card back to Desmond. "Take this to the cashier's office. Oh, yes, your family is a remarkably long-lived one, isn't it? Your father died accidentally, but his father lived to be one hundred and two. Your mother is eighty, but she should live to be over a hundred. And you, you could have forty more years of life as *you've known it*."

Desmond was enraged but not so much that he dared let himself show it. The gray air became black, and the old man's face shone in it. It floated toward him, expanded, and suddenly Desmond was inside the gray wrinkles. It was not a pleasant place.

The tiny figures on a dimly haloed horizon danced, then faded, and he fell through a bellowing blackness. The air was gray again, and he was leaning forward, clenching the edge of the table.

"Mr. Desmond, do you have these attacks often?"

Desmond released his grip and straightened. "Too much excitement, I suppose. No, I've never had an attack, not now or ever."

The old man chuckled. "Yes, it must be emotional stress. Perhaps you'll find the means for relieving that stress here."

Desmond turned and walked away. Until he left the

building, he saw only blurred figures and signs. That ancient wizard... how had he known his thoughts so well? Was it simply because he had read the biographical accounts, made a few inquiries, and then surmised a complete picture? Or was there more to it than that?

The sun had gone behind thick sluggish clouds. Past the campus, past many trees hiding the houses of the city were the Tamsiqueg hills. According to the long-extinct Indians after whom they were named, they had once been evil giants who'd waged war with the hero Mikatoonis and his magic-making friend, Chegaspat. Chegaspat had been killed, but Mikatoonis had turned the giants into stone with a magical club.

But Cotoaahd, the chief giant, was able to free himself from the spell every few centuries. Sometimes, a sorcerer could loose him. Then Cotoaahd walked abroad for a while before returning to his rocky slumber. In 1724 a house and many trees on the edge of the town had been flattened one stormy night as if colossal feet had stepped upon them. And the broken trees formed a trail which led to the curiously shaped hill known as Cotoaahd.

There was nothing about these stories that couldn't be explained by the tendency of the Indians, and the superstitious eighteenth-century whites, to legendize natural phenomena. But was it entirely coincidence that the acronym of the committee headed by Layamon duplicated the giant's name?

Suddenly, he became aware that he was heading for a telephone booth. He looked at his watch and felt panicky. The phone in his dormitory room would be ringing. It would be better to call her from the booth and save the three minutes it would take to walk to the dormitory.

He stopped. No, if he called from the booth, he would only get a busy signal.

"Forty more years of life as *you've known it*," the chairman had said.

Desmond turned. His path was blocked by an enormous youth. He was a head taller than Desmond's six feet and so fat he looked like a smaller version of a the Santa Claus balloon in Macy's Christmas-day parade. He wore a dingy sweatshirt on the front of which was the ubiquitous M.U., unpressed pants, and torn tennis shoes. In banana-sized fingers he held a salami sandwich which Gargantua would not have found too small.

Looking at him, Desmond suddenly realized that most of the students here were too thin or too fat.

"Mr. Desmond?"

"Right."

He shook hands. The fellow's skin was wet and cold, but the hand exerted a powerful pressure.

"I'm Wendell Trepan. With your knowledge, you've heard about my ancestors. The most famous, or infamous, of whom was the Cornish witch, Rachel Trepan."

"Yes. Rachel of the hamlet of Tredannick Wollas, near Poldhu Bay."

"I knew you'd know. I'm following the trade of my ancestors, though more cautiously, of course. Anyway, I'm a senior and the chairperson of the rushing committee for the Lam Kha Alif fraternity."

He paused to bite into the sandwich. Mayonnaise and salami and cheese oozing from his mouth, he said, "You're invited to the party we're holding at the house this afternoon."

The other hand reached into a pocket and brought out a card. Desmond looked at it briefly. "You want me to be a candidate for membership in your frat? I'm pretty old for that sort of thing. I'd feel out of place…"

"Nonsense, Mr. Desmond. We're a pretty serious bunch. In fact, none of the frats here are like any on other campuses. You should know that. We feel you'd provide stability and, I'll admit, prestige. You're pretty well known, you know. Layamon, by the way, is a Lam Kha Alif. He tends to favor students who belong to his frat. He'd deny it, of course, and I'll deny it if you repeat this. But it's true."

"Well, I don't know. Suppose I did pledge—if I'm invited to, that is—would I have to live in the frat house?"

"Yes. We make no exceptions. Of course, that's only when you're a pledge. You can live wherever you want to when you're an active."

Trepan smiled, showing the unswallowed bite. "You're not married, so there's no problem there."

"What do you mean by that?"

"Nothing, Mr. Desmond. It's just that we don't pledge married men unless they don't live with their wives. Married men lose some of their power, you know. Of course, no way do we insist on celibacy. We have some pretty good parties, too. Once a month we hold a big bust in a grove at the foot of Cotoaahd. Most of the women guests there belong to the Ba

Ghay Sin sorority. Some of them really go for the older type, if you know what I mean."

Trepan stepped forward to place his face directly above Desmond's. "We don't just have beer, pot, hashish, and sisters. There're other attractions. Brothers, if you're so inclined. Some stuff that's made from a recipe by the Marquis Manuel de Dembron himself. But most of that is kid stuff. There'll be a goat there, too!"

"A goat? A *black* goat?"

Trepan nodded, and his triple-fold jowls swung. "Yeah. Old Layamon'll be there to supervise, though he'll be masked, of course. With him as coach nothing can go wrong. Last Halloween though…"

He paused, then said, "Well, it was something to see."

Desmond licked dry lips. His heart was thudding like the tom-toms that beat at the ritual of which he had only read but had envisioned many times.

Desmond put the card in his pocket. "At one o'clock?"

"You're coming? Very good! See you, Mr. Desmond. You won't regret it."

Desmond walked past the buildings of the university quadrangle, the most imposing of which was the museum. This was the oldest structure on the campus, the original college. Time had beaten and chipped away at the brick and stone of the others, but the museum seemed to have absorbed time and to be slowly radiating it back just as cement and stone and brick absorbed heat in the sunlight and then gave it back in the darkness. Also, whereas the other structures were covered with vines, perhaps too covered, the museum was naked of plant life. Vines which tried to crawl up its gray-bone-colored stones withered and fell back.

Layamon's red-stone house was narrow, three stories high, and had a double-peaked roof. Its cover of vines was so thick that it seemed a wonder that the weight didn't bring it to the ground. The colors of the vines were subtly different from those on the other buildings. Seen at one angle, they looked cyanotic. From another, they were the exact green of the eyes of a Sumatran snake Desmond had seen in a colored plate in a book on herpetology.

It was this venomous reptile which was used by the sorcerers of the Yan tribes to transmit messages and sometimes to kill. The writer had not explained what he meant by "messages." Desmond had discovered the meaning in another book, which had required him to learn Malay, written in the Arabic script, before he could read it.

He hurried on past the house, which was not something a sightseer would care to look at long, and came to the dormitory. It had been built in 1888 on the site of another building and remodeled in 1938. Its gray paint was peeling. There were several broken windows, over the panes of which cardboard had been nailed. The porch floorboards bent and creaked as he passed over them. The main door was of oak, its paint long gone. The bronze head of a cat, a heavy bronze ring dangling from its mouth, served as a door knocker.

Desmond entered, passed through the main room over the worn carpet, and walked up two flights of bare-board steps. On the gray-white of a wall by the first landing someone had long ago written, *Yog-Sothoth Sucks*. Many attempts had been made to wash it off, but it was evident that only paint could hide this insulting and dangerous sentiment. Yesterday a junior had told him that no one knew who had written it, but the night after it had appeared, a freshman had been found dead, hanging from a hook in a closet.

"The kid had mutilated himself terribly before he committed suicide," the junior had said. "I wasn't here then, but I understand that he was a mess. He'd done it with a razor *and* a hot iron. There was blood all over the place, his pecker and balls were on the table, arranged to form a T-cross, you know whose symbol that is, and he'd clawed out plaster on the wall, leaving a big bloody print. It didn't even look like a human hand had done it."

"I'm surprised he lived long enough to hang himself," Desmond had said. "All that loss of blood, you know."

The junior had guffawed. "You're kidding, of course!"

It was several seconds before Desmond understood what he meant. Then he'd paled. But later he wondered if the junior wasn't playing a traditional joke on a green freshman. He didn't think he'd ask anybody else about it, however. If he had been made a fool of, he wasn't going to let it happen more than once.

He heard the phone ringing at the end of the long hall. He sighed, and strode down it, passing closed doors. From behind one came a faint tittering. He unlocked his door and closed it behind him. For a long time he stood watching the phone, which went on and on, reminding him, he didn't know why, of the poem about the Australian swagman who went for a dip in a waterhole.

The bunyip, that mysterious and sinister creature of down-under folklore, the dweller in the water, silently and smoothly took care of the swagman. And the tea kettle he'd put on the fire whistled and whistled with no one to hear.

And the phone rang on and on.

The bunyip was on the other end.

Guilt spread through him as quick as a blush.

He walked across the room glimpsing something out of the corner of his eye, something small, dark, and swift that dived under the sagging mildew-odorous bed-couch. He stopped at the small table, reached out to the receiver, touched it, felt its cold throbbing. He snatched his hand back. It was foolish, but it had seemed to him that she would detect his touch and know that he was there.

Snarling, he wheeled and started across the room. He noticed that the hole in the baseboard was open again. The Coke bottle whose butt end he'd jammed into the hole had been pushed out. He stopped and reinserted it and straightened up.

When he was at the foot of the staircase, he could still hear the ringing. But he wasn't sure that it wasn't just in his head.

After he'd paid his tuition and eaten at the cafeteria—the food was better than he'd thought it would be—he walked to the ROTC building. It was in better shape than the other structures, probably because the Army was in charge of it. Still, it wasn't in the condition an inspector would require. And those cannons on caissons in the rear. Were the students really supposed to train with Spanish-American War weapons? And since when was steel subject to verdigris?

The officer in charge was surprised when Desmond asked to be issued his uniform and manuals.

"I don't know. You realize ROTC is no longer required of freshmen and sophomores?"

Desmond insisted that he wanted to enroll. The officer rubbed his unshaven jaw and blew smoke from a Tijuana Gold panatela. "Hmm. Let me see."

He consulted a book whose edges seemed to have been nibbled by rats. "Well, what do you know? There's nothing in the regulations about age. Course, there's some pages missing. Must be an oversight. Nobody near your age has ever been considered. But... well, if the regulations say nothing about it, then... what the hell! Won't hurt you, our boys don't have to go through obstacle courses or anything like that.

"But, jeeze, you're sixty! Why do you want to sign up?"

Desmond did not tell him that he had been deferred from service in World War II because he was the sole support of his sick mother. Ever since then, he'd felt guilty, but at least here he could do his bit—however minute—for his country.

The officer stood up, though not in a coordinated manner. "Okay. I'll see you get your issue. It's only fair to warn you, though, that these fuck-ups play some mighty strange tricks. You should see what they blow out of their cannons."

Fifteen minutes later, Desmond left, a pile of uniforms and manuals under one arm. Since he didn't want to return home with them, he checked them in at the university book store. The girl put them on a shelf alongside other belongings, some of them unidentifiable to the noncognoscenti. One of them was a small cage covered with a black cloth.

Desmond walked to Fraternity Row. All of the houses had Arabic names, except the House of Hastur. These were afflicted with the same general decrepitude and lack of care as the university structures. Desmond turned in at a cement walk, from the cracks of which spread dying dandelions and other weeds. On his left leaned a massive wooden pole fifteen feet high. The heads and symbols carved into it had caused the townspeople to refer to it as the totem pole. It wasn't, of course, since the tribe to which it had belonged were not Northwest Coast or Alaskan Indians. It and a fellow in the university museum were the last survivors of hundreds which had once stood in this area.

Desmond, passing it, put the end of his left thumb under his nose and the tip of his index finger in the center of his forehead, and he muttered the ancient phrase of obeisance, *"Shesh-cotoaahd-ting-ononwa-senk."* According to various texts he'd read, this was required of every Tamsiqueg who walked by it during this phase of the moon. The phrase was unintelligible even to them, since it came from another tribe or perhaps from an antique stage of the language. But it indicated respect, and lack of its observance was likely to result in misfortune.

He felt a little silly doing it, but it couldn't hurt.

The unpainted wooden steps creaked as he stepped upon them. The porch was huge; the wires of the screen were rusty and useless in keeping insects out because of the many holes. The front door was open; from it came a blast of rock music, the loud chatter of many people, and the acrid odor of pot.

Desmond almost turned back. He suffered when he was

in a crowd, and his consciousness of his age made him feel embarrassingly conspicuous. But the huge figure of Wendell Trepan was in the doorway, and he was seized by an enormous hand.

"Come on in!" Trepan bellowed. "I'll introduce you to the brothers!"

Desmond was pulled into a large room jammed with youths of both sexes. Trepan bulled through, halting now and then to slap somebody on the back and shout a greeting, and once to pat a well-built young woman on the fanny. Then they were in a corner where Professor Layamon sat surrounded by people who looked older than most of the attendees. Desmond supposed that they were graduate students. He shook the fat swollen hand and said, "Pleased to meet you again," but he doubted that his words were heard.

Layamon pulled him down so he could be heard, and he said, "Have you made up your mind yet?"

The old man's breath was not unpleasant, but he had certainly been drinking something which Desmond had never smelled before. The red eyes seemed to hold a light, almost as if tiny candles were burning inside the eyeballs. "About what?" Desmond shouted back. The old man smiled and said, "You know." He released his grip. Desmond straightened up. Suddenly, though the room was hot enough to make him sweat, he felt chilly. What was Layamon hinting at? It couldn't be that he really knew. Or could it be?

Trepan introduced him to the men and women around the chair and then took him into the crowd. Other introductions followed, most of those he met seeming to be members of Lam Kha Alif or of the sorority across the street. The only one he could identify for sure as a candidate for pledging was a black, a Gabonese. After they left him, Trepan said, "Bukawai comes from a long line of witch doctors. He's going to be a real treasure if he accepts our invitation, though the House of Hastur and Kaf Dhal Waw are hot to get him. The department is a little weak on Central African science. It used to have a great teacher, Janice Momaya, but she disappeared ten years ago while on a sabbatical in Sierra Leone. I wouldn't be surprised if Bukawai was offered an assistant professorship even if he is nominally a freshman. Man, the other night, he taught me part of a ritual you wouldn't believe. I... well, I won't go into it now. Some other time. Anyway, he has the greatest respect for Layamon, and since the old fart is head of the department, Bukawai is almost a cinch to join us."

Suddenly, his lips pulled back, his teeth clenched, his skin paled beneath the dirt, and he bent over and grabbed his huge paunch. Desmond said, "What's the matter?"

Trepan shook his head, gave a deep sigh, and straightened up.

"Man, that hurt!"

"What?" Desmond said.

"I shouldn't have called him an old fart. I didn't think he could hear me, but he isn't using sound to receive. Hell, there's nobody in the world has more respect for him than me. But sometimes my mouth runs off... well, never again."

"You mean?" Desmond said.

"Yeah. Who'd you think? Never mind. Come with me where we can hear ourselves think."

He pulled Desmond through a smaller room, one with many shelves of books, novels, school texts, and here and there some old leather-bound volumes.

"We got a hell of a good library here, the best any house can boast of. It's one of our stellar attractions. But it's the open one."

They entered a narrow door, passed into a short hall, and stopped while Trepan took a key from his pocket and unlocked another door. Beyond it was a narrow corkscrew staircase, the steps of which were dusty. A window high above gave a weak light through dirty panes. Trepan turned on a wall light, and they went up the stairs. Trepan unlocked another door with a different key. They stepped into a small room whose walls were covered by bookshelves from floor to ceiling. Trepan turned on a light. In a corner was a small table and a folding chair. The table had a lamp and a stone bust of the Marquis de Dembron on it.

Trepan, breathing heavily after the climb, said, "Usually, only seniors and graduates are allowed here. But I'm making an exception in your case. I just wanted to show you one of the advantages of belonging to Lam Kha Alif. None of the other houses have a library like this."

Trepan was looking narrow-eyed at him. "Eyeball the books. But don't touch them. They, uh, absorb, if you know what I mean."

Desmond moved around, looking at the titles. When he was finished, he said, "I'm impressed. I thought some of these were to be found only in the university library. In locked rooms."

"That's what the public thinks. Listen, if you pledge us,

you'll have access to these books. Only don't tell the other undergrads. They'd get jealous."

Trepan, still narrow-eyed, as if he were considering something that perhaps he shouldn't, said, "Would you mind turning your back and sticking your fingers in your ears?"

Desmond said, "What?"

Trepan smiled. "Oh, if you sign up with us, you'll be given the little recipe necessary to work in here. But until then I'd just as soon you don't see it."

Desmond, smiling with embarrassment, the cause of which he couldn't account for, and also feeling excited, turned his back, facing away from Trepan, and jammed his fingertips into his ears. While he stood there in the very quiet room—was it soundproofed with insulation or with something perhaps not material?—he counted the seconds. One thousand and one, one thousand and two...

A little more than a minute had passed when he felt Trepan's hand on his shoulder. He turned and removed his fingers. The fat youth was holding out to him a tall but very slim volume bound in a skin with many small dark protuberances. Desmond was surprised, since he was sure he had not seen it on the shelves.

"I deactivated this," Trepan said. "Here. Take it." He looked at his wristwatch. "It'll be okay for ten minutes."

There was no title or byline on the cover. And, now that he looked at it closely and felt it, he did not think the skin was from an animal.

Trepan said, "It's the hide of old Atechironnon himself."

Desmond said, "Ah!" and he trembled. But he rallied. "He must have been covered with warts."

"Yeah. Go ahead. Look at it. It's a shame you can't read it, though."

The first page was slightly yellowed, which wasn't surprising for paper four hundred years old. There was no printing but large handwritten letters.

"Ye lesser Rituall of Ye Tahmmsiquegg Warlock Atechironunn," Desmond read. *"Reprodust from ye Picture-riting on ye Skin lefft unbirnt by ye Godly.*

"By his own Hand, Simon Conant. 1641.

"Let him who speaks these Words of Pictures, first lissen."

Trepan chuckled and said, "Spelling wasn't his forte, was it?"

"Simon, the half-brother of Roger Conant," Desmond said. "He was the first white man to visit the Tamsiqueg and not leave with his severed thumb stuck up his ass. He was also with the settlers who raided the Tamsiqueg, but they didn't know who his sympathies were with. He fled with the badly wounded Atechironnon into the wilderness. Twenty years later, he appeared in Virginia with this book."

He slowly turned the five pages, fixing each pictograph in his photographic memory. There was one figure he didn't like to look at.

"Layamon's the only one who can read it," Trepan said.

Desmond did not tell him that he was conversant with the grammar and small dictionary of the Tamsiqueg language, written by William Cor Dunnes in 1624 and published in 1654. It contained an appendix translating the pictographs. It had cost him twenty years of searching and a thousand dollars just for a xerox copy. His mother had raised hell about the expenditure, but for once he had stood up to her. Not even the university had a copy.

Trepan looked at his watch. "One minute to go. Hey!"

He grabbed the book from Desmond's hands and said, harshly, "Turn your back and plug your ears!"

Trepan looked as if he were in a panic. He turned, and a minute later Trepan pulled one of Desmond's fingers away.

"Sorry to be so sudden, but the hold was beginning to break down. I can't figure it out. It's always been good for at least ten minutes."

Desmond had not felt anything, but that might be because Trepan, having been exposed to the influence, was more sensitive to it.

Trepan, obviously nervous, said, "Let's get out of here. It's got to cool off."

On the way down, he said, "You sure you can't read it?"

"Where would I have learned how?" Desmond said.

They plunged into a sea of noise and odors in the big room. They did not stay long, since Trepan wanted to show him the rest of the house, except the basement.

"You can see it sometime this week. Just now it's not advisable to go down there."

Desmond didn't ask why.

When they entered a very small room on the second floor, Trepan said, "Ordinarily we don't let freshmen have a room to themselves. But for you… well, it's yours if you want it."

That pleased Desmond. He wouldn't have to put up with

someone whose habits would irk him and whose chatter would anger him.

They descended to the first floor. The big room was not so crowded now. Old Layamon, just getting up from the chair, beckoned to him. Desmond approached him slowly. For some reason, he knew he was not going to like what Layamon would say to him. Or perhaps he wasn't sure whether he would like it or not.

"Trepan showed you the frat's more precious books," the chairman said. It wasn't a question but a statement. "Especially Conant's book."

Trepan said, "How did you...?" He grinned. "You felt it."

"Of course," the rusty voice said. "Well, Desmond, don't you think it's time to answer that phone?"

Trepan looked puzzled. Desmond felt sick and cold. Layamon was now almost nose to nose with Desmond. The many wrinkles of the doughy skin looked like hieroglyphs.

"You've made up your mind, but you aren't letting yourself know it," he said. "Listen. That was Conant's advice, wasn't it? Listen. From the moment you got onto the plane to Boston, you were committed. You could have backed out in the airport, but you didn't, even though, I imagine, your mother made a scene there. But you didn't. So there's no use putting it off." He chuckled. "That I am bothering to give you advice is a token of my esteem for you. I think you'll go far and fast. If you are able to eliminate certain defects of character. It takes strength and intelligence and great self-discipline and a vast dedication to get even a B.A. here, Desmond.

"There are too many who enroll here because they think they'll be taking snap courses. Getting great power, hobnobbing with things that are really not socially minded, to say the least, seems to them to be as easy as rolling off a log. But they soon find out that the department's standards are higher than, say, those of MIT in engineering. And a hell of a lot more dangerous.

"And then there's the moral issue. That's declared just by enrolling here. But how many have the will to push on? How many decide that they are on the wrong side? They quit, not knowing that it's too late for any but a tiny fraction of them to return to the other side. They've declared themselves, have stood up and been counted forever, as it were."

He paused to light up a brown panatela. The smoke curled around Desmond, who did not smell what he expected. The odor was not quite like that of a dead bat he had once used in an experiment.

"Every man or woman determines his or her own destiny. But I would make my decision swiftly, if I were you. I've got my eye on you, and your advancement here does depend upon my estimate of your character and potentiality.

"Good day, Desmond."

The old man walked out. Trepan said, "What was that all about?"

Desmond did not answer. He stood for a minute or so while Trepan fidgeted. Then he said goodbye to the fat man and walked out slowly. Instead of going home, he wandered around the campus. Attracted by flashing red lights, he went over to see what was going on. A car with the markings of the campus police and an ambulance from the university hospital were in front of a two-story building. Its lower floor had once been a grocery store according to the letters on the dirty plate-glass window. The paint inside and out was peeling, and plaster had fallen off the walls inside, revealing the laths beneath. On the bare wooden floor were three bodies. One was the youth who had stood just in front of him in the line in the gymnasium. He lay on his back, his mouth open below the scraggly mustache.

Desmond asked one of the people pressed against the window what had happened. The gray-bearded man, probably a professor, said, "This happens every year at this time. Some kids get carried away and try something no one but an M.A. would even think of trying. It's strictly forbidden, but that doesn't stop those young fools."

The corpse with the mustache seemed to have a large round black object or perhaps a burn on its forehead. Desmond wanted to get a closer look, but the ambulance men put a blanket over the face before carrying the body out.

The gray-bearded man said, "The university police and the hospital will handle them." He laughed shortly. "The city police don't even want to come on the campus. The relatives will be notified they've OD'ed on heroin."

"There's no trouble about that?"

"Sometimes. Private detectives have come here, but they don't stay long."

Desmond walked away swiftly. His mind was made up. The sight of those bodies had shaken him. He'd go home, make peace with his mother, sell all the books he'd spent so much time and money accumulating and studying, take up writing mystery novels. He'd seen the face of death, and if he did what he had thought about, only idly of course, fantasizing for psychic therapy, he would see her face. Dead. He couldn't do it.

When he entered his room in the boarding house, the phone was still ringing. He walked to it, reached out his hand, held it for an indeterminable time, then dropped it. As he walked toward the couch, he noticed that the Coca-Cola bottle had been shoved or pulled out of the hole in the baseboard. He knelt down and jammed it back into the hole. From behind the wall came a faint twittering.

He sat down on the sagging couch, took his notebook from his jacket pocket, and began to pencil in the pictographs he remembered so well on the sheets. It took him half an hour, since exactness of reproduction was vital. The phone did not stop ringing.

Someone knocked on the door and yelled, "I saw you go in! Answer the phone or take it off the hook! Or I'll put something on you!"

He did not reply or rise from the couch.

He had left out one of the drawings in the sequence. Now he poised the pencil an inch above the blank space. Sitting at the other end of the line would be a very fat, very old woman. She was old and ugly now, but she had borne him and for many years thereafter she had been beautiful. When his father had died, she had gone to work to keep their house and to support her son in the manner to which both were accustomed. She had worked hard to pay his tuition and other expenses while he went to college. She had continued to work until he had sold two novels. Then she had gotten sickly, though not until he began bringing women home to introduce as potential wives.

She loved him, but she wouldn't let loose of him, and that wasn't genuine love. He hadn't been able to tear loose, which meant that though he was resentful, he had something in him which liked being caged. Then, one day, he had decided to take the big step toward freedom. It had been done secretly and swiftly. He had despised himself for his fear of her, but that was the way he was. If he stayed here, she would be coming here. He couldn't endure that. So, he would have to go home.

He looked at the phone, started to rise, sank back.

What to do? He could commit suicide. He'd be free, and she would know how angry he'd been with her. He gave a start as the phone stopped ringing. So, she had given up for a while. But she would return.

He looked at the baseboard. The bottle was moving out from the hole a little at a time. Something behind the wall was working away determinedly. How many times had it started to leave the hole and found that its passage was blocked? Far too many, the thing must think, if it had a mind. But it refused to give up, and some day it might occur to it to solve its problem by killing the one who was causing the problem.

If, however, it was daunted by the far greater size of the problem maker, if it lacked courage, then it would have to keep on pushing the bottle from the hole. And...

He looked at the notebook, and he shook. The blank space had been filled in. There was the drawing of Cotoaahd, the thing which, now he looked at it, somehow resembled his mother.

Had he unconsciously penciled it in while he was thinking?

Or had the figure formed itself?

It didn't matter. In either case, he knew what he had to do.

While the eyes passed over each drawing, and he intoned the words of that long-dead language, he felt something move out from within his chest, crawl into his belly, his legs, his throat, his brain. The symbol of Cotoaahd seemed to burn on the sheet when he pronounced its name, his eyes on the drawing.

The room grew dark as the final words were said. He rose and turned on a table lamp and went into the tiny, dirty bathroom. The face in the mirror did not look like a murderer's; it was just that of a sixty-year-old man who had been through an ordeal and was not quite sure that it was over.

On the way out of the room, he saw the Coke bottle slide free of the baseboard hole. But whatever had pushed it was not yet ready to come out.

Hours later he returned reeling from the campus tavern. The phone was ringing again. But the call, as he had expected, was not from his mother, though it was from his native city in Illinois.

"Mr. Desmond, this is Sergeant Rourke of the Busiris Police Department. I'm afraid I have some bad news for you. Uh, ah, your mother died some hours ago of a heart attack."

Desmond did not have to act stunned. He was numb throughout. Even the hand holding the receiver felt as if it had turned to granite. Vaguely, he was aware that Rourke's voice seemed strange.

"Heart attack? Heart…? Are you sure?"

He groaned. His mother had died naturally. He would not have had to recite the ancient words. And now he had committed himself for nothing and was forever trapped. Once the words were used while the eyes read, there was no turning back.

But… if the words had been only words, dying as sound usually does, no physical reaction resulting from words transmitted through that subcontinuum, then was he bound?

Wouldn't he be free, clear of debt? Able to walk out of this place without fear of retaliation?

"It was a terrible thing, Mr. Desmond. A freak accident. Your mother died while she was talking to a visiting neighbor, Mrs. Sammins. Sammins called the police and an ambulance. Some other neighbors went into the house, and then… then…"

Rourke's throat seemed to be clogging.

"I'd just got there and was on the front porch when it… it…"

Rourke coughed, and he said, "My brother was in the house, too."

Three neighbors, two ambulance attendants, and two policemen had been crushed to death when the house had unaccountably collapsed.

"It was like a giant foot stepped on it. If it'd fallen in six seconds later, I'd have been caught, too."

Desmond thanked him and said he'd take the next plane out to Busiris.

He staggered to the window, and he raised it to breathe in the open air. Below, in the light of a street lamp, hobbling along on his cane, was Layamon. The gray face lifted. Teeth flashed whitely.

Desmond wept, but the tears were only for himself.

AFTER KING KONG FELL

BY PHILIP JOSÉ FARMER

In the aftermath of Kong's plunge from the Empire State Building, some interesting characters appear on the scene: a powerful-looking, golden-eyed man and his five companions, and a hawk-nosed man with blazing eyes and a lovely female companion. These are, firstly, Doc Savage and his five stalwart aides (Ham Brooks, Monk Mayfair, Renny Renwick, Johnny Littlejohn, and Long Tom Roberts), and secondly, The Shadow (likely in his Lamont Cranston guise) and his assistant Margo Lane. Doc, Monk, and The Shadow are all members of the Wold Newton Family, descendants of those exposed to meteoritic ionization at Wold Newton, England, in December 1795, thus placing the tragic events surrounding Kong squarely in the Wold Newton Universe.

Sharp-eyed readers will note that Margo did not make her pulp debut as one of The Shadow's assistants until 1941, while "After King Kong Fell" takes place in 1931 (the radio versions of The Shadow and Margo were different from the pulp versions—

on the radio shows, Lamont Cranston *really was* The Shadow—so it should be noted here that Farmer added the pulp version, not the radio version, to the Wold Newton Family). Margo's anachronistic 1931 appearance has been addressed by some of Farmer's readers in various "creative mythography" essays.

A young man who is visiting New York and witnesses Kong's fall is one Tim Howller of Peoria, Illinois, age thirteen. Perhaps not coincidentally, Farmer, also of Peoria, was also thirteen in 1931. Tim Howller makes another appearance in Farmer's short story, "The Face That Launched a Thousand Eggs."

The first half of the movie was grim and gray and somewhat tedious. Mr. Howller did not mind. That was, after all, realism. Those times had been grim and gray. Moreover, behind the tediousness was the promise of something vast and horrifying. The creeping pace and the measured ritualistic movements of the actors gave intimations of the workings of the gods. Unhurriedly, but with utmost confidence, the gods were directing events toward the climax.

Mr. Howller had felt that at the age of fifteen, and he felt it now while watching the show on TV at the age of fifty-five. Of course, when he first saw it in 1933, he had known what was coming. Hadn't he lived through some of the events only two years before that?

The old freighter, the *Wanderer*, was nosing blindly through the fog toward the surflike roar of the natives' drums. And then: the commercial. Mr. Howller rose and stepped into the hall and called down the steps loudly enough for Jill to hear him on the front porch. He thought, commercials could be a blessing. They give us time to get into the bathroom or the kitchen, or time to light up a cigarette and decide about continuing to watch this show or go on to that show.

And why couldn't real life have its commercials?

Wouldn't it be something to be grateful for if reality stopped in midcourse while the Big Salesman made His pitch? The car about to smash into you, the bullet on its way to your brain, the first cancer cell about to break loose, the boss reaching for the phone to call you in so he can fire you, the spermatozoon about to be launched toward the ovum, the final insult about to be hurled at the once, and perhaps still, beloved, the final drink of alcohol which would rupture the abused blood vessel, the decision which would lead to the light that would surely fail?

If only you could step out while the commercial interrupted these, think about it, talk about it, and then, returning to the set, switch it to another channel.

But that one is having technical difficulties, and the one after that is a talk show whose guest is the archangel Gabriel himself and after some urging by the host he agrees to blow his trumpet, and…

Jill entered, sat down, and began to munch the cookies and drink the lemonade he had prepared for her. Jill was six and a half years old and beautiful, but then what granddaughter wasn't beautiful? Jill was also unhappy because she had just quarreled with her best friend, Amy, who had stalked off with threats never to see Jill again. Mr. Howller reminded her that this had happened before and that Amy always came back the next day, if not sooner. To take her mind off of Amy, Mr. Howller gave her a brief outline of what had happened in the movie. Jill listened without enthusiasm, but she became excited enough once the movie had resumed. And when Kong was feeling over the edge of the abyss for John Driscoll, played by Bruce Cabot, she got into her grandfather's lap. She gave a little scream and put her hands over her eyes when Kong carried Ann Redman into the jungle (Ann played by Fay Wray).

But by the time Kong lay dead on Fifth Avenue, she was rooting for him, as millions had before her. Mr. Howller squeezed her and kissed her and said, "When your mother was about your age, I took her to see this. And when it was over, she was crying, too."

Jill sniffled and let him dry the tears with his handkerchief. When the Roadrunner cartoon came on, she got off his lap and went back to her cookie-munching. After a while she said, "Grandpa, the coyote falls off the cliff so far you can't even see him. When he hits, the whole earth shakes. But he always comes back, good as new. Why can he fall so far and not get hurt? Why couldn't King Kong fall and be just like new?"

Her grandparents and her mother had explained many times the distinction between a "live" and a "taped" show. It did not seem to make any difference how many times they explained. Somehow, in the years of watching TV, she had gotten the fixed idea that people in "live" shows actually suffered pain, sorrow, and death. The only shows she could endure seeing were those that her elders labeled as "taped." This worried Mr. Howller more than he admitted to his wife and daughter. Jill was a very bright child, but what if too many TV shows at too early an age had done her some irreparable harm? What if, a few years from now, she could easily see, and even define, the distinction between reality and unreality on the screen but deep down in her there was a child that still could not distinguish?

"You know that the Roadrunner is a series of pictures that move. People draw pictures, and people can do anything with pictures. So the Roadrunner is drawn again and again, and he's back in the next show with his wounds all healed and he's ready to make a jackass of himself again."

"A jackass? But he's a coyote."

"Now…"

Mr. Howller stopped. Jill was grinning.

"Okay, now you're pulling my leg."

"But is King Kong alive or is he taped?"

"Taped. Like the Disney I took you to see last week. *Bedknobs and Broomsticks*."

"Then *King Kong* didn't happen?"

"Oh, yes, it really happened. But this is a movie they made about King Kong after what really happened was all over. So it's not exactly like it really was, and actors took the parts of Ann Redman and Carl Denham and all the others. Except King Kong himself. He was a toy model."

Jill was silent for a minute and then she said, "You mean, there really *was* a King Kong? How do you know, Grandpa?"

"Because I was there in New York when Kong went on his rampage. I was in the theater when he broke loose, and I was in the crowd that gathered around Kong's body after he fell off the

Empire State Building. I was thirteen then, just seven years older than you are now. I was with my parents, and they were visiting my Aunt Thea. She was beautiful, and she had golden hair just like Fay Wray's—I mean, Ann Redman's. She'd married a very rich man, and they had a big apartment high up in the clouds. In the Empire State Building itself."

"High up in the clouds! That must've been fun, Grandpa!"

It would have been, he thought, if there had not been so much tension in that apartment. Uncle Nate and Aunt Thea should have been happy because they were so rich and lived in such a swell place. But they weren't. No one said anything to young Tim Howller, but he felt the suppressed anger, heard the bite of tone, and saw the tightening lips. His aunt and uncle were having trouble of some sort, and his parents were upset by it. But they all tried to pretend everything was as sweet as honey when he was around.

Young Howller had been eager to accept the pretense. He didn't like to think that anybody could be mad at his tall, blond, and beautiful aunt. He was passionately in love with her; he ached for her in the daytime; at night he had fantasies about her of which he was ashamed when he awoke. But not for long. She was a thousand times more desirable than Fay Wray or Claudette Colbert or Elissa Landi.

But that night, when they were all going to see the premiere of *The Eighth Wonder of the World*, King Kong himself, young Howller had managed to ignore whatever it was that was bugging his elders. And even they seemed to be having a good time. Uncle Nate, over his parents' weak protests, had purchased orchestra seats for them. These were twenty dollars apiece, big money in Depression days, enough to feed a family for a month. Everybody got all dressed up, and Aunt Thea looked too beautiful to be real. Young Howller was so excited that he thought his heart was going to climb up and out through his throat. For days the newspapers had been full of stories about King Kong, speculations, rather, since Carl Denham wasn't telling them much. And he, Tim Howller, would be one of the lucky few to see the monster first.

Boy, wait until he got back to the kids in seventh grade at Busiris, Illinois! Would their eyes ever pop when he told them all about it!

But his happiness was too good to last. Aunt Thea suddenly said she had a headache and couldn't possibly go. Then she and Uncle Nate went into their bedroom, and even in the front room, three rooms and a hallway distant, young Tim could hear their voices. After a while Uncle Nate, slamming doors behind him, came out. He was red-faced and scowling, but he wasn't going to call the party off. All four of them, very uncomfortable and silent, rode in a taxi to the theater on Times Square. But when they got inside, even Uncle Nate forgot the quarrel, or at least he seemed to. There was the big stage with its towering silvery curtains and through the curtains came a vibration of excitement and of delicious danger. And even through the curtains the hot hairy ape-stink filled the theater.

"Did King Kong get loose just like in the movie?" Jill said.

Mr. Howller started. "What? Oh, yes, he sure did. Just like in the movie."

"Were you scared, Grandpa? Did you run away like everybody else?"

He hesitated. Jill's image of her grandfather had been cast in a heroic mold. To her he was a giant of Herculean strength and perfect courage, her defender and champion. So far he had managed to live up to the image, mainly because the demands she made were not too much for him. In time she would see the cracks and the sawdust oozing out. But she was too young to disillusion now.

"No, I didn't run," he said. "I waited until the theater was cleared of the crowd."

This was true. The big man who'd been sitting in the seat before him had leaped up yelling as Kong began tearing the bars out of his cage, had whirled and jumped over the back of his seat, and his knee had hit young Howller on the jaw. And so young Howller had been stretched out senseless on the floor under the seats while the mob screamed and tore at each other and trampled the fallen.

Later he was glad that he had been knocked out. It gave him a good excuse for not keeping cool, for not acting heroically in the situation. He knew that if he had not been unconscious, he would have been as frenzied as the others, and he would have abandoned his parents, thinking only in his terror of his own salvation. Of course, his parents had deserted him, though they claimed that they had been swept away from him by the mob. This could be true: maybe his folks had actually tried to get to him. But he had not really thought they had, and for years he had looked down on them because of their flight. When he got older, he realized that he would have done the same thing, and he knew that his contempt for them was really a disguised contempt for himself.

He had awakened with a sore jaw and a headache. The police and the ambulance men were there and starting to take care of the hurt and to haul away the dead. He staggered past them out into the lobby and, not seeing his parents there, went outside. The sidewalks and the streets were plugged with thousands of men, women, and children, on foot and in cars, fleeing northward.

He had not known where Kong was. He should have been able to figure it out, since the frantic mob was leaving the midtown part of Manhattan. But he could think of only two things. Where were his parents? And was Aunt Thea safe? And then he had a third thing to consider. He discovered that he had wet his pants. When he had seen the great ape burst loose, he had wet his pants.

Under the circumstances, he should have paid no attention to this. Certainly no one else did. But he was a very sensitive and shy boy of thirteen, and, for some reason, the need for getting dry underwear and trousers seemed even more important than finding his parents. In retrospect he would tell himself that he would have gone south anyway. But he knew deep down that if his pants had not been wet he might not have dared return to the Empire State Building.

It was impossible to buck the flow of the thousands moving like lava up Broadway. He went east on 43rd Street until he came to Fifth Avenue, where he started southward. There was a crowd to fight against here, too, but it was much smaller than that on Broadway. He was able to thread his way through it, though he often had to go out into the street and dodge the cars. These, fortunately, were not able to move faster than about three miles an hour.

"Many people got impatient because the cars wouldn't go faster," he told Jill, "and they just abandoned them and struck out on foot."

"Wasn't it noisy, Grandpa?"

"Noisy? I've never heard such noise. I think that everyone in Manhattan, except those hiding under their beds, was yelling or talking. And every driver in Manhattan was blowing his car's horn. And then there were the sirens of the fire trucks and police cars and ambulances. Yes, it was noisy."

Several times he tried to stop a fugitive so he could find out what was going on. But even when he did succeed in halting someone for a few seconds, he couldn't make himself heard. By then, as he found out later, the radio had broadcast the news. Kong had chased John Driscoll and Ann Redman out of the theater and across the street to their hotel. They had gone up to Driscoll's room, where they thought they were safe. But Kong had climbed up, using windows as ladder steps, reached into the room, knocked Driscoll out, grabbed Ann, and had then leaped away with her. He had headed, as Carl Denham figured he would, toward the tallest structure on the island. On King Kong's own island, he lived on the highest point, Skull Mountain, where he was truly monarch of all he surveyed. Here he would climb to the top of the Empire State Building, Manhattan's Skull Mountain.

Tim Howller had not known this, but he was able to infer that Kong had traveled down Fifth Avenue from 38th Street on. He passed a dozen cars with their tops flattened down by the ape's fist or turned over on their sides or tops. He saw three sheet-covered bodies on the sidewalks, and he overheard a policeman telling a reporter that Kong had climbed up several buildings on his way south and reached into windows and pulled people out and thrown them down onto the pavement.

"But you said King Kong was carrying Ann Redman in the crook of his arm, Grandpa," Jill said. "He only had one arm to climb with, Grandpa, so... so wouldn't he fall off the building when he reached in to grab those poor people?"

"A very shrewd observation, my little chickadee," Mr. Howller said, using the W. C. Fields voice that usually sent her into giggles. "But his arms were long enough for him to drape Ann Redman over the arm he used to hang on with while he reached in with the other. And to forestall your next question, even if you had not thought of it, he could turn over an automobile with only one hand."

"But... but why'd he take time out to do that if he wanted to get to the top of the Empire State Building?"

"I don't know why *people* often do the things they do," Mr. Howller said. "So how would I know why an ape does the things he does?"

When he was a block away from the Empire State, a plane crashed onto the middle of the avenue two blocks behind him and burned furiously. Tim Howller watched it for a few minutes, then he looked upward and saw the red and green lights of the five planes and the silvery bodies slipping in and out of the searchlights.

"Five airplanes, Grandpa? But the movie…"

"Yes, I know. The movie showed abut fourteen or fifteen. But the book says that there were six to begin with, and the book is much more accurate. The movie also shows King Kong's last stand taking place in the daylight. But it didn't; it was still nighttime."

The Army Air Force plane must have been going at least two hundred and fifty miles an hour as it dived down toward the giant ape standing on the top of the observation tower. Kong had put Ann Redman by his feet so he could hang on to the tower with one hand and grab out with the other at the planes. One had come too close, and he had seized the left biplane structure and ripped it off. Given the energy of the plane, his hand should have been torn off, too, or at least he should have been pulled loose from his hold on the tower and gone down with the plane. But he hadn't let loose, and that told something of the enormous strength of that towering body. It also told something of the relative fragility of the biplane.

Young Howller had watched the efforts of the firemen to extinguish the fire and then he had turned back toward the Empire State Building. By then it was all over. All over for King Kong, anyway. It was, in after years, one of Mr. Howller's greatest regrets that he had not seen the monstrous dark body falling through the beams of the searchlights—blackness, then the flash of blackness through the whiteness of the highest beam, blackness, the flash through the next beam, blackness, the flash through the third beam, blackness, the flash through the lowest beam. Dot, dash, dot, dash, Mr. Howller was to think afterward. A code transmitted unconsciously by the great ape and received unconsciously by those who witnessed the fall. Or by those who would hear of it and think about it. Or was he going too far conceiving this? Wasn't he always looking for codes? And, when he found them, unable to decipher them?

Since he had been thirteen, he had been trying to equate the great falls in man's myths and legends and to find some sort of intelligence in them. The fall of the tower of Babel, of Lucifer, of Vulcan, of Icarus, and, finally, of King Kong. But he wasn't equal to the task; he didn't have the genius to perceive what the falls meant; he couldn't screen out the—to use an electronic term—the "noise." All he could come up with were folk adages. What goes up must come down. The bigger they are, the harder they fall.

"What'd you say, Grandpa?"

"I was thinking out loud, if you can call that thinking," Mr. Howller said.

Young Howller had been one of the first on the scene, and so he got a place in the front of the crowd. He had not completely forgotten his parents or Aunt Thea, but the danger was over, and he could not make himself leave to search for them. And he had even forgotten about his soaked pants. The body was only about thirty feet from him. It lay on its back on the sidewalk, just as in the movie. But the dead Kong did not look as big or as dignified as in the movie. He was spread out more like an ape-skin rug than a body, and blood and bowels and their contents had splashed out around him.

After a while Carl Denham, the man responsible for capturing Kong and bringing him to New York, appeared. As in the movie, Denham spoke his classical lines by the body: "It was Beauty. As always, Beauty killed the Beast."

This was the most appropriately dramatic place for the lines to be spoken, of course, and the proper place to end the movie.

But the book had Denham speaking these lines as he leaned over the parapet of the observation tower to look down at Kong on the sidewalk. His only audience was a police sergeant.

Both the book and the movie were true. Or half true. Denham did speak those lines way up on the 102nd floor of the tower. But, showman that he was, he also spoke them when he got down to the sidewalk, where the newsmen could hear them.

Young Howller didn't hear Denham's remarks. He was too far away. Besides, at that moment he felt a tap on his shoulder and heard a man say, "Hey, kid, there's somebody trying to get your attention!"

Young Howller went into his mother's arms and wept for at least a minute. His father reached past his mother and touched him briefly on the forehead, as if blessing him, and then gave his shoulder a squeeze. When he was able to talk, Tim Howller asked his mother what had happened to them. They, as near as they could remember, had been pushed out by the crowd, though they had fought to get to him, and had run up Broadway after they found themselves in the street because King Kong had appeared. They had managed to get back to the theater, had not been able to locate Tim, and had walked back to the Empire State Building.

"What happened to Uncle Nate?" Tim said.

Uncle Nate, his mother said, had caught up with them on Fifth Avenue and just now was trying to get past the police cordon into the building so he could check on Aunt Thea.

"She must be all right!" young Howller said. "The ape climbed up her side of the building, but she could easily get away from him, her apartment's so big!"

"Well, yes," his father had said. "But if she went to bed with her headache, she would've been right next to the window. But don't worry. If she'd been hurt, we'd know it. And maybe she wasn't even home."

Young Tim had asked him what he meant by that, but his father had only shrugged.

The three of them stood in the front line of the crowd, waiting for Uncle Nate to bring news of Aunt Thea, even though they weren't really worried about her, and waiting to see what happened to Kong. Mayor Jimmy Walker showed up and conferred with the officials. Then the governor himself, Franklin Delano Roosevelt, arrived with much noise of siren and motorcycle. A minute later a big black limousine with flashing red lights and a siren pulled up. Standing on the running board was a giant with bronze hair and strange-looking gold-flecked eyes. He jumped off the running board and strode up to the mayor, governor, and police commissioner and talked briefly with them. Tim Howller asked the man next to him what the giant's name was, but the man replied that he didn't know because he was from out of town also. The giant finished talking and strode up to the crowd, which opened for him as if it were the Red Sea and he were Moses, and he had no trouble at all getting through the police cordon. Tim then asked the man on the right of his parents if he knew the yellow-eyed giant's name. This man, tall and thin, was with a beautiful woman dressed up in an evening gown and a mink coat. He turned his head when Tim called to him and presented a hawklike face and eyes that burned so brightly that Tim wondered if he took dope. Those eyes also told him that here was a man who asked questions, not one who gave answers. Tim didn't repeat his question, and a moment later the man said, in a whispering voice that still carried a long distance, "Come on, Margo. I've work to do." And the two melted into the crowd.

Mr. Howller told Jill about the two men, and she said, "What about them, Grandpa?"

"I don't really know," he said. "Often I've wondered… well, never mind. Whoever they were, they're irrelevant to what happened to King Kong. But I'll say one thing about New York— you sure see a lot of strange characters there."

Young Howller had expected that the mess would quickly be cleaned up. And it was true that the Sanitation Department had sent a big truck with a big crane and a number of men with hoses, scoop shovels, and brooms. But a dozen people at least stopped the cleanup almost before it began. Carl Denham wanted no one to touch the body except the taxidermists he had called in. If he couldn't exhibit a live Kong, he would exhibit a dead one. A colonel from Roosevelt Field claimed the body, and, when asked why the Air Force wanted it, could not give an explanation. Rather, he refused to give one, and it was not until an hour later that a phone call from the White House forced him to reveal the real reason. A general wanted the skin for a trophy because Kong was the only ape ever shot down in aerial combat.

A lawyer for the owners of the Empire State Building appeared with a claim for possession of the body. His clients wanted reimbursement for the damage done to the building.

A representative of the transit system wanted Kong's body so it could be sold to help pay for the damage the ape had done to the Sixth Avenue Elevated.

The owner of the theater from which Kong had escaped arrived with his lawyer and announced he intended to sue Denham for an amount which would cover the sums he would have to pay to those who were inevitably going to sue him.

The police ordered the body seized as evidence in the trial for involuntary manslaughter and criminal negligence in which Denham and the theater owner would be defendants in due process.

The manslaughter charges were later dropped, but Denham did serve a year before being paroled. On being released, he was killed by a religious fanatic, a native brought back by the second expedition to Kong's island. He was, in fact, the witch doctor. He had murdered Denham because Denham had abducted and slain his god, Kong.

His Majesty's New York consul showed up with papers which proved that Kong's island was in British waters. Therefore, Denham had no right to anything removed from the island without permission of His Majesty's government.

Denham was in a lot of trouble. But the worst blow of all was to come next day. He would be handed notification that he was being sued by Ann Redman. She wanted compensation to the tune of ten million dollars for various physical indignities and injuries suffered during her two abductions by the ape, plus the mental anguish these had caused her. Unfortunately for her, Denham went to prison without a penny in his pocket, and she dropped the suit. Thus, the public never found out exactly what the "physical indignities and injuries" were, but this did not keep it from making many speculations. Ann Redman also sued John Driscoll, though for a different reason. She claimed breach of promise. Driscoll, interviewed by a newsman, made his famous remark that she should have been suing Kong, not him. This convinced most of the public that what it had suspected had indeed happened. Just how it could have been done was difficult to explain, but the public had never lacked wiseacres who would not only attempt the difficult but would not draw back even at the impossible.

Actually, Mr. Howller thought, the deed was not beyond possibility. Take an adult male gorilla who stood six feet high and weighed three hundred and fifty pounds. According to Swiss zoo director Ernst Lang, he would have a full erection only two inches long. How did Professor Lang know this? Did he enter the cage during a mating and measure the phallus? Not very likely. Even the timid and amiable gorilla would scarcely submit to this type of handling in that kind of situation. Never mind. Professor Lang said it was so, and so it must be. Perhaps he used a telescope with gradations across the lens like those on a submarine's periscope. In any event, until someone entered the cage and slapped down a ruler during the action, Professor Lang's word would have to be taken as the last word.

By mathematical extrapolation, using the square-cube law, a gorilla twenty feet tall would have an erect penis about twenty-one inches long. What the diameter would be was another guess and perhaps a vital one, for Ann Redman anyway. Whatever anyone else thought about the possibility, Kong must have decided that he would never know unless he tried. Just how well he succeeded, only he and his victim knew, since the attempt would have taken place before Driscoll and Denham got to the observation tower and before the searchlight beams centered on their target.

But Ann Redman must have told her lover, John Driscoll, the truth, and he turned out not to be such an understanding man after all.

"What're you thinking about, Grandpa?"

Mr. Howller looked at the screen. The Roadrunner had been succeeded by the Pink Panther, who was enduring as much pain and violence as the poor old coyote.

"Nothing," he said. "I'm just watching the Pink Panther with you."

"But you didn't say what happened to King Kong," she said.

"Oh," he said, "we stood around until dawn, and then the big shots finally came to some sort of agreement. The body just couldn't be left there much longer, if for no other reason than that it was blocking traffic. Blocking traffic meant that business would be held up. And lots of people would lose lots of money. And so Kong's body was taken away by the Police Department, though it used the Sanitation Department's crane, and it was kept in an icehouse until its ownership could be thrashed out."

"Poor Kong."

"No," he said, "not poor Kong. He was dead and out of it."

"He went to heaven?"

"As much as anybody," Mr. Howller said.

"But he killed a lot of people, and he carried off that nice girl. Wasn't he bad?"

"No, he wasn't bad. He was an animal, and he didn't know the difference between good and evil. Anyway, even if he'd been human, he would've been doing what any human would have done."

"What do you mean, Grandpa?"

"Well, if you were captured by people only a foot tall and carried off to a far place and put in a cage, wouldn't you try to escape? And if these people tried to put you back in, or got so scared that they tried to kill you right now, wouldn't you step on them?"

"Sure, I'd step on them, Grandpa."

"You'd be justified, too. And King Kong was justified. He was only acting according to the dictates of his instincts."

"What?"

"He was an animal, and so he can't be blamed, no matter what he did. He wasn't evil. It was what happened around Kong that was evil."

"What do you mean?" Jill said.

"He brought out the bad and the good in the people."

But mostly bad, he thought, and he encouraged Jill to forget about Kong and concentrate on the Pink Panther. And as he looked at the screen, he saw it through tears. Even after forty-two years, he thought, tears. This was what the fall of Kong had meant to him.

The crane had hooked the corpse and lifted it up. And there were two flattened-out bodies under Kong; he must have dropped them onto the sidewalk on his way up and then fallen on them from the tower. But how explain the nakedness of the corpses of the man and the woman?

The hair of the woman was long and, in a small area not covered by blood, yellow. And part of her face was recognizable.

Young Tim had not known until then that Uncle Nate had returned from looking for Aunt Thea. Uncle Nate gave a long wailing cry that sounded as if he, too, were falling from the top of the Empire State Building.

A second later young Tim Howller was wailing. But where Uncle Nate's was the cry of betrayal, and perhaps of revenge satisfied, Tim's was both of betrayal and of grief for the death of one he had passionately loved with a thirteen-year-old's love, for one whom the thirteen-year-old in him still loved.

"Grandpa, are there any more King Kongs?"

"No," Mr. Howller said. To say yes would force him to try to explain something that she could not understand. When she got older, she would know that every dawn saw the death of the old Kong and the birth of the new.

WOLD NEWTON PREHISTORY

THE KHOKARSA SERIES

KWASIN AND THE BEAR GOD

BY PHILIP JOSÉ FARMER
AND CHRISTOPHER PAUL CAREY

In this tale of the ancient African civilization of Khokarsa, the mad giant Kwasin has returned to the island of his birth after eight long years of exile and has just escaped from the dungeons of the tyrannical King Minruth. Kwasin is a cousin to the hero Hadon, whose adventures are told in the first two novels of the Khokarsa trilogy, *Hadon of Ancient Opar* (Titan Books, 2013) and *Flight to Opar*. Both Hadon and Kwasin are descendants of Sahhindar, the Gray-Eyed Archer God, who is also the Khokarsan god of plants, bronze, and Time. Readers of Farmer's Wold Newton novel *Time's Last Gift* (Titan Books, 2012) will likely recognize from the author's many hints that Sahhindar is an alias of the time traveler John Gribardsun, who, under yet another alias, was also a certain well-known jungle lord of the nineteenth and twentieth centuries. More importantly, Sahhindar/Gribardsun is a prominent member of the Wold Newton Family, whose genetic relationship to Hadon and Kwasin goes a long way to explaining their almost superhuman abilities and deeds. What follows is one of Kwasin's stranger adventures, which fits chronologically between the first and second chapters of the concluding novel of the Khokarsa trilogy, *The Song of Kwasin*, by Farmer and Christopher Paul Carey.

When Kwasin crawled from the tiny fishing boat and began hauling it up the sandy slope, he did not know he trod upon the City of the Snake. If he had, he thought later, he might have rowed back out to sea as quickly as his great muscles could carry him, eager to face the boatload of Minruth's sailors headlong rather than risk disturbing the demons and spirits rumored to haunt this place.

But then again, he was Kwasin, defiler of the Temple of Kho. Even the fact that the Goddess had cursed the grounds of these timeworn ruins might not have been enough to give him pause. Still, in his heart, he had never forsaken Kho, even when the oracle had cast him from civilization and doomed him to exile in the Wild Lands. And secretly he knew he could not escape the superstitions of his people. Though Kwasin was as brave and free a spirit as any that walked the land, the folktales instilled in him during childhood sometimes spoke with a voice louder than that of his adult rationality.

By the time he had hidden the boat amid the thorny flora that grew along the seaside cliffs, Kwasin was already beginning to have misgivings about his chosen landing site. Looking down the beach to his right he could make out in several places broad and flat outcroppings of granite emerging from the sand at irregular angles. Surely these were the remnants of an ancient quay. Farther up the slope shadows arched eastward from vague but towering projections vaulting slantingly in what seemed an unnatural fashion out of the uneven landscape. The shadows were darker emanations within the penumbra of the mountains that rose sharply from the site's western periphery.

The mountains were the Saasanadar. In order to get to Dythbeth he would either have to go around them by boat along the northern coast of the island or head deeper inland and pass to their south. Both routes carried great risk. Minruth's forces were everywhere, including on the waters at the mouth of the Gulf of Gahete. Only minutes ago Kwasin had barely escaped the notice of one of the king's galleys. Or he hoped he had. The bireme had appeared just as Kwasin was rounding the narrow cape that curved into the sea just east of the beach where he had then landed.

His boat now safely hidden, Kwasin sprinted up the slope and into the shadows. Here the land leveled out, although dark, barrowlike mounds rose in places out of the grassy mud and all around him jutted the immense, shadow-spawning projections. A breeze was blowing steadily from the northwest in advance of a storm front. In the distance, lightning flashed, followed a few moments later by a deep booming.

A closer examination of the projections quickly confirmed his suspicions. The giant outcroppings were not natural formations but rather great monoliths of ancient construction, and the drawings carved upon them, though but faintly visible in twilight's shadow, only heightened his fears about the place.

The symbols on the stones did not resemble modern hieroglyphs. Rather, they were crude, pitted images, graven by primitive hands and likely dating to an era long before Awines invented his syllabary. Some of the petroglyphs depicted Kho as the Bird-Headed Mother; that is, as a steatopygic and large-breasted woman with the head of a fish-eagle. Many of the monuments, however, bore another image: that of a long-fanged serpent coiling tightly as if its deathly embrace meant to draw blood from stone. Everywhere the serpent carvings were surrounded by swarms of spiral pictographs.

He recalled the scribe Hinokly once remarking upon the ancient spiral found in the early stonework of the Klemreskom, the Fish-Eagle People who first populated the island of Khokarsa. The scribe had said Awines had adapted the symbol into the Khokarsan syllabary to represent Kho, in correspondence to the ancient glyph's original meaning. Then Hinokly had laughed darkly and said that Awines had not wanted the glyph in the syllabary to match too closely the primitive image, so he had altered it, for it was said that he who gazed too long at the deasil spiral would become as the living dead, lost for all eternity enraptured by Great Kho's terrible beauty.

Kwasin had scoffed at the latter notion, but he told the scribe he had seen similar spiral pictographs carved into the cliffs near where he had lived along the southern sea as a youth. Hinokly had told him the images were doubtless carved there by the aborigines long before the priestess-heroine Lupoeth first explored the region, and their existence so far south was proof that the symbol was ancient indeed.

Kwasin shuddered in the cool shadow of the black stones that rose about him. Were the carvings of the Goddess and clockwise-spinning gyres warnings from Kho to avoid this place or else risk facing the snake demons said to inhabit the ruins?

He did not know, but gazing up at the whorls and slithering creatures decorating the age-old monoliths, he was sure of one thing—he indeed stood among the moldering ruins of fabled Miterisi, the City of the Snake.

Kwasin started as a parrot screeched and flew out at him from behind one of the great columns of stone. He shook his head as if awakening from a trance and forced himself to turn away from the spirals. How long had he been standing here? He could not say for sure, but the scribe's superstitious yarn about getting lost in the vortex of Kho's ancient symbol had apparently played upon his ingrained fears about the site.

He cursed. Looking back to the beach, he saw two sailors emerging from a skiff in the shallows. Now they were dragging the craft toward shore. A second skiff—empty—already lay upon the beach, its crew nowhere in sight.

Since he had begun gazing at the stones, the temperature had dropped several degrees and the breeze from the approaching storm now blew with increasing force. If it had not been for the bird, how much longer would he have stood there unknowing?

Kwasin dropped the thought from his mind and slipped behind the nearest monolith, swearing silently.

For a brief moment he had again felt drawn to stare at the whorls.

He crouched behind the enormous stone and listened. Other than the occasional parrot's chittering caw, the sea breeze, the occasional clap of thunder, and the surf lapping in the distance, he could hear nothing. He slipped the leather thong of his ax from around his shoulder and relished the comfortable feel of the weapon's half-petrified antelope-bone handle in his grip. Then he peered from behind the stone.

A sword thrust violently upward from the shadows, sheening in a flash from the heavens. If the lightning had not illuminated the blade, Kwasin might have missed it amid the rapidly diminishing twilight.

He swung his ax. Earthly iron clanked against the meteoritic iron of Kwasin's weapon. His attacker, whom Kwasin could make out only vaguely in the dimness of the gully below him, grunted at the blow. Overcome by fury, Kwasin leaped downward.

If his attacker had also held a sword in his off-hand, it might have been Kwasin's final action. But the man didn't, and instead of meeting instant death, Kwasin kneed his assailant in the abdomen with the full force of his downward leap. The man sprawled on his back in the sloping ditch, momentarily stunned, while Kwasin finished him off with a single blow of his ax.

Something whirred past Kwasin's head as he rose from the corpse. A loud crack came from the monolith above him and small bits of stone showered down upon his head and naked shoulders. Then Kwasin was running for the next monolith. Though the monument he had just jumped from behind was nearer cover, it was not in his nature to remain on the defensive, even against an opponent wielding a sling. He would face his attackers head-on.

Kwasin almost stumbled mid-stride. For an instant, he thought he had seen a naked female figure standing tall upon one of the stone monuments, lit up in the fleeting brilliance of another heavenly flash. The figure had held forth what looked like a crooked, snake-headed staff. Or it could have been a real snake. He could not be sure. The whole thing might have been a false apparition, conjured in his mind by the unnerving images of Kho and the coiling pythons upon the tall, black stones.

He made it to the monument but paused only briefly behind it. Then he was running again, this time toward the shore, jumping over the rocks and small boulders that littered the scape between the barrowlike mounds. If any sling-stones whirred past him, he did not notice.

Cold rain sprinkled Kwasin's face as he ran. A moment later, the darkened heavens clamored with fury, and in the next, a deluge of hail and sleet assailed him in what was surely a bad omen. The sungod Resu—who, in his rage at his mother and ex-lover Kho, had sided with King Minruth in the bloody civil war—was also the god of rain.

A javelin hurtled at Kwasin out of the dark but its deadly point missed him, thudding into the muddy ground before him. Kwasin jumped over the weapon and veered to his left toward where he judged the javelin had come.

Then he saw the thrower emerge from behind a mound not twenty strides away, winding up his sling for a throw.

Kwasin looked for cover, but seeing none, roared in competition with the heavens' din and charged the slinger. Kwasin knew it was a desperate act, but maybe the sight of the furious seven-foot-tall giant charging forward would cause the slinger to flee or to fumble his throw.

The tactic had worked for Kwasin in the past, but the slinger who confronted him now seemed frustratingly cool and levelheaded. He continued to whirl his sling as Kwasin closed upon him, tightening the revolutions of the weapon's cradle to compensate for the changing proximity of his target.

Blood drained from Kwasin's face. He would take the full brunt of the projectile at close range.

Suddenly, the man reeled. The sling-stone shot out of its cradle, flying off harmlessly into the night.

Kwasin ran forward and examined the man, who had pitched forward into the slick, gravelly mud, facedown and unmoving. For a moment, Kwasin saw no wound upon the man. Then, running his hand over the man's back in the freezing rain, he felt something protruding from the skin: a thistle-fletched bamboo dart, impaled deeply.

He grabbed the fallen man by his long hair, lifted up his head, and placed a hand before the man's nose and mouth. Though frigid rain pelted Kwasin's palm, he felt warm, shallow breaths upon it.

The dart was doubtless tipped with a paralytic.

Kwasin dropped the man's face into the mud and looked about. Perhaps he had not imagined the woman atop the monolith after all.

After dispatching the man, Kwasin got up and again made for the shore. This time, however, he proceeded at a cautious jog, his roving eyes seeking to penetrate the gloom of night and storm.

Kwasin arrived at the shore to find it unoccupied except for the two empty skiffs. Grinning darkly, he went to work with his ax smashing great holes in the bottoms of the boats, all the while keeping watch inland, though he could no longer see farther than a few yards in the storm-wracked night. Finished with his sabotage, he looked out to sea, wondering what had become of the bireme that had landed the party of marines on shore. Doubtless she was having a hard time of it on the storm-lashed waves, and he could only hope her captain had taken the vessel back out to sea to avoid being driven onto the shallows.

A man's throaty cry turned Kwasin's attention away from the sea and back inland. Still thwarted by darkness, he took off rapidly toward the ruins and the direction of the shout, his great ax held ready in both hands.

When he came to the top of the slope he could just make out the form of a woman in the murk of the ruins ahead. Her long, dark hair whipped wildly in the wind and in her hands she held a long tube. In a crouched stance, she crept forward toward a crumpled form several paces before her on the ground. The form could have been an outcropping for all Kwasin could tell, but in context of the cry he had heard only moments earlier, the scene told it all: the woman had struck down a marine with her blowgun and she was quietly advancing to ascertain whether her dart had fully immobilized its target.

Then, to his horror, he perceived amid the shadows a dark, man-sized figure moving up just behind the woman. Kwasin bellowed a warning but it was too late. The woman screamed as the shadowy figure enveloped her. The bamboo tube of the blowgun clunked hollowly as the woman flailed it against an adjoining pillar in an attempt to repel her attacker. Then the tube clattered to the stony ground. The woman grunted as if struck and went limp.

Kwasin was already running into the ruins at the first glimpse of the woman's attacker, but by the time he arrived at the spot, he found the man had slipped into the shadows, apparently dragging the woman with him. For a moment, Kwasin bent low and looked for prints in the muddy ground, but the black night made the endeavor impossible. He got up and began running frantically from monument to monument, rapidly circling behind the stones in search of the marine and his captive.

As Kwasin stepped momentarily out of the rain beneath the protection of a half-toppled monolith, something cold and soft slithered across his ankle. He froze. Looking down he saw a grotesque and bloated wormlike form glide across the black ground, its pale skin patterned evenly with darker diamond-shaped markings. The priestess's python, free of its mistress, must have sought out the relative dryness provided by the vaulting pillar.

He shuddered, thinking of his mother's death by snake bite when he had been but ten years old. While the serpent that had struck and killed his mother had not been a python, the pictographs on the surrounding monuments unnerved him. That, and the dreams that had assailed him since his return from the Wild Lands—horrendous visions of his mother's death, played over and over until he thought he might go mad. What did they mean? Might the nightmares presage his death in the ruins of cursed Miterisi?

But adversity, rather than daunting him, more often served Kwasin as a catalyst to overcome what he considered self-weakness. And so, biting back his revulsion, the giant leaned over, lifted up the snake, and looped it over his great shoulders. Despite the cause of his mother's death, he held no deep fear of snakes. It was only Goddess-forsaken Miterisi that now unsettled him in this regard. Following his mother's death, he had frequently forced himself to handle serpents, much to his cousin Hadon's dismay, who awoke all too often to find a slithering companion in his bed.

This last thought brought a grin to Kwasin's face, and thus distracted, he almost stumbled into a narrow opening in the ground that he had overlooked in the dark. A fortuitous lightning flash, however, prevented the accident, and also revealed a distinct handprint in the mud that ringed the stone-lined, circular hole. The marine had taken his captive down into the underground chamber—perhaps an ancient storage bin for grain or some other harvest—in the hope that he could wait out the giant who sought to slay him. The man had apparently taken the woman as a fail-safe—if Kwasin cornered him, the man would threaten to kill his hostage.

For a moment, Kwasin considered his options. He could

move one of the small boulders that littered the site overtop the opening and thus seal the marine in a living tomb. This would require the least risk and effort on his part, but he would also be entombing the woman who had risked her life to defend him. He could also drop down into the hole, hoping the element of surprise would aid him. The marine, however, would be waiting below to dispatch Kwasin with his sword. But it was a third option that Kwasin found the most appealing.

Slowly and carefully, he knelt down beside the hole and uncoiled the python from his shoulders. As the snake slithered down an arm, Kwasin lowered the creature toward the opening in the ground. The python paused briefly; then, finding a ledge of rough stone cropping from one side of the hole's interior, it slid down into the earth.

A fleeting guilt tinged Kwasin's conscience as he thought of the woman, a guilt he quickly cast off. To live, one often had to do unpleasant things, even if that meant risking the life of a potential ally. Besides, he had seen the woman handle the snake when she stood illuminated by lightning atop the stone pillar— the python appeared to be her familiar. Had he not also seen the oracle at Dythbeth seemingly command her sacred serpent before his very eyes upon the occasion of the pronouncement of his exile to the Wild Lands? The priestesses of Kho—and this woman was certainly one—seemed to have an affinity with their ophidian pets. Surely the woman's own snake would not harm her.

But doubt returned as Kwasin stood above the hole, the rain running in small waterfalls off the colossal column of black stone. For a long while he stood there waiting, until the fury of the storm abated to a gentle drizzle and he began to wonder if the man had indeed crawled into the pit. Then, at last, it came—a choked-off male scream of utter terror.

Kwasin grinned. His inspired decision had been the right one. After all, in cursed Miterisi, was it not best to ally with the local snake god than to fight against him?

A short time later the woman crawled slowly up out of the dark mouth in the earth, the whitish-scaled, diamond-spotted python draped over her back and coiling around a shoulder and arm. She was indeed a priestess, as evidenced by the jewel-studded ceremonial dagger sheathed upon her shapely hip. She must have recovered the blade from her captor after the snake had strangled him.

Kwasin made the sign of Kho and the priestess's strong white teeth glistened back at him in the darkness.

He had been about to speak but stopped himself abruptly. Did the woman's canines look a little too long, a little too sharp? A little too… snakelike?

Kwasin frowned at himself, then laughed—a trifle nervously, he thought. No, it was just these cursed ruins playing tricks on his mind once more. When he saw the woman in the bright daylight he was sure she would appear as ravishingly and humanly beautiful as the darkness of the night hinted.

"What are you looking at?" the priestess said. "We must hurry. Now that the storm's abated, the shipmates of the sailors we've killed will likely come ashore looking for their men. Let's go!"

The woman reached out for his hand, but Kwasin hesitated. When the woman had spoken, had he merely imagined that her tongue flicked out from between her luscious lips in a most unmistakably reptilian fashion?

Kwasin frowned again. Then, uttering a half-facetious—and half-serious—prayer to Kho, he took her cold, tiny hand in his own warm, giant one and headed out into the night.

Kwasin awoke the next day in the little temple that rose from the center of the sacred grove of the pythoness. Through the little window beside his bed of sleeping furs, he could hear the gentle tinkling of the creek that wound around the temple and through the forest. With a heavy sigh of contentment, he flung aside the furs, sat up, and regarded the lithe form of the priestess that lay sleeping beside him.

The sight of the naked woman aroused him, but not enough for him to wake her for more lovemaking. Although the priestess was of uncommon beauty, that beauty also was of uncommon strangeness. The darkness had not deceived him about her teeth—her canines had indeed been filed to points resembling those of a serpent's fangs. He lightly touched the numerous scrapes on his shoulders and chest where she had raked him with those teeth while in the throes of passion.

A chill ran through him as he recalled his night with Madekha. Her movements during foreplay had been eerily snakelike, and though she had kissed him as lovingly as any warm-blooded woman, he could not mistake the soft hissing between kisses. But then, he should not have been surprised—what did one expect from the high priestess of the Spotted

Python Totem? And he could not say he did not enjoy himself at the time.

The woman reached out to pull the furs back over herself, then groaned lightly and opened her eyes with a silent yawn. Seeing Kwasin, she smiled.

"Sinuneth welcomes you this morning, O Giant Warrior." The priestess now looked past Kwasin to the pile of furs and linens piled up at the head of the oak-framed bed.

Kwasin's skin crawled as he slowly turned his gaze to where she looked. Then he jumped up out of the bed, cursing loudly.

The priestess's diamond-spotted familiar glided out from the deep mass of coverings to coil caressingly around its mistress's outstretched arm.

The woman laughed and said, "You did not seem to mind Sinuneth's company last night."

"You mean the snake was in our bed while we—" Kwasin bellowed another curse and began donning his lion-skin kilt.

"I don't advise you to leave the temple by daylight." Madekha let the snake slither from her arm and back onto the bed, then arose and continued. "If a worshiper from the village sees you, it might get back to T'agoqo and his jealousies will be all the more enflamed. Though he and his fellow priests have thus far resisted King Minruth's blasphemies, I hold little faith they will continue to do so. T'agoqo has only maintained a thin façade of faithfulness to Kho because he desires me and I have dangled out the thread of hope. He knows he will never have me if he publicly turns against the cause of the Goddess, but if he learns I am harboring a legendary criminal and that I have invited him into my bed…"

Madekha arose and rang a small iron bell, and before long two young, raven-haired priestesses entered the chamber. "See to his needs," she ordered them, and then regarded Kwasin.

"We have much to discuss, O Kwasin. You are a criminal, exiled by the oracle at Dythbeth for crimes against a daughter of Kho, and we must address that fact before we speak any further. But we are also in a Time of Troubles, and even the Goddess must seek aid where she can find it." She motioned to the priestesses to escort Kwasin from the chamber, but as he passed through the doorway she called out to him.

"Behave yourself with my priestesses," she said as he turned back. "They will clean you up and take care of your desires, but if you harm them in any way, you will awake in Sisisken's dark house before you even know what has struck you."

Kwasin smiled innocently and traced the sign of Kho with his fingers, but deep inside he felt troubled at the snakewoman's words.

A little over two hours later, Kwasin met with Madekha beneath a portico behind the temple overlooking the well-tended grove to Terisikokori, the local pythoness goddess. The storm had passed and the strong, late morning sun shone down through the trees, causing the leaves that had blown to the ground during the previous night's torrent to glisten with a golden light. Already the day's oppressive heat fought to break through the shade of the trees.

Above, Kwasin heard the cry of *datoekem*, then spied one of the large, white-winged gulls arcing overhead through the trees. It reminded him of the proximity to the shore of the temple and the adjoining village of Kaarkor. Madekha had told him the sea-girt cliffs of the Saasanadar lay not a quarter mile north of the hallowed grove.

With a nod, Madekha dismissed her attendant, who had come with news of Khowot's recent eruption and the devastation it had once again wrought upon the capital. It seemed that Minruth blamed the disaster on the prisoners who had just escaped from his prison, proclaiming their breakout had precipitated a great shouting match between Kho and Resu. But though the prisoners had made their getaway, Minruth asserted that Resu had won out in the end, for had not the god of the sun and rain quickly brought the blessed showers that saved much of the city from the fires that threatened to destroy it? Still, Resu was angry that the escapees had succeeded, and if they were not caught soon, the sungod would punish the mortals in the capital for their incompetence. Further, Minruth had sworn vengeance on any city, village, or individual that came to the aid of Kwasin and the other escapees. The priestess was taking a great risk by harboring him.

"You look refreshed," Madekha said, not unpleasantly, though her face betrayed worry at her attendant's news. "But then you will need to be, for you have much work ahead of you in the days to come, O Kwasin."

"It is not my intention to stay here, O Priestess," Kwasin said. "I can't tarry here and fight your battles. Those I have yet to face lie westward, on the road to Dythbeth, where I intend to clear my name."

Madekha smiled grimly. "There is truth in what you say, but do you think you can just walk into Dythbeth and demand forgiveness from Queen Weth?"

Kwasin said nothing. He had not truly thought out his plans for accomplishing his goal once he arrived at his birth city. Not that he had had the time to do so since his flight from the capital.

"But the oracle did pronounce that you would be permitted to return to the land when Kho so decrees," Madekha went on. "I, of course, am not in a position to speak for Kho on this matter, but that is not to say I cannot aid you. After all, you saved my life in the old city, although it is true I would have been in no danger had it not been for you. But it was my decision to enter the ruins of Miterisi all the same, prompted as I was to go there by a vision from the sacred pythoness herself, and I don't regret slaying the followers of Minruth's new order. I owe you... well, if not a favor, then an opportunity."

As the priestess spoke, Kwasin had the sinking feeling he was about to be pulled into a business of which he wanted no part. What she said next convinced him of it.

"Much has changed across the land even since you returned from your exile and were imprisoned. Minruth's profane revolt has spread to the outermost corners of the empire. While it is true that Dythbeth yet holds out against the sun worshipers, the cities and towns all around her are falling fast. And though the rural areas and mountain villages remain in large part stolid against the ambitions of Minruth and his wicked priests, that is not to say they have gone untouched. One such village—profaned by the blasphemers, and very dear to me for reasons I will soon explain—lies in the path of your journey westward across the island: the village of Q'okwoqo."

Kwasin nodded in the Khokarsan negative, feeling as if one of the *nukaar*, the long-armed hairy half-men of the trees, had reached down out of the jungle, taken hold of him in its viselike grip, and pulled him up into its dark abode. The woman meant to trap him with her so-called opportunity.

"I have no interest," Kwasin said, "in the age-old struggle between the priestesses of Kho and the priests of Resu. Kho helps him who helps himself! She cares nothing for the mortals who merely get in Her way or who attribute their own self-serving prattle to Her divine lips!"

"Hear me out, Kwasin!" Madekha snapped. "Do you forget I can turn you in to the priests in the village if you displease me?"

He recognized the desperation in the woman's voice as well as her conviction. She would not hesitate to execute her threat if he crossed her. Besides, he was desperate as well. If she could truly help him make amends with the Great Mother at Dythbeth, could he resist her offer, no matter the task given him?

"Go on," he said at last, but he did not hide his displeasure.

"Only two days ago," Madekha continued, "my cousin Tswethphe—an acolyte serving the village priestess—arrived from Q'okwoqo. She reports that a small band of soldiers has taken the village, and that the priestess escaped into the wilderness with only my cousin by her side as the soldiers struck. The priestess sent Tswethphe to neighboring Dythbeth to ask for succor, but King Roteka is too busy fighting off Minruth's legions to be bothered with the troubles of a small mountain village.

And so my cousin left Dythbeth and crossed the island to throw herself upon my mercy."

"Why does this backwoods village concern you, priestess? Your cousin is safe in your arms, and Q"okwoqo is but an insignificant abode of mountain-dwelling yokels." Kwasin had heard of the rustic mountain village, having lived out his early years in Dythbeth at the foothills of the Saasamaro. He could think of no strategic importance the place might bear upon the struggle against the sun worshipers.

"Alas, I do not disagree with your assessment of Q"okwoqo, but my twin sister, Adythne, the priestess of the village, is as stubborn-headed and dogged as Kopoethken herself. She will not leave her village to the blasphemers and says she will singlehandedly launch a campaign of guerrilla warfare against the soldiers if no one comes to her aid. She will get herself killed!"

Madekha, her face flushed with emotion, paced the granite blocks that composed the portico's floor, but Kwasin only roared with laughter.

"I like the sound of your sister! Are you sure you want to trust me with her?"

The priestess of the sacred pythoness glared at him, the points of her sharpened teeth whitening her otherwise sensuous crimson lips.

"What would you have me do?" Kwasin offered when she said nothing. "Bring her back to you, against her will?"

"No, she would have none of it. I know her too well. Even if you tied her up and carried her here, she would only fly back to her village at the earliest opportunity. You must aid her in her quest. That is the only way. It's a fool's errand, I know, but what other choice have you? If you agree to help her, I shall whisper into Queen Weth's ear of your efforts to free Q'okwoqo, as well as your act of heroism in defending a daughter of Kho in the ruins of Miterisi—both deeds which will go a long way toward forgiveness of your crimes against the Goddess. But if you refuse to help my sister, I may tell Weth another story, of how in a murderous rage you sought to slay me with your ax amid the ruins. And lest you think I carry no weight with the queen, know that I trained with Weth in the college of priestesses. She will listen to me."

The woman was clearly distraught. And as desperate as her sister if she thought Kwasin could liberate the village from a band of disciplined and entrenched soldiers with an ax as his only ally. Kwasin did not know whether to cry out in laughter or outrage at her opportunity-turned-threat.

"Why not send some of your own men from Kaarkor to help your sister?" Kwasin countered. "Surely some of the villagers remain faithful to you. The priests cannot have corrupted your entire flock."

"Yesterday I was weighing just that," Madekha said, "but concluded that to weaken my forces now, when T'agoqo is readying his own forces to strike, would be foolhardy. And then Terisikokori visited me in my sleep and told me to go to the ruins. And lo, there I found you, perhaps the greatest warrior in all the land! Next to your cousin Hadon, that is, the hero of the Great Games. Perhaps if you are too cowardly to help me, I should seek him out and ask him for help. He escaped from prison with you, did he not? Surely he is somewhere nearby and such a champion would not shirk the challenge I set before him."

Though he knew the woman was manipulating him, it was too much for Kwasin. "Good luck with my cousin!" he roared. "He flew like a frightened hare before Minruth's soldiers while I remained behind to slay a whole company! Had I not, then your beloved queen, Awineth, would have perished. Tell me who is the greatest hero of the land!"

"Then you accept the challenge?"

Before he could stop himself, Kwasin found himself shouting out his prideful assent.

Madekha smiled like a sly snake. "Good," she said. "In any case, I have a feeling you will find the village of Q'okwoqo more palatable than you have found Kaarkor and the moldering ruins of Miterisi. The villagers there worship Old Father Nakendar, a great *klakoru*[4] rumored to have made its lair in the caves near the village for over four hundred years. Perhaps the Bear God himself led you to me so that you would journey to the village and help his children. And besides, the Q'okwoqo are of your totem—the Klakordeth—so you cannot treat my... request to aid them as some distasteful chore. It is your duty to help your Bear brothers and sisters!"[5]

Kwasin did not argue with her. The sooner he was on his way and far away from the snakewoman the better. By now, his

---

[4] "Cave bear" in Khokarsan, or literally, "great devourer of honey."
[5] Given the reputation of the Q'okwoqo as bear worshipers, it may be no coincidence that the name of their tribe and village is strikingly reminiscent of "Ngoloko," another name for the legendary East African cryptid known as the Nandi Bear (note that the Khokarsan character transcribed as the letter "q" is pronounced roughly as the "ng" in the English "sing").

pride had settled and he had no intention of undertaking her charge, though when she summoned a priestess to bring her a map showing the location of Q"okwoqo and proceeded to spread it out before them on the stone floor, he knelt beside her and nodded as if he were studying his mission in earnest. When Madekha asked him to memorize a passphrase she said would convey to her sister that Kwasin was her emissary, he did so as if it were the most important thing in the world. Observing that he seemed to be taking his newfound mission so solemnly, the woman beamed.

He smiled back at her widely. Besides being the greatest hero of the land, Kwasin was also a passable actor.

And so it was that as the sun fell behind the western mountains and Kwasin prepared for his departure, the village priest, T'agoqo, arrived at the temple to call on the high priestess of the sacred pythoness. Madekha immediately ordered Kwasin into a back chamber in the temple. Only moments later Kwasin heard violent shouting erupt on the other side of the door. Then, as he almost anticipated, he heard the temple's outer doors bang open and the sound of many feet marching into the building.

Kwasin grabbed his ax and flung wide the door, which opened onto the temple's central chamber. Before him lay chaos. Two temple guards lay dead before the great door on the opposite side of the chamber. T'agoqo stood before Madekha, whose back was to the altar. Madekha's ceremonial dagger gleamed in the torchlight as she thrust it at the priest, who cried out, looking like a betrayed lover, as the blade sank into his scarlet-blossoming robes. Behind them came a group of twelve sailors, recognizable from the fish-eagle insignia of the Khokarsan navy painted on the faces of their small round shields. They must have been from the galley that hunted Kwasin, having provided T'agoqo and his priests with all the reason they needed to at last make their move against the followers of the Goddess.

Kwasin was about to hurl himself into the fray when a rapid succession of muted and airy thwocks sounded in the chamber. Six of the sailors reeled, then crumpled unmoving to the brightly colored mosaic floor. At seeing their comrades fall about them, and having witnessed the death of the priest, the remaining sailors fell into a disorderly retreat, practically tripping over themselves as they scrambled to get out of the temple.

Though Kwasin surveyed the room, he could see no sign to indicate who had blown the poisoned darts. The blowgun-wielding priestesses must have hidden themselves in secret chambers behind the walls, Madekha having likely outfitted the room in case of just such an attack upon the temple.

When he approached the altar, Kwasin found Madekha wiping her blade on the lifeless form of T'agoqo, something akin to satisfaction crossing her features. Then her expression turned to one of urgency.

"T'agoqo has sent his priests to the garrison at the foothills to summon more soldiers," she said, already leading him out of the altar room and through the two adjoining antechambers toward the temple steps. "He told me he did so this morning, so we have little time before they arrive. You must leave in haste if you are to avoid becoming entangled in Kaarkor's affairs." Seeing the unfulfilled battle lust smoldering in his eyes, she added, "As you told me earlier, it is not your desire to stay here and take up the local quarrels. I can take care of myself. Already my courier speeds to the village to bring aid. Much blood will be spilt, but the cause is not a lost one. Kho's faithful do marginally outnumber the followers of the sungod in the village, and they will obey the high priestess of Terisikokori without question. And many in the garrison have wives and lovers in the village—he who turns against the faithful will feel the sting of an angry pythoness!"

Kwasin did not doubt Madekha's conviction, but a mob of untrained country folk against a hardened Khokarsan garrison seemed like long odds on a bet. Still, he had a feeling the high priestess of Terisikokori would not be easily subdued, and further, she was right: he had no interest in remaining here among the People of the Snake. His destiny lay to the west in Dythbeth.

As they stood upon the temple steps, pinpoints of fiery torchlight flickered through the trees on the forest's edge, accompanied by the yapping of approaching dogs. It was the direction from which the soldiers would come if summoned from the garrison.

"Go, Kwasin, fly!" Madekha cried. "Fulfill your charge to me and you shall be rewarded! I have made arrangements—even should I be killed—to get word to Weth that will lobby on your behalf! Now go!"

Kwasin took hold of the woman and kissed her passionately. Then, grinning with the sense of adventure that had seized him, he sped into the forest in the opposite direction to the coming soldiers, bearing only the ax he had brought with him.

He intended to head inland and pass well south of the Saasanadar Mountains on his journey to Dythbeth, perhaps stealing a boat and accomplishing a lengthy stretch of his journey floating down the river that fed the island's great lake. But the presence of the soldiers to the south meant he would not be able to take the direct route. Right now his primary concern was getting the soldiers and their dogs off his trail.

With no plan other than to open as much distance as he could between himself and the enemy, Kwasin cut a beeline north through the grove of the sacred pythoness. His great strides carried him quickly through the knee-high grasses that grew between the dark trees, but the soldiers were closing on him. If they released the dogs from their harnesses, the unbridled canines would quickly catch up with him.

Then, abruptly, the forest ended and Kwasin found himself almost barreling headlong off the soaring granite cliffs into the sea. He reeled back, his wildly swaying arms spread behind him as he teetered on the precipice. Far below—though he could not see it—he heard the surf crashing violently against the cliffs.

Despite the coolness of the evening sea breeze, he broke out in a sweat. Without knowing it, he had almost entered Sisisken's dark queendom.

Behind him in the forest the hellacious barking of the dogs drew nearer. As far as he could see to either side, the moonlight revealed only a level span of the stark and unfaltering granite cliff top.

By the sound of the barking, he judged the dogs could only be three or four hundred yards off. And now he saw two, then six, then a dozen torches flaming in a wide arc across the forest—the soldiers had fanned out in their pursuit and were now almost upon him.

Swallowing back the sick feeling that rose from the pit of his stomach, Kwasin backed up several paces. Then, clutching his ax with all his oxlike might, he charged toward the cliff's granite rim, howling like a mad gorilla. He kicked off from the edge, and then the night air took him.

He fell for what seemed far too long. Perhaps dread Sisisken would yet entertain him in her dark house.

Just over a week later saw a very much alive Kwasin climbing the mid-reaches of the northeastern Saasamaro on the far western corner of the island. Tall though the cliffs above Kaarkor had been, the precipitous plunge had ended in what amounted to a perfect high dive as Kwasin parted the cold, dark waters with a precision that would have won him a gold crown and a standing ovation had he performed the feat in the Great Games.

The journey after that had not been easy. When Kwasin circled back inland and reached the wide river that flowed south of the Saasanadar, he had been unable to find a boat to steal and carry him on his way. So instead, with the ax given to him by the manling Paga, he had chopped down a great teak and, with a backbreaking and laborious effort he never wanted to repeat again, fashioned from it a crude dugout canoe. The craft, however, was barely riverworthy, and after many frustrating mishaps in which the boat capsized and he nearly drowned, Kwasin was forced to finally abandon his wayward creation and proceed on foot.

Not long after this, while passing south of the vast and waving emmer fields of Awamuka, Kwasin had spied a large contingent of soldiers marching out of the north. After some reconnoitering, he determined the assemblage belonged to Minruth's Sixth Army, the division representing the capital itself and the most battle-hardened of them all. Despite Madekha's threat to malign him to Queen Weth if he failed to aid her sister's village, Kwasin had intended to head south as the *kagaga* flies, taking the shortest route to Dythbeth by passing along the shores of the island's great lake. But seeing that the massive body of soldiers would quickly bisect his path, he had been forced to make haste and detour far to the west. Before long, the heights of the Saasamaro, blanketed in green swaths of cedar and pine, loomed before him.

Here he had thought of Madekha's sister and shrugged. He might as well check in on her village and ascertain the situation. Perhaps the soldiers had moved on and he could beseech Adythne to speak on his behalf to Weth—the priestess was, after all, of his totem, and he had saved her sister's life. More likely, the woman had died of starvation in the wilderness or been captured by Minruth's men. If he could, he would find out, to satisfy his curiosity if nothing else.

In any case, he wanted to see if the stories about the Bear God were true. Long ago, the young Kwasin had listened as his godfather, Pwamkhu, related to him the legend of Old Father Nakendar. It was said the Bear God had lived in his cave near Q''okwoqo for over four hundred years, brought to the island by the hero Rimasweth, whose soldiers had captured the enormous cave bear in the mountains near Kethna during their historic expedition to free the poetess Kwamim from Gokasis, the legendary pirate-king who once almost toppled the empire. Kwasin had believed the tale as a child, but he now knew better: the elders of his totem said bears lived no more than half the lifespan of the average human. But even so, there could be some shade of truth in the matter. Perhaps the original cave bear's descendants lived on in the isolated mountain area. Small, though rapidly dwindling, populations of brown bears were known to exist on the island, brought here long ago from the far northern mainland; it would not be impossible for the beast to have bred successfully with these bears, thereby producing progeny that kept the legend of Old Father Nakendar alive.

And so, recalling the maps Madekha had shown him of the region, Kwasin footed his way up the long arm of the northern Saasamaro that would, if he was not mistaken, eventually lead him to the valley of the Q''okwoqo. Passing higher and deeper into the mountains, he saw evidence of recent encroachment by soldiers: the charred remains of a cooking fire here, an ax-toppled cedar there. These could have been attributed to a band of local hunters, but the orderliness of the sites convinced him otherwise; soldiers almost always kept their camps tidier than the average backwoods hunting party.

The next afternoon, having descended into a forested valley on the eastern side of the range, Kwasin spied a group of ten soldiers bathing in a natural hot spring in a clearing overlooked by a rocky slope. With the men were six women—likely locals from the village he sought—who seemed to bear the soldiers no ill will, and, if their giggles and frolicking meant anything, were even enjoying themselves.

Kwasin watched the party from a distance for some time, taking passing note of what appeared to be a cave blocked off by a boulder-slide at the top of the slope. He was on the verge of sneaking into the clearing and making off with the soldiers' kilts, harnesses, and weapons—which lay upon the edge of the steaming pool of turquoise water—when suddenly the men and women drew themselves from the spring, their bathing finished, and began donning their clothes.

Slowly, Kwasin withdrew into the woods. He had no desire to take on the soldiers without knowing if they were part of a larger force stationed nearby, which, if Madekha's intelligence was accurate, they were. That the soldiers were Khokarsan and not from Dythbeth, he had no doubt; he had listened to them long enough to determine that from their accents.

Kwasin did, however, cautiously follow the party, which took up a well-worn trail through the trees that, after about a half-hour of walking, led to a little village in the forest circled by an intimidating thorn boma. The party entered the boma through its only means of ingress, a stout wooden, bronze-reinforced gate, after speaking a password to a sentry through a speak-hole in the door.

Curious about the situation in the village, Kwasin climbed a thickly leaved oak on the perimeter of the village clearing. From this vantage, he observed three clusters of huts: the longhouse where undoubtedly were held the rituals of the Klakordeth; a large mess hall likely erected after the soldiers seized the village; and a high interior cedar stockade that encompassed a quarter of the village and seemed to be the designated living area for those natives who had resisted the soldiers. But not all of the villagers were confined within the pen; some were at work, under the close watch of their guards, beginning construction on a watchtower near the gate, while others—by far the minority—moved about the village more or less freely while they carried out various chores for their new masters.

The reconnoitering told him all he wanted to know: the situation was grim for the bulk of the villagers. Madekha's hope that he could emancipate Q"okwoqo from Minruth's forces was nothing but a wishful dream.

He climbed down from the oak and faded into the woods, intent on getting away from the village as quickly as possible. He would go to Dythbeth as he had originally intended and take his chances with Queen Weth.

When Kwasin was not yet a half-mile from the village, he thought he heard a woman's voice come to him upon the warm forest breeze. Yes, there it was again. He froze and listened. The words were singsong, almost as if the speaker addressed a child:

"In the beginning was a formless substance which gave birth to Kho, the Great Goddess. She fashioned the earth, the air, the sky, the stars, the moon, and the sun…"

Quietly, Kwasin moved through the forest in the direction of the speaker.

"After eons, being lonely," the voice continued, "she copulated with the world and had daughters. These she assigned as watchers over the air, the sky, the stars, the moon, and the sun. She created a great tree with many fruits and birds which rested on the tree. The daughters ate the fruit and copulated with the birds, and from these were born all manner of life, including Old Father Nakendar, who mated with his mother's sister, Besbesbes, the goddess of honey, and produced a great variety of bear children, which is why you, my magnificent friend, can't get enough of the nectar of your bee cousins."

A meadow opened up before Kwasin and, wide-eyed, his jaw hanging, he peered through the underbrush at an incredible site. Indeed, there was a woman in the wood—a beautiful, young woman, her lustrous hair night-black, with a delicate face that was identical in every way to Madekha's, though perhaps somewhat more wholesome, and not at all serpentlike. But lo! It was not a child the woman addressed with all the affection of a doting mother—but rather a great brown bear, standing upright, fully ten feet tall on its hind legs, as the woman reached up and fed it honey from her dripping hand!

In the tiny hand went, into that great fanged mouth, to be licked by an enormous pink tongue, and then out again it came, miraculously unharmed. Then the woman dipped her hand into the ceramic jar she held nestled in the crook of her arm, withdrew the now honey-covered hand, and plunged it again into that terrible maw.

To see the tiny creature before him do what he, the mighty Kwasin, would never think to do astounded him. He had heard folktales in the lodges and halls of the Klakordeth of an ancient trickster-hero of the totem who had donned bearskins and went to live among a sloth of bears, creating trouble for all the humans and mythological creatures that encountered him; but never had Kwasin believed old Klaklaku to be other than a fable. Now, his heart thrumming with envy at seeing this woman interact so intimately with his totem animal, he wondered.

But soon Kwasin's heart beat rapidly for a different reason as the bear dropped to all fours and began huffing and growling in his direction, swinging its long-snouted head wildly and baring its awful fangs. The woman quickly stepped back from her ferocious companion and swung about to face Kwasin, who, having heard from his totem brothers about what to do if one unexpectedly encountered a hostile bear in the wild, remained as still as he could. If the animal came any closer, however, he would stand up, making himself as tall and threatening as possible, and roar like a demon. There was no sense trying to run—even the fastest sprinter in the empire could not hope to outpace a charging bear.

Now the woman spoke sternly to the bear, telling it to lie down. The bear continued to huff until she repeated the command again, this time pointing assertively at the ground. To Kwasin's surprise, the bear complied, placing its chin on the carpet of grass and whining like a chided dog.

"You, in the woods!" the woman shouted. "Come out, slowly, or you'll anger Parbho and he will eat you."

Kwasin crawled out from behind the lavender where he had been hiding and stepped slowly into the meadow. The bear whined louder as Kwasin advanced, but stopped when the woman admonished it with a command of "Stay!"

"You don't look like a soldier," she said, her eyes narrowed. "But I will have Parbho kill you all the same if you don't tell me what you're doing in these woods."

Kwasin smiled disarmingly and, spreading his arms wide, made an exaggerated bow, keeping his eyes on the woman, and, of course, the bear.

"I am Kwasin," he said, "an emissary of Madekha, high priestess of the sacred pythoness at Kaarkor and holy daughter of Kho." And then Kwasin spoke the words Madekha had said would convince her sister he spoke the truth.

The woman started upon hearing the secret phrase, and then her face, surrounded by the dark firmament of her hair, lit up like the most radiant star in the night sky, her lips parting in a gleaming smile. If not for the bear, Kwasin doubted he would have been able to resist taking her up in his arms and covering her with his hot kisses. Then he thought, if not for the bear, of course he would not resist it.

"My sister sent you?" the woman asked, hope ringing clearly in her voice. "You have brought men from Kaarkor to wage war on the soldiers who have taken my people?"

"No, O Fair Adythne," he replied, "for I can only assume

that is your name. Your sister faces troubles of her own in Kaarkor, and needs all the men she has to protect her sacred office. She's sent only me, Kwasin, slayer of men and monsters, and the greatest lov—"

For a moment the woman had looked forlorn, but now she cut him off, her vision seeming to turn inward as if already she plotted a scheme and his boasting words were but bothersome spores upon the wind.

"It is just as well," she said over his words. "A large and unwieldy band would only cause the soldiers to garrison themselves in the village and threaten to execute hostages until the attackers departed. And you are indeed a giant, and one man may sometimes achieve what an army cannot. Especially if that man is made invincible."

"I don't know of what you speak, O Priestess," Kwasin said, "but let us first understand one another before we talk of—"

"Yes, yes," the woman said eagerly, "you are foreign to these parts, unfamiliar with our village, and want to know how it is that I am so friendly with Parbho here."

It was not what Kwasin was thinking. He only wanted to make clear to the priestess that she was delusional if she thought he would fight her battles for her—that the only sensible thing was to accompany him to Dythbeth, where she could give testimony to clear his name, and also ask for assistance for her village from King Roteka and his army. But the woman gave him no opportunity to make his case.

"Parbho," Adythne continued without pausing, "is one of seven bears we have trained in the village. We, the Klakordeth of Q'okwoqo, have a long tradition of intimate dealings with our sacred animal, going back almost half a millennia. Oh, how you should see them dance and jump through hoops of fire during the festival days of Kho-wu! But they are much more than just pets—they are our spirit guides, and we of the village could not go on without them. That is why, when the soldiers stormed Q'okwoqo, I set the bears free from their cages—I could not risk that they might slay the spirit guides and use their meat for stew."

Here the woman paused to coddle Parbho's glossy brown neck, and, at seeing the bear react by licking her hand like a playful pup, Kwasin's intended words vanished from his mind.

Now Adythne's beautiful features darkened. "But the soldiers have blocked up Old Father Nakendar in his cave. He would have starved by now had I not fed him what slim morsels I've been able to catch in the woods, dropping them down through the sacrificial opening at the summit above his cave."

"The Bear God is real?" Kwasin said, somewhat dubiously.

"Of course he is," Adythne snapped. "He lairs in the cave above the northern hot springs—the sacred waters the soldiers defile with their ritually unclean bodies." Then the priestess's expression grew yet darker. "But I hold an even greater fear than for Nakendar, who, being divine, is surely just biding his time in his cave while the mortals about him bicker. I have just been to the village and exchanged messages with one of my acolytes by means of the mirror code employed by the daughters of Kho. She has told me that late one night, about a week ago, a gang of drunk soldiers slipped into the stockade without their commanding officers' permission and at sword-point marched away with a half-dozen children while their mothers cried and screamed and pulled at their hair in dismay. Two men were killed, and a third gravely injured, trying to stop the soldiers. Now, a week has passed and the children have not returned.

"The days grow dark for the people of Q"okwoqo," Adythne said, looking weary, "and I, their priestess, have been unable to help them. Indeed, if not for the presence of the spirit guides, madness would have consumed me by now. But now that you have arrived, O Mighty Kwasin, we will set things right. And yes," she added, regarding him slyly, "I know who you are, and of your larger-than-life—if outright criminal—reputation. But that is something I intend to wield to our advantage."

At these last words, the beautiful Adythne beckoned Kwasin forward, took his hand in hers, and led him past the suspicious, beady red eyes of her bear to the edge of the shaded meadow. Here she knelt on the ground before a pile of dead underbrush, which she proceeded to move aside until a smooth, round stone was revealed half embedded in the reddish-brown soil. She leaned forward, dug her fingers into the earth around the stone, and, groaning, pulled aside the covering. From the deep hole beneath where the stone had been, she drew forth a large bundle sealed tight in waxed antelope hide. Then she stood up and held out the bundle with an air of reverence.

"It is the sacred pelt of a she-bear once worshiped by the Klemklakor in the lands far north of the Saasares, near the Ringing Sea. The she-bear killed and ate my great-great-grandfather, but then choked on his bones and died. Or at least that was the story told by my great-great-grandmother, who brought back the bear's hide when she returned to her home village of Kaarkor. The pelt was passed to me from my mother, who, while not of the Klemklakor, had inherited it from her mother and understood the sacramental nature of the pelt. And it was while I was partaking of the laurel leaf during the orgiastic rites of my former totem that the old she-bear came to me and told me I must travel to Q'okwoqo to become a sister of the Klemklakor. She also said that neither blade nor spear nor fire would touch him who wore the she-bear's pelt into battle."

Adythne untied the antelope-sinew strings that bound the bag and unfurled a magnificent black-furred bearskin, its cured head still attached and serving as a sort of coif. Sinew cords hung from the hide, allowing the wearer to secure the pelt to the arms and shoulders.

"And for that reason," she said, proffering the pelt to Kwasin, "I pass the holy mantle to you, O Great Warrior, to wear for your protection until you have freed my people from the wicked followers of the sungod. You must, of course, relinquish the pelt after you have achieved our goal, for I intend to pass it along to a daughter of my own one day."

Kwasin took the pelt—for indeed it was a splendid specimen, one he could not help but admire as a member of the Thunder Bear Totem—and swept it over his great bronzed and muscled shoulders. He smiled appreciatively at Adythne, but only briefly.

"Like your sister," he said, sloughing the cloak from his shoulders, "you make a compelling argument. But I can't take up your local burdens. I'm steadfast on a mission to see Queen

Weth, and—if she still lives—the oracle Wasemquth, who exiled me from the land nine years ago. For too long have I wandered the wilds, distracting my lonely soul with whatever trouble I happened to stumble across. But our causes lead to the same place. You can't make the dangerous journey to Dythbeth without escort, but I can take you there. There you can ask the queen to urge her husband, King Roteka, to send a force into the mountains and free the good people of Q'okwoqo from the soldiers of Minruth the Mad. And it would be but little trouble for you to put in a good word for me, who saved your sister from certain death—or worse—in the ruins of cursed Miterisi."

Since Kwasin had encountered her, Adythne had paused in neither thought nor action long enough to entertain the possibility that Kwasin might not be interested in joining her single-minded quest to free her village from the soldiers. Now, upon hearing Kwasin's little speech, the woman's face flushed with anger and resentment.

"You are the mad one, O Kwasin the Ill-fated!" Adythne snatched the sacred pelt from Kwasin's hands and shook it out with an angry flourish as if his mere touch had defiled it. "For Weth—the very priestess whose ravaging by you doomed you to exile from the land—will have you executed upon sight! And were I to be seen in your company, my loyalties too would be thrown into question, and no hope would my people have of succor from Dythbeth." Behind them the bear, roused by his mistress's anger, began growling lightly as Adythne continued. "No! We must fight the soldiers now, with as much stealth and cunning as I can design—for it is clear your dull-witted mind is not made for either. Your course would do nothing but condemn us to imprisonment in King Roteka's dungeons!"

Adythne was certainly spirited, but Kwasin had known that even before he laid eyes on her. Who else would abandon her mother's totem in favor of adoption into a foreign one? He knew, however, that such things were done in certain rare cases. Sometimes, in a remote village, an infant's or toddler's mother died leaving behind no direct living matrilineal relatives. If no member from the mother's clan stepped forward to adopt the child, the village priestess had leeway to reassign the child to another totem. There was almost always a great-aunt or a distant cousin able to adopt the child, and if the child was old enough, someone from the mother's totem would adopt it, no matter the hazy nature of the relation—for were not all totem brothers and sisters of the same spiritual blood? But Adythne had not only switched totems; she had become a high priestess among her adopted people—how Kwasin would love to hear the tale behind that!

The thought of being spiritually separated from his birth totem disturbed Kwasin. Though he had not been among his bear brothers during his eight years in exile, he could not imagine cutting himself off from the Klakordeth forever. The spirit of the bear ran too deeply within him.

He could not, however, blame the woman for her decision to switch totems. The Thunder Bear Totem was of heady stock, the cream of the crop as far as Kwasin was concerned, even if its members did tend to indulge a bit too heavily in alcohol and, from time to time, killed one another in drunken rages, or in ritual games of strength and endurance. But they were bears at heart, his spiritual brothers and sisters—and bears liked their honey, and were also prone to outbursts of violence when the mood set upon them—so how could anyone hold it against them? Because of this, Kwasin did not begrudge the woman her stubbornness either.

And so, instead of arguing with Adythne, Kwasin merely bellowed with laughter.

"You are courageous, O Priestess, and I wish you luck," he said, "though I doubt you will find it." And with that he slung his ax over a shoulder and strode leisurely into the forest.

Through the trees he heard the priestess curse him, and then, loud enough that he knew she meant him to hear it, she said, "Come, Parbho, we shall free the village ourselves. You, at least, are no coward."

Kwasin walked on through the cedars for some time, trying to keep his thoughts on his goal of reaching Dythbeth and seeking exoneration from his crimes. Soon, however, his conscience began to prickle. He could not keep Adythne's final words from his mind.

Had he not accused Hadon of exactly the same sort of cowardice for failing to remain behind with him to fight Minruth's soldiers in the capital? Had his desire to clear his name and abrogate his exile—strengthened by the dreams of his mother's death that wracked his sleep—at last squelched his seemingly bottomless well of boldness and spontaneity? Not to mention—and here his pride truly stung—his fearlessness?

He muttered a curse. Then, he laughed.

Truly had the priestess worked a spell over him, one that had almost succeeded. No, he thought, not just Adythne, but her sister as well. Both, he mused, had shrewdly and cunningly worked their magic on him—the snakewoman had planted the seed and the bearwoman had sought to harvest it. But he would not be distracted from his mission. Maybe, if the oracle did pardon his crimes, he would return to the Saasamaro with a stalwart band of King Roteka's soldiers and rout the enemy from Q"okwoqo. But not until he again walked free within the empire.

Kwasin continued on through the woods. Soon he found his mood had lifted and again he began to feel like his old self.

Then came the tart stink of death amid the strong smell of the cedars.

When he found the bodies of the children, blackness consumed him.

Kwasin knew now that he could not go to Dythbeth. Not yet anyway. He could not let the atrocity go unpunished, no matter his previous plans.

That so-called civilized citizens of the empire had committed such a profane act against the innocent made him feel ashamed of his desire to return to civilization—he had never seen such vile barbarism in all his years among the savages in the Wild Lands. But war, Kwasin knew, sometimes made people commit atrocities they would never conceive of enacting in peacetime. Still, that did not forgive the soldiers who had done this. He would make them pay for their actions. He had no doubt the corpses were those of the children abducted by the drunken soldiers about whom Adythne had raged.

What had set him on the path that had led here? He might have set off from the meadow on any number of paths through the forest, but he had taken this one. Had the Bear God truly guided him here, as Madekha had suggested, so that Kwasin would remain and help Old Father Nakendar's people? Or perhaps the Goddess Herself wanted him to stay and fight, for Her own unknowable reasons. He did not know, but the end result was the same. One moment, he had been on the road to Dythbeth, caring little for anything but his own self-interest; in the next, a path of blood and death lay before him.

Though a dark rage had seized him, he set about the task of burying the dead innocents. He had no tool but the sharpened head of his ax to dig the graves, but he could not turn away from the unpleasant chore, notwithstanding the furious urge to take up the war trail straightaway. What these children could not expect of life, he would assure they received in death. When he could, he would hunt down a wild boar and sacrifice it so that their spirits would not hunger and thirst. But now he had only the time to bury their mortal remains.

The early afternoon having passed at his grim labors, Kwasin set off for the meadow where he had last seen Adythne. It took him longer than he would have liked to find the place, and when he did, the priestess was not there. He did, however, find her spoor, as well as that of the bear. The two had set off in different directions, the bear toward the southwest where the forest deepened as the valley widened, and the woman, not surprisingly, in the direction of the village.

After following Adythne's trail for fifteen minutes, the

spoor disappeared beneath the fresh bootprints of many men. He tracked the party a short distance before noticing a woman's footprints diverging from the group. He followed her tracks but found they made only a little loop through the woods before rejoining the prints of the main party.

Standing beneath the vaulting cedars, Kwasin reconstructed what had transpired. Adythne had set off from the meadow and quickly parted with the bear. Perhaps she had commanded the bear to head into the deep woods, where the animal would be less likely to have a confrontation with the soldiers. About a half-mile from the meadow, Adythne had spied a group of soldiers in the forest, at which point she turned to the east. From the length of the woman's stride, as well as the shallow impression of her heels, Kwasin could tell she was at this point running, as if the soldiers had seen her. She had gone a distance and then stopped beneath a sprawling pine amid the cedars before finally turning back in the direction of the soldiers. Then she had been caught.

But why had the woman detoured from the party of soldiers only to return to be captured by them? Unless…

Kwasin jogged back to the great pine and looked up into its array of widely spread limbs. He grunted approvingly when he spied what he sought, then pulled himself up among the branches and climbed high into the pine.

When he neared the top of the tree he plucked from between two joining limbs what the woman had cached there: the tightly wrapped antelope-hide bundle that contained the sacred bear pelt. Then he returned to the ground with his prize.

Kwasin removed the pelt from the waxen hide, eddied the pelt over his well-muscled shoulders, and sat down glumly beneath the great pine. His head couched in his hands, he sighed deeply. He thought of how he had abandoned Adythne in the forest against her urgings that he help her defeat the soldiers occupying her village. Now those soldiers had caught her.

That the all-too-determined priestess would have been apprehended by the soldiers sooner or later did nothing to assuage Kwasin's guilt that he had not assisted her. He was not one to live his life imprisoned by feelings of remorse—he did what his heart told him and bore the consequences. But since he had returned from the Wild Lands, something had changed in him. His actions no longer seemed as certain as they once had. Perhaps he had become unaccustomed to civilized companionship. Or possibly the feeling of uncertainty was due to the dreams that plagued his nights, or maybe the furious battle between Great Kho and Resu that shook the land. Why, he wondered, had he so desired to return to the empire that spurned him to begin with?

Of course, he knew the answer. He had suffered a terrible, soul-aching loneliness while in the wilds. But when he had returned to civilization, a stark feeling of *nothingness* had rapidly descended upon him, even more smothering than the isolation he had faced in the far-flung land of the savages. In the hope of filling that void of nothingness, he had seized upon the idea of returning to Dythbeth and obtaining a pardon for his crimes. But now, in the mountains above his homeland, the emptiness remained and he wondered if he would ever find that which would satisfy the cravings of his soul.

As Kwasin sat brooding thus, his head cradled deeply in his hands, something cold and wet nudged his forearm. He lifted his head and nearly leaped to his feet when he found himself looking into the large and terrible dark eyes of a great brown bear. It was all he could do to keep from jumping up, but he knew that if he moved suddenly, the bear would become enraged and all would be over for the mighty Kwasin—the bear's horrible fangs would devour both body and soul, and even dread Sisisken, goddess of the underworld, would be left wondering what had become of him. The nothingness that he feared most would blot him out forever.

And so Kwasin sat there, unmoving, watching the bear. That it was Parbho, the bear that had accompanied the priestess Adythne, he had no doubt. In fact, the bear had a forlorn look about it, as it sat on its haunches, snorting and nudging Kwasin gently with its cold, black nose. Almost, Kwasin thought, as if the bear understood its mistress had been captured by the soldiers—as if, finding Kwasin in the forest with the sacred pelt of the she-bear draped about his shoulders, the bear sought comfort from the man-thing. Did the bear believe, because its mistress had commanded it not to attack the man-thing, that Kwasin was consequently its mistress's friend? And by extension, the bear's friend?

Kwasin did not question his attribution of human emotions and motivations to the bear; all living things were by extension the children of Kho, the Mother of All, and even the deities felt love and hate and greed and sorrow. The bear was no different.

Of course, Parbho's playful nosing of Kwasin might simply

have been due to the pelt the human wore. As a holy artifact, it was likely used in the sacred rituals of the Klakordeth, and Adythne had said the villagers thought of their trained bears as spirit guides. Doubtless Parbho had taken some role in the totem's rites and was accustomed to the scent of the pelt, which must have reassured the bear in the absence of its mistress.

Boldly, though hardly sure of the wisdom of his action, Kwasin reached out a hand and scratched Parbho behind an ear. The bear tilted its head and, if Kwasin was not mistaken, smiled at him as it whined affectionately.

Kwasin smiled back with genuine delight, but he was careful not to bare his teeth. He did not want the bear to mistake his grin for a threatening snarl.

For some time Kwasin sat with Parbho, caressing the beast as friskily as he dared. The bear even rolled onto its back in apparent jollity, and then back onto its feet to push Kwasin with a playful nudge that was at the same time forceful enough to almost send the human sprawling.

Finally, Kwasin decided he had to get to his feet and assert himself at some point or he might be trapped playing with the frolicsome bear until it grew tired of playing and turned on him. Slowly, the sacred she-bear pelt still about his shoulders, he rose. As he did so, the bear got to its feet as well and let out a deep growl that froze Kwasin where he stood.

Then inspiration struck him. He would not merely wait to see what the bear would do next. Adythne had, after all, said her people had trained the animals to dance. And so Kwasin crouched down on all fours and began to act out one of the ritual dances of the Bear people. As he danced, Kwasin also began chanting in gruff tones a primordial song of his totem. The ritual was, in fact, the Dance of Klaklaku, reputed to depict the same motions of that legendary hero of the Klakordeth, who, donning bearskins, had convinced a sloth of bears to adopt him. If the dance had worked for his ancient totem ancestor, Kwasin thought, perhaps it would work for him as well.

At first the bear just watched him. Kwasin thought that from its look the animal believed the human to be mad, that at any second the bear would leap upon him and tear him to bloody pieces with its great claws and teeth. But then, much to his surprise, Parbho jumped in behind Kwasin and began following him in his dance, acting out the same motions that had been passed from Bear brother to Bear brother down from the time of Klaklaku himself!

Kwasin was amazed. But he also understood he had been lucky. Bears, whether trained or not, were by their very nature wild and deadly animals, and he had encountered this one under just the right circumstances. The villagers must have taught Parbho just this same ritual dance, one of the most ancient of his people. Seeing Kwasin attired in the sacred pelt, doubtless worn by Adythne or another totem member during the local rituals, and then watching the man-thing enact the familiar dance of Klaklaku, the bear was probably only doing what he had been taught to do as a cub.

Just when Kwasin felt the day could not grow stranger, he heard a rustling from the forest. Suddenly, out walked another brown bear, just as giant as his brother Parbho. Still Kwasin did not stop his dancing and singing. He feared too much what would happen if he did.

In the same manner as Parbho had at first done, the newcomer sat on his haunches and watched Kwasin intently. Then, as if waiting for just the right timing in the ritual display, the newly arrived bear rose up on all fours and swayed in behind Parbho, mimicking the exaggerated motions of the dance.

When the third bear, and then a fourth and a fifth, arrived Kwasin did not question it. Nor did he do so after all seven of the bears mentioned by Adythne had come and joined in the ritual. By this time Kwasin had lost himself in the dance and now fully believed himself possessed by the spirit of his ancestor, Klaklaku the Man-Bear. And who could have doubted it to see Kwasin thus, leading bear after bear in that erratic dance upon the forest floor! Sometimes he stopped and rose up on two legs, hands lifted up like raking claws; at other times he fell back again upon all fours, swaying back and forth and huffing and growling no differently than the great ursines that trod so closely behind him in the circling path of the dance.

How long the impromptu ritual went on, Kwasin was unsure, but at last he—and he believed the bears as well—grew tired. He knew the dance could not go on forever, and if stopping his wild motions would cause the bears to turn violently upon him, so be it. If he had to die, then at least he would exit this world directly following one of the most supremely satisfying experiences of his life—the exalting of his ancient ancestor's soaring spirit in communion with the spirit guides of his people. If his bear cousins devoured him, Kwasin knew in the utter conviction of the moment that old Klaklaku would be there to welcome him into the afterlife.

Following the traditional means to conclude the dance, Kwasin leaped high into the air with a roar and then collapsed upon the ground and lay still. Through slitted lids he watched the bears as they attempted to imitate his closing leap—they were, of course, too heavy to jump fully off the ground as he did—and then flopped onto the forest floor in apparent exhaustion. For several minutes the ursines lay there with Kwasin. Eventually, one bear arose and sniffed one of its companions before finally swaying off at a leisurely pace into the woods. Then the other bears followed suit, one after another, until only Parbho remained lying next to Kwasin. Finally that great beast too rolled up onto his feet. He walked over to where Kwasin lay, sniffed him, and padded off toward the north upon some errand only the bear could know.

Contented in a way he had never before known, Kwasin stood up and watched the bear disappear into the woods.

The next few days were busy for Kwasin, and though he regretted leaving Adythne in the hands of the soldiers while making no attempt to free her, he knew he needed to invest some time and much patience if his plan to help the priestess and her people was to succeed. Still, if he waited too long, he would be too late.

Though he worked hard at his preparations during the day, at night he lingered outside the village walls eavesdropping on the villagers. On the first night he learned nothing of importance, but on the second he overheard two sentries discussing how their commandant, a captain named Riwaphe, intended to sacrifice Adythne to the sungod as an example to the people of Q"okwoqo. The ceremony was to occur at dawn on the morning of the second fire day of the month, in only five days.

Because of this intelligence, Kwasin was forced to speed up his preparations, working well under a timeframe he considered wise. But then, luck—and the Bear God—was on his side. What other sign did he need of the god's favor than the bizarre congregation of the dancing bears of Q"okwoqo that had communed with him? Old Father Nakendar was looking after him. He hoped. He would need the Bear God's help if his daring plan was to succeed.

On the morning of the month's second cloud day— the sixth day since his arrival in the area and the day before Adythne's scheduled execution—Kwasin set out for the nearby hot spring. His experience with the bears had struck him profoundly, and he wanted to pay his respects to the Old Father before the night of trials that lay ahead and ask the god for his blessing and for strength.

Kwasin made sure to keep a watchful eye out during his journey to the spring. Over the course of the preceding days, he had observed the officers in command at Q"okwoqo make something of a daily ritual out of hiking out to the spring and soaking in the soothing hot waters. Always did the soldiers leave the village at the point when the sun had descended approximately halfway from the zenith of Kho's blue bowl, filing along the same forest path with a number of local women who, from their attitudes, seemed to be seeking the favor of the officers so that they might elevate their social status in the new order of things. Today Kwasin arrived at the spring in the late morning, well ahead of the soldiers' expected visit.

He climbed the high, rocky prominence that overlooked the spring, stopping briefly at the ledge upon which rested the great boulder that sealed off the entrance to the Bear God's cave. After examining the obstruction for a few minutes, he continued on. At the slope's summit, the land leveled out and Kwasin walked only a short distance before coming upon a scattering of branches and dead brush. He cleared these away and examined the sacrificial opening about which Adythne had told him.

The circular opening was just over five feet in diameter and rimmed with expertly fitted blocks of white, red-veined marble. A thick bear smell came up out of the hole from the black abyss of the cave, and though Kwasin strained his eyes, he could see nothing in the darkness below. Perhaps the Bear God had at last succumbed to the very mortal afflictions of starvation and thirst. It had been at least six days since the priestess had last visited the god and fed him, and for all Kwasin knew it could have been much longer.

"I am Kwasin, brother of the Klakordeth!" he shouted down the shaft. "I have come to help your people, O Nakendar!" His own words came hollowly back at him from the enormous cavern below, but other than the echo, he heard nothing.

"Hear me, Old Father!" he cried again. "I seek your blessing in destroying the enemies of the Q'okwoqo!"

Finally, Kwasin grew tired of staring down into the murk. Concluding sadly that the cave bear must have really died, he rearranged the dead foliage over the opening and went off to look for lunch.

He ultimately found his meal in the form of a termite colony nested high in a tree. He would have preferred to roast the insects but he could not take the chance of building a fire, which might alert the nearby soldiers to his presence. But he needed his strength for what was to come, and so he had to make do fishing the insects out of their nest with a stick and eating them raw. This was not much of a concession; many Khokarsans ate their termites raw by choice.

His belly full, Kwasin climbed down from the tree and lay down in the shade of a great boulder on the rock-strewn slope overlooking the spring, where he thought to rest for but a few minutes. Soon, however, his meal made him sleepy and he drifted off into a deep slumber.

When the sound of laughter and splashing water below awakened him, his first impulse was to pull the sacred pelt of the she-bear over his head and continue sleeping. Then, remembering his whereabouts, he cursed groggily.

He rose to discover Resu's weltering red eye had already slipped below the western mountains, the heavens staining the forest a dim crimson. Beneath him at the foot of the slope, the band of officers, their two foot soldiers, and the women who accompanied them frolicked in the warm waters, oblivious to the giant that observed them from behind a boulder.

Kwasin cursed again. His hopes to assail the village while Captain Riwaphe and his officers were absent at the spring were now dashed. But then, as the sleep-fog cleared from his mind, he remembered that the Bear God had come to him while he slept.

Or rather, Kwasin had come to the god, for in the dream he had sat before Nakendar in the darkness of his cave. All that Kwasin had been able to see of the god was the eerie glow of his terrible red eyes; the Old Father, however, had spoken to him in a series of huffing growls that, somehow, Kwasin understood. And he had told Kwasin that the sleep that had overcome him was not due to a lapse in the mortal's determination. No, the god had cast the slumber over Kwasin that he might advise him. There was, according to the Old Father, a more effective way to keep the officers from the village, and one that would not leave the god hungering in his cave-prison.

Recalling the task with which Nakendar had charged him, Kwasin grinned widely.

There was no use in wasting time. He stepped from behind the boulder in full sight of the party below, stretched wide his arms, and let out a cavernous yawn.

Instantly, the laughter and chitchat of the frolickers ceased. The soldiers stood up in the steaming waters, their naked forms glistening redly in the fading twilight, their mouths dark circles of surprise. Then, at an order from the captain, the men scampered out of the pool and began donning their clothes and picking up their weapons.

Kwasin smiled broadly and waved down at the soldiers; then he turned about, lifted his kilt, and mooned them. He stood thus only long enough to hear the soldiers' curses, then lost no time in ascending the slope. He did not think the men carried slings, but he was uncertain.

When he reached the summit, he waited. The soldiers would have to get much closer if the Bear God's plan was to succeed.

He grinned when he saw that, as he had hoped, the captain led the charge up the rocky incline, with the four other officers and two infantrymen just behind him. Kwasin felt relieved to discover they carried only their swords.

Finally, the captain, red-faced and panting heavily, pulled himself up onto the summit. As the man did so, Kwasin feigned a startled expression, then turned and sprinted across the plateau. He did not, however, sprint too quickly as he did not want to get too far ahead of the man.

Kwasin looked over a shoulder and saw the captain only a couple of yards behind him, with the other soldiers in a tight-knit group directly behind their superior. Then Kwasin leaped over the scattering of branches before him, swung around, and stopped.

There was a crash as the captain fell through the fragile lattice of brushwood that covered the stone-lined sacrificial opening, then the heavy thud of a body hitting the stone floor of the cave below. The other soldiers, directly on the heels of their captain, could not stop their forward momentum. Kwasin grinned like a demon at seeing their dumbfounded faces just before they tumbled as one into the black pit. Their bodies too thumped hollowly as they made a series of rapid impacts upon the cavern floor.

He bent over the hole and shouted down at the groaning men.

"That is your punishment for sealing up Old Father

Nakendar and leaving him to die! May his spirit gnaw on your shinbones for all eternity!"

Kwasin remained at the edge of the hole, listening to the continued groaning and sobbing of the men below. He felt no remorse for dooming the men to die in the cave. After what the soldiers had done to the children and to the Old Father, he only regretted that they would not suffer more.

Suddenly, from somewhere deep in the cave came a hideous, moaning scream. The hair rose stiffly on the back of Kwasin's neck and the men below began to shout out in terror.

The bloodcurdling scream came again, now nearer to the bottom of the marble shaft. Kwasin bent over the hole, trying to penetrate the darkness, his giant frame trembling. It was not every day that one heard the scream of a god.

The men were now shrieking in utter fright. Then came the sound of slashing claws and a gut-wrenching chomping of bone, followed a few moments later by complete silence.

No, the silence was not absolute. He thought, if he strained his hearing, he could just make out a faint rasping of breath. Then he saw, caught faintly in the evening's fading light, what appeared to be the glimmer of two large, reddish eyes looking up at him.

Kwasin backed away from the hole, his heart pounding, his body covered in a cold sweat.

Half numb with shock, he stumbled back down the slope to retrieve the sacred she-bear pelt where he had left it by the boulder. Briefly, he looked for the women who had accompanied the soldiers, but they were nowhere to be found. Doubtless they had run off into the woods after hearing the hideous cry of the Old Father.

Shaken to his core by what he had seen and heard, Kwasin could not say he blamed them.

Kwasin knew he had to move fast. The sky had already darkened and he needed to get back to his camp near the village as quickly as possible. He hoped the bears had not wandered off. If they had, his plan would fail.

As he ran through the dark woods, the preposterousness of what he hoped to do made him wonder at his sanity. But it also exhilarated him. If he was able to beat the incredible odds and succeed at his intent, then his name would forever be sung in the halls of his totem. A new ritual dance would be initiated to record his great deeds for the posterity of all Bear people. They might call it the Dance of the Imprudent Giant, and he would become as legendary as Klaklaku himself.

But more than just vanity drove Kwasin on. When the Old Father had come to him in the dream, he had told Kwasin it was time to choose sides. To stand on the side of Kho, the Mother of All, and give sustenance to the great tree from which all life sprang. Or to turn his back on the Goddess and kindle the smoldering flames that were the lies and arrogance of Resu— to stand with the sungod until his blistering gaze reduced the world-tree to nothing more than a dried and blackened husk. The Bear God had told Kwasin he must either help the people of Q"okwoqo or turn against his totem brothers and sisters and slay them. According to Old Nakendar, it was because Kwasin had for so long remained a disinterested party in the conflict between Kho and Resu that his soul so greatly feared oblivion. Kwasin's own petty goals and desires were but nothing compared to the flowering of Great Kho's will or the sungod's burning desire to murder his mother and former lover, the Creator and Replenisher of all things.

And so it was that Kwasin—defiler of the temple of Kho, exile from the land by order of the Voice of Kho herself—took the side of the Great Mother in the war between the deities. He now recognized the battle for Q''okwoqo for what it was—not merely a local matter, but rather the touchstone of his destiny. Perhaps in his heart he had known this all along but his head had denied it. Was this why, since his return from the Wild Lands, his mother had plagued his dreams with visions of her death? Had she been trying to send him a message from her shadowy station in Sisisken's dark house—to urge him to stand with the Goddess against the blasphemers or risk the extinguishing of his soul as the snake that had bitten her had struck down her own life? If the nightmares now ceased, he would know.

At last he came to his camp, about a half-mile from Q''okwoqo. This was his new camp, the original having been positioned far enough away from the village that the soldiers would not detect the smoke from the training fires he lit. He had relocated here only yesterday, the site's proximity to the village being crucial to his plan.

For a moment, his heart sank. Where were the bears? He began to think they had loped off into the forest as they were wont to do at night after their training sessions, knowing that if they had, Adythne was doomed to die at sunrise upon the altar of Resu. But then, as he searched the woods just beyond the camp's perimeter, he saw in the dim starlight cast down between the branches seven large, dark forms upon the forest floor. He sighed with relief. The bears had not fled after all.

Now came one of the most dangerous parts of his scheme—and there were many. When he had trained with the bears, it had always been in the light of day, as his plan was to task the animals early that afternoon when the contingent's officers were away from the village and soaking in the hot spring. He did not know how the bears would react to a disruption in their routine. Bears were for the most part diurnal. Would they follow their training in the pitch black of night? Or, when he woke them, would they revert to the untamed beasts they were at heart and attack him?

There was only one way to find out. Kwasin donned the sacred pelt of the she-bear, which he had carried with him from the spring. Quietly, at first, so as not to startle the bears, he began to sing the crude ballad he had composed to accompany the bears' training. This he had set, rather wryly, to the tune of "Bear Mother Mistakes Her Teeth for Her Anus," an ancient and bawdy folksong about a popular heroine of his totem.

At hearing Kwasin's crass singing, the bears awoke, one by one, some of them huffing as they were roused. This set Kwasin's heart racing, as he knew the sound indicated the animals felt threatened. A few moments later, however, the huffing ceased, and he felt a great hairy body brush up friendlily against his bare thigh. He continued his singing and began dancing in the same manner as he had during the bears' training, first in a wide orbit around the camp, and then, after the bears had begun to follow behind him, off into the forest in the direction of Q"okwoqo.

Every so often Kwasin looked back to make sure his outlandish company was still in tow. But he did not need to do so; he could hear well enough the sounds of their heavy bodies crashing through the forest. He hoped the sentries in the village would not hear them coming, but there was nothing Kwasin could do about it if they did. Perhaps the sentries would be so startled at seeing the giant and his ursine entourage emerge from the woods that they would be temporarily immobilized. It might even buy him enough time to launch his attack.

But Kwasin did not need to worry about being heard. Even before he reached the village, the sound of great revelry came to him through the trees. The jubilant shouting, laughter, clapping, and singing was loud enough to cover any noise made by the bears, and also of such volume that he began to worry it would disrupt the spell he had succeeded in casting over the animals with his song and the movements of the ritual dance. The soldiers must have been celebrating Adythne's coming execution upon the altar of Resu at sunrise.

By the time Kwasin and his companions arrived at the edge of the village clearing, the deep throoming of drums had erupted from inside the surrounding thorn boma. Kwasin tried to calm the bears as best he could with both song and gentle cooings, but his hairy cohorts were obviously upset by the noise and celebratory fires within the village. Knowing he had little time before the animals became so agitated that they would either turn on him or break for the woods, Kwasin went into action.

He began by removing himself a short distance from the bears and laying upon the ground a half-dozen torches saturated with the fat of an antelope he had speared a few days earlier. He had carried these from his camp in the same antelope-hide sack Adythne had used to hold the sacred she-bear pelt. Out of the same bag he removed tinder, a flint, and a piece of iron; the latter he had stolen from a farmer's hut on his journey across the island. Crouching on the ground, he struck flint against iron until the tinder caught a spark and smoldered into flame. He dipped one torch, then another, into the burning tinder. Then, having gathered up the unlit torches in an arm and holding the two burning ones in his other hand, he ran boldly into the clearing and stopped directly before the gate, in full sight of the sentry stationed atop the newly constructed watchtower.

The sentry stood up on the narrow platform on which he had been squatting and looked down at Kwasin, surprise apparent on his long face. For a moment, the man seemed too startled to act, but then he cried down at the revelers below. No one, however, seemed to be able to hear him over the drums and raucous clamor of the festivities.

Kwasin couldn't have hoped for better circumstances. While the man yelled down trying to catch the attention of the oblivious celebrants, Kwasin cast one of the burning torches at the wall of the thorn boma just to the left of the iron-reinforced gate. Thanks to a lack of rain over the past few days, the wall bloomed almost instantly with fire. He lit another torch with the one remaining in his hand and threw it onto the wall to the right of the gate, grinning wickedly as it caught fire just as quickly as his first throw. A third torch went flaming into the village where he judged the hall of the Klakordeth was situated. Although it pained him deeply to set fire to the sacred lodge of his Bear brothers, he had earlier reconnoitered the camp and discovered the soldiers were using it as a barracks. He suspected many of these would be celebrating in the hall and hoped he might trap a great number of them in the burning building.

He lit the fourth torch and hurtled it over the gate at the watchtower just as a soldier carrying a sling mounted the narrow deck and joined the sentry at the tower's top. Though the torch disappeared from view as it fell behind the top of the fifteen-foot-tall gate, Kwasin knew it must have landed and ignited the dry wood of the tower when the two men hastily abandoned the platform and began climbing down. Before passing from sight, the slinger paused and shook his fist angrily at Kwasin.

Quickly, Kwasin ignited the remaining torch and began whirling it in wide circles in unison with the torch already burning in his hand. He did this following the same motions he had employed in his training sessions with the bears over the past few days, having gotten the idea from the priestess Adythne, who had told him the bears had been taught to jump through hoops of fire during the annual festival days of Kho-wu. As he whirled the torches, Kwasin sang, with all the passionate gusto he could summon, his crude, part-improvised lyrics to the tune of the ancient folksong about Bear Mother.

Parbho, who in his mistress's absence seemed to have taken a special liking to Kwasin, was the first of the bears to emerge from the woods. He bounded up to Kwasin and stood up on his hind legs, as he had been taught to do, just as the bronze-plated wooden gate swung open. Behind the open gate, two dozen panicked-looking soldiers and villagers were stampeding forward. At the sight of the growling, upright bear that confronted them, those in front screamed and tried to turn back into the unbridled exodus pouring from the gate. Then all hell let loose as Parbho's dark-furred friends gamboled out of the woods and followed their brother's example, rearing up on their hind legs directly before the mass of fleeing, panic-stricken humans. Still bellowing his bawdy song, Kwasin swung both of the burning torches simultaneously forward in the direction of the gate. This was the motion he had used to signal the bears during their training sessions to charge forward and leap between two blazing practice fires.

Again, Parbho was the first to obey. He came down on all fours and bounded toward the gate at frightening speed. The soldiers and villagers tried to break to either side of the charging bear, but many were knocked to the ground and trampled by their terrified comrades. Others went down beneath the clawed feet of the eight-hundred-pound animal.

One man, an older fellow in priestly robes, kept his cool and stood to one side of the gate, shouting at Parbho in an authoritative tone to stay. He must have been one of the bears' trainers or was mimicking commands he had witnessed other trainers use with the animals. It was a valiant effort, Kwasin thought, but too late. Already Parbho was past the man and leaping between the burning walls into the village. And behind him, one after another, came the other bears.

Two soldiers broke from the chaotic mass of screaming fleers and ran directly for Kwasin, who threw his remaining torches in their faces. The action bought Kwasin enough time to unsling his ax from his shoulder and smash both of their skulls with a single swing of his weapon. Then he ran, roaring, his ax whirling, through the throng of frightened humans, following the last bear through the flame-ringed gate.

Inside the village walls chaos met him. Tongues of reddish-orange fire licked the night sky above the watchtower and totem hall. Hysterical villagers stood outside the hall shrieking frantic prayers at the deities to save those trapped inside. Though dark smoke billowed from the windows and doorways, a few of these ran heedlessly into the burning building after loved ones they believed to be inside. The bears were in a frenzy now; if they recognized any of the villagers who had once trained and fed them, they did not show it. The spirit guides were angry, and many lay dead or horribly mauled beneath their great fangs and claws.

Suddenly, the wind gusted from the west and the flames from the hall of the Klakordeth swept out over the gulf separating the building from the village's stockaded quarter. Kwasin swore. The faithful of Kho who had resisted the invading soldiers were still penned up in the stockade. Almost instantly, the cedar poles that walled in the prisoners—baked dry from the recent hot spell—began crackling with rapidly spreading flames.

Kwasin made for the stockade but found himself confronted on all sides by panicked villagers and soldiers. He roared like a demon and swung his ax in an attempt to clear a path before him. The tactic worked to some degree, as many in the mob fell back before his mad charge. He must have made a terrible figure, he thought—a seven-foot-tall giant, cutting down his foes with his glittering ax and dressed in the sacred pelt, the snout of the dead she-bear jutting up behind his head like some dreadful cowl. Still, some of the soldiers tried to take him on, and one of these succeeded in slicing a nasty wound in Kwasin's thigh before the giant's great iron ax swept down and crushed the man's face.

The deeper into the village Kwasin passed, however, the fewer foes he found in his way, until, at last, he stood before the roaring inferno that was the stockade. Desperate shouts to unlock the gate came from the prisoners on the other side of the wall. Kwasin yelled back that he was trying to get them out, but that the stockade's gate, along with the entire wall, was afire and he'd have to find another way. This did not stop the frantic pleading.

Great waves of sweltering heat singed the hair on Kwasin's arms and chest as he stalked up and down the fiery wall, looking for an opening in the flames. Finally, he stopped where the wall burned most furiously. There he stood for some time, peering into the blaze, trying to see how much of the wood in that section had been burned out. It was not easy to tell, but now the wind had shifted again and was sweeping the flames back into the pen where the prisoners were trapped. They would not survive much longer.

Again, he swore. Then, drawing the sacred pelt protectively over his head and torso, he barreled headlong into the hellish conflagration.

Kwasin choked on the dense, sickeningly sweet cedar

smoke as he crashed heavily into half-charred timbers. The wall held, though it had buckled under the impact of his ax, which he had swung before him as he ran. He roared as the sacred pelt burned and crackled, the flames searing his back and shoulders. He fought to breathe.

Again, he swung his ax. This time, the burned-out cedar posts splintered. Screaming wrathful obscenities at Klykwo, the goddess of fire, Kwasin shouldered his way through to the other side of the wall.

For a moment, he could see nothing through the thick, black smoke that sought to smother him. Then the wind shifted yet again, blowing the scorching flames and choking smoke to the south, away from the prisoners' enclosure.

He tore off the still-burning bear pelt and threw it on the ground. Then he bent over and began coughing uncontrollably. When he looked up between coughs, a frightened-looking Adythne was standing before him. She looked distraught at seeing the remains of the sacred she-bear pelt smoldering on the ground, but then she grinned.

"It is as the old she-bear spirit told me in my dream! He who wore her pelt into battle would be invincible! Even fire would not touch him!"

The painful reddish burns all over Kwasin's body and the gruesome wound in his thigh argued against the priestess's assertion, but he could say nothing to refute her. He was still too busy coughing.

While Kwasin was recovering, a large group of prisoners came up behind Adythne, their frightened faces straining to look hopeful as they regarded the newly arrived giant.

"Quickly," Adythne said. She took Kwasin by the hand and began leading him back from the fiery wall, motioning her people to follow. "If the winds shift again," she said to Kwasin, "we'll all die beneath the flames and smoke. You, O Giant Bear Man, must use your gleaming ax and break through the stockade's outer wall!"

Though his lungs felt like they had been raked repeatedly with a rusting iron file, Kwasin accompanied the priestess to the outlying wall and began chopping at it with his ax. After a wearisome effort, and not a few glances back at the burning enclosure to motivate him, Kwasin succeeded in hewing down three cedar poles near their bases, creating a wide enough space for him and the prisoners to pass through.

Kwasin and Adythne in the lead, the group ran across the clearing and assembled in the woods a short distance from the village. Here the priestess gathered the escapees about her. These amounted, all told, to about sixty men, women, and children, though Kwasin estimated that perhaps only twenty-five of them might make able warriors.

"Though we are all tired," Adythne said to the group, "we must strike the enemy while they are routed! We cannot falter now when our victory over the sun worshipers is so near! We must reenter the village and get weapons from the armory." To Kwasin, she said, "The weapons are stored in an outbuilding in the southeast corner of the village, untouched by flames."

"What of the spirit guides?" a man asked, his worried face making it clear he had no desire to reenter the blazing village.

"They have been angered and will eat us!"

Adythne scowled at the man. "It is the spirit guides who have freed us, Tethwa. They will not harm the faithful. And if Nakendar's children do devour us, our flesh will only strengthen them as they rise up to slay the enemies of Kho."

Tethwa grumbled something beneath his breath, but he shook his head in obeisance to his priestess.

Kwasin, for his part, did not relish the idea of returning to the hellhole that was Q"okwoqo any more than Tethwa. But he had come this far against staggering odds. Why not, one way or another, see it through to the end?

After a deep sigh and a silent prayer to Kho, Kwasin led the party back to the fiery main gate.

When dawn broke, few of the survivors of the previous night's devastation were happy. Q"okwoqo lay in ruins. The longhouse of the Klakordeth, many huts and outbuildings, the stockade, and a long stretch of the defensive wall had all been reduced to little more than ash and smoldering cinders. Villagers and soldiers alike stood about looking tired and dejected, their feet and hands stained gray-black with soot.

During the night, Kwasin had succeeded in reentering the village and recovering the weapons from the armory, and with these he led a guerrilla force against the soldiers who had regrouped outside the walls. Many of these men fled into the forest upon being attacked, but Kwasin and his band of twenty men and four women slingers managed to hole up a number of soldiers in the village. These had huddled in an area not beset by fire, deciding to wait it out there until morning rather than risk being killed by the guerrillas in the dark.

Now, as Kwasin and Adythne entered through the main gate in the dawn light, the soldiers looked up as if their very souls sought to flee their bodies. When Adythne began hurling holy curses at them, they bolted for the main gate and fled into the woods. Kwasin, utterly exhausted and relieved that he did not have to fight them, only laughed at the men as they ran past and shouted a number of disparaging epithets about the manhood of Minruth's soldiers.

After the soldiers and a handful of traitorous villagers had been chased into the woods, Kwasin accompanied the priestess as she poked about in the ashes searching for the remains of the sacred she-bear pelt. Finally, looking defeated, Adythne sat down on a half-burned post.

"It is no use," she said. "The sacred pelt has returned to the spirit world." Then Adythne's smoke-reddened, dark-circled eyes brightened. "But not all is lost. By a divine miracle of the Bear God himself, the spirit guides have all escaped the flames and now wander the woods. You, O Kwasin, will help me round them up, and then, with your ax, you can help my people cut down enough lumber to rebuild the totem hall. And when you have finished constructing it, you will lead a glorious dance in the new hall, after which I shall take you into my hut and show you my gratitude."

Kwasin sighed heavily. The priestess was certainly beautiful and the thought of the reward waiting for him in her hut was, without question, enticing. But he knew staying here and rebuilding the village was not in his future.

He did, however, have one last chore he felt obligated to perform before he left the valley of Q"okwoqo.

The evening before Kwasin took his leave of the priestess and her village, Kho and Resu pealed the heavens with great blinding flashes of lightning and fearsome claps of thunder as they waged war against one another. Who won the battle, Kwasin could not say, but the heavenly tumult only strengthened his resolve for the task that lay ahead.

The next morning Kwasin ascended the steep, rain-sodden slope overlooking the local hot spring. The climb was a treacherous one. The ground, powdery and brittle from the recent dry spell, had given way in many places to small mudslides. Twice, Kwasin lost his hold and slid painfully down the face of the rocky escarpment. But he was determined. He had a debt to repay.

At last, he pulled himself up over the ledge that jutted out from the slope before Old Father Nakendar's cave. Kwasin stood up and examined the boulder that blocked the entrance. The size of the great stone was daunting. He could not begin to guess its weight, but it was certainly more than even his prodigious strength might hope to move.

But he had an idea. If he could not move the boulder by himself, perhaps Great Kho, goddess of the Earth, could give him a little help.

He unslung his ax and began assailing the dirt at the base of the boulder with the weapon's massive iron head. Soon, the earth began to give way.

Too late, Kwasin realized the flaw in his plan. After several swings of his ax, the ledge as a whole—already weakened from the recent downpour on dry soil—began to crumble beneath his feet.

He fell to his knees as the ground on which he stood yielded, the ax falling out of his grip and tumbling end over end down the escarpment. The great boulder groaned as it teetered forward, the soil beneath it sieving down the slope in great rivers of earth. Then, the boulder gave.

Kwasin kicked off just before the ledge completely collapsed, barreling his chest into the sharp rocks that rimmed the lower edge of the newly opened cave entrance. There he hung, his dust-covered, muscular arms thrust out over the edge, clinging with the barest of holds to the face of the escarpment. For a few moments, he could still hear the roar of the boulder as it wreaked havoc on the slope.

Now the lower edge of the cave's base began to crumble beneath his weight. He slipped down another foot before desperately flailing out and finding another hold.

He looked down. The landslide resulting from the great boulder's tumble had sloughed off a huge portion of the slope directly below him, a deep and narrow gouge that dropped fifty feet to the rocky base of the escarpment.

Again, dirt crumbled and he felt his hold giving way.

He breathed a prayer to Kho. Soon he would see Sisisken's terrible face and be led down to her shadowy underworld. He only hoped the people of Q"okwoqo would from time to time sacrifice a bull or a goat to his spirit so that he would not hunger. If they did not, who would?

Something warm gripped his wrist. An overpowering, rank bear smell saturated the dusty air. Suddenly, he felt himself being pulled upward as the earth crumbled beneath him. Then, he was sitting on the firm ground inside the cave, peering through a cloud of sunlit dust and out over the rocky scape. In the distance lay the clear and steaming turquoise waters of the sacred spring.

Although it took all his will to do so, Kwasin turned and looked up at the towering dark form beside him. When he did, he gasped, his heart pounding.

The thing that met Kwasin's eyes smiled down at him. Or it might have been a grimace. It was hard to tell with those terrible teeth and the unnerving, red-rimmed, all-brown eyes. Its jaws protruded, more than a man's but less than an ape's. Still, the face was unmistakably bearlike, and when the creature spoke a single word, Kwasin gasped again, though he did not at first understand it.

Then the hairy form stepped to the rim of the cave and lowered itself gracefully over the edge. Kwasin watched, stupefied, as the creature climbed slowly but nimbly down the rock-tumbled slope to the western side of the great abyss, finding holds where Kwasin could discern none. When it reached the bottom of the escarpment, it headed southwest, toward the deep mountains. Finally, it disappeared in the dark trees.

Kwasin's heart went on beating heavily as he sat for a great while at the mouth of the cave looking out over the spring.

Eventually, a wide smile stretched across his face. Though the word spoken by the Old Father had been strangely pronounced, Kwasin believed he understood it at last.

His mother had once told him, after all, that divine blood ran in his veins, though she had not elaborated on the matter.

Yes, there could be no mistaking it.

The Bear God had called him "Brother."

WOLD NEWTON PREHISTORY

PREHISTORY

JOHN GRIBARDSUN & TIME'S LAST GIFT

INTO TIME'S ABYSS

BY JOHN ALLEN SMALL

Philip José Farmer was known for writing many different series, even once stating that he had twelve going at the same time. However, the standalone novel *Time's Last Gift* (Titan Books, 2012) has proven to be one of his most popular works. Perhaps "standalone" is not a completely accurate description; the novel also serves as an unstated prelude to the Khokarsa series: *Hadon of Ancient Opar* (Titan Books, 2013), *Flight to Opar*, and *The Song of Kwasin*. And who is to say that Farmer might not have revisited the characters in *Time's Last Gift*? He certainly left an opening, as one can see in the excerpt on the following page, an opening John Allen Small deftly uses to relaunch the time travelers on a quite different adventure.

When the H. G. Wells I *voyaged into time (again), he felt sorry for John II, Rachel, Drummond, and Robert. This trip would not take them to the France of 12,000 B.C. Somewhere along the transit, the vessel and its passengers would disappear. He did not know how or to where... He liked to think that Rachel and the others had not just disintegrated. Perhaps they were shunted off into a parallel world...*

—Philip José Farmer, *Time's Last Gift*

The explosion *should* have been as loud as a seventy-five-millimeter cannon's.

The fact that it was not was the second bit of evidence that something might have gone awry.

The first had occurred en route. All available data and preliminary testing had indicated that the timeship's transition from A.D. 2070, spring, to circa 12,000 B.C., spring, should have been instantaneous. The expected explosion, caused by displacement of air upon the vehicle's arrival, should have been the only physical sensation proving that the transition had taken place at all.

Instead there was a sickening feeling of momentary nonentity—as if the *H. G. Wells I* and all four members of her crew had briefly phased out of existence altogether—followed not by a deafening boom, but by a sound vaguely reminiscent of an electrical short circuit. Or, perhaps, of bacon frying.

"That... didn't seem right, somehow," Rachel Silverstein managed to stammer. She brought up her hands, placed the palms against her chest, her shoulders, the sides of her face, as if making certain she was real. Her pretty face was twisted into a slight grimace. "Or am I just imagining things?"

Drummond Silverstein, her husband, slowly exhaled as he opened his eyes. Releasing his grip on the arms of his chair, he drew in a new breath as the color slowly returned to his ashen features. "If you are, you aren't the only one," he said in response to Rachel's question.

At his station on the other side of the craft, Robert von Billman shifted in his seat and nervously cleared his throat. "Indeed," he concurred, his unease making his slight German accent seem a bit stronger than usual. He glanced around the ship and added, "Is it safe to get up and move about?"

John Gribardsun turned in his seat and took a moment to look at each of his crewmates. "Physically we all appear to be unharmed," he said at last. "As for the ship..." He swiveled back around and began twisting dials on the instrument panel before him. As his fingers played upon the controls he felt a momentary flash of—what, exactly? Not so much a sense of déjà vu as of a vague, unsettling sensation that the situation should somehow be more familiar than it actually was.

The feeling passed quickly, and did not distract from the task at hand. Gribardsun's hands danced expertly across the panel, pushing buttons and flipping switches as he watched the readouts and studied the controls' responses. "Everything seems to be functioning normally," he finally reported. "Let's take a look outside."

With that Gribardsun twisted the dial that activated the ship's viewscreen and exterior cameras. His crewmates gathered around his chair as the picture shimmered into view.

That view was spectacular—a pristine, virgin woodland which reminded Rachel of the way she'd pictured the Garden of Eden when she was a child. Even the seemingly unflappable Gribardsun appeared visibly moved by the sight, but he and his crewmates barely had time to enjoy it. Rachel was the first to notice the tiny figure dash out of a clearing about halfway up the right side of the screen. "Look there," she said, pointing. "Is that a man?"

Gribardsun looked where Rachel had pointed, then pressed a button to increase the camera's magnification. Sure enough, it seemed to be a Magdalenian—followed by three more, all running in more or less the same direction. The primitives ran at an angle away from the general direction of the timeship. One turned and looked behind him, a look of fear etched into his features as he stumbled and almost fell. He managed to right himself, though the effort nearly caused him to career into one of the other runners.

These men were running for their very lives.

"What are they afraid of?" Drummond asked. "Us?"

Gribardsun shook his head. "No," he answered. "I don't believe they are even aware of our presence. Something is chasing them. But what?"

As if in answer, there was a rippling in the air behind the runners, as if some sort of invisible projectile had been fired in their direction. An explosion like the bursting of a small artillery shell rocked the ground at the heels of the runner who had nearly stumbled before, sending him sprawling face-first into the ground as his companions continued to flee. The one who had fallen managed to roll over and sit upright, but that was as far as he got; his eyes grew wide, his face frozen in an expression of utter horror that none besides Gribardsun had ever seen before.

There was another rippling of the air, and this time whatever projectile had been fired struck the poor fellow full in the center of the chest. It hit with such force that the time travelers thought it should have ripped a hole in his midsection; instead the victim's body began to spasm violently, as if gripped by an epileptic seizure. The seizure lasted roughly three seconds; on the fourth second the seizure ceased, and the man's body suddenly turned white and slightly crystalline in appearance. As Gribardsun watched he was reminded of the old story about Lot's wife turning into a pillar of salt...

That thought had scarcely entered Gribardsun's head when the fallen man's body suddenly popped out of existence. Not an explosion, but more like the bursting of a soap bubble—with only a small trace of a white, powder-like substance drifting to the ground to mark that the man had ever existed.

"My God!" von Billman exclaimed. Rachel gasped and

buried her face in Gribardsun's shoulder, who had jumped up out of his seat like a jungle cat ready to spring into action. Unconsciously, perhaps, he slipped a protective arm around Rachel; Drummond saw this and grimaced, but said nothing.

The four of them watched as the remaining runners suddenly stopped short, then turned in an effort to go back. They stopped again, their heads moving back and forth in either direction as the three of them seemed to press into one another for protection. Von Billman was just about to ask again what they might be running from when the viewscreen provided the answer: a pair of huge four-legged creatures, one emerging from either side of the clearing. The behemoths looked like some kind of cross between a wolf and a bear; both were saddled like a horse and ridden by humanoids wearing what appeared to be battle armor. The riders were quite a bit larger than the average man—Gribardsun guessed them to be somewhere between eight and nine feet tall, though it was difficult to be certain—and each carried a hand-held firearm, the likes of which none of the crew had ever seen before.

One of the riders dismounted and walked toward the three who had been running, now huddled together on the ground like frightened children. One of them mustered up enough courage to pull away from the others and swipe his arm toward the rider in a gesture of defiance; the gesture was rewarded by his meeting the same grisly fate as the earlier victim, thanks to a short burst from the rider's gun. The two remaining runners fell forward with their arms outstretched in surrender; the rider stepped forward and yanked them up to their feet, his weapon held ready to fire again as he and the other rider herded them to a place outside the camera's field of vision.

"Who are they?" von Billman demanded. "What are they doing to those poor people?"

"I don't know," Gribardsun responded, gently pushing Rachel toward her husband as he spoke. He moved toward the exit hatch and added, "But I intend to find out."

"John?" Rachel called after him, barely masking the concern in her voice. "What are you going to do?"

This time Gribardsun did not answer. He paused long enough to unlock the expedition's weapons box and remove an automatic pistol, as well as a leather belt and scabbard holding the old hunting knife he had insisted upon bringing along. Securing the belt and scabbard around the waist of his single-piece tunic, Gribardsun opened the portal and waited as the timeship's stairway platform slid down into place. Once the platform was secure, he stepped through the hatch and started down the steps.

The others hesitated for a moment before following him, Drummond stopping long enough to grab a .30-caliber automatic rifle from the weapons locker. They reached the foot of the stairs and stood behind Gribardsun, where they were met by a sight none could have anticipated during the many months of planning and preparation for this voyage.

An entire platoon of riders like those they had seen on the viewscreen—twenty in all—stood in formation approximately two hundred yards from the timeship, lined up in four rows of five and facing Gribardsun and the others. Between the second and third row stood a group of about forty or fifty men, women and children who appeared to be from the same tribe as the two just captured. They were also lined up in rows, and bound together by large chains attached to clasps secured around their necks and the ankles of their right legs. One was a young female child whose neck was similarly chained but rode on the shoulder of a man Gribardsun assumed was her father. The two new additions were shepherded toward the group by their capturers, and barely struggled now as they were chained into place.

"Slavers," Rachel gasped. Gribardsun nodded grimly.

"But who are they?" von Billman asked again. He turned to Gribardsun and added, "And where do they come from? Look at the size of them—it's like a race of giants."

"What about those guns they carry?" Drummond queried. "They seem to turn the very air around them into some kind of missile. Technology like that doesn't exist in our time; how can it exist in 12,000 B.C.?"

Gribardsun held up a hand to silence them. "Perhaps some of our questions are about to be answered," he half whispered.

The others followed his gaze and watched as the front row of slavers nudged their steeds forward toward them. Four of the riders carried large banners, bearing an insignia resembling a starburst. The rider in the middle was obviously the leader; he rode about half a length in front of the others and held himself with an air of superiority. When the quintet reached a point about midway between their fellows and the Gribardsun party, the leader held up a hand and they came to a halt.

The leader reached up with both hands and removed his armored helmet, revealing a face both human and leonine in appearance. The skin had a reddish-brown tint, and the head was topped by a shock of bright white hair like an unkempt Mohawk. He sat there quietly for a moment, his eyes gazing upon each of the time travelers one at a time. His eyes lingered upon Rachel a bit longer than the others, a fact that did not escape her notice— nor that of her husband. She took a half-step backward as both Drummond and Gribardsun assumed protective stances on either side of her, an act which brought a trace of a smile to the leader's face.

Finally he spoke. "Which among you is in command?"

Rachel and Drummond's eyes grew wide, and von Billman—the linguist of the group—for a moment appeared as though he was about to faint. "English!" he exclaimed. "He speaks *English*! But how?"

Gribardsun alone appeared unfazed by this discovery. Gently pushing Rachel closer to her husband, he took several steps forward and gazed up at the leader. "I am John Gribardsun," he said simply.

"I don't care," was the leader's response.

For one of only a very few times in his life, Gribardsun did not know how to react. He had never really considered himself an egotist, but over the years had learned to put his natural sense of self-confidence to good use and had become accustomed— unwittingly, perhaps—to a certain type of reaction when he did. Those rare occasions when he failed to elicit such a reaction tended to stay with him—necessary reminders that, no matter how much he might wish to deny it, he was only human after all.

But now was not the time to dwell upon that. Changing the

subject, he said simply, "You speak our tongue."

"Do I?" the leader retorted. "Or would it be more precise to instead say that you speak ours?" He paused for a moment as if letting that suggestion sink in before continuing. "But that is a mystery to be considered later. For the moment the only thing you are required to know is that you and your companions are now the property of Seris Dourn."

Although he dared not show it, Gribardsun couldn't help but be amused by the haughtiness in the other's tone of voice; it reminded him of so many of his fellow dukes in the days before England had abolished titles. Gribardsun asked, "I assume you are Seris Dourn?"

"Your assumption is flattering but inaccurate. I am Teran Lynd, the emperor's representative and humble servant."

"I see. Then allow me to ask the emperor's representative and humble servant a question." Gribardsun took another step toward Lynd's steed. "By what right do you enslave these people, or claim ownership over my companions and myself?"

A great, booming laugh erupted from Lynd. "By what right?" he repeated. "The right of superior power, of course. We can conquer, therefore we conquer. What other right does one need?" He raised one hand and gestured; the two riders Gribardsun's party first saw on the viewscreen rode up to join him. "Take them," Lynd commanded. "The men will join the ranks of our slaves. The woman…" His voice trailed off as his gaze moved back in Rachel's direction, then he added, "The woman I have other plans for."

The riders nudged their steeds in unison, but the great

beasts had barely taken a step when Drummond brought up his rifle and fired. The shot bounced harmlessly off Lynd's armor; the entire front line of his command responded by raising their own weapons and firing in Drummond's direction.

"No!" The scream came from von Billman. He grabbed Rachel by the arm and managed to pull her down to the ground out of the line of fire. As he rolled atop Rachel to protect her, von Billman caught a quick glimpse of the expression on her husband's face as one of the blasts hit him full in the chest. He couldn't remember ever seeing anyone look so surprised…

Drummond Silverstein died not knowing that there would be no voyage home for his companions. One of the marauders' shots had struck the time traveler; the others impacted against his ship. The *H. G. Wells I* shuddered violently as though located at the epicenter of an earthquake, then seemed to fold into itself before imploding like a planet caught in the throes of a black hole. Rachel screamed, and von Billman struck the ground with an angry fist.

All this happened within the course of only a few seconds. Gribardsun took advantage of the confusion to launch himself up and forward, striking Teran Lynd with his shoulder and knocking him off his mount onto the ground. Both men jumped quickly to their feet, and a roar erupted from the back of Lynd's throat like the jungle cat he resembled. Gribardsun brought up his pistol, only to have it knocked out of his hand by a swing of Lynd's massive right hand. Lynd charged forward, striking Gribardsun full force and sending him sprawling backward into the grass.

They struggled there, rolling around on the ground as each

battled to gain the upper hand. At one point Gribardsun was able to maneuver himself up on top of his adversary, locking his well-muscled legs around the bigger man's arms. Holding his left forearm against Lynd's throat, he reached down with his right hand in an attempt to draw his hunting knife. But Lynd managed to free one of his arms and thrust it upward, ramming Gribardsun hard in the jaw. Gribardsun tumbled in one direction and his knife in the other, as Lynd jumped back to his feet. Momentarily dazed, Gribardsun raised himself up onto his hands and knees, shook his head and managed to stand up as well.

"John! Look out behind you!"

At Rachel's cry, Gribardsun whirled around in time to see one of the other riders advancing on him, his rifle drawn. Before he could fire, Gribardsun jumped at him and grabbed the barrel of the weapon with both hands; he yanked the gun out of the rider's hands, sending him up over the head of his mount and onto the ground. The mount was unable to stop in time and ran directly over the rider, killing him instantly.

Gribardsun swung the rifle up like a club and brought it crashing down onto a large nearby rock, splintering it into dozens of pieces. He turned again, just in time to see Lynd pull back his fist in preparation to strike. Gribardsun avoided the fist and lunged at Lynd again, and as the two continued to trade blows, one of Lynd's standard bearers rode forward and brought his pole down across the back of Gribardsun's head.

The last sound Gribardsun heard before sliding into unconsciousness was Rachel screaming again…

* * *

He awoke to find himself seated on the ground with his arms pulled behind him, secured by leather straps around the trunk of a small tree. A campfire provided the only illumination, and several tents dotted the nearby landscape. Gribardsun's jumpsuit, tattered in the fight with Teran Lynd, had been replaced while he was unconscious by a loincloth fashioned from the hide of some manner of beast. There was a soft metallic rustling sound off to his right. Gribardsun glanced in that direction and saw the small throng of aborigines who had been taken captive earlier, still chained together as they slept on the cold dirt.

One of the captives sat upright, kneeling forward with his face buried in his arms, which lay folded across his raised knees. Gribardsun recognized the man and called out to him. "Robert?"

Von Billman raised his head and turned in the direction of the other's voice. The corners of his mouth curved up into a slight smile. "John! Thank God you're all right, man. I was beginning to fear that I might have lost you as well."

"I still live," Gribardsun replied. Then, recalling von Billman's comment, he asked, "Where is Rachel?"

Von Billman's smile disappeared. "In one of the tents, I think," the linguist responded. "She and several of the other women were separated from the rest of us after our captors made camp. I overheard a bit of conversation between two of our fellow prisoners; it seems this Lynd fellow has developed quite the affinity for the local women." He paused briefly before adding, "From what I gather, Rachel and the others are to be the latest additions to his harem."

That last comment caused Gribardsun to see something

that had escaped his notice before. While the male captives' ages ranged from very young to very old, and everything between, the females were all either small children to prepubescent teens or middle-aged and older. Women between the ages of around fourteen or fifteen to twenty-five or thirty were nowhere to be seen, save for several who appeared sickly or in some other way unappealing to someone with certain activities on their mind.

Von Billman watched as Gribardsun glanced around the camp. "Not exactly the sort of situation a person might typically expect to find himself in, is it?"

This time it was Gribardsun's turn to offer a slight—albeit grim—smile. "For most people, I suppose," he replied. "You said you overheard some of the Magdalenians talking. Do they also speak English?"

"Only a few of them, and those few not very well," von Billman answered. "Apparently these marauders have been a presence here long enough for a few of them to pick up some of the language. Although it is still a mystery to me where our captors might have learned it, given that they are obviously not native to the area."

Gribardsun asked, "Have you been able to learn anything about our hosts?"

"Just enough to deepen the mystery, I'm afraid," von Billman said glumly. "They appear to be extraterrestrial in origin, which would certainly explain their appearance. One of the Magdalenian children—a little girl named Anana—spoke of a 'great boat that came down from the sky.' Roughly a year and a half ago, if I understood her correctly. Shortly after they arrived they raided this tribe's village and at least two others located not far away. A number of men and women from each village were captured and apparently enslaved—for what reason, no one seems to know—and there have been several more raids since then..."

Before von Billman could say more, the door flap to the largest of the tents opened and Teran Lynd stepped out, flanked by a pair of guards. In addition to the firearms seen earlier, each guard wore a large broadsword strapped across his back and carried a smaller dagger in a belt wrapped around his tunic.

Lynd wore a knife as well—Gribardsun's hunting knife, its scabbard secured to Lynd's waist like a trophy. Gribardsun looked from the knife up into the eyes of his captor and said simply, "That belongs to me."

In response, Lynd merely smiled. He knelt down in front of Gribardsun as if to speak, then brought the back of his hand hard against Gribardsun's face. Despite the force of the blow, the time traveler barely flinched; a tiny trickle of blood ran down from the corner of Gribardsun's lip, but he did not speak.

Lynd rose to full height and stood silently for a moment. He announced, "I believe I am going to enjoy watching you die."

"You are not the first to have expressed such sentiments," Gribardsun replied evenly. "I doubt you shall be the last."

"We shall see." Lynd turned and took a couple of steps away, then whirled back to face Gribardsun. "You should consider yourself fortunate," he said. "I wanted to merely kill you and be done with it. But my warriors were so impressed by your fighting skills that they felt a simple execution would be..."

He paused as if searching for the right words, then concluded, "a terrible waste."

"No doubt you'll be able to think of something appropriately entertaining," Gribardsun observed.

Lynd smiled, his lion-like teeth and eyes gleaming in the firelight. "I believe I already have," he stated. He turned and pointed at a tent at the far end of the camp. "In that tent we are holding one of my people—a criminal and traitor, found guilty of treason against his emperor. I've been trying to think of a punishment befitting his transgressions. It occurs to me that pitting the two of you against one another in battle would be a worthy solution to both questions. And so tomorrow morning that is exactly what will occur."

"A battle to the death, then," Gribardsun said. "And what becomes of the winner?"

Lynd smiled again. "The 'winner' is given the opportunity to live long enough to return with us to our city, and witness my marriage to that exquisite female who accompanied you here," he replied. "Then he shall be chained to an altar and sacrificed as an offering to our gods."

A look of horror fell over von Billman's features. Gribardsun glared at Lynd. "Where is Rachel?" he demanded.

"In the tent next to mine, being attended to by several of my other wives," Lynd told him. He knelt down in front of Gribardsun again. "Whatever other reason you might have had for coming here, I am grateful to you for bringing this Rachel to me. She's not like the other women here. There's a fire in her that I find most appealing."

He stood up and added, "Yes, I shall indeed enjoy watching you die."

"As you said, we shall see," Gribardsun told him.

Lynd merely laughed as he turned and strode back toward his tent, his guards right behind him. Von Billman watched until they entered the tent, turned to Gribardsun with a distressed expression. "I have an uneasy feeling, my friend, that you may have made too strong an impression upon our host."

Gribardsun nodded. "I seem to have that effect on some people," he said humorlessly. Both men fell silent, and eventually drifted off to sleep.

A stinging cloud of loose dirt, kicked up into his face by one of Lynd's guards, roused Gribardsun from his slumber. For a moment he forgot he was bound to the tree, causing the guard to laugh when Gribardsun was unable to stand. The guard loosened the leather straps and pulled Gribardsun to his feet. Von Billman, awakened by the guard's laughter, opened his eyes in time to see Gribardsun being led toward a clearing on the opposite side of the camp where the rest of Lynd's party was assembled.

At the same time, from the tent Lynd had pointed out the previous night, another guard emerged with a second member of his race, this one with his arms secured behind him and a heavy chain binding his ankles together. Both prisoners were brought to the center of the clearing and stood before Lynd, seated and posturing like Caesar at the Colosseum, flanked by two guards and several Magdalenian women Gribardsun guessed to be favorites from his harem. To Lynd's immediate left stood Rachel, her uniform tunic replaced by a halter top and loincloth made of some silken-type fabric, the latter held in place by an ornate belt of gold.

Rachel's expression was one of both fear and defiance of this monster who claimed her as his bride. Her face first seemed to brighten as she saw Gribardsun, but that light faded and her shoulders sagged as the realization of what was about to happen hit home.

Lynd peered up at the prisoners but said nothing. Instead he gestured toward their escorts, who reached behind and drew their broadswords from the scabbards strapped across their backs. After handing their swords to the prisoners, the guards turned and marched to opposite ends of the clearing to stand with their comrades.

Rising from his chair, Lynd took a step forward and addressed the prisoners. "Soon enough, the gods will feast upon both your souls," he said softly, before stepping back again and holding one arm up over his head. Looking around at his followers, Lynd announced loudly, "Let the battle begin!"

He dropped his arm, and Gribardsun barely managed to sidestep the blow as his opponent brought up his sword and swung it down at Gribardsun's skull. He swung again, and Gribardsun parried and caught the blade upon his own. He stuck one leg out, causing the other to stumble and drop down to one knee. At first the fall seemed to have little effect as he and Gribardsun exchanged blows, sparks flying as their swords crashed repeatedly against one another. Because of his greater height, the kneeling alien stood eye to eye with Gribardsun; it was only due to his own extraordinary strength and prowess—the product of his unique upbringing and a lifetime of experience— that Gribardsun was able to hold his own in the face of such a formidable adversary.

Eventually, Gribardsun managed to press a slight advantage, pushing his crouching rival further backward as he held his blade against the other. Then Gribardsun's blade slid up toward the tip of the other sword. His opponent used the shift in weight to drop below Gribardsun's sword and roll to one side, his elbow striking the back of Gribardsun's knee. The action knocked Gribardsun off balance, allowing his adversary to jump back to his feet and assume an offensive stance. Gribardsun whirled and quickly brought his blade up to meet the other at mid-swing.

For several minutes they battled back and forth, and Gribardsun thought he saw remorse in the other's expression. "I have no wish to kill you," the alien warrior told him.

"That is good," Gribardsun answered as they continued exchanging blows, "for I do not plan to die." He brought his sword up over his head and swung down, only to have the blow parried again.

"You do not understand," the warrior said. "We will both die this day."

"Perhaps," Gribardsun conceded. "But if it is to be, let it not be at the whim of one such as Teran Lynd." He took a step backward and lowered his sword. "I have no fight with you," he said. Then he threw down his sword, turned and began to walk back toward where Lynd was sitting.

His opponent stood there for a moment, unsure how to react, and a roar of disapproval swept through the group of spectators. Lynd leaned forward in his chair and frowned. "It would seem that your champion is a coward after all," he told Rachel, who merely closed her eyes in despair but said nothing.

Gribardsun had taken nine or ten steps when he suddenly stopped and gazed forward, his eyes locked on Lynd's. For a moment the corners of Gribardsun's mouth pulled up into just the slightest trace of a smile. He took one step backward and broke into a sprint, leaping forward and knocking Lynd out of his chair. Rachel and the other women managed to jump aside just before impact. Lynd fell to the ground and was knocked unconscious when his head struck a rock. Gribardsun quickly jumped to his feet and found himself facing the two guards who had been at Lynd's side, both of whom darted forward with daggers drawn to protect their leader.

But Gribardsun was too fast for them. He grabbed one guard's wrist and swung him around, forcing his dagger deep into the chest of the other. As the second guard fell dead Gribardsun twisted the first's arm behind his back, breaking the limb in the process and pushing him to the ground. Gribardsun then spun round and retrieved the dagger from the other guard's chest, taking time to also grab both the guard's firearm and the keys.

Gribardsun rose and fired the weapon in the direction of the warriors who had been watching the fight, felling four of them in rapid succession. In the ensuing confusion the other warriors drew their own guns, but because of their close proximity to one another they were unable to return fire without the risk of hitting their own comrades. Several of them instead drew their daggers and rushed forward to battle Gribardsun hand to hand, but the time traveler fought with a ferocity none of them had anticipated.

Gribardsun drove his sword into the chest of one of the warriors, pulled it out and swung around to sever another opponent's leg just above the knee. The wounded warrior toppled into the path of one of his comrades, knocking him off balance. Gribardsun seized the moment and sliced through the warrior's torso, his sword moving upward from just above the right hip to the left shoulder.

The two halves of the body fell in opposite directions. A battle roar issued from the throat of a fourth warrior as he charged in Gribardsun's direction. Gribardsun picked up the leg he had severed earlier and threw it at the charging combatant. The soldier dodged the detached limb but stumbled over part of the body that had been cleaved in two. He landed on his face and rolled over in time to see the tip of Gribardsun's sword driving downward into his face.

In rapid succession Gribardsun dispatched three more warriors, two with his sword and the third with the gun as he dodged a death blow from that fighter's blade. Gribardsun whirled round to face yet another opponent, but stopped short when he realized the latter was the warrior Lynd had forced him to fight. At his feet lay the soldier whose leg had been cut off, the sword Gribardsun had earlier tossed aside protruding from his chest. Without a word the warrior withdrew the sword and held it out toward Gribardsun. Shifting the gun to his other hand, Gribardsun took back the sword, and together the two of them continued battling against Lynd's troops.

After running his sword through one of the warriors, Gribardsun turned and caught a glimpse of Rachel cowering by one of the nearby trees. He sprinted in her direction and she rushed forward to meet him, wrapping her arms around him and pulling herself close. "Are you all right?" he asked.

He could feel her nod. "I am now," she said softly, and Gribardsun could tell that she was trying mightily not to cry. Rachel clung tightly to him for just a few seconds, then pulled away and looked at him. She smiled and started to say something more, but suddenly pulled away and screamed. Gribardsun whirled around in time to see one of Lynd's warriors bring up one of those strange firearms and point it in their direction. The guard's finger twitched on the trigger, but he did not fire; instead his eyes grew wide as the blade of a broadsword suddenly erupted from the center of his chest.

The guard dropped his gun and fell forward, dead. Behind him stood Gribardsun's erstwhile opponent, who brought a hand up to his forehead in a gesture of salute. Gribardsun returned the gesture, and the warrior drew his sword from the body of his victim before turning to stand against more of his own kind.

Gribardsun turned back to Rachel. "Take these," he said, handing her both the gun and the key. "Go release Robert and the others. Then you and he go with them back to their village."

Rachel shook her head. "I won't go without you," she told him.

"Yes you will," he answered, as he gave Rachel a gentle push in the direction of the captives. "I won't be far behind, I promise." As she darted away Gribardsun was waylaid from behind. Gribardsun and his opponent struggled as they rolled around in the dirt, until Gribardsun found himself with his back to the ground and a pair of massive hands around his throat. It was at that moment Gribardsun realized he was fighting Lynd, who had regained consciousness and was determined to rend Gribardsun limb from limb.

Placing his hands around Lynd's wrists, Gribardsun pulled and finally managed to free himself from the large alien's grip. He brought one knee up sharply into Lynd's gut, then kicked Lynd up and over his head. As Lynd landed on his back with a thud, Gribardsun rose to his feet. Weakened slightly by the attempted strangulation, Gribardsun nonetheless rushed forward and brought the fight to Lynd again. As they fought, another of Lynd's warriors rushed forward to join in the fray—but was prevented from doing so by Gribardsun's newfound ally, who engaged the warrior as Gribardsun and Lynd continued to fight.

Following Gribardsun's instructions, Rachel and von Billman worked to release the captive Magdalenians, who wasted little time fleeing the campsite. Rachel and von Billman followed behind them, von Billman pausing long enough to turn and fire a couple of shots to cover their escape before running off into the forest.

Angrily balling his massive hands into fists, Lynd swung at Gribardsun several times but failed to land a blow. Gribardsun punched Lynd in the gut, and as the alien fell forward from the force of the blow, Gribardsun brought his knee up into Lynd's groin. Lynd fell to his knees and Gribardsun drew back his leg to kick him in the face. But Lynd recovered more quickly than Gribardsun expected, grabbing the time traveler's leg and flipping him violently into the air. Rolling onto the ground in such a way as to avoid broken bones, Gribardsun quickly jumped up and charged his foe.

Lynd stopped that charge with a powerful swipe of his hand, his nails clawing across Gribardsun's face in the process. The blow knocked Gribardsun aside and drew blood from the gouge marks across his cheek, but failed to knock him off his feet. He darted around and jumped onto the alien's back, passing his arms under Lynd's from behind and clamping his hands on the back of his opponent's neck in a full nelson.

Gribardsun squeezed in an attempt to press the advantage, but Lynd started spinning around in order to break the Earthman's hold on him. He finally managed to shake free of Gribardsun, who again tumbled to the ground. The alien was on him in an instant, and the pair rolled around back and forth in the dirt as they continued trading blows.

Eventually, Gribardsun managed to roll over on top of Lynd, at the same time retrieving the hunting knife that Lynd had taken from him. Gribardsun held the knife menacingly in front of Lynd's face and said in a near-growl, "This belonged to my father." Then he plunged the knife forward into Lynd's throat. At almost the exact same moment, his ally dispatched the other warrior with a swing of his sword, severing the warrior's head from his body. With one knee pressed upon his dead foe's chest, Gribardsun threw back his head and raised his voice to the sky. The sound that issued forth was like the battle cry of a great beast, and the warrior who now stood beside him looked upon Gribardsun with an expression showing equal parts awe and respect.

"Truly you are a mighty warrior," he said as Gribardsun rose to his feet, securing his reclaimed scabbard around his own waist.

"As are you," Gribardsun answered, sliding his knife into the scabbard. "I am glad we fight side by side, rather than against one another." He held out his hand in a gesture of friendship. The warrior clasped it firmly in his own as Gribardsun said, "My name is John."

"I am Gar Duno," the other responded. He was about to speak again when they both heard the sound of footfalls racing away from the camp. They looked up and saw three surviving members of Lynd's squadron running after Rachel, von Billman and the natives. Gribardsun moved forward to give chase, but stopped as his companion placed a firm hand on his shoulder. Gar Duno quickly bent down and snatched another gun from the holster of one of his dead kinsmen. He stood back up and fired at the warriors, deliberately missing but drawing their attention from the fleeing natives. As the warriors turned and started running back in their direction, Gar snapped, "Quickly, we must go!"

The two raced into the forest, heading in the opposite direction from the path that Rachel and the others had taken. Although slightly fatigued from the battle, they continued running for roughly two miles and managed to put some space between them and their pursuers, who continued the chase despite losing ground. Gribardsun could still hear the warriors following them even though they were no longer in sight.

He and Gar slowed down to rest for a moment. Glancing around at their surroundings, Gar spied a natural path through the woods that veered around a large rock formation and back in the general direction they had come from. He pointed out the path to Gribardsun.

"Go this way," Gar directed. "The natives' village is about a day's march from here. If I am right, you should rejoin your friends in less than half that time."

"What about you?" Gribardsun queried.

In response Gar motioned back toward the warriors who were chasing them. "I'll remain here long enough to draw them in the other direction, to allow you to make good your escape. I know this area better than they do. In time they will grow weary of the chase, and will return to our city."

"Good idea," Gribardsun said. "Once you've lost them you can make your way back and join us as well."

Gar shook his head. "You and your friends may be strangers here, but the natives are your people," he said. "I am an outcast among my people, but I doubt I would be accepted among yours."

"I accept you," Gribardsun told him. "That should be enough."

"Perhaps, in time, it will be," Gar answered with a shrug. "For now that should not concern you. When those warriors return home having lost Teran Lynd, most of his command, *and* a new group of slaves, the consequences will not be good for the natives. They will look to you for leadership—and protection. You must convince them to relocate, to find a place where they can be safe. Such a place may well not exist, but you must try. Teran Lynd merely intended to subjugate these people. After today it is unlikely that whoever succeeds him as the emperor's emissary will be quite as merciful. I fear you have made a dangerous enemy today, my friend."

"So it would seem," Gribardsun acknowledged, recalling a lifetime of exploits that had led him to this moment in time— or, perhaps more appropriately under the circumstances, out of time. "I have made dangerous enemies before, and have lived to tell the tale," he said. "If it is indeed my destiny to remain here among these people, I will do what I can to help them. If I must make war to do so, I shall."

Gar smiled and clasped his hands upon Gribardsun's shoulders. "If that day should come, I pray to my gods that Gar Duno is there to battle at your side again." With that he glanced back in the direction they had come from. In the distance they could hear the pursuing warriors coming closer toward them. "Now go, friend John. Go!" Gribardsun nodded in silent thanks, then turned and began the trek to rejoin his comrades.

The afternoon sun was just preparing to make its descent when Gribardsun caught up with Rachel, von Billman and the Magdalenians. They had stopped to rest and were discussing the idea of making camp for the night when Rachel happened to look up and saw Gribardsun walking toward them. She stood up and ran to him, wrapping her arms around his muscular frame and hugging him close. She did not speak at first, but the tears she had fought back earlier finally spilled from her eyes.

Gribardsun held her for a moment, then gently released her and stepped back. "I'm sorry about Drummond," he told her.

Rachel nodded in acknowledgment. "He was a good man," she said. "We'd had our problems over the past year or so; I think he hoped being part of this project would bring us closer together. I guess we'll never know…"

Just then von Billman came forward to join them. "Welcome back, John," he said. As he shook Gribardsun's hand a sad smile worked its way across his features. "I almost said 'welcome home.' I suppose that's what it is now, isn't it?"

Gribardsun nodded. "I suppose so," he said. He told them of how he and Gar Duno had acted as decoys to help the others escape, of the flight into the jungle, and Gar's admonition regarding the natives' safety.

A mournful expression crossed Rachel's face. "What's to become of us?" she asked.

"We survive," Gribardsun answered simply. "With the timeship destroyed we cannot return; everything and everyone we left behind are lost to us. As much as it pains us, that is the reality we face. We can accept it and move forward, or give in to despair. The latter has never been an option in my life and I do not plan to make it one now."

Rachel reached up to wipe the tears from her eyes. "In that case," she said, hoping to exhibit a confidence she did not yet truly feel, "we face reality together."

"Agreed," von Billman stated. He turned to Gribardsun and asked, "So where do we begin?"

"By leading our new friends to safety, and doing what we can to help them remain free," Gribardsun said. "Gar was correct when he warned that the slavers are bound to strike back. Simply returning these people to their village will not be enough to keep them out of harm's way. We must do what we can to assist them: relocate the tribe, teach them to better protect themselves, whatever it takes."

"But how much can we do, realistically?" Rachel inquired. "There are only the three of us. And any tools or equipment we might have put to use were lost when the ship was destroyed."

"True," Gribardsun admitted. "But we still have one very important weapon at our disposal, something that no one else here can lay claim to: millions of years' worth of knowledge. The crew of the *H. G. Wells I* was selected in part because we represented the top minds of our era. What better way to put that talent to use? And in the process, perhaps we can find the answers to the questions we've found ourselves faced with. To start with: where are we? I'm not completely convinced we arrived at our planned destination. We all felt something not quite right occurred in transit. But what happened, and why?

"Then there is the matter of the slavers. I agree with your assessment, Robert, that they have come here from some other planet. But from where? And why? And if this is truly 12,000 B.C., how does a band of invading aliens speak an Earth language that will not exist for thousands of years? Our survival—and that of our hosts—could well depend upon the answers."

Gribardsun fell silent then, and for the briefest of moments he felt a sense of grief for the friends and family left behind. But the tide of sorrow passed as quickly as it came. "There is much to do," he told his friends, "but first we must rest and we must eat. I'll find some food. You two help set up a temporary camp, but make sure our new friends understand that we cannot stay long if they are to remain safe. I'll be back within the hour."

With that he drew his knife and turned to march back off into the woods. Rachel took a single step after him, but stopped and called out. "Hurry back, John," she said as he turned back to face her. "Please."

"I will," he told her. Then he turned again and was gone.

Rachel stood there for a moment, looking at the place where she had last seen him and hoping she would be able to summon the courage she knew Gribardsun would expect of her. She took a deep breath and turned to help von Billman, who was already busy trying to explain the situation to several of the Magdalenians.

And thus did their future begin...

THE LAST OF THE GUARANYS

BY OCTAVIO ARAGÃO AND CARLOS ORSI

In Philip José Farmer's novel *Time's Last Gift*, a scientific research team is transported from 2070 A.D. back in time to 12,000 B.C. on a four-year expedition. However, at the end of the novel, the leader of the team decides to stay behind and not return with the group. He will meet them again in future, preferring to take the long way back. Thus, the jungle lord John Gribardsun, an immortal, looks forward to 14,000 years of adventure on an uncrowded world, similar to the Africa he knew as a child in the late nineteenth-century.

In his time, Gribardsun was known as the Khokarsan the god of plants, bronze, and Time; as the historical Hercules; and as Quetzalcoatl, among others.

Now Peri, the last of the Guarany Indians, from José de Alencar's 1857 Brazilian novel *O Guarani*, has been added to the list.

The dosimeter, a small square that would darken in the presence of ionizing radiation, he had made from his cache of photographic film. Quite easy. The fluorescent lamp had been trickier.

John Gribardsun had had to evaporate his own urine to obtain the phosphorus. He'd also had to make an impromptu vacuum pump with the guts and bladders of assorted animals and, the trickiest part, to seal the glass bulb with fire without losing the vacuum inside.

But it had been done, nonetheless, and now he was ready to visit one of only two known nuclear reactors on the face of the Earth created not by human (or even alien) hands, but by a whim of Mother Nature. Both had been already inactive when discovered by man.

The one in Africa had been shut down by natural processes two billion years before discovery. But the one in South America had been dead for just a few centuries when scientists found it, in the 2030s. Which meant that in Gribardsun's present today—the beginnings of the seventeenth century—it was still generating power.

He'd been somewhat surprised to find civilized people—as far as sixteenth-century petty European nobility might be considered civilized—already in the place.

The Rio de Janeiro Sierra, which would someday be called Serra dos Órgãos National Park, was relatively close to the Brazilian shore, and the Portuguese had claimed the Brazilian coast for themselves more than a hundred years before.

Even so, Gribardsun had surmised that the new European masters of the land would be quite daunted by the sheer mountains—part naked granite, part impenetrable forest—and equally entranced by the riches easily found closer to the beach. And that this mixture of awe and greed would prevent them, for at least one more century, from trying to live uphill.

The time traveler had been quite surprised when he discovered the imposing structure, a commixture of medieval castle and Neolithic fort, perched on a rock shelf high above the great river, Paquequer, which coiled around the mountains and jumped down gorges.

His first instinct had been to avoid the Europeans completely—he was quite sure the natives, the fierce Aymoré people, would give him all the trouble he would need. Although recently, while he was performing an autopsy on a mutant jaguar, some white men, slavers or smugglers perhaps, had happened upon him, assumed he was just another Indian performing some primitive rite, and continued on their way. Which was just fine.

But then he'd seen Cecilia. Naked. Having a long, delightful bath. She was in her late teens but Gribardsun had been without a female sex partner for more than a year now, since the end of his quite intense, but finally doomed, affair with the regrettably flea-infested self-appointed vampire-princess of Machu-Picchu. So, Cecilia seemed gorgeous enough. The problem was, how could he try and engage her attentions (and favors) without scaring her to death? Could it be possible she had something to do with the strange fortress he had seen the day before? That place, with its massive stone walls and circular design, few windows no more than holes, and large, solid wooden doors, was so like some early civilized domes he saw millennia ago, down by the rivers Tigris and Euphrates. Could it be possible that some ancestral architectural concepts had survived for so long? But that was for later. Now, he had more important matters to deal with.

He'd been going consistently upriver for quite a while when he found the pool and waterfall with the naked Portuguese girl in it. Without a GPS network in orbit and with some four hundred years of geological evolution and human intervention to discount, he'd been counting on the flora and fauna to clue him toward the reactor's precise location.

His idea was to photograph it, to document it thoroughly, and perhaps to collect a few samples. He was curious about the impact of time travel on the radioactive decay of isotopes, among other things. He had puzzled, from time to time, about the carbon-14 content of his own cells.

Marching upriver had presented him with more and more mutant life forms. He'd spotted the jaguar a few weeks before, and tracked the animal to a thick part of the bush. The huge cat had jumped into the trees to stalk its pursuer, believing itself the hunter, not the hunted.

The arrival of the smugglers distracted the predator, perhaps inducing it to ponder if horse meat might offer a more substantial meal than the well-muscled, tanned frame of Gribardsun.

One of the white men, and a particularly ugly one, raised his musket to the beast. This man had an uncouth black beard falling to his chest and eyes that shone, perhaps in an unconscious—but nevertheless doomed—attempt to conceal the propensity to violence therein. It was clear that he wasn't trying to save the "Indian," only to have some sport with the big cat.

But the time traveler dismissed such an abortive "rescue" with a gesture and a word. The troop then left, the coarsely bearded one derisively calling him "chief" before vanishing into the woods. Gribardsun retained the man's scent and face in his memory for future reference and then returned to the jaguar.

The cat delayed its gaze on the horses for a while. The moment of distraction was ended by three small darts, quickly shot from Gribardsun's bow into the cat's body, piercing an eye, an ear, and a shoulder. The effect was just what the hunter wanted: focusing the attention of the beast to the business at hand, and goading it to attack.

Like a thunderbolt, the animal jumped for Gribardsun's throat.

The jaguar was probably used to having its prey duly impressed and generally horror-stricken, fear-pissed by its fierce appearance, quick action, lightning leap, long white teeth, and astonishing claws. With this particular piece of human flesh, however, it was in for a surprise.

The time traveler had at his side a long dependable and quite strong fork of fire-hardened wood, which he raised as soon as his eyes detected the slight contraction of muscle under the cat's skin—the unconscious and almost imperceptible movement that marked, as a split-second warning, the creature's decision to jump.

The animal's neck was caught in midair between the two prongs of the fork, and in the next second both prongs had penetrated the soil, being forced almost a foot under the earth by Gribardsun's powerful arms and quite effectively pinning the cat, belly up, to the ground. It was the biggest specimen he'd ever seen, with longer paws than average and fearsome claws that retracted into soft sheaths. The fangs were also longer than those of the average jaguar, and sharp as knives. But the eyes were the *pièce de résistance*, black and yellow, but with a curious blue glow.

With a quick shot of the bow, the time adventurer killed a fat rodent that scurried nearby. Pressing the dead furry creature as if it were a ripe orange above the cat's mouth, he created a trickle of blood that fell between the jaguar's teeth.

The eerie blue glow in the eyes intensified. Even with its neck pinned down, the animal might have tried to roar, but it didn't, keeping perfectly silent. Gribardsun nodded to himself and, feeling a small pang of regret but recognizing the need, killed the beast mercifully with the long, Spanish-steel-bladed knife that he had obtained during his stint among the Incas. For a few centuries now he'd started collecting blades here and there, so he might spare the knife he'd brought from the future. Ten thousand years of sharpening could wear even the finest steel too thin after all.

Then he proceeded with the autopsy.

It was immediately obvious why the animal had not vented its hatred with a powerful roar: it couldn't. If its throat could emit any sound, it would have been outside the human spectrum of hearing. A most curious adaptation.

The blue glow to the eyes came from nictitating membranes, translucent third eyelids in each eye. Polar bears had them to protect themselves from snow blindness and beavers used them to see underwater, but it was unheard of in felines. Until now. The belly was one-third full of raw meat, not quite fresh, and not human. This jaguar was slow in digesting its meals.

Finishing the examination, Gribardsun skinned the animal—its fur would provide a nice coat against the cold he expected to find at the top of the mountains—and partook of some of the hard raw muscle of the cat in a rite of respect for the fallen enemy. Old habits die hard, he told himself, and those pertaining to proper etiquette in killing are those that die hardest.

He then lit a fire to prepare a proper meal from the flesh of the smaller, softer, and more palatable rodent. Finishing dinner, he poured some herbs on the fire, creating a dark, pungent smoke, and using sticks for support, spread the cat's skin over it. It wasn't proper tanning, but that would have to do.

A few hours passed before he was quite confident that it would be possible to wear the jaguar mantle without offending all the noses for miles. As soon as the smoke cleared, Gribardsun sniffed the wind that blew in his direction. There was a faint smell of human bodies. Diluted, weak, but increasing. He then placed his ear on the ground, and heard the approach of the Aymorés. At least a dozen pairs of feet treading softly, but surely coming.

He'd seen signs that the mutant beasts were somehow sacred to them, and knew that his treatment of the jaguar had been, in such a perspective, nothing less than sacrilegious. Gribardsun had no idea what the Aymoré penalty for heresy and blasphemy would amount to, and wasn't especially curious to find out. So, tying the skin over his shoulders, he took to the canopy and vanished.

From the highest branch of a tall tree, Gribardsun watched the fearsome group of Indians. The Aymorés used wooden discs under their lower lips and in the earlobes, a decoration that made them look like living gargoyles, as if some medieval stone demons had turned into flesh.

He'd seen all kinds of body ornamentation and modification during his travels of nearly fourteen thousand years. Besides, his training as an anthropologist and his peculiar upbringing in Africa had made him somewhat impervious to prejudice, and strongly non-judgmental. Even so, Gribardsun couldn't figure out why that tribe had their noses decorated with strange blue, shining metal rings. Blue, he thought with irony, seems to be the color of jungle fashion these days.

Few human communities had, through history, developed the habit and the skill to live and move upon trees. Gribardsun was quite sure that the Aymorés wouldn't be able to track him if he kept to the canopy and did not do anything to call their attention. So, treading softly and silently, he moved on.

Even now, perched on one of the tallest trees close to the pool's perimeter and entranced by Cecilia's beauty, he was aware of the movements in his surroundings. It would not do, after all, to let a cousin of the dead jaguar sneak up on him.

He noticed the Aymorés approaching the pool a few minutes before the girl. He had always felt protective toward women—beautiful young women, especially—and this one was naked and alone, with a troop of armed savages bearing down on her location. But he refrained from acting too early: after all, he didn't know enough about the situation. She might be their nymph, their goddess; they might be her lovers.

It was only when she screamed with terror and the arrows started to fly that he decided to enter the fray. The idea was to save the girl and to impress the heck out of her in the process. He left the Spanish knife in the tree, along with the leather bag he used to carry his other possessions, and jumped down armed only with a heavy piece of wood.

Twirling the club above his head, Gribardsun hit the closest Indian right in the face, splitting it from forehead to chin and producing an ample arc of blood and teeth fragments.

The unnatural sound of the exploding skull—comparable to a ripe coconut falling on hard ground from a very tall tree—made the other attackers stop in their tracks and turn toward the source of the *bang!*—just to have arms and ankles dutifully clobbered, the pain—and one broken bone or another—making them fall down, or at least to drop their weapons.

Heavily tanned, with longish, matted hair and a foot taller than the average Indian, wearing nothing but a one-shoulder tunic of coarse cotton that left a good part of his broad chest and abdomen naked, bound at the waist by a cord of feathers, Gribardsun looked like nothing but the hero of some old Italian sword-and-sandal flick. A reference which would have been lost on the scattered, scared, and smashed Indians.

Then the largest of the Aymorés made a feint in Gribardsun's direction and quickly jumped back, trying to get out of the mysterious man's reach and perhaps to compromise his balance. But the time traveler was also, by inclination and necessity, an experienced warrior. With a quick turn of the torso he almost overstepped himself, but instead kept both feet firm on the ground and smashed the cudgel into the Aymoré's ribs, cracking at least two of them and sending him backwards, splashing into the lake where Cecilia was.

Flying into the water in pursuit, Gribardsun grabbed the Aymoré's hands and, with a swing, lifted him over his head, as if the man was a prize cup he had just won.

The Indian was shorter than the time traveler, but heavier: his body was dense, well-muscled, and compact. He was called Aymberê by his peers, meaning hard, unflinching, immovable. He was considered a powerful hunter. He'd once killed a huge tapir, ten feet long and weighing six hundred pounds, with his bare hands, breaking the animal's neck in his grip.

But now this bold, strong and unflinching hunter was screaming for help. His companions, however, fled—limping and crawling, but fled, nonetheless—leaving him to his doom.

The time traveler knew that even if he killed the Indian, the rest of them—probably all the rest of them—would soon lick their wounds and return for revenge.

He needed to put the fear of god—or, at least, the fear of Gribardsun—in their hearts. A good strategy would be to break the Aymoré's spine, leaving him crippled but able to talk. But that would certainly terrorize the girl more than the remaining warriors of Aymberê's tribe, and he didn't want to be labeled, in her eyes, as someone as savage as his foes.

So he talked to Aymberê in his own tongue. The Indian's face assumed a ghastly gray hue as he listened. When he was finished, Gribardsun—who had kept the Indian in the air all this time—merely threw him clear of the water. Aymberê fell outside of the pool, his shoulders connecting painfully with a flat rock, and he then scampered, rolling at first, and then running.

"Are you... Are you a Guarany? My father told me about a legend of the last of the Guaranys... A noble people, exterminated by these hideous Aymorés..."

The musical voice, a mixture of tinkling crystal and bird song, came from behind him, formulating the question in Portuguese. The girl.

He decided to play it cool and feed her fantasies. It was better to be thought of as a mythical last of the *Bon Sauvages* than to explain that he had come from five hundred years in the future, had travelled fourteen thousand years into the past and that, now, he was going back to his own time like everybody else, one year every three hundred and sixty-five days.

And, of course, that he was impervious to disease and old age.

"Yes." He probably could speak Portuguese better than she.

He'd even met the putative founder of Portuguese literature, Luis de Camões, in Goa, some five or six decades earlier. They'd done a lot of drinking and whoring together. Camões would call him "Adamastor," for no reason he could discern. But if he was to play the savage, he'd do it to the hilt. She'd have the whole Johnny Weissmuller routine.

"Me Peri," he said, choosing the name at random. Or was he thinking about his friend Joe Periton, captain of the 1925 rugby team of England? "Me last of Guaranys." He then turned to face her.

She was beautiful. And excited: the water was cool, but not cool enough to have such an effect on her breasts and nipples. She tried to raise her arms to shield her nakedness from his devouring eyes, but then his body found hers under the water, touching her, hard and warm. She trembled, electrified, her mouth wet, half open, a pink tongue touching the lower lip.

"Are… are you a Christian?" she asked in something that was half a sigh, half a whimper.

His only reply was a kiss.

"Peri told, Peri would not eat him."

They were lying side by side on the flat rock by the pool, her head on his chest, the fingers of her right hand playing with him—he, half smiling, but somewhat worried: the girl had a lot of stamina, but Gribardsun wasn't sure that she could take any more of the kind of thing she was provoking. But the strokes were gentle and pleasurable, so he let her.

"Eat?" She screwed her nose in disgust.

"Eat enemy flesh sign of respect. Body not eaten is body of coward to the gods. Spirit of coward goes to hell."

"So you are not a Christian." The idea seemed to worry her in a vague kind of way. "But you have a hell just like us. So, you told him you wouldn't eat him. If you killed him, he would be like a coward in the eyes of the gods, his corpse left for the vultures and the like, and he would go to hell. It made him afraid. Hell."

This girl was sharp, thought Gribardsun. He'd have to keep his eyes open around her. Not that it wouldn't be a pleasure.

"Álvaro is a Christian," she said, tauntingly.

"Who Álvaro?"

"My fiancé, silly."

"Ceci has a Man Promised?" Gribardsun did his best to sound dumbfounded. *Bon Sauvages* are always monogamous, after all, and quite punctilious on points of honor.

She laughed.

"He is not a man, hardly more than a boy. He still thinks I'm a virgin. Now, come."

She was on her feet, collecting her clothes.

"Come?"

"You saved my life. I must introduce you to my father. Dom Antônio. The master of the castle." She made a gesture in the direction of the fortress.

The "castle," as she called it, was upriver, and Gribardsun had reasons to believe that part of the Paquequer flowed through a cave just behind the natural rock wall that buttressed the rear of the structure. It would be useful to take a look inside. Or was he just rationalizing his desire to stay close to the girl?

"Peri go with Ceci," he said. "But not now."

"Why not…?" She turned from her clothes to look at him. As he was still naked, she saw his motive. And smiled. "Okay," she complied. "We go in a little while."

"Not so little. While."

Afterward, as he was collecting his stuff, Gribardsun noted something.

The cloak of jaguar skin was missing.

He was quite sure he had had it on his shoulders when he dropped from the tree and smashed the first Indian's head. It must have fallen then, or a little afterward. Perhaps during the big guy's attempted feint. If one of the fleeing warriors had taken it, the tribe would soon have proof positive that Gribardsun was the perpetrator of a sacrilege.

So, the threat of non-cannibalism might not be enough after all.

He knelt by the body of the skull-crunched Aymoré. The curious blue ring had snapped out of the nose and rolled a few inches away, but Gribardsun had no difficulty in finding it. He took it, feeling that it might be useful in the future.

Dom Antônio, father of Cecilia, was a strong man. And a shrewd one, too. He knew, for instance, that the tale of the "Last of the Guaranys," a noble, strong Indian who protected the oppressed and the innocent from the cannibalistic fury of the Aymorés, was a fantasy. Bunkum. He knew because he'd invented it himself, a white lie, a myth to keep Cecilia calm.

But he also knew that the giant his daughter had brought home was a potential ally, and he needed one. Badly. His fortress in the hills was highly coveted by smugglers and slavers. The only thing that prevented the criminals and outcasts from slicing his throat and raping Cecilia to death was the fear of a common enemy, the fierce Aymorés. White men, he thought wryly, are only to be trusted to band together when men of a different color come killing.

But even this solidarity in the face of dire straits might fail him. He'd used Cecilia's wiles to seduce a silver smuggler named Álvaro to his side. As far as smuggling goes, silver was a benign merchandise, certainly better than Indian women or slave labor. And Álvaro commanded a strong party of thugs.

Not any longer, however. Shortly before Cecilia's arrival with the supposed Guarany, Álvaro's second in command, a hideously bearded Italian expatriate called Loredano, had brought the "sad news" of his leader's demise. Dom Antônio could almost see, in his mind's eye, Loredano's bullet piercing Álvaro's heart—coming from the back, obviously.

The development meant two things: first, that Loredano had finally found where the map to the silver mines was kept. Second, that after a decent period of mourning, Dom Antônio would have to use Cecilia to find himself a new rascal who could provide men and swords to defend the fortress.

But now it seemed that his daughter was a step ahead of him. This faux Guarany had no posse with him, but he was so large and strong—and radiated so much confidence—that by his side a bunch of warriors would look almost superfluous.

They were alone in the Dom's library—study would be a better word, since there were not very many books there, besides a huge Bible and some books in degenerate Latin, cheap romances and the like. There was an Ovid and a copy of the *Aeneid*, but nothing in Greek. By 1600s standards, Dom Antônio was a barbarian, almost an illiterate. But then, most of the aristocracy fell in the same category.

Gribardsun had his eyes firmly locked on his host's. What he saw was a man of wealth, strength, and stubbornness—much too stubborn for his own good, and for the good of his own family. If his memory of world history served him right, the time traveler believed that in this specific year Portugal was no more, the country and its New World colonies absorbed into the Spanish Empire. But the fortress was decorated with Portuguese flags and symbols, and there were no Spanish signs to be seen anywhere.

So, Dom Antônio was a patriot. Which explained why he was here up in the hills, and not by the more civilized shores. And which explained his predicament and his weaknesses.

Gribardsun was only marginally interested in the old man, however. His main interest was in the fact that his dosimeter, which he kept tied around his neck, had blackened, a sure sign of the presence of radiation.

As a matter of fact, it was as if the whole fortress was flooded with ionizing rays. Not enough to cause the common symptoms of radioactive poisoning, like nausea or hair loss, but sufficient to abbreviate the lives of everyone present by one or two decades. Philosophically, the time traveler considered that most of them would die of tetanus, sepsis, diarrhea, childbirth, or an eventual Indian arrow in the eye long before the cancers they were nursing had a chance to show up anyway. No need to spread warnings that would not be heard.

One other thing that caught Gribardsun's attention was the fact that the blue nose ring he had taken from the dead Aymoré was strongly magnetic: it had stuck to his Spanish knife, and he could feel it being pulled by the steel swords that decorated the study. The traveler recalled that strong magnetic fields could deflect some kinds of radiation.

It opened some interesting avenues of thought: could the Indians have evolved a culture that allowed them to tolerate, perhaps even to live together with the reactor? And the dosimeter suggested that the burning uranium had to be in the same mountain that contained the fortress. Gribardsun formed the decision to inspect the back of the property, where it was buttressed by the slope. There might be a cave entrance somewhere.

The time traveler was, of course, also worried about the Europeans. It would be inhumane of him not to be. Even if the Aymorés had some cultural scheme that inadvertently protected them from the radiation, the magnetic rings would be only part of it, and Dom Antônio's family had nothing of the sort. But he coldly saw that there could be no hurry in removing them, not with the Indians going down the warpath, which they would almost certainly do, after finding out that Gribardsun had skinned the sacred jaguar.

Now, if he could find a cave through the mountain, with

an opening at the back of the fortress, there might be a chance of escaping from the Indians. The selfsame cave would probably take them close to the heart of the reactor, so they'd have to move fast, very fast.

Cecilia was now in her room, weeping for her dead fiancé. She seemed to have been really fond of him, even if more like a sister than anything else.

Before getting the news from her father, she'd been exultant, introducing Gribardsun to Dom Antônio with beaming happiness.

"Father, this is Peri," said Cecilia with a smile that shone amidst the candlelight. "He is the last Guarany you talked so much about! And he saved me from the dirty hands of those ominous Aymorés and pledged alliance to our family. Could we have him with us? Please?"

Anyone listening to her could think she was talking about some pet tapir she found in the woods, thought Gribardsun. *But maybe this is for the best. Or for the beast.*

Dom Antônio then broke the news to her in a tone that was subdued, but firm. She had paled, and ran away, leaving the two men alone. The old nobleman was no fool, and he knew that Gribardsun had as much Guarany blood as himself. The man was a Saxon, he surmised, perhaps a Scot. A very large and a very tanned one, but that's what he was.

But he also knew that the British hated the Spanish as much as he did. He knew he needed help and, more importantly, he knew to what lengths men of a virile disposition would go to wipe the tears from Cecilia's eyes.

"Be welcome, then, brave Peri," he said, giving his verdict. "I just hope you were baptized."

Religion was the least of Gribardsun's worries. Nonetheless, despite all his layers of Western education, down there, in his so-called soul, he still believed that somewhere lived a horrifying entity that would eventually eat the Moon and the Sun in a day of rage. That was the belief and the primal fear of the beast: an all-powerful, blood-crazed hunter God that devours everything at the end. The only baptism the ancient Thing asked for was a baptism of blood. On an ocean of red blood.

"Yes, Peri baptized."

"Fine," said the Portuguese landlord. "Then we are friends."

For "friend," Dom Antônio meant something like "special agent with a license to kill anything or anyone who meant a threat, even slightly," and, after a substantial meal, and a mute but wet promise from Cecilia's blue eyes, Gribardsun received his first official mission as Dom Antônio's aide: to stalk Loredano.

Dom Antônio's property was composed of a front wall, a main building and, behind that, an open area dotted with stables, barns and lodgings for the smugglers' rabble (the leaders used guest rooms in the castle proper). From there, if one looked up, it would be possible to see the cataract of the Paquequer crashing down to the side. The sound of the waterfall was part of the fortress environment, and it was loud. There was no chance of silence there.

Passing this area, one would find three squat stone buildings, seemingly cut directly into the mountain's slope. Closed with hardwood doors reinforced with bronze and iron padlocks, two of them were quite close to each other. Of these, one contained some of the crude guns of the period, a few spare pieces, plus a little ammunition, oil, tools, and some ten leather bags with small amounts of gunpowder. The other one contained the main reserve of gunpowder of the castle, kegs and kegs of it.

The third stone hut, also with a reinforced, padlocked door, was Dom Antônio's dungeon, complete with a small cell and the implements necessary for branding human flesh with metal and fire. For the present, unused and unoccupied, but if Gribardsun did a good job, soon to receive Loredano in its embrace.

The dawn was still three or four hours in the future when Gribardsun tied on a loincloth, got his leather bag, and silently left Cecilia's chamber. She was sleeping a satiated sleep. She'd used the night activities to exorcise her sorrow and her anger for Álvaro's death. Having Peri in her bed that night had been a bittersweet, almost physically painful experience, but a liberating one.

Now, she slept.

The corridor was dark and empty. There was only a distant torch on the wall, giving light. Gribardsun noted how the flame moved—there was a draft. He went quickly there, and found the cause. Loredano's door was only half closed. Without hesitation, he pushed it fully open and entered.

Empty. The place was saturated by the man's foul smell, but he was nowhere to be seen. Gribardsun knew the stench from his meeting with the smuggler's group in the forest. He remembered the one who had called him "chief."

It was a very distinctive smell. Not hard to track at all.

After leaving the main building, Gribardsun—*Peri*, he thought. *Peri. I must keep this name fresh on my mind and stop thinking of myself as Gribardsun or even John. I must believe that I am Peri, the last of the Guaranys*—Peri melted with the night shadows and became invisible to the civilized men.

After a while, in complete silence, the trail led him to the powder deposit. Peri climbed to the roof of the closest hut, and watched.

Loredano's men were taking the powder kegs and putting them on a group of horses that waited, silently, near the door. There was a smell of fresh blood in the air.

"There's a tunnel hidden in here, all right," said a voice, nothing more than a whisper, coming from the shadows between the two huts, the one with the powder and the one with the guns. "The old man was smart in concealing it. The door is almost seamless. If it wasn't for the map…"

"The old man must have known you would take the map from Álvaro's body," interjected another voice. "How come he didn't place any extra security around here?"

"Who said he didn't?" Now it was Loredano talking. Peri recognized both the tone and the bad breath. "He used the best two guards money could buy. My money, that is."

"Your gold bought only one of us." A new voice.

"Your colleague preferred a price paid in steel. It's all the same for me."

The laughter was subdued, but cruel. For Peri, it explained the aroma of recently shed blood. He now had a decision to make: it would be easy to fall among the bandits, surprise them, kill some, demoralize the others, and have the thing done.

But he was also curious. What map were they talking about? Dom Antônio had told him that he believed that Loredano had killed Álvaro out of envy and sheer malevolence. Those might very well be real motives, but now it seemed there were other motivations the old man had kept to himself.

And, of course, Peri wanted to explore the entrails of the mountain. If he sounded the alarm now, it was possible that Dom Antônio would act to preserve whatever secret he thought worth preserving and to deny him the opportunity.

So, he decided to keep quiet for the time being.

The tunnel was tall, broad and irregular, a natural fissure in the rock. It had slanted walls, with a narrow ledge near the top. Peri was able to follow Loredano's men and horses by silently climbing and then crawling on this ledge. It was almost like crawling in a ventilator shaft, something he had done a few times before.

It was also short, ending abruptly behind a screen of trees and bushes, in a patch of forest that hugged the mountainside. There they took a trail among the trees. Peri jumped to the canopy and followed them from there.

After thirty minutes trailing those clumsy men, Peri surmised their intention. They were taking the powder to Álvaro's silver mine—he recalled Cecilia saying something about her fiancé being a silver entrepreneur, and the mention of a "map" made sense in this light—probably to blow another vein.

It didn't take long for Peri to notice that, as stupid as all white people were when trying to negotiate the jungle, map or no map, they were as lost as blind birds in a death trap. He noticed the jaguar following them as soon as they went into the foliage, but saw that the animal was pregnant and decided to let fate take its course. He wouldn't help one side or the other and when it attacked the last of Loredano's men—a fat, slow one, who smelled of molasses—Peri felt nothing but admiration for the fast and lethal feline. The man died without a sound, his neck broken as a result of a precise slap, the powder keg lost in the jungle.

When Loredano called for the dead man and, after some confusion, decided to turn around and try to find him, the maneuver sealed their destiny. They would never be able to return to their original path, walking in circles and making more and more noise, alerting all the beasts nearby.

It will be a miracle if they survive this night, thought Peri, forgetting that, as his own life bore witness, miracles sometimes happen. That was one of those unlikely moments. The party—without any help from its pursuer—found another path in the woods, one that led them into another cave. A more dangerous, deadlier hole in the mountain. It wasn't a miracle after all, just another bad joke from that treacherous God of the Beasts.

The two things Peri noticed as soon as he managed to get down from the trees and enter the second cave were the sound of flowing water—a stretch of the Paquequer river ran inside this hole, which meant they were somewhere above the Europeans' fortress—and the warmth of the stone walls.

The heat in the walls meant energy. And energy meant…

Again, there was an inward slanting of the walls, giving the tunnel the appearance of a prolonged triangle. There was also a ledge close to the ceiling, convenient for crawling. This cave, he deduced, must be part of the same system as the one behind the castle. It was highly probable that the whole mountain was interconnected by a labyrinth of tunnels.

He quickly remembered all he knew about natural fission reactors. There ought to be the right isotopes of uranium, the proper mass, and a neutron-slowing medium. The slowing was necessary to regulate the reaction. If not, the neutrons issued by the naturally radioactive element would be moving too fast to be assimilated into other atomic nuclei, forcing them to decay and to issue more neutrons, and so on.

The slowing medium usually took the form of water. So, the presence of the river checked. There was also the question of criticality: if a too-large mass of radioactive material is brought together, it may cause a sudden blue glow and a lethal spike of radiation and heat. If the critical mass is formed too quickly, it may result in an explosion—an atomic blast.

The first atomic bombs used conventional explosives to fire a radioactive bullet against a radioactive target. When the target was hit, there was a critical mass instantly assembled, and then, *boom*.

This fact gave Peri some mixed feelings about the powder kegs the smugglers were carrying. He decided that it would be better to get closer to the smugglers, so he would be at hand to intervene if they tried something really stupid.

The tunnel was quite dark. The men in front were carrying

torches; those behind, with the gunpowder, had no light source with them, and just followed the reddish glow ahead. Peri surmised that if he stayed ten to twelve steps behind the hindermost man, he'd be virtually invisible in the darkness.

In silence, he climbed down from the ledge. There were a few thick stalagmites the time traveler might use for extra cover, but he was convinced that it would not be necessary.

He was wrong.

Things started happening quickly.

The river flowed down the middle of the corridor, and when his eyes were properly adjusted, Peri noticed that there was a thin blue glow in the waters. He supposed that it might be caused by Cherenkov radiation, a byproduct of the nuclear reactions taking place there, or perhaps a sign of the presence of trace amounts of the same kind of blue-glowing magnetic mineral the Aymorés used. He recalled that the mutant jaguar had the selfsame glow in its eye membranes. If the thing was being assimilated into the bodies of animals adapted to life near the reactor, he surmised it might offer some real protection. Evolution, after all, may be blind, but it is also economic and supremely efficient.

So, he kept an eye on the river, deciding to rub his whole body with any blue-glowing sand he might find. Taking survival lessons from animals was almost second nature with him. His attention, however, was divided, thus explaining the extra second it took for him to register the long, thick shadow slithering under the water's surface.

There was a violent splash about twenty meters ahead,

followed by an eruption of screaming, cursing, and shots, and the whole group was surging back in his direction.

He had time to jump on and behind a stalagmite, but too late noticed that the cover was less than perfect.

"There!" one of the smugglers cried. "Another glowing beast!"

Shots came in his direction. The rate of fire was lousy—muskets and pistols—but it only took one hit to do a lot of damage. And now they were all crowded around the kegs.

Glowing, Peri mused, as he felled two of his assailants with a couple of well-placed arrows. *How am I glowing?*

"It's a giant monkey!" another screamed. "Its tail is bright!"

Now Peri understood; his fluorescent lamp had betrayed him. He'd made one so it would light up in the presence of intense radiation. It was in his bag. If the bag had been punctured, it might explain the "bright tail."

One arrow found its home through the eye of a gunman. Another one pierced the right arm of the man at his left. The rest of the group just fled, running blindly and forgetting all about big blue beasts dangling from the ceiling.

"It's not a monkey! Monkeys don't shoot arrows!"

He recognized the voice: Loredano, the bearded leader.

"It's just a fucking lousy Indian!" If the goal was to bolster the morale of his men, it didn't work. Soon, even Loredano's voice vanished.

Gribardsun grabbed the last one to run, but the roar that echoed behind them made the time traveler forget the man. By the sound, this noise came from something very different from all the animals he had seen before.

A few torches had been left behind, scattered on the floor. These puddles of yellow light, combined with the blue hue emanating from the water, did as little to assuage the darkness as the white glow of the lamp that he finally took from his bag and raised as a lantern. The lights, however, only seemed to accentuate the shadows.

Now he felt a trembling of the ground; there were waves on the river. The beast emerged suddenly from the water, almost as if pushed from behind, and paused, standing head and shoulders taller than a black bear, in front of the two men. It was the biggest ugliest son of a bitch Gribardsun had ever encountered. Its fiery, flashing eyeballs didn't actually seem to see, but were rolled up like the eyes of a blind animal. The creature's claws flailed out, ripping chunks from the walls and the ground. Its fur seemed thick and sharp, as if small razors were growing from the end of each strand of fur. Snarling and undulating his bulbous head, moving back and forth along the ceiling, knocking stalactites, it moved its body violently to shake the river from its chinking fur, sending out a wave of blue river water and showering the men with a glittering mud.

Gribardsun let his inner beast take control of his body and acted without thinking. Two jumps took him away from the first attack, and placed him far from the claws. For his next move, he grabbed his knife and pressed his legs against the wall, creating the necessary tension to propel himself, bouncing like a rubber ball, under the legs of the creature. As he rolled under the animal's hindquarters, he raised the blade, forcing it against the soft flesh of the beast's underbelly. Blood and guts spilled all over the place.

The wound was deep, but the animal became more ferocious as the scent of blood reached its sensitive nose. Turning its huge body around with far more speed than Gribardsun considered it capable of, the monster dog howled and, with a twist of its giant forepaw, caught Gribardsun on the side, marking his torso with four red cuts.

Snarling in pain and fury, Gribardsun jumped on the same paw that had wounded him and, climbing the limb faster than the creature could react, got to its neck, opening it from chin to breast, stopping at the breastbone with a loud crack. The large jaw snapped three times, searching for Gribardsun and missing, but the claws of the free paw opened four more bloody scratches, now on his back.

Gribardsun didn't let go and pressed the knife against bone till the last breath of the hideous beast. Then, after its final shudder, Gribardsun pressed his foot over the carcass and howled as if he were a big cat claiming its prey. Blood and blue dust merged, forming rivulets that covered his bruises, and it felt good.

Then, the whole world came down on his head.

A great explosion sent Gribardsun reeling into the river as the ceiling fell. Even in a state of semi-consciousness, the reflexes conditioned by a thousand previous adventures made him hold his breath before submerging. He rolled in the water, the gentle flux made violent by the sudden impact of the heavy stones and stalactites. The vicious speed probably saved the time traveler's life, since the creatures that might've been attracted by his bleeding wounds were themselves caught by the violence of the current.

In a sudden movement, the wild waters made him break the surface for some seconds, allowing him to fill his lungs with a welcoming breath. Fighting to keep his head above the ferocious river, he became aware of a white-yellow light some distance ahead. The rest of the dizziness then left him. It was the light of dawn or early morning, he knew, which meant that the cave ended somewhere ahead. Could it be possible that he was rushing toward a high waterfall?

He searched for something to grab on to. Then he saw a rock outcrop, in the form of a crescent moon, which marked the mouth of the fall. Gribardsun struggled against the current to reduce his speed as he approached it.

The time traveler grabbed the rock with his remaining strength as the rushing water tried to yank him out. For a moment he thought his arms would be disjointed at the shoulders, but then all he had to support was his own weight and the bag was yet dangling from his shoulder.

Gasping for air, he pulled himself into a sitting position on the rock crescent. He was battered, cut, bleeding, bruised. His aches had aches. He concluded that the laggard smuggler, upon hearing the awful victory scream Gribardsun had let loose, had decided that he'd rather be blown to pieces than be eaten alive by the beast responsible for the beastly cry, and had thrust the flaming head of a torch into one of the barrels.

But he still lived! As fresh air filled his lungs and he caught the cold wind on his face and saw the sun rising gloriously over the sierra, Gribardsun knew, once more, the ecstasy of living a life on the edge. He'd partaken of such joy countless times in thousands of years, and it still energized him.

The ecstatic peak fading, he evaluated his situation: the bag was still with him, its contents somewhat shaken, but the most precious parts of his equipment were intact. Those things were sturdy, made to last the centuries. He'd lost bow and arrows, but still had the knife.

He noticed that the rock he was sitting on was getting warmer. There was also some steam coming, under pressure, from the waterfall, as if the falling water itself was becoming hotter.

He looked down.

Gribardsun was perched high above Dom Antônio's fortress, and could survey the whole area around it. The tactical situation was crystal clear: the castle was under siege by the Aymorés. There was a skirmish at the rearguard of the attacking Indians—he surmised that the surviving smugglers had tried to return to the white man's refuge and found the path blocked by the native force.

He took a moment to sort out his equipment and materials, adjusting his camera in a nook close to the tip of the crescent and pointing it in the general direction of the source of the rushing water. Judiciously placing pebbles on and around the shutter button, he created a system that, he believed, would take a series of a dozen snapshots as soon as the ground moved in response to some big upheaval. He then decided to enter the fray on the side of the smugglers. The Aymorés, after all, were a threat to Cecilia, and if the warming rock and steaming water meant what he thought, any second there could be their last.

So, knife firmly grasped in his clenched teeth, he jumped.

* * *

The first Aymoré never knew what killed him. The knife went into his spine at the bottom of the skull and he fell instantly, dead silent. Gribardsun then used a trick he had learned back in his infancy, when he had wanted to mock the savages that had slain his ape-mother. For a whole month he had played the role of a trickster jungle spirit. After each attack, Gribardsun jumped back to the nearest tree, far from the sight of the Indians.

In this jump-kill-jump routine, it took him less than forty-five minutes to wipe out a sizeable part of the Aymoré troop. Enough to give the smugglers a fighting chance to get behind the walls, but only barely: the war party was huge. He might have kept the game going for a while more, but the tree cover was becoming scarce as they approached the walls, forcing him to do longer and longer jumps. And, in one of them, someone grabbed his left ankle and dashed him to the ground.

The impact caught Gribardsun in the shoulders, not on the head, which was partially luck and partially well-honed reflexes. Even so, the knife fell from his hand.

He was back on his feet in almost no time, quickly slipping back into his Peri persona, automatically assuming the typical crouch of the Indian wrestler. Facing him, equally crouched and with a maniacal light in his eyes, stood Aymberê, the giant of the Aymorés.

And, with a roar, the giant plunged to the attack.

The roar gave Peri an unwanted taste of Aymberê's breath, enough for his awareness to register a peculiar scent, an acetous edge. The man had gorged himself on ant-poison liquor. He was drugged into a berserk rage.

And, of course, behind the red haze of fury that clouded his mind, he recalled the previous humiliating defeat at Gribardsun's hands.

His plunge was not that of a wrestler: the crouch propelled him forward with balled fists, his thighs stretching like high-tension coils. His powerful blows caught Peri's face and midsection, knocking the air out of him.

Aymberê was possessed and powerful, and Peri was tired, dazed by the sudden fall and still sore with the many wounds he had sustained in the caves. Aymberê's mad punches were hurting him more than they should; and his counter-punches had no effect he could discern.

So, Peri went down, felled like an old oak.

The glee in his opponent's eyes was fearful to see. Aymberê's smile was a hideous rictus, and spittle drooled from his lower lip as he loomed over Peri's body, the eyes closed, the head turned to the side.

He came closer, savoring the moment, the berserk rage fueling a sadistic, anticipatory pleasure, a monstrous gloating. He would do unmentionable things to this inert body before dismembering it. Power surged to his loins.

It was when Aymberê's shadow fell on Peri's face, blocking the red glare of the sun that filtered through his eyelids, that the time traveler, who had been pretending defeat, flashed into action, raising his bent knee with the speed, strength, and determination of a Norse god brandishing his magic hammer, smashing his enemy's genitalia.

Blood shot into Aymberê's eyes, and his crazed wide-eyed rictus was turned into a desperate, thin-lipped scowl as he fell to the ground. Rolling to one side, Peri connected his elbow with the Indian's jaw, and Aymberê was knocked unconscious, his face broken.

Peri then started hearing explosions. The smugglers couldn't have had time to reload their muskets and pistols, but finally there was someone at the walls using the cannons.

There was an explosion quite close, and chips of broken rock and hot lead embedded themselves in Peri's cheek.

Someone, it seemed, had found the time to reload.

"Die, pagan bastard!" cried Loredano, a brace of pistols in his arms. Two guns, two barrels per gun, one shot fired. Three to go then.

As his mind evaluated the tactical aspects of the situation, Peri kept rolling on the ground, hoping the smuggler would keep firing at a moving target, wasting shots. The smuggler then raised his right arm above his head, and started, slowly, to lower it, bringing the barrels in line with the blurring motion that was the half-naked savage in front of him.

"Die, and Cecilia will be mine!"

Not today, thought Peri, changing direction and using his legs as pistons to jump over Loredano's head, passing so close to him he could smell the stink of old layers of dry sweat. As he passed over the man's oily hair, Peri grabbed the still raised weapon—barely taking notice of Loredano's scream when his forefinger, caught in the trigger guard, was broken by the sudden lurch—and, on landing behind the enemy, crouched, turned, and used its heavy wooden handle as a club, cracking Loredano's right knee.

"Nor ever."

Turning Loredano with a shove of his left hand and grabbing him by the hair before he fell, Peri launched two punches from his right into Loredano's nose and left eye, blinding him and cutting off his breathing. The man even tried to claw at Peri's eyes with his muddy nails, but failed and started to choke.

Peri finally smashed Loredano's face against the nearest tree, cutting the blabbing and gurgling off and leaving a red blot on the trunk.

He felt the earth trembling under his feet. He knew that if the sequence of collapses and landslides happening right now in the caves ended up creating a critical mass of uranium, the possible outcomes would be a "China syndrome"—the fissile material boring a hole into the earth and burying itself—or an explosion. Whichever would happen, might happen quickly.

Now his goal was to take Cecilia, and if possible her family, out of this doomed land.

The time traveler had a way paved with dead bodies in front of him. The Aymorés had been scattered by the cannon fire from the castle, and demoralized by the second defeat of Aymberê, but apparently not before slaughtering all of the remaining smugglers.

Which meant that Cecilia would be alone in the fortress, with only her father and the servants, and maybe one or two other bandits who perhaps had remained behind when

Loredano's party ventured outside to find the mine. But would anyone wish to be left behind? These men were cutthroats, and none would trust the others with the secret location of the silver, Peri surmised.

He ran.

There were no more defenses on the walls. The gates were closed, but the cannons were silent, and Gribardsun got there without being challenged or hailed. He climbed the stone barrier with the ease of one long adjusted to steep hills and even steeper trees, jumped inside, breaking his fall by grabbing a wooden shaft that projected at an angle from the structure, and landed, silently, on his two feet and left hand.

He thought of inspecting the inside of the walls, finding out what may have happened to the men who had manned the artillery, but his priority was to locate Cecilia and, if possible, Dom Antônio. The rest could wait.

As he ran into the castle, the great hall seemed empty. This first cursory impression almost cost Peri his life. He moved quickly toward the stairs, failing to notice the giant snake slowly uncoiling from the roof beams to the floor behind him, ready for the attack.

It was only Gribardsun's almost unconscious, instinctive attention to every scrap of information around him that allowed him to detect the barely audible sound of the reptile slithering on the flagstones of the floor. He turned just in time to see the monster launching two coils of its scaly body around his torso and legs, and to use the heel of his left hand to stop its jaws from closing on his head.

The thing had the thickness of an old tree, and a body as hard as mahogany. The general appearance was that of a gigantic boa constrictor, but the head was triangular—an almost sure signature of the venomous snake. The eyes had the eerie blue glint of the radiation-immune animals, and with both hands employed in keeping the thing's mouth open, he was able to feel the swelling poison bags behind the needle-like teeth.

The poison started to flow onto his hands and down his wrists as he pressed the jaws open and back. The liquid was dark-golden, like honey, and burned at the touch. At the same time, the muscular coils were closing around him: his breath became short and, suddenly, his ribs seemed quite brittle. He'd taken his knife back after the fights with Aymberê and Loredano, and even had a charged two-shot pistol in his sash, but both were useless now.

The whole thing would be decided by a contest of brute force and resistance: what would break first—his ribcage or the creature's mandible? The pain in his chest at least distracted him from the smoldering burn of the acidic poison on his arms, but the lack of oxygen, combined with the extenuating effort, was starting to exact a price. His vision was tunneling; he would black out in no time.

Suddenly, there was a violent crack, and the coils around him went limp. Gribardsun fell to the ground—the only thing that had kept him erect for the last few minutes being the muscular strength of the snake—and gasped. The skin of his forearms was fiery red.

The beast was dead, its mouth open in an unnatural angle of much larger than 180 degrees.

He went into the kitchen, looking for something that might mitigate the chemical burns, and found some ashes and coarse soap—as well as dead bodies and a gaping hole in the floor.

There was a track of bluish mud coming from the hole, and Peri did not need special deductive powers to conclude that the snake had come from there. The corpses were crushed, or blackened by poison, or both. It seemed obvious that the creature hadn't killed them out of hunger, but out of fear and anger. Its world had been destroyed, and someone—even perfectly innocent servants—had to pay.

Satisfied that his hands and arms were in good working condition and the pain had subsided enough, he decided to follow the tracks, fearful of what other bodies he might find along the way.

The remains of Dom Antônio were in the library. He still had a sword in his hands, but his legs were crushed beyond description and his belly was swollen and black, split open. The snake had injected an astounding amount of venom there.

Gribardsun took the time to close the old nobleman's glazed eyes before proceeding. The snake's trail, however, only led back to the main hall. So, hopeful that Cecilia might still be safe upstairs, he bolted up the steps.

But the rooms were all empty.

Might she be in one of the huts in the back yard? Perhaps even in the torture cell?

Gribardsun was preparing to run down and find out when

a great blast, followed by a shock that shook the castle to its foundations, launched him against the corridor wall. He banged his head, and lost consciousness.

Mud and water! Everywhere!

The time traveler awoke with the fresh spray that came from a crack in the corridor lightly striking his eyelids. There was a torrent coming down on the castle from on high, filling the space between the building, the defensive wall, and the mountainside.

It was already filling up the lower levels of the structure: the main hall, kitchen, and library already had water close to the ceiling.

Gribardsun's lips twisted in a sad smile. He believed he knew what had happened: his fear of a "China syndrome" against a full-blown nuclear explosion had been a false one. There was a third option, a so-called fizzle—a small blast, caused by a critical mass that takes form too quickly for a "syndrome" scenario, but too slowly to free the whole power of the nuclear fuel.

The relatively small blast hadn't been enough to pulverize the mountain, but it had destroyed part of the stone wall that kept the river on course, and now the Paquequer was falling, with all its might, directly over Dom Antônio's home.

As it dawned on Gribardsun that anyone who'd been in the huts behind the castle had certainly drowned by now, he felt a weight in his chest for Cecilia. She'd been not only young and beautiful and delightful, but there was also a fire in her, in her eyes, in her heart, that he could relate to and, even admire. But now…

Her scream pierced his thoughts.

There was already water bubbling up from the stairwell. Peri ran into one of the bedrooms in the corridor, found a window, and jumped out. His body hit the water after a fall of less than a meter and he swam in the direction of the screams.

They came from the external wall. Looking, he saw that Cecilia was there, on the top of a pillar somewhat higher than the surrounding structure. She was crouching over it, surrounded by water on one side, and by a sheer drop on the other. She had both hands behind her head, fingers intertwined. She screamed in utter despair.

"Peri coming!" Gribardsun cried back, crossing the distance between them with powerful strokes, allowing the current to drag him a while, but always fighting to keep control. She looked at him. Her eyes went wide, and something that might be construed as a smile touched her lips.

As soon as he got onto the wall, she started, "I was in there, with the cannons. I…"

"Ceci shot fireballs?" The time traveler wasn't drifting out of character, not yet. He would be Peri as long as Cecilia stayed with him. She'd lost her fiancé, her father, her land, her house; he wouldn't deprive her of her imaginary friend.

"Father brought the ammo and gunpowder… Told me to stay. Said it would be safer if… if…"

As she started to cry, Gribardsun noticed that the waters, crashing in small waves against the top of the wall, were depositing blue mud in the cracks and depressions of the stone. He scraped some of it up and started to rub it on Cecilia's body.

"Peri... what...?"

"Medicine. Good medicine," he replied.

The rubbing was quite professional, the traveler's powerful hands manipulating nerve nodes and muscle groups, inducing a deep sense of relaxation. And the mud had a good chance of really being medicinal. It might even save her from radiation-induced diseases, if his deductions were correct.

The water kept rising. It was already high on the outside of the fortress; it was almost level on both sides, which meant that the current must have weakened substantially.

He looked at her, smiling.

"Ceci wait. Peri will get boat."

"What...?"

Before she could complete the question, he jumped. Holding his breath, down and down he went. Dead bodies floated all around, most of them too weighted down with weapons and gear to rise all the way to the surface. One day, they'd rot enough so that the heavy materials would sink all the way down, while the buoyant flesh went all the way up. Until then, however, they'd stay there suspended in the middle.

Down and down Peri went. He'd seen what he wanted: a good-sized tree. He dived to its roots and dug into its sides with his powerful, acid-burned fingers. It pained him, and the stale air he stubbornly kept in his lungs cried for release, but he paid no heed. He dug his fingers in the bark, in the wood. And pulled. The flood, the impact of the rushing waters, had already destabilized the tree. And for years small animals had burrowed around and under its roots. Now, the tunnels were full of water, sapping it, loosening its grip on the earth underneath.

Once, twice, he pulled. The sheer effort kept his feet firm on the muddy ground, despite the tendency of his body to float.

His lungs ached. Burned. He kept pulling.

Then, in what seemed like one powerful lurch, it came out at the roots and shot upward, propelled by the natural buoyancy of the wood. Gribardsun just kept his fingers dug in, and went with the ride.

Cecilia saw the tree suddenly breaking the water's surface a few meters ahead. For a moment it seemed that the shaft would fly away, but no: it fell in a horizontal position, rolled a bit, and stayed.

"Ceci! Come!" Peri's voice came from the tree.

"Peri made boat, we float to safety!"

She jumped in the water, swimming without much elegance. But it was a short stretch. Peri helped her to get aboard.

They were both tired and in pain, and Cecilia had just lost everything she had ever known. She was shaking and nearly slid off the trunk more than once. Peri decided to carry her to the canopy, where the soft branches and leaves the current hadn't swept away made a kind of safety net that would support her slender body.

This was a tricky proposition, since walking on a wet trunk with the girl in his arms was somewhat akin to walking on a tightrope, and a slippery one. He might've tried to swim along the tree with her, but to put her back in the water didn't seem a good idea.

The feeling of her cold, wet, trembling flesh, of the

goosebumps on her skin, against his bare chest was certainly pleasurable, however. And his warmth was doing her some good. Her teeth unclenched, and her lips regained some color.

When he kneeled to lay her down on the leaves, she grabbed him by the arms. Cecilia wasn't letting him go. She needed human warmth... his warmth... too badly. Her breasts heaved.

He smiled. "Ceci need rest."

She shook her head, saying, "I need you."

And he felt the need, too. Among all that death, the need for a reaffirmation of life. And of the pleasures and of the reasons for being alive.

So, he grabbed Cecilia, raising her once more and, as she cried in surprise, made a dangerous and exhilarating maneuver, turning on tiptoes while holding her above his head. In the end, he had his back to the canopy net and she was in front of him.

And then Peri let himself down, pulling the girl above him as he felt the strength of the branches and leaves, allowing the net bedding to slowly adapt to his weight. And hers.

The girl would have to stay on top, and to do most of the effort, and to do it lightly. Otherwise, they would just buck themselves through the canopy and to the bottom of the flood.

"I understand," she said, smiling delightfully, even a little wickedly. "I promise to be gentle to my poor little Peri."

A few hours later, the sun was setting right in front of them, the tree trunk moving almost imperceptibly downstream, the glint of twilight everywhere in a world fresh and ready to be made whole again. The Spirit of God floated on the waters just before the Creation, after all. Cecilia noticed that Peri was looking not ahead, where nature offered its performance, but behind, to the blasted mountain they had left.

"What are you thinking, my love?" she asked.

He turned to look at her, and smiled. Gribardsun had been thinking about the camera setup he'd left on the stone ledge before jumping into the fight, after his adventures inside the mountain tunnel. He'd been wondering if the equipment had been destroyed and, if not, maybe he would have a picture of a miniature atomic mushroom—the first one of all time. He'd have to come back, someday, to check.

But not now.

"Peri not thinking," he replied. "Peri just waiting."

"Oh? And waiting for what?"

"Ceci's kisses."

The trunk kept floating on for quite a long time after that.

WOLD NEWTON ORIGINS/ SECRETS OF THE NINE

THE WILD HUNTSMAN

BY WIN SCOTT ECKERT

Philip José Farmer was nothing if not ambitious. He wrote biographies—so meticulously researched they were worthy of Ph.Ds.—of two of his heroes, Tarzan and Doc Savage. More amazing still was his discovery during these researches of the Wold Newton Family, a group of influential men and women—and their descendants—who happened to be in Wold Newton, England on the fateful day when a meteor fell from the sky: the heroes and heroines of the Wold Newton Universe.

In his introduction to *Lord of the Trees* (Secrets of the Nine #2, Titan Books, 2012), Win Scott Eckert posited that the continuity of Lord Grandrith and Doc Caliban was in fact parallel to that known as the Wold Newton Universe. In his chronology in *The Mad Goblin* (Secrets of the Nine #3, Titan Books, 2013), he expanded on that notion, suggesting that the two universes shared a common past which diverged in distant ages, as a river branches into two, and that the secret cabal of immortals known as the Nine predated the divergence.

"The Wild Huntsman" brings the two universes back together, in a tale that ties the Secrets of the Nine series to Farmer's *Time's Last Gift* (Titan Books, 2012), *The Other Log of Phileas Fogg* (Titan Books, 2012), Christopher Paul Carey's prequel to the Khokarsa trilogy, *Exiles of Kho* (Meteor House, 2012), and the present volume's "Into Time's Abyss" (by John Allen Small), and reveals exactly why seven couples in two carriages, their coachmen, and several others on horseback were at the precisely correct location, at the precisely correct time, to be exposed to the ionization of a meteorite in the out-of-the-way village of Wold Newton, Yorkshire, England, on 13 December 1795—an event that led to a beneficial genetic mutation that was reinforced by their descendants, the supermen and superwomen of the Wold Newton Family.

The Greystokes, like the present Queen of England, can trace their ancestry through Egbert, king of Wessex, to the great god Woden in Denmark of the third century A.D.... The founders of the Greystoke line were secret worshippers of Woden long after their neighbors had converted to Christianity...

Thus, Tarzan has as ancestor Woden. It would be difficult to find a more highly placed forefather than the All-Father.

Perhaps the great god of the North is not dead but is in hiding. It pleased the Wild Huntsman to direct the falling star of Wold Newton near the two coaches. Thus, in a manner of speaking, he fathered the children of the occupants. The mutated and recessive genes would be reinforced, kept from being lost, by the frequent marriages among the descendants of the irradiated parents.

— Philip José Farmer, *Tarzan Alive:*
A Definitive Biography of Lord Greystoke

AFRICA, REMOTE MOUNTAINS
NEAR UGANDA, 1720

The Old Man sat quietly in his secluded cavern. His one good eye was closed and he appeared to be meditating. His other eye was covered by a black patch.

The Old Man was a giant. Or rather, although he was a large man, there was a strength about him that gave the impression he was a giant. His white beard fell to his waist. His hazel eye was strong, and protean, shifting color in the flickering candlelight.

He wore a double-headed raven headpiece. The headpiece looked heavy for a man of his age—he appeared to be ninety, or perhaps even older. Despite the deep lines, like tiny crevasses crisscrossing his face, his neck was thick and strong, and cords of muscle banded his arms and legs.

He had been known by countless names, many of which even he had forgotten through the ages, and he had inspired legends, folktales, and myths. In these were varying degrees of truth.

For he truly deserved the appellation "Old Man." He had been born in the Old Stone Age, and was at least twenty-five thousand, and perhaps thirty thousand, years old.

The candles wavered in a slight breeze and one extinguished.

There should have been no breeze here, twenty caverns deep in the labyrinth of the Nine.

The Old Man opened his eye and looked into the mirror directly across from him.

The cavern had had no mirror when he had closed his eye in meditation.

The Old Man and the reflection, the Other in the mirror,

watched each other for a long, long time. It was an admirable exercise in motionlessness.

Then the Old Man extended a finger and tapped his own eyepatch pointedly. The Other's eyepatch was on the opposite side of the Old Man's, rather than on the same as in a true mirror image.

In the mirror, the Other Old Man grinned ruefully and gave a slight shrug of the shoulders, as if to say, Good one. You got me!

Then the Other in the mirror swiftly reached into the folds of his ancient robes, withdrew a horn-handled dagger, and launched it at the Old Man.

The wickedly sharp blade flew through the mirror, causing a slight ripple like that of a pebble tossed in a pond. It slipped between the Old Man's ribs and penetrated his heart, causing instantaneous death.

Death. Thirty thousand years of breathing, fighting, lovemaking, scheming, thinking, killing, dreaming... snuffed out, with the flick of a wrist.

The Old Man slumped to the cavern's dirt floor. His one eye, no longer protean, stared at the ceiling.

The Other Old Man stepped gingerly through the mirror and bent down over his counterpart. He lifted his own eyepatch, revealing a perfectly good hazel eye, in which gold flecks seemed to swirl and eddy. Singing quietly to himself—"I am he as you are he as you are me, And we are all together"—he closed the Old Man's unseeing eye and winked at the corpse.

A gentle knock came at the heavy wooden door separating the Old Man's private chambers from the rest of those of the Nine. It was the Speaker for the Nine, summoning him to the annual ceremonies.

He told the Speaker to return in five minutes. Then he hefted the corpse with the ease of lifting an infant, hopped through the mirror, and landed in a substantially identical cavern. He concealed the body under a pile of furs and blankets, to be disposed of later.

He retrieved a pocket mirror—a real mirror—from a small wooden box carved with crawling and twisted serpents, and adjusted the eyepatch and the double-headed raven headpiece. He touched up his makeup, ensuring it exactly duplicated the crags and valleys on his late counterpart's face.

Satisfied, he again bounded through the mirror that was not a mirror. He pulled an oversized nineteenth-century pocket watch from deep within the folds of his robes. The pearlescent lid was as protean as his eyes, the embossed constellation of Auriga—the charioteer—shifting around a tiny blue sapphire representing the brightest star, Capella.

He worked at the watch and the mirror-gate closed in upon itself, just as the Speaker called him once more.

"XauXaz, Old Father, it is time."

BLAKENEY HALL, EAST RIDING OF YORKSHIRE, NEAR THE VILLAGE OF WOLD NEWTON
11 DECEMBER 1795

Shortly after the nine terrible and shattering clangings came again, John Gribardsun found the dead man hanging in the library.

To those the clangings summoned, the tolling was as loud as if it had been made while they were standing under the bourdon bell of the cathedral at Notre Dame de Paris. The unexplained, horrific clamor brought the men running from all over Sir Percy's estate.

Sir Percy Blakeney, General Sir Hezekiah Fogg, and Dr. Siger Holmes arrived first, followed by some of Sir Percy's other guests: Colonel Bozzo-Corona (accompanied, as always, by his man, Lecoq), Sir Hugh Drummond, and Honoré Delagardie, whom Sir Percy had saved from Madame la Guillotine.

The men stood in silence for a moment, watching the swaying corpse hanging from a stout rope which in turn was fastened to the high ceiling by the chandelier.

Sir Percy turned to Holmes. "Get a knife," but before the latter could act Gribardsun, who was known to them as Sir John Gribson, had leapt like a jungle cat upon a side table and was already cutting down the unfortunate deceased. He passed the corpse down to the others and regained the floor with ease.

Sir Percy turned the body over to get a good look at his face. "Iain Bond, aide-de-camp to de Winter, the King's representative at our little congregation…"

The men gathered around while Holmes made a quick examination. The hawk-nosed doctor, lean and wiry, looked up after a cursory survey. "Strangled, just as one would expect with hanging."

"The second murder in as many days," Fogg said.

"But each one different," Bozzo-Corona noted.

"Both heralded by that demmed bell ringing," Sir Percy countered.

"Indeed, but each carried out by different methods," Drummond said. "Gerolstein was found with a knife in his heart."

"Perhaps no great loss," Delagardie added.

"Now, now, my boy," Sir Percy said, "the last thing you want to do now is cast suspicion on yourself, eh?"

"But Percy, he insulted Philippa with his base attentions!"

"My sister as well as your wife," Drummond reminded Delagardie, "but Gerolstein's insults are not worth the gallows. And his brother may arrive at any moment; the last thing needed at the moment is a challenge to a duel."

"Right now suspicion is cast on everyone," Colonel Bozzo-Corona said. He pointed to Gribardsun. "This one is clearly strong enough to have committed both murders."

Gribardsun shrugged. "Just about anyone is."

"I am not," the Colonel said with a sardonic smile. "I am but a frail, old man."

"Demme me, sir! We're not going to find the killer slinging accusations at each other," Sir Percy said. "Call some footmen and we'll store the body with Gerolstein's. And someone fetch de Winter; as His Majesty's representative, at least he can assist in dealing with the parish constabulary."

Gribardsun padded around the estate, weaving through hidden garden paths and hedges. His passing was utterly silent, as befitted his jungle upbringing and years of experience as a woodsman, although of course he could do little to prevent his scent from being detected downwind.

He thought about the terrible din that portended the two murders. He had heard a similar clangor several other times in the past one hundred and fifty years, and while he hadn't discovered the source, it always seemed to accompany some misfortune or unfortunate occurrence.

In his long life, Gribardsun had generally taken pains—with a few exceptions—to avoid involvement in key historical events, not always with success. Besides, as scientists he had worked with reasoned, who was to say that his involvement was not part of the natural flow of history? That the unnatural pealing of unseen bells had come to this place, at this time, reinforced his decision to attend Sir Percy's conclave. If he didn't solve the mystery of the clanging here and now, it seemed likely he'd have more opportunities in the years to come.

He stopped.

He scented a vaguely familiar smell, one that tickled the edges of his memory. He had an extraordinary sense of smell, almost equal to that of the higher primates among whom he had been raised. Some few who knew the particulars of Gribardsun's background—the real story, not the fictionalized and romanticized tales written for popular magazines—speculated that these were an unknown line of australopithecines; others postulated they were Bili apes, a species of large chimpanzee first identified some one hundred years after his birth.

He tracked the scent, circumnavigating the estate once on the ground, and again after taking to the trees.

Gribardsun stopped, turned, scented the air once more, and gave up. The trail had gone cold. He dropped easily from the high branches of a large beech tree, retrieved his boots, and made for the house.

As he passed through a small terraced garden, he heard the low strain of several voices in deep conversation. The exchange came from the drawing room, on the other side of high windows which had been closed against the December chill.

He leapt to a balcony, from it caught a tangle of vinery, and stealthily scrambled to a short overhanging roof. He flipped over the roof ledge with ease and silently scuttled over to a window. He clung upside down and dipped his head just past the top of the window, and peered into the room.

Gribardsun's hearing was almost as uncanny as his sense of smell, and he hung there, at ease, listening to the men inside. Sir Percy Blakeney. Fitzwilliam Darcy. Sir Hezekiah Fogg. George Edward Rutherford, the 11th Baron Tennington. Dr. Siger Holmes. William de Winter. John Clayton, the 3rd Duke of Greystoke.

With the exception of Fogg and Holmes and de Winter, all the men in the room were his great-great-grandfathers. Siger Holmes' granddaughter was, or would be, his great-aunt.

Coming to Blakeney Hall was a great risk.

But he couldn't leave.

He eavesdropped.

"This was supposed to be a gathering of the best minds, the most politically astute. Men of power, those who could influence statesmen." Sir Percy tossed his snuff box down in disgust. "Demme me! Things are going to hell on the Continent. The Revolution's excesses in the Reign of Terror, the Thermidorian Reaction, and the White Terror in response. And the Red Reign of Terror. I brought the best and brightest here to strategize—how to end the violence, the endless cycles of revenge?

"Instead," Sir Percy concluded, "it's a farce. More violence, more death."

"Someone seeks to sabotage your assembly before it starts," Lord Tennington said.

"And who would do that?" Lord Greystoke asked.

"Who has the most to gain?" de Winter countered.

"Colonel Bozzo-Corona, perhaps," Holmes said.

"With what motive?" Darcy asked.

"Unknown," Holmes said. "But I witnessed the Colonel's man Lecoq meet with Countess Carody in Paris last month."

"Interesting, yes, my dear Holmes," Sir Percy said. "But that doesn't necessarily implicate the Colonel in any wrongdoing."

"Their meeting was illicit," Holmes replied, "conducted at the Calyx Bar."

"Perhaps Lecoq and the Countess…" Sir Hezekiah said.

"I'm afraid not, Fogg," Sir Percy said. "I think the Countess does not prefer such company."

"Certainly she is a noble and he a commoner, and yet it is not unheard of—"

"I mean, Fogg, that Countess Nadine Carody does not prefer *any* such company."

Darcy flushed with embarrassment at the turn the conversation had taken. "Surely such speculation…"

"Marguerite and Alice have assured me that it is so," Sir Percy said.

"All the more reason to assume Lecoq met the Countess on behalf of the Colonel," Holmes said. "No other conclusion fits the facts at hand."

"If you are correct," de Winter said, "then, as Darcy pointed out, we still have no idea why."

"As I said," Tennington interjected, "sabotage the meeting."

"But to what purpose?" Darcy asked.

"Perhaps Colonel Bozzo-Corona doesn't share Sir Percy's vision of peace on the Continent," Greystoke said.

"And yet," Sir Percy replied, "we seem to be aligned. The Colonel and his Brothers of Mercy gave Marguerite and Alice the Heart of Ahriman to help us defeat Baron de Musard."

"I still say that lot—the Colonel, Kramm, Carody, Gerolstein—bear further watching," Tennington said.

"But Gerolstein's own brother was murdered!" Sir Hezekiah said.

"What better way to cast suspicion away from themselves than to sacrifice one of their useless pawns?" de Winter asked. "I agree with Tennington, beware of them."

Sir Percy nodded in reluctant agreement. "I'll tell Sir Hugh and Delagardie and Gribson—he's a distant relative of yours, eh what, Greystoke?—to keep their eyes open as well."

He took a pinch of snuff, and sneezed. "To think Marguerite gave up wintering at the Crescent for this…"

Gribardsun left his perch and crept along the rooftop to the other side of the estate. The tinkling of a piano drew him to the music room, where another gathering and opportunity to listen in seemed likely.

He found a toehold, lowered his head to peer into the frosted windows, and saw a large group of the estate's female guests—many of them his ancestresses, and many of them currently in the common state of pregnancy. Alice Clarke Raffles played the piano, while Lady Blakeney and Elizabeth Darcy watched her play.

Two small groups held quiet conversations. In one corner Countess Carody, Miss Caroline Bingley, and Philippa Delagardie, née Drummond, were sitting with Lady Alicia Clayton. Lady Tennington, Violet Clarke Holmes, and Elizabeth de Winter formed another small group, while Lady Drummond sat by herself, reading.

There was no one thread of conversation to follow, but he did pick up several interesting pieces of information.

Several of the ladies were put out by the short notice of the invitation to Blakeney Hall; such affairs usually called for months of preparation.

Caroline Bingley, in particular, seemed intent on complaining that the quickly arranged gathering was in poor taste, to which her sister-in-law, Elizabeth Darcy, replied with a rebuke, at once gentle and sharp, that it was a shame there weren't nearly as many unattached nobles in attendance as Miss Bingley might have hoped.

Lady Blakeney laughed it off, blaming Sir Percy for the timing. Alice supported her, and spoke of men's affairs waiting for no one.

Gribardsun supposed that not all the women had been brought into confidence regarding the true nature of the gathering, and Sir Percy's plans to end the Continental strife once and for all.

He also sensed a tension in the air, which was perfectly natural, given the two unexplained killings. Most of the ladies had no prior acquaintance with danger. And many of them were pregnant, and understandably apprehensive that something dreadful might happen to them and their unborn children.

Some few of the women had encountered danger and adventure, however, and appeared more at ease, if not sanguine, in the wake of the terrible events. Gribardsun focused his attention on them.

Two of these were Lady Marguerite Blakeney and Alice Clarke Raffles, whom Gribardsun gathered had shared an exploit last month in France, battling a baron called de Musard. Gribardsun had also confronted a Baron de Musard once, killed him in fact, in the late 1500s in France. He resolved to learn more about this if he could.

Elizabeth de Winter also seemed less affected by the past days' events, although this was perhaps natural given her husband's high position in the government.

Countess Nadine Carody appeared outright indifferent to the murders, and Gribardsun noted that she had also not been offended in the least by the expedient invitation to England. In fact, she had seemed glad to come on short notice.

Many roads appeared to lead to the Countess. She had conducted a strange meeting with Lecoq in Paris last month, and apparently was in league with Colonel Bozzo-Corona in some way.

Gribardsun focused on her. She watched Lady Blakeney the way a lioness regarded her next meal.

He recalled that she smelled… strange. Almost like a corpse, but he could smell the lifeblood pumping through her veins.

Countess Carody was mysterious. But was she the key to the mystery at hand?

It warranted further investigation.

Nighttime, and a new moon.

And what was the Continental contingent doing wandering the grounds, taking advantage of the pitch-black night?

Nothing good, Gribardsun decided. He swung from his perch to a lower branch, still out of sight of those he spied upon, and settled in to listen.

"I must have satisfaction!" Gerolstein cried.

"Meaning what?" Gustavas Kramm asked.

"Delagardie must pay."

"We have no proof Honoré Delagardie killed your brother," Kramm replied. "And why would he also kill Bond?"

"To cover his tracks, throw us off his scent," Gerolstein said.

"Nonsense. You give the boy too much credit," the Colonel said. "Have a care. We must tread lightly here."

"But—"

"Enough!" the Colonel said. "Kramm, take him to his rooms and keep him there. We cannot afford a misstep now."

Gribardsun watched Kramm march off with the reluctant Gerolstein in tow. He elected to stay with Bozzo-Corona, Lecoq, and Countess Carody, and his decision was rewarded a moment later.

"Do you suppose Sir Percy and the others suspect us of these murders, my father?" Lecoq asked.

Gribardsun watched carefully as the supposedly feeble old man, the patriarch of the Brothers of Mercy, answered: "They'd be fools not to, my son."

"Perhaps," Countess Carody said, "they are dimly beginning to realize that you were behind Baron de Musard all along."

"And that through setting Blakeney and de Musard against each other," the Colonel said, "I manipulated Blakeney into convening this so-called 'conclave' of his? As I said, Sir Percy is no fool, but I doubt he is that perceptive."

"Perhaps not, my father, but if you'll forgive me, his friend Holmes may be," Lecoq said. "And Blakeney's friend. Fogg. There is something… something not quite right about him. I beg you leave to spy upon them further."

The sinister old man regarded his lieutenant, then said: "Very well, my son, you may go. But remember your longer-term mission. Ingratiate yourself with Delagardie. He will need another coachman once Lupin moves on. You will be our man inside once Sir Percy's conclave disbands—if we can manage this unforeseen situation of murder and death, and can all part as trusted allies."

"Or at least part leaving them thinking we are all trusted allies," Countess Carody amended.

Lecoq nodded his thanks to the Colonel and returned to the house, followed by the silent Gribardsun, who took a circuitous route through the shadows and yet kept his quarry in sight.

Lecoq soon discovered, however, that his targets had retired for the evening, and took himself to his own quarters.

And Gribardsun... John Gribardsun kept the silent night watch over Blakeney Hall.

BLAKENEY HALL, EAST RIDING OF YORKSHIRE, NEAR THE VILLAGE OF WOLD NEWTON 12 DECEMBER 1795

The dreadful clangings, and death, summoned them the next morning. Sir Percy, Siger Holmes, and Gribardsun arrived first.

Miss Caroline Bingley lay in her bed, blue of face, limbs bloated and distended. The body had been discovered by her chambermaid.

Holmes examined her fingernails, peeled back her eyelids, and sniffed at the corpse's face. He pulled a sheet up over the gruesome discovery. "A fast-acting poison. Body's still warm. I'd say she's been dead ten minutes, maybe fifteen."

"Which coincides with those demmed bells," Sir Percy said. He turned to the others. "Did anyone see anything? You, Sir John—" he gestured to Gribardsun "—you were up, prowling these halls early this morning. Did you notice anything?"

Gribardsun shook his head, expressionless. Inside, he burned. Another killing, and he had failed to prevent it. Each slaying heralded by the ominous tolling, as of funeral bells, but funeral bells which pierced the brain as if one were standing directly under them.

And that maddeningly familiar scent...

"Miss Caroline Bingley," Sir Percy said, bringing Gribardsun's attention back to the cadaver. "Demmed wretched woman. Darcy will have a deuced time composing a letter of condolence to her brother."

"And I'm having a deuced time explaining all this and keeping the local constabulary at bay," William de Winter declared as he entered the death chamber. "I saw the value of this assembly of yours when you first described it to me, Sir Percy, but I declare that any benefit which may result from this meeting is being quickly diminished by these abominable murders."

"I agree, de Winter—"

"I've already lost my best man, Iain Bond," de Winter continued, "and His Majesty is rapidly losing patience with this conclave. We must have results, and soon, or I'll order this assembly adjourned." He turned to the two footmen who stood quietly in the hallway. "Meantime, store this body with the others. I'll be in my rooms, concocting some story or other about Miss Bingley's untimely demise. Apoplexy, or some such, I suppose." He stalked out.

The sun sank toward the horizon, washing Blakeney Hall in a blazing orange-red burn, as Gribardsun stalked the grounds searching for a clue, for the slightest scrap or hint of information. It could not be said that he stalked his prey, for he couldn't even scent his target.

That morning, in Miss Bingley's chambers, he had caught that scent again. He sifted through millennia of memories both ancient and recent, and still could not place it.

He had left the estate and spent the day patrolling the outskirts, haunting the surrounding woods and gardens, hoping to pick up the spoor again.

It was all to no avail, but his head was clear and he felt energized by the outdoor air. He thought of ages past and the unspoiled, savage world he had sought out, found, and which he was slowly losing once again. Civilization was slowly, but inexorably, closing in upon him as the centuries passed.

The day had seen the denizens of Blakeney Hall keep to their rooms, a growing sense of dread and anxiety hanging over the entire estate. Very few felt safe enough to venture out, and the pregnant women—a few of them, at least—fretted over themselves and their unborn. Some of the others, Gribardsun knew, such as Lady Blakeney and her friend Alice, were not given to fretting under any circumstances.

The sun disappeared and twilight encroached, bringing the first hint of starlight. The waxing crescent moon, soon to rise, would provide little light, which suited him, for he intended to resume his watch over Colonel Bozzo-Corona's man Albert Lecoq this night.

Gribardsun found the supposed coachman with one of his peers at the stables. Swinging to the roof, nimbly and silently, he crept in an upper window, and swung between the rafters until he reached a spot where he could observe and listen to the two men, Lecoq and Louis Lupin, ostensibly coachmen to Honoré Delagardie. Of the other coachmen, Arthur Blake and Etienne Austin—Sir Percy had rescued the latter from Madame la Guillotine several years ago—there was no sign.

Lecoq and Lupin sat on short wooden stools, a dark lantern on a barrel casting a sliver of luminescence as they played *vingt-et-un* and spoke in harsh whispers.

"So they suspect the Colonel set up Sir Percy in that de Musard matter, only to then come to the heroic rescue by supplying the Heart of Ahriman?" Lupin asked.

"We don't believe so, not yet anyway," came Lecoq's reply. "Dr. Holmes may be perceptive enough to land on the truth, but I've been keeping my ears open, and they don't seem to have put it together yet.

"But we do believe they suspect us in these bizarre murders," Lecoq continued. "Sir Percy, and Greystoke, and the rest have become singularly close-mouthed in our presence. As a result, the talks have stalled. The Colonel grows impatient, and speaks of departing within the next few days."

"Then is all lost?" Lupin implored. "Will we not all agree to give Napoleon the signal, and put an end to this madness in France?"

"Your half-brother has been perfectly positioned, and the time is ripe, it is true, for action," Lecoq replied. "He can impose stability in France, and on the Continent. The Colonel and the Brothers of Mercy had hoped to protect their flanks by bringing the British in on the plan, and indeed, making them think it was their own idea. But these inexplicable killings…"

"And if the Colonel decides that we are to leave, that the British will not join us?" Lupin asked.

"I imagine he will act anyway, giving your sibling the go-ahead," Lecoq said. "But it would be better to have the British on our side."

Gribardsun heard a scrape, so slight that the two Frenchmen would not have been able to detect it. He shifted stealthily in the rafters and identified the source: Arthur Blake, covertly observing Lupin and Lecoq from the main entrance to the stables, and not realizing that he, in turn, was being observed.

This was getting interesting. Gribardsun was sure that Blake had only just arrived; otherwise, he would have detected the coachman earlier.

"Then perhaps we should try to solve the mystery of these 'ringing bell murders' ourselves," Lupin said, "and put a stop to them before any more damage is done."

"And just how do you propose to do that?" Lecoq asked, skepticism painting his rough features.

"Well…" Lupin turned over his cards.

"*Vingt-et-un*," Lecoq declared, revealing his cards with a triumphant grin.

Arthur Blake left his place of concealment at the main stable door and made for the estate.

Gribardsun decided there was more profit in hearing what the coachman would report to his master. He decamped from the stable rafters, as soundlessly as he had entered, leapt to the ground with the sleek grace of a black panther, and trailed Blake at a discreet distance.

The coachman entered the main house, and Gribardsun

took a chance that Blake would seek out Sir Percy in his private study. He scaled the stone walls and once again traversed the roof as easily as if it were the upper levels of the jungle forest he knew so well.

He came to the spot above Blakeney's private chambers, found a grip, and as he had several other times in the past few days, hung upside down from the gable, with his ear close to the study windows.

Gribardsun's gamble paid off. He heard Blake knock and his master bid him enter.

As the latter did so, however, it was not Sir Percy who spoke first but Sir Hezekiah Fogg. "Well, Blake, what is your report?"

There was a long pause, and Sir Hezekiah spoke again. "Go ahead, we've swept the room for listening devices."

"Very well, Sir Hezekiah, I've just come from the stables," Blake replied.

"Ah, and what do our French 'coachmen' have to say for themselves, cousin?" Sir Percy drawled. Gribardsun heard Blakeney take a snort of snuff.

"Well, as you say, Sir Percy, they're no more coachmen than I am. But as to what I heard, they're of a mind to solve these murders themselves. They seem to think if they can do so, it will mitigate some damage, although I missed the beginnings of their conversation and can't tell exactly what they meant by that."

"If these Frenchies start meddling," Sir Hezekiah interjected, "it could ruin everything."

"Well," Sir Percy replied, "at least we can be pretty well assured they're not Capelleans. They don't seem to recognize that the clangings are caused by a distorter."

"Or distorters," Blake said.

"But they wouldn't admit knowing the sounds if they did," Sir Hezekiah said.

"True, sir," Blake said, "but Lecoq and Lupin didn't know they were being observed, and spoke as if they didn't know what the tolling was. My opinion is they're not Capellean."

"Well," Sir Percy said, "*somebody* around here is a Capellean. I've never seen or held an actual distorter, but I know the meaning of these clamorous sounds."

"Aye," Sir Hezekiah said. "Someone must know you are an Eridanean agent, and that I am an Old Eridanean. For whatever reason, they mean to disrupt the assembly you've brought together here."

"Is it really in the Capelleans' interest to foment further discord, or rather prevent us from quelling the discord, in France?" Sir Percy asked. "I'm not so sure."

"What else could it be?" Sir Hezekiah said. "We have the tolling which signals the use of a distorter; murders in which no sign of the culprit can be found, and thus which can only be explained by someone transmitting in and out using a distorter; and the consequent disruption of your secret meeting. The Eridaneans prefer that your conclave succeed. The only logical conclusion is Capellean sabotage."

"Yes, it makes sense when you put it that way..." Sir Percy said. "Y'know, Fogg, you could give Dr. Holmes some lessons in logic."

"A brilliant man," Sir Hezekiah conceded. "Perhaps we

should recruit him to the Eridanean cause."

"Perhaps, someday," Sir Percy said. "Here and now, we need to prepare for tomorrow. A murder a day. We have to suppose there'll be another, or at least an attempt, tomorrow."

"What do you have in mind, Sir Percy?" Blake asked.

"We need to keep everyone together, for the whole day. Everyone within view of everyone else. No demmed transmitting in and out, sight unseen."

"And…?" Sir Hezekiah asked.

Gribardsun listened to Sir Percy take another snort of snuff.

"I think," the man who had also been known as the Scarlet Pimpernel said, "that we should get away from Blakeney Hall for a bit. I do believe a carriage ride is in order."

Gribardsun's ebony hair hung in his face, covering his piercing gray eyes, as he sat alone in his room, staring at the floor, brooding.

He reflected back on the other occasions he'd heard the strange clanging, and went over again in his head the conversation he'd just heard. The information he'd gleaned from Blakeney, Fogg, and Blake—these "Eridaneans"—answered many questions and raised as many new ones.

Eridaneans and Capelleans. Some sort of competing secret societies, so-called because their membership, rituals, and purpose were clandestine?

Perhaps related to the Illuminati? The Rosicrucians? These groups were supposedly interested in gathering secret knowledge from all over the world. Listening devices (unknown in 1795) and "distorters" which "transmitted" people or things (unknown even in his own time—although he supposed that his ship, the *H. G. Wells I*, was, after all, a sort of teleportation device) certainly could be characterized as "secret knowledge."

He had also heard rumblings, through the ages, whispered in the darkness when the fire fell to crackling embers, of a society, truly secret, in that no one, or almost no one, knew of its very existence. The Nine.

The nine bell tolls that signaled each murder.

His brain raced now, unbidden, and another part of his mind, compartmentalized, knew he was making stream-of-consciousness connections, stitching seemingly unrelated items together into a grand tapestry.

He thought of the importance of the number nine in Khokarsan culture, and of the nine-sided temple of Kho. The Door of the Nine, which gave unto the temple. And the nine primary aspects of Kho.

Gribardsun blinked, shook his head, coming out of his fugue.

He almost had it. Not quite, but it was almost there.

Khokarsa. Africa. thirteen thousand years ago. And the tickling, niggling scent that accompanied each slaying.

He put it aside, not forcing it, and came back to the Eridaneans and Capelleans. Were they secret societies? What other explanation was there? Teleportation technology was extremely advanced. Too advanced, in fact, to reasonably have been developed in this time and place, even by progressive intellectuals operating surreptitiously. The scientific and technological infrastructure just wouldn't support it.

Extraterrestrials?

Could celestial races be interfering in human affairs? It certainly would not surprise him, given his prior experiences in Africa of exotic plants and the massive crystalline root system—both clearly of alien origin—which had infested large swaths of the continent, leading to the great calamity and the end of the Khokarsan civilization.

But were they extraterrestrials? Blakeney, Fogg, and Blake—the Eridaneans, as they called themselves—seemed fully human and appeared to be on the side of right. And Blakeney was his great-great-grandfather.

Gribardsun decided he'd reserve complete judgment for the future, but would still investigate the ungodly clangings which signaled teleportation—"transmission"—if he came through this tomorrow, and if he heard them again in the future. And he'd put a stop to the strange rivalry between the Capelleans and Eridaneans if he could.

Gribardsun thought about tomorrow, the momentous day. Blakeney had proposed a carriage ride; certainly no one bent on sabotage would propose that.

But if sabotage was the murderer's object, sabotage of *what*, precisely?

Sabotage of Sir Percy's conclave, of his attempt to quell the raging fires in France and prevent them from spreading to the rest of Europe?

Or sabotage of... tomorrow itself?

EAST RIDING OF YORKSHIRE, NEAR THE VILLAGE OF WOLD NEWTON
13 DECEMBER 1795, 2:00 P.M.

True to his word, Sir Percy Blakeney had rousted the inhabitants and guests for a day away from the grim pall that overhung Blakeney Hall.

Two huge carriages leisurely passed through the village of Thwing and turned onto Rainsburgh Lane.

The first was occupied by Greystoke, Tennington, Honoré Delagardie, Fitzwilliam Darcy, and their wives. It was driven by Delagardie's two coachmen, Lecoq and Lupin.

The second held Sir Percy, Lady Blakeney, and Alice Clarke Raffles, as well as Alice's sister Violet and Violet's husband, Dr. Holmes. Rounding out the passengers were Sir Hugh Drummond and his wife, Lady Georgia Dewhurst Drummond. Driving the coach were Albert Blake and Etienne Austin.

Gribardsun—Sir John Gribson, to the carriage party—rode alongside on horseback, as did a physician friend of Holmes, Sebastian Noel. Noel had arrived in the area yesterday and was staying at an inn in the nearby village of Wold Newton, toward which they were now circling back. At the party's restful pace, the village was perhaps half an hour or slightly more away.

Colonel Bozzo-Corona, Kramm, and Gerolstein had not elected to join the party. The wizened old Colonel had seen Sir Percy and the others off, and before they departed, Gribardsun had overheard them speaking frankly about the situation they faced. The upshot had been that if there was no progress on the negotiations and plans within the next two days, the Colonel and his party would take their leave of Blakeney Hall.

Shortly thereafter, Gribardsun observed Sir Percy speaking quietly to Fogg and de Winter; as the latter two had not joined the carriage party, Gribardsun assumed they had agreed to keep an eye on the Colonel and his associates and ensure no mischief ensued back at Blakeney Hall while the others were absent.

Countess Carody also begged off, to the chagrin of Marguerite and Alice and Lizzie Darcy, claiming too much sun would be unfavorable to her complexion—this despite the enclosed carriages.

At 2:25 P.M., a light cloud cover hovered in the distance. There was a crisp and refreshing chill in the air as the party traversed the gently rolling farmland. Gribardsun rode alongside Sir Percy's carriage and listened as the baronet pointed out Major Edward Topham's Wold Cottage in the distance on the left, and regaled his fellow passengers with slightly risqué accounts of the unmarried Topham, the actress Mrs. Mary Wells, and their three surviving daughters, to the accompaniment of many chuckles and some outright laughter. Sir Percy was quick to note the loveliness of Major Topham's three children, Juliet, Harriet, and Maria.

Blakeney's tale-telling was affectionate. It was clear he held his friend Topham, as well as his amorous exploits, in high regard. This came as no surprise to the other carriage passengers, who well knew that his lady loves, Lady Blakeney and Alice, were both among the foremost actresses of their day.

At 2:30, nine ominous clangings rang out across the countryside.

The two carriages stopped amidst the uneasy chatter of the occupants, as they attempted to hone in on the source.

After a brief pause, the nine bells tolled again, seemingly coming from everywhere and nowhere.

While the party, nerves on edge, debated the meaning of the ear-splitting clangor and the wisdom of further investigation, particularly given the presence of the many gravid ladies, John Gribardsun galloped away, leaving the others far behind.

The bells pealed again, and the cycle of nine clangings repeated on a regular cadence as he rode hard down Rainsburgh Lane and turned into the short drive leading to Wold Cottage.

How could anyone, other than himself, know about today? And were they—whoever they were—here to sabotage?

Gribardsun urged his horse on past Topham's abode. He had come to observe the momentous event of December 13, and now it seemed that someone—whoever was associated with, or causing, the clangings and the murders—might succeed in stopping what history said had happened. Gribardsun had been stalking his prey, getting closer and closer, trying to ensure that each incident, each death, did not result in an alteration in the streams of Time—and now it seemed that catastrophe loomed over him.

What would happen if he failed? Would he just… wink out of existence?

The scientists who had worked on Project Chronos said no, that whatever he or other time travelers did in the past would be a natural part of the fabric of history. Dr. Jacob Moishe, the scientist leading the project team that had invented the time machine later utilized by Gribardsun's expedition, had demonstrated that if time travel were going to change history, it had already done so.

Moishe, however, had not taken an immortal, now some fourteen thousand years old, into account in his calculations. With that in mind, Gribardsun had tried to keep a low profile throughout history, but on the other hand had been unable to resist selectively intervening—a push here, a tug there—in some key events. Particularly key events that pertained to his own history.

The regular clanging became louder and louder as he closed in on it, heading in the direction of a field past Major Topham's cottage. He calculated that it was 2:40. Sir Percy's party—the carriages and the horses—were not close to the impact site. Not close enough, anyway.

If they were not there at three o'clock, all was lost.

Gribardsun came over a low rise, making for the field which was empty save for some scattered farmhands. In four years, the field would not be quite so empty; the site would be marked by an obelisk erected by Topham commemorating the event. Gribardsun had visited the site several times, the last in the 2060s.

Then Gribardsun saw *Him*. Smelled *Him*. The scent clicked, and he remembered. *He* looked now the same age as *He* had then, so long ago.

Thirteen thousand years ago.

10,814 B.C. (786 A.T.)

John Gribardsun couldn't believe his nose.

The way other men relied primarily on their sense of sight, and yet often couldn't believe their eyes, despite the evidence in front of them, he could not believe his nose.

Gribardsun picked up the man's spoor before he saw him. No two men, or women, had the exact same scent. Each was unique, among billions, and Gribardsun could recognize the distinctive scent signature of a specific human as easily as a normal man would recognize someone he knew and had seen before.

But this scent defied belief. It was impossible. From his personal perspective, it had been over one thousand years since he had encountered the human being with that scent signature. Perhaps his memory was faulty.

And yet he must trust the evidence before his nose.

Gribardsun had come to this area, a jungle thick with vegetation thousands of miles south of Khokarsa, on the unexplored shores of the inland sea, to investigate the uncanny root system which seemed to be infesting much of this part of Africa. He suspected it might now be extending from Khokarsa to these lands, and he had set a tribe of Gokako—a squat and hairy slant-browed group of Neanderthals, very rare in these far southern lands—to excavating key areas in his search for the root system.

Gribardsun knew of the devastation which could and would be caused in Khokarsa by the alien organism—for alien it was—and hoped to prevent the destruction from reaching these lands. He had had direct experience with similar patterns of annihilation caused by the crystalline roots, having lived through a series of shattering earthquakes in central Africa in 1918. The city which would arise here, which would be founded by Lupoeth, a priestess of Kho, was, and would be, very important to him. He hoped to prevent the spread of ruin, the great cataclysm which was inevitable elsewhere, to these lush lands.

A push here, a nudge there.

The wind shifted, and Gribardsun picked up the scent again, the scent which he could not believe. He whirled.

"You cannot be here," he said in Khokarsan. He was too surprised to consider any alternative languages, but in any event Khokarsan was a probable choice for this time and place—even if the man he spoke to could not be of this time and place.

"Why not?" the other replied, in the same language. Then: "Do you know me?"

Gribardsun did know the man. How come the knowledge was not reciprocal?

The last time Gribardsun had seen the man, in Africa, in 1912, the man had looked like a native witch doctor. Gribardsun, a young man of twenty-three, had saved the witch doctor from a lion. In gratitude, the witch doctor had offered him everlasting life. Gribardsun had laughed, but said why not. He didn't believe the man, but if there were any truth to the claims, he'd have been a fool to decline the offer.

After a procedure which lasted a month, and greatly sickened him, he'd wondered if he had been a fool to accept. The process involved multiple blood transfusions from the witch doctor and continuous imbibing of a concoction brewed from rare herbs.

But, as he had learned over decades, centuries, and finally millennia, it had worked.

Gribardsun thought about the man's question, "Do you know me?" The man smelled exactly like the witch doctor, but looked nothing like him, which he didn't understand. When Gribardsun had met the man in 1912, the man must have been very, very old. This made sense, if he thought about it. The man was an immortal, and had passed the secret of immortality on to Gribardsun.

The man before him was the younger version, although he could not explain the difference in appearance. This man was Caucasoid, a large man, with hazel eyes, heavy brows, and a Roman nose. His hair was dark, his skin bronzed, and he looked to be in his late thirties or perhaps early forties. Like Gribardsun, he wore clothing appropriate for the jungle, which is to say, very little: a loincloth of antelope hide, a leather pouch, and tough moccasins.

Gribardsun responded to the man's question: "Perhaps."

"I don't know you," the man replied. "Or rather, I should say, I have never met you. But I know who you are. I've been looking for you, Sahhindar."

Gribardsun shrugged. "Some call me that."

"Sahhindar, the Gray-Eyed Archer God," the man continued, and he smiled broadly. "Also the god of plants, of bronze, and of Time. As I've listened to the legends and stories about you over the centuries, it's become clear to me that you are a fellow immortal. I confess that I did not connect the dots, however, until this very minute, that you are also a time traveler. I had never assumed that 'the god of Time' was a literal appellation. That was my mistake."

"What do you want?"

"Perfect." The man grinned at him again. "Straight to the point. I sought you out to discover your source of youth."

Gribardsun's mind raced. "Why?"

"Because it may be more effective than my own."

"Meaning?"

The man smiled his infernal smile.

Gribardsun put his hand on the hilt of the big steel hunting knife which hung in a sheath on his belt and said, "Tell me, or I will remove that smile and replace it with a red one."

"Now *that* would be a grievous mistake, and I think you know it," the man said. "But, I will tell you. There is no point in not being forthright, for once, because this *must* happen.

"If I am correct," the man continued, "you do not age at all. I do age, albeit extraordinarily slowly, and barring accident or murder, someday my body will be very, very old, and it will die. This day may come after millennia, or tens of millennia, but it will come. I would prefer that it didn't."

"And why would I help you with anything, assuming I'm in a position to do so?" Gribardsun asked, his gray eyes piercing the other man's.

"I think," the man replied, "you are beginning to suspect that you have no choice. *If*, that is, you would like me to reciprocate in the future. That's the crux of it, isn't it?"

"If you are correct," Gribardsun said, "how were you—will

you—be able to appear to me in the guise of a native African witch doctor?"

"I have no idea," the man said, grinning, "but now that you've told me that's what I need to do, it appears I'll have plenty of time to figure it out."

"You never told me the precise herbs needed, the exact recipe," Gribardsun said.

"Aha! *Herbs*. The god of plants. Well?" the man prodded.

"I am observant. And an expert botanist. But my knowledge of the herbs used is nonetheless imperfect, and is based on best guesses at the plants and herbs which were growing nearby when I received the treatment."

"But these plants and herbs do exist in this time as well?"

"Yes, or at least some that are very closely related."

"Tell me, show me, and I will be on my way."

"It won't be that simple," Gribardsun said. "The herbal mixture is a vile brew, and I look forward to forcing it down your throat, but it is useless without the other component of the treatment."

"Which is?"

Gribardsun's eyes were hooded. The other man may have had him over the proverbial barrel, but likewise he too had the man over a barrel. He was in control now.

Gribardsun patted the hilt of his steel knife again. "A blood transfusion. From me to you."

The man's perpetual grin faded a few degrees.

"Whatever it takes," he said. "I've endured far worse."

"I cannot guarantee the treatment will work as perfectly on

you as it has seemed to work on me," Gribardsun warned. "There *are* slight differences in the plants and herbs, as I mentioned."

"I'll take the risk," the man said dryly. "Can we get on with it?"

"What is your name?" Gribardsun asked.

A sly look came over the man's face and his eyes seemed to shift color, taking on a faint yellowish tint. "I've many names, just as you seem to have, Sahhindar. But you can call me Kethnu. It's as good a name as any other right now."

"*Kethnu.* 'Head man.' High opinion of yourself."

Kethnu shrugged, and his infernal grin broadened again.

"Kethnu, sit down," Gribardsun ordered. "I hope you don't have anyone who will miss you for the next month or so."

He smiled and drew his blade.

EAST RIDING OF YORKSHIRE, NEAR THE VILLAGE OF WOLD NEWTON 13 DECEMBER 1795, 2:40 P.M.

The man Gribardsun had known as Kethnu stood alone in the middle of the field. He was a large man, although perhaps not quite as tall as Gribardsun, and exuded an air of power in the same way Gribardsun did. He still looked to be in his late thirties, and wore his sideburns long. A bushy mustache perched under a Roman nose.

He wore riding dress, similar to Gribardsun's, appropriate for the cold December day and weather: a white, high-collared double-breasted waistcoat, and snug leather riding breeches reaching almost to the tops of his boots.

Unlike Gribardsun, who was no dandy, Kethnu wore around his neck a sterling silver quizzing glass attached to a long black ribbon. The quizzing glass's handle was six-sided and crafted from a pearlescent blue material which Gribardsun couldn't identify.

In his right hand, Kethnu held a large pocket watch attached to a silver chain which disappeared into a pouch on his waistcoat. The pocket watch's lid was of the same pearlescent material as the quizzing glass's handle, and was embossed with an elaborate pattern highlighted by a brilliant blue star sapphire. The blue sapphire reminded Gribardsun of the *nethkarna*, the seed of the Tree of Kho, which the Khokarsan oracles had planted beneath their temples to tap into the root system across Africa, thus gaining their oracular powers.

It was from this watch that the terrible clangings emanated.

"It's been a long time," the other immortal greeted Gribardsun, in between cycles of the riotous nine clangs. There was no trace of irony in the comment. His gray eyes, touched with green, glinted.

"It has," the Englishman acknowledged. "I don't suppose you call yourself 'Kethnu' any longer."

"No indeed," the other man replied. "So much time, and so many names. One which I keep coming back to of late—*of late* being relative, of course—is XauXaz."

"From 'head man' to 'high one.'"

"You are a linguist, my friend. You know your Proto-Germanic."

"The millennia have not taught you humility," Gribardsun said.

"You expected otherwise?" XauXaz asked. Chuckling, he sketched a bow and gestured theatrically to the pocket watch. "Now I am also a time traveler."

"I don't believe you," Gribardsun replied. "It is not possible for anyone else to travel to any time during my lifetime—which is to say, all the way back to 12,000 B.C."

"It is only prevented for *you*," XauXaz answered. "This time distorter works on different principles. It opens gates, and allows one to pass through them, rather than simply shifting stationary masses in time."

Gribardsun gestured to the distorter. "Turn it off."

XauXaz smiled and shook his head slowly.

Gribardsun turned and looked in the distance. Even with his excellent eyesight, he could barely make out the carriage party, still out on Rainsburgh Lane. The horrendous tolling, symbol of murder and death to those carriage passengers, was a deterrent. There was no doubt they would avoid this place, from which the din originated, in an effort to keep the ladies and their unborn children safe.

It was 2:43 P.M.

At three o'clock it would be too late.

Gribardsun attacked.

XauXaz parried, and the two men gripped each other's hands, boots digging into the earth as they thrust against each other.

They pressed back and forth, each struggling for an advantage, and Gribardsun was inwardly surprised to discover the other man seemed to nearly match him in strength.

As if reading his mind, XauXaz grunted, "My bones are thicker than any modern man's, with greater surface area for muscle attachment. Remember, I am a Cro-Magnon."

Gribardsun thrust his right arm downward, caught XauXaz's lower thigh in a crushing grip in his strong fingers, and hoisted the other man above his head as if lifting a barbell. He spun around a few times to disrupt XauXaz's equilibrium and catapulted him headfirst to the ground.

No follower of gentlemen's rules of civilized fighting, Gribardsun followed up with a sharp kick to the abdomen, causing XauXaz to expel a great rush of air, and another kick to the face.

XauXaz rolled away and came back up on his feet, blood streaming from his mouth. "Of course, your bones are much thicker as well." He grinned. "I've been visiting the Ladies Greystoke in their bedchambers for quite some time now. I am your grandfather several times over. How does that make you feel, my boy?"

Gribardsun dived at the other man and took his feet out from under him. XauXaz fell on top of him and they tangled and rolled. The jungle man thrust powerful legs and flipped his opponent over his head, but XauXaz landed deftly on his feet.

The Englishman came back to his feet as well but the other man was at him, and he took a solid one-two punch to the kidneys.

He barely twitched at the pain, side-stepped a third punch, and jackhammered his foot into XauXaz's jaw.

XauXaz was momentarily stunned and the other man pressed the advantage, slamming his opponent's face down in the dirt. He put an elbow firmly in the back of the Old Stone Age man's neck, and wrenched his arm behind his back at an increasingly unnatural angle.

Gribardsun tugged at the twisted arm and simultaneously pressed down with his elbow, eliciting a grunt. He reached under XauXaz's torso, felt for the silver chain, and pulled the outsized pocket watch from underneath the other man's body. Still holding XauXaz immobile, he worked the clasp, popped the watch lid, and started to fumble at the buttons inside.

"I wouldn't," XauXaz said. His voice was low and firm, belying his current position.

"Then you do it," Gribardsun said. "Turn it off, or I'll snap your arm, followed by your neck." He placed the watch on the ground next to the hand that was not attached to XauXaz's twisted arm.

XauXaz worked at the mechanism with his free hand, and the clangings stopped.

Still holding the Cro-Magnon's left arm firmly behind him, Gribardsun grabbed him by the nape of his neck with his right hand and lifted him bodily to his feet. He threw his right arm around the other man's neck and exerted pressure on his throat with the crook of his elbow.

He peered into the distance. The carriage riders had halted at the intersection of Rainsburgh Lane and the short drive leading to Wold Cottage.

"They've stopped to discuss it," XauXaz said. His voice remained calm. "They were following the bells to their source, to investigate, but now the bells have stopped. They've stopped also, to discuss and debate it."

Gribardsun watched, saying nothing.

"Are you here to observe, or stop it from happening?" XauXaz asked.

Gribardsun considered the wisdom of being drawn into conversation with this man. He continued to watch the carriage party, which remained stalled at the distant, too distant, driveway.

"I was here to observe," Gribardsun finally replied. "Now I'm here to ensure it happens."

"Then let me go and restart the distorter." XauXaz's voice was mild.

Gribardsun tightened his arm around the other's neck.

"I estimate it is now 2:48 P.M.," XauXaz said. Was that the tiniest note of desperation creeping into his voice? "Time is running out. Quite literally running out."

Still, Gribardsun said nothing.

"See the small rise behind us?" XauXaz asked.

"What of it?" Gribardsun's voice was as immovable as the steel-corded muscles holding XauXaz fast.

"At least let us climb up there and conceal ourselves—in case Blakeney and the rest do head this way," XauXaz said.

Gribardsun considered this. Then he bent down, grabbed the distorter, threw XauXaz to the ground and dragged him up the hillock.

Reaching the top, Gribardsun took XauXaz in a firm handgrip about the throat and forced him to crouch down. Gribardsun knelt beside him. His strong fingers remained tight around XauXaz's windpipe.

XauXaz gestured to speak and Gribardsun loosened his clutch slightly.

"You don't trust me," XauXaz croaked, mock reproach in his voice.

"Say something worth saying," Gribardsun said.

"Well, you're right not to trust me, of course. Except now. It's ten minutes to three o'clock. Do you see those farmhands approaching from a nearby field?"

Gribardsun gave a curt nod.

"Their names are John Shipley and Kevin Cook," XauXaz said. "If you know your history, you know they witnessed it too. The moment is approaching.

"Now," XauXaz continued, "look at the two carriages. They're still at the driveway into Wold Cottage—about ten minutes away."

Gribardsun was silent. The wind gusted and coal-black hair whipped in his face.

XauXaz pressed his point. "They're too far away. They're not going to make it. Give me back the distorter."

Gribardsun watched. The carriages sat idle while the men, tiny stick figures in the distance, appeared to confer.

"You came here to watch it happen. Instead, you're stopping it from happening," XauXaz said. "Why would I have given you the elixir in 1912, if I intended to go mucking about with the timeline?"

Gribardsun still watched. A man remounted his horse— Sebastian Noel. The coachmen clambered back onto their perches atop the carriages.

The vehicles turned, pointing away from Wold Cottage and oriented back toward the village of Wold Newton.

"*Give it to me.*"

Gribardsun handed over the distorter.

XauXaz worked at it and a riotous clanging ensued, reverberating in the air and shaking them to the bone.

They watched as, in the distance, the carriage riders spurred into action. The coachmen turned the carriages back toward Wold Cottage and drove at high speed, seeking the source of the noise which had, to them, signaled death over the past three days.

From the other direction, the farmhands also came their way, seeking the cause of the din.

John Gribardsun and XauXaz crouched down at the top of the rise, out of sight, to observe.

The distorter's awful pealing continued for several more minutes. The carriages came carefully down a dirt trail—it could hardly be called a road—and pulled up below the rise where XauXaz and Gribardsun were hidden.

XauXaz worked at the distorter's controls and the din ceased. The two men out of time watched as Sir Percy ordered the carriages to a halt in the middle of the field.

The carriage party hardly had time to gather their wits when from the air all around came a series of loud claps, like pistol reports. A light like burning phosphorous blazed and streaked across the sky, hissing through the air, leaving what looked like sparks trailing behind it.

The leading edge of the burning light struck the ground

near the carriages, spewing dirt and mud and earth everywhere. The blazing light and the sizzling noise caused the horses to panic, and the passengers cried out in alarm as the carriages were pulled and tugged, but the coachmen swiftly brought the terrified beasts under control.

The passengers were still shaken, but quickly came out of their shock. Gribardsun and XauXaz watched silently as Sir Percy, Greystoke, Holmes, Darcy, and the other men alighted and followed the burrowed trail in the ground to the end of its trajectory. They saw Topham's shepherd, as well as the farmhands, John Shipley and Kevin Cook, come alongside. The group cautiously began digging. Eventually, as nothing untoward transpired, the women also descended and came to watch as a large stone, smoking and smelling of sulfur, was dug out from where it had buried itself almost two feet deep in the earth.

Atop their perch, still crouching down out of sight, Gribardsun looked at XauXaz. "Why?"

XauXaz grinned at him. He lifted the quizzing glass to a yellow-tinted eye and arched a thick dark brow, giving him a superior air. "Why what?" he queried.

"What is your motivation? Why lead them all to the meteor crash site? Why do you care?"

XauXaz shrugged. "A lot happens in thirty thousand years—give or take. A man makes friends, and enemies. Enemies who become friends and allies. Friends and allies who become enemies. Perhaps one of their descendants—" he gestured to the crowd below, gathered around the smoking meteor "—will be in a position to assist me one day."

"Their children, and grandchildren, and great-grandchildren," Gribardsun replied, "will all be born as history recorded, whether or not these people witnessed the meteor today."

"Not necessarily," XauXaz said. "You know as well as I that these people are now special. Their children will have special abilities, abilities they may need just to survive. Who is to say you would have survived your jungle upbringing if your great-great-grandfathers were not here today, close to the meteor, being exposed to its heat and energy?"

"You seem to know much about me and my upbringing. But never mind that," Gribardsun said. "You can't count on help from one of their descendants—"

"You helped me by sharing the elixir of your blood, so many millennia ago."

"I had no choice. If I hadn't, then you would not have been alive to share the elixir with me in 1912."

"Perhaps someone else, someday, will also have no choice, and will help me," XauXaz said.

"No, there is more to it than that. What is the real reason behind your intervention here today?"

XauXaz smiled again. He pulled a mother-of-pearl and silver snuff box from a vest pocket. It was inlaid with symbols similar to those on the pocket watch distorter. He took a pinch, snorted, and wiped his nose with a silk handkerchief. He looked at Gribardsun, as if calculating.

Then he spoke.

"The elixir I received from you was much better than that

which my friends who are also my enemies had given me. It conferred eternal youth. With the other elixir, I aged, but very, very slowly. And I needed repeated doses of the other elixir. Not so with yours.

"But even your elixir, I have found, was imperfect. Or it worked imperfectly on me."

"I did warn you that might be the case," Gribardsun said. "The differences in the plants and herbs thirteen thousand years ago."

"Indeed, you did warn me," XauXaz agreed mildly. "And I have had little reason to complain, at least to this point. Your elixir kept me young, while my friends who are also my enemies, with their lesser elixir, continued to age. I would be quite elderly now, had I only taken their lesser elixir. In fact, if you believe in the theory of divergent timelines, then I have—or is it had?—a parallel universe counterpart who indeed continued to age in the very way I describe.

"As it was, I had to pretend to age alongside my friends who are also my enemies, as I should have done if I were using their elixir.

"However, as I said, your elixir has started to fail me. About one hundred years ago—one hundred from my perspective—I came to realize this. I was, at the time, playing the part of a seal-hunting schooner captain named Larsen. I started experiencing blinding, debilitating headaches. Eventually, they proved my undoing and those who served under me revolted." XauXaz laughed. "You might say the headaches were the 'death' of me. It was time to move on and create a new identity anyway. But I instinctively understood that the elixir was failing me."

"So you thought to find me here?" Gribardsun asked. "You thought to earn my good graces by luring Sir Percy and his guests to the meteor site, in the hopes that I would return the favor and give you another dose? If so, you are sadly misguided."

XauXaz shook his head and laughed softly. "No, no. I know you have no reason to help me. And no reason to have any love for me—although you should. As I mentioned, I am your grandfather, many times over, and you owe me a genetic debt. But no, I know you will not."

"You are right," Gribardsun said simply. "You murdered unnecessarily to create this scenario."

"What—you, purveyor of the law of the jungle, of kill or be killed? You are judging me for this, of all things?"

"I kill when attacked, to defend myself. And I kill for food, as Nature dictates."

"You kill to live, which is nothing more than I have done. Those small people who died, you will find if you dig deep into the historical records, actually did die at this time. Although the records were altered by de Winter and his cronies as to the place of death. I have altered nothing; Time unfolded as intended."

"You are a murderer," Gribardsun repeated.

"They were *dead already*, you fool." XauXaz was no longer grinning. "What are their small, piggish lives compared to those who travel in time as we do? Everyone you meet is already dead."

"Everyone I meet is vibrantly alive."

"Then why not share your blood elixir with all of them? Make them all immortal?"

Gribardsun stared at him.

"I'll tell you why," XauXaz said. "Because you want to *live*. You *can't* share the elixir with many others, because you *didn't*. You weren't born in, didn't grow up in, a world where the elixir was commonplace. Therefore you didn't share it around during the long, long life you've lived from 12,000 B.C. until now. Who can say why you didn't share it? I think it's because you want to live, and too many other immortals running around could jeopardize that.

"But for whatever reason, whether I'm right or wrong about the reasons, the fact remains that you didn't share it, and you're stuck with that.

"And of course," XauXaz concluded, "I agree with your decision. The elixir should not be shared lightly."

"Then you know that I will not share the elixir with you again," Gribardsun said. "I'm glad that it's failing you now."

"Perhaps it's unnecessary to share it with me again," XauXaz said. "Perhaps it was your genetic legacy, the altered genes you carry as a result of your great-great-grandfathers being exposed to the meteor, which makes the elixir work so perfectly in you."

A shrewd look swept across his face. "And now I have been exposed to the meteor's effects as well. Perhaps that alone will have a positive effect on the elixir's efficacy. Perhaps that's all I needed."

"But if not, then you will die," Gribardsun said flatly.

"If not," said XauXaz, "then perchance a descendant, or descendants, of those down there digging up that celestial stone will provide what I need to unlock the secret of the perfect elixir. Their genes themselves may help me derive, or distill, the formula.

"They'll be brilliant, of course. The geniuses flourishing from the event we just witnessed will be unmatched in the annals of history. Perhaps one of them will beat me to creating the perfect elixir. Many of them have tried—or will try. Most of their elixirs are imperfect to one degree or another, but intriguing nonetheless.

"For instance, the Royal Jelly treatment requires several elements which were difficult to obtain—including a shard of the very meteor we just watched plummet from the sky."

Gribardsun tensed and XauXaz laughed. "Not to worry. I'd be pleased to grab a piece of it now, but history says I didn't. So I won't try. I did try once, however, and ended up jousting with Sherlock Holmes over it in 1917, and again a few years later when he caught up with me.

"Then, of course, there's the nefarious Mastermind from the Far East—the grandson of the 3rd Duke of Greystoke, there—who's reputed to have an 'Oil of Life.' A very dangerous man, and he has a large organization at his command. I've skirmished with him once or twice, and may yet take him on directly." XauXaz smiled wistfully. "It might almost be a fair fight.

"But it's another of these geniuses—I think you know him, my own grandson, James Clarke Wildman—in whom I place the most hope. In fact, it was in my guise as a German Baron that I clashed with him, near the end of the Great War, and opened his mind to the possibility of an elixir—among other things. Wildman and his wife have not been seen publicly for many years, but I have reason to believe he may be as young as he ever was."

Gribardsun's gray eyes had narrowed during this recitation. XauXaz was oversharing. Why? Perhaps the fellow immortal was lonely, and this had been the first chance in millennia to unburden himself.

More likely he was simply a sociopath.

XauXaz's next words bore this out. "If one of them succeeds in developing the elixir before I do, I'll crush them and take it, of course.

"You know," XauXaz's voice lowered to a mock-confidential whisper, as if sharing secrets among treasured friends, "it's not only time travel that makes everyone dead to people like you and me. It's the elixir. Once you're immortal, you're walking among the dead. Kill them as they clutch and scrabble for their piggish lives. Love them, hurt them, do whatever you want to them. It just doesn't matter if you help them along to *Niflheimr*, because sooner or later—mostly sooner—they die anyway and there you are still breathing. And you are consequently more alive than they ever can be."

"Enough," Gribardsun said. "You've done what you came here to do, and your incessant talk is tiresome."

"Yes, I did what needed to be done. Did you know, John," XauXaz said slyly, "that *you* needed to be here, at Wold Newton, as well as I did? Even when you were young, very young, you had special qualities. Your own British Secret Service was quite interested in you. You exhibited instances of what their scientists called the 'human magnetic moment.'"

XauXaz went silent and stared at Gribardsun, a trace of mockery in his protean eyes.

"Say what you have to say or begone," Gribardsun said. "I have no more patience for your serpentine gamesmanship."

XauXaz continued to regard him, as a scientist would regard an interesting specimen. Then he shrugged, as if in acquiescence.

"What an amazing chain of events we've witnessed here today," he said. "Do you suppose the meteor would have fallen, *right here in this particular spot*, if you hadn't been *right here* as well to guide it?"

Then—XauXaz was gone, the only sign of his passing an inrush of air filling the vacuum of space he had occupied.

Gribardsun peered over the ridge, and watched the men and women below, watched his own past and future being made, watched as the history of all humanity took a great leap forward.

1972

XauXaz was tired.

He didn't tire easily, but time travel tended to take it out of him. Much as modern humans who flitted over time zones in a matter of hours suffered from jet-lag, he suffered from distorter-lag.

He had discovered the Capellean distorter in the 1930s. The following decade, he had modified it to suppress the telltale "clangings," if and when he so desired. He recalled with fondness how his impossible comings and goings had baffled the Gray Man of Ice during their clashes.

Just this year, prompted by rumors of similar advances with other distorters, he had succeeded in improving the device to also serve as a time distorter.

And thus he was finally able to scratch the itch that had been festering at him for over two hundred and fifty years, since it had first begun plaguing him in 1720.

XauXaz had become aware of the existence of the parallel universe in 1720 when the Shrassk entity tapped into his mind. He had learned that the other world had been created tens of thousands of years ago when one universe had split into two, as a cell divides.

Since he had been alive when the universe divided, he, and everyone else living at the time, was also divided. The only others from that time still alive now were his allies-enemies in the Nine, Anana and Iwaldi, and so they too existed in both universes.

Since 1720, he had known that he had a living counterpart, an exact twin in another world.

This he could not bear.

It drove him mad, madder than even twenty thousand, or twenty-five thousand, or more, years of life had driven him.

He had to kill his Other.

For XauXaz, a decision made was a decision implemented, a fait accompli, *even two hundred and fifty-two years after making that decision. He could afford to take the long view.*

With the distorter—now a time distorter—he traveled back to 1720, the earliest time he could access the other world. The Shrassk entity, which had been invoked by the Nine of that other world in 1720, had been brought forth to their world from its nether-space, acted in concert with his distorter to create a dimensional gate, a gate only he could access.

Thus he crossed the boundary, killing his counterpart.

This done, he was greatly relieved.

Of course, the Nine in this parallel universe could be as

dangerous to him—perhaps even more dangerous—than his own Nine. It would pay to keep tabs on them.

Living as two people in two different worlds for the past year had been complicated, but had been worth the risk, doubling his chances of finding a more permanent elixir.

He thought of the other two with whom he had comprised the Germanic trinity, his brothers Ebnaz XauXaz and Thrithjaz. They were still alive at the time of the universe's division, and thus also existed in both worlds. It was fortunate for him they had died before the advent of Shrassk. The Other Ebnaz XauXaz and Other Thrithjaz might have seen through his deception. On his own world, he had simply kept Sahhindar's elixir from his brothers; he had pretended to age alongside them, as if he were using their elixir, and watched them die of old age.

Nonetheless, it had been exhausting, traveling to the other world day after day for the past two hundred and forty-eight days, while two hundred and forty-eight yearly ceremonies passed deep in the Nine's caverns below central Africa.

When the Nine of that other world finally became suspicious, in 1968, he had been forced to give up his imposture and fake the Other XauXaz's death. Still, he was proud of what he had accomplished in that world, in so short a time.

He was particularly pleased that he had injected himself (he laughed to himself, silently amused at his own pun) into the bloodline of John Cloamby, Lord Grandrith and Cloamby's half-brother, Doctor James Caliban, with midnight visits—in the guise of the elderly and charismatic Mister Bileyg—to their more-than-willing grandmother, and then set the brothers against each other so that they had, in turn, both revolted against the Nine.

Once he found the more permanent elixir, he'd need to ensure the Nine on both worlds were eliminated. This was a good first step. He couldn't wait to see how it turned out.

Once more, he lived the life of just one XauXaz.

The one and only.

And now, he had done what needed to be done in 1795, and could rest before the next phase.

He put down the newspaper. The story of the supposed deaths of Doctor James Clarke Wildman and his wife in their private plane far above the Arctic Circle was a fascinating ruse, but much too coincidental given the alleged deaths of Greystoke and his wife Jane just a few months before.

He thought of his prior engagements with his grandson, who had known him as Baron von Hessel.

If Wildman was on to him, aware of his existence and the threat he posed, then it was time to go after Wildman, before Wildman found him first...

A private clinic in upstate New York was Wildman's last known location. Perhaps there were clues to be found there. There was a daughter, Patricia Wildman. His own great-granddaughter.

She could be made to talk.

A candle flickered with a soft movement of air. There should have been no air movement here.

XauXaz heard a soft scuff behind him.

He turned.

John Gribardsun stepped out of the shadows.

POSTSCRIPT

I would be more than remiss if I failed to acknowledge and pay tribute to the extraordinary speculative essays which inspired this tale. First and foremost among these is Christopher Paul Carey's "The Green Eyes Have It—Or Are They Blue? or Another Case of Identity Recased" in my *Myths for the Modern Age: Philip José Farmer's Wold Newton Universe*, which, not incidentally, also inspired the appearance in other stories of a certain Trickster once called Baron von Hessel: he appeared as Baron Ulf von Waldman in "The Adventure of the Fallen Stone" in *Sherlock Holmes: The Crossovers Casebook*; as Dr. Karl Walden in "Happy Death Men" in *The Avenger: The Justice, Inc. Files*, and "According to Plan of a One-Eyed Trickster" in *The Avenger: Heart of the Roaring Crucible*; and as Dr. Stipier in the forthcoming Honey West novella, *A Girl and Her Cat*.

Other creatively mythological essays from which I drew are: Dennis E. Power's "The Royal Jelly Problem," "Triple Tarzan Tangle," and "The Root of the Wold Newton Family Tree" (all available at Power's *The Wold Newton Universe: A Secret History*, www.pjfarmer.com/secret/index.htm); and Jean-Marc Lofficier's "Will There Be Light Tomorrow?" (*Shadowmen: Heroes and Villains of French Pulp Fiction*).

Minor, but important, elements were taken from Cheryl L. Huttner's "Name of a Thousand Blue Demons" and Rick Lai's "The Secret History of Captain Nemo" (both in *Myths for the Modern Age*).

It's important to note that while I adopted many of the speculations presented in the essays noted above, I just as often deviated from them to follow my own path. None of the articles listed above were adopted wholesale; I am nothing if not an equal-opportunity deviant.

I also owe a debt to my fellow "fiction" scribes. The notion that a distorter could be modified into a time distorter comes from Paul Spiteri's "Time Distorter" tales in *Farmerphile* no. 15 and *The Worlds of Philip José Farmer 1: Protean Dimensions*, although the time distorter herein works differently. "The Wild Huntsman" also has ties to John Allen Small's "Into Time's Abyss" and Christopher Paul Carey's novella *Exiles of Kho*, which I'll let readers suss out for themselves.

Readers of *Myths for the Modern Age* may note that "The Wild Huntsman" contradicts my own "Who's Going to Take Over the World When I'm Gone? (A Look at the Genealogies of Wold Newton Family Super-Villains and Their Nemeses)" in its treatment of Baron von Hessel. My only defense in this regard is that someone, somewhere along the way, must have been lying. It happens.

Readers may also need help in sorting out the tangled branches of the various official Wold Newton Origins stories and unofficial "sideways" tales.

The first story, "Is He in Hell?" was published in *Tales of the Shadowmen 6: Grand Guignol* (January 2010). It was revised to include its intended ending and was published as an official Wold Newton tale in *The Worlds of Philip José Farmer 1: Protean Dimensions* (Meteor House, June 2010); this is the preferred text. Thereafter, two short sideways follow-ups to "Is He in Hell?" "Nadine's Invitation" and "Marguerite's Tears," appeared in *Tales of the Shadowmen 7: Femmes Fatales* (December 2010) and *Tales of the Shadowmen 8: Agents Provocateurs* (December 2011), respectively. These sideways tales can be read separately from the main storyline, and conclude with a third story, "Violet's Lament," in *Tales of the Shadowmen 9: La Vie en Noir* (December 2012).

"The Wild Huntsman" in this volume carries forward the official Wold Newton Origins storyline and is a direct sequel to "Is He in Hell?"

To anyone reading "The Wild Huntsman" who has not read Philip José Farmer's *Tarzan Alive: A Definitive Biography of Lord Greystoke*, *Doc Savage: His Apocalyptic Life*, *Time's Last Gift*, *The Other Log of Phileas Fogg*, and *A Feast Unknown*... One: for shame. Two: you might be a little lost at this point. Three: that's all right, go out and find and devour those books immediately, and then follow them up with *Escape from Loki: Doc Savage's First Adventure*, *The Dark Heart of Time: A Tarzan Novel*, *The Peerless Peer*, *Ironcastle*, *The Evil in Pemberley*

House, Lord of the Trees, The Mad Goblin, and *Gods of Opar: Tales of Lost Khokarsa.*

Go on, we'll be waiting right here for you.

The Whitechapel Horrors
by Edward B. Hanna

Dr Jekyll and Mr Holmes
by Loren D. Estleman

The Angel of the Opera
by Sam Siciliano

The Giant Rat of Sumatra
by Richard L. Boyer

The Peerless Peer
by Philip José Farmer

The Star of India
by Carole Buggé

The Web Weaver
by Sam Siciliano

The Titanic Tragedy
by William Seil

Sherlock Holmes vs. Dracula
by Loren D. Estleman